EVERYTHING IS NOT ENOUGH

EVERYTHING IS NOT ENOUGH

Bernardine Kennedy

HEADLINE

First published in Great Britain in 2000 by
HEADLINE BOOK PUBLISHING

10 9 8 7 6 5 4 3 2

British Library Cataloguing in Publication Data

Kennedy, Bernardine
  Everything is not enough
  I.Title
  823.9'14[F]

ISBN 0 7472 7010 4

Typeset by
Letterpart Limited, Reigate, Surrey

Printed and bound in Great Britain by
Clays Ltd, St Ives plc

HEADLINE BOOK PUBLISHING
A division of Hodder Headline
338 Euston Road
London NW1 3BH

www.headline.co.uk
www.hodderheadline.com

For Stevie B and Katie K. Simply the best son and daughter in the whole wide world. Naturally.

Also, of course, for Ian, my soul mate, my best friend and favourite travelling companion. LYFY.

Special thanks to my friend Martina for her encouragement, and to my best cat, Jo-Jo, for silently keeping me company at the WP.

All my love to you all, and please, please continue to keep those fingers (and paws) crossed.

Prologue

The immigration officer barely glanced at Angie as she took her place at the desk and handed over her dog-eared passport. He checked her forms and turned to his screen.

'Purpose of your visit, Miss Kavanagh?'

'Work. I'm a journalist on assignment; I'm here for a week.' She smiled as she answered politely, remembering the first lesson of international journalism – never upset immigration or custom officials.

Formalities completed, she waited for her companion to go through the same routine.

'Purpose of your visit, Mr Oliver?'

'Work, I'm a photographer on assignment; I'm here for a week.'

As Dave joined her Angie smiled, knowing exactly what he was going to say. He didn't disappoint her.

'You know, it would be so much quicker if we were married. We could go through together. Think of the time it would save.'

'Yeah right, all of two minutes,' she laughed as they made their way through to the baggage claim area.

They had been exchanging the same words for years and although it was a long-standing joke, Angie knew that Dave meant it every time. She took his arm affectionately.

'Come on, you. Let's just get out of here as quick as poss and grab a cab. Work beckons.'

They looked an unlikely couple: the woman dark and casually elegant, with black afro hair cropped close to her head; he tall and well-built with long grey hair pulled back in a ponytail. No one could ever call Dave elegant.

Formalities complete and luggage collected, they jumped into a yellow cab and headed out from JFK Airport towards Manhattan.

Angie loved New York. She loved the constant buzz of enthusiasm, the hustle and bustle of the city, the traffic-clogged streets and the seething sidewalks, and she always felt that she belonged.

1

Dave joked that it was because both she and New York were hyperactive.

'New York and Angie Kavanagh never sleep, they just lull occasionally,' he would declare.

The familiar cab ride passed in companionable silence, interrupted only by the occasional question fired at them by the driver.

When Angie was on assignment she took everything about it seriously; only when it was over would she relax and enjoy the time with Dave. They always stayed at the same hotel; by US standards it was small and compact but the central location on Lexington was convenient, and they both loved the eccentric décor.

'Right, let's get to it.' Angie dumped her suitcase on the bed and reached immediately for her briefcase. 'We've got a lot of planning to do.'

Within minutes the hotel room was awash with papers and photographs, and she was totally in work mode. When it came to her job Angie was single-minded and driven.

'Rebekah Alari is holed up on Park Avenue and no one has seen hide nor hair of her since she left the clinic three weeks ago. She's agreed to see me; it's just a matter of waiting for the call. I'll dig around a bit more tomorrow to see if I can find out anything else beforehand.'

Dave looked uneasy. 'Doesn't this make you feel intrusive? The girl is only twenty-five. Her mother and father are ill and she's tried to top herself – is this really a big story? Isn't it just voyeurism?'

'It's my job, in case you've forgotten. If I don't talk to her then someone else will and then it won't be an exclusive. Rebekah Alari isn't the type to shy away from publicity for long. Anyway, I'm not forcing my way in; she's agreed to see me!' Angie snapped.

'OK, OK, but it still makes me feel uncomfortable.' Dave sighed and turned his attention to the coffee machine.

'Look, Dave, I'm sorry but she let herself be set up. This is a big story, and journalists and photographers in this city are scavenging around for any snippets they can get. The girl is where she is because she's always grabbed any publicity she can. She can't expect us to forget about her when it suddenly suits.'

As he poured the coffee Dave heard the laptop snap open and fire up. It was business as usual.

Rebekah Alari gazed out of the floor-to-ceiling window at the New York skyline. She was looking but not seeing. Her long chocolate-brown hair was pulled back in a band, missing the regular loving touch of a personal hairdresser, and her face was totally nude of make-up. With her skinny arms wrapped tightly around her pyjama-clad body she looked like a little girl, lost and bewildered.

The door opened but she didn't even bother to look round; only one other person was in the apartment.

'Beka, please, you have to have something to eat. Let's call room service and order something up—'

'Fuck off, Lewis. I'm not hungry. Just leave me alone.' She didn't glance round at the young man so she was oblivious of the grief-stricken look on his face.

'No, I won't leave you alone. You've got to snap out of this. Think of Mum and Dad. They'd hate to see you like this—'

She spun round. 'Hate to see me like this? Hate to fucking see me like this?' she screamed. 'It's all their fault, the lying bastards. They've wrecked my life. I hate them. If it wasn't for them none of this would have happened . . .'

'Don't be so pig selfish. You've only ever thought of yourself. Try considering someone else, for a change. It's hard on all of us.'

Rebekah picked up the silver ice bucket from the table and threw it full force across the room. 'Arsehole!'

Lewis stood his ground and the bucket landed on the carpet at his feet with a dull thud, scattering ice.

'Rebekah, you're my sister and I love you but you've got to get a grip on this. Nothing has changed really. We're still the same people we were. So are Mum and Dad.'

Lewis turned on his heel and left the room, closing the door quietly behind him. Rebekah had always been the strong one, the leader, the one who loved life and lived it to the full. Now he knew he was having to take charge. Rebekah was out of control.

He sat silently in his bedroom listening to the crashing and thudding next door. From an early age she had always thrown things about when events didn't go her way – and usually it had worked. Everyone gave in to Rebekah. But this was different; no tantrum could alter what had happened.

As soon as it quietened down Lewis went back in.

'Are you still going to talk with Angie Kavanagh? If you are, I have to phone and arrange it.'

'Why should I talk to anyone, Lewis? It's fuck all to do with them . . . Bloody vultures, they're enjoying it.' She paced back and forth, angrily waving her arms about and running her fingers through her hair.

3

'But you agreed to it, Beka. Angie Kavanagh's in New York for that reason.'

'Read my lips, you stupid bastard. I . . . will . . . not . . . talk . . . to . . . the . . . press, I will not!'

Lewis walked over and put his hands on her shoulders. 'If you don't they'll keep hanging around and digging. Remember this affects me too. Just give her a line and send her on her way, then we can get back to normal.'

The crack of her hand on the side of his head made his ears buzz.

'How can I ever get on with my life now? How can anything ever be normal again?'

Rebekah stood up as the journalists entered the vast open-plan apartment. She looked fantastic and she knew it. This was Rebekah the party animal, who left quivering wrecks of besotted men in her wake, this was the persona that kept her at the top of the invitation A-list. The skin-tight black trousers and cap-sleeved tee shirt didn't quite meet in the middle, showing a glimpse of the diamond stud in her belly button that twinkled suggestively in the chandelier light, the only jewellery she was wearing. The kitten-heeled suede boots added to her height and she towered over her visitors.

Walking towards the couple she smiled broadly and held out one perfectly manicured hand while flicking her hair behind her ear with the other. Angie was impressed by the performance that she knew it was.

'Hi, I'm Rebekah. I know you're Angie, and this must of course be Dave?' She pouted suggestively at Dave and struck her familiar model pose.

Angie's instinct for a good story told her there was one here. It was out of character for Rebekah Alari to fall to pieces over her parents' accident. She was just too self-centred and egotistical. And now she was trying too hard to be charming. Why? What was she hiding?

The smiling mouth was betrayed by the lifeless dark-ringed eyes. Angie had seen that look of despair before – on her own face, a long time ago, when she had very nearly tipped over the edge.

There was much to be discovered behind the smile, and if anyone could do it Angie Kavanagh could.

BOOK ONE

Chapter One

1969

Louise had tried everything over the past few months to block out the incessant shouting and fighting. Locked in her bedroom with the radio turned up, the sound of battle still seeped through but at a distance it was more bearable than being in the firing line.

Concentrating on her English homework was difficult but it provided an escape from the emotional turmoil in her life. She turned the radio's volume up as the shouting got louder but it carried easily through the paper-thin walls of the council flat.

'This is the last time you do this to me, Fran. You're a slag, a useless lazy slag, and I've had it up to here with you. You're making a right fool out of me.'

'You don't need any bleedin' help from me to look a fool, you can do it all by yourself,' snarled Louise's mother. 'Just bugger off, why don't you? Just bugger off, you bastard, and let me have some fun. God knows, I need it married to you.'

'I might just do that.'

'I can't wait.'

Louise listened for the front door crashing shut. It was always the same after her mother had been out the night before, and lately she was out most nights. Fran came in late sometimes and slept in the spare bedroom on the Put-u-up, but Louise never knew where she went or who with. She never asked, aware that she wouldn't be told anyway.

Louise was nothing if not a realist. Born and brought up in Leytonstone, the only child of mixed-race parents, she knew a lot about life. Her father had come over from Barbados in the fifties and struggled hard to make a living and a life. But he alienated himself from both the black and white communities by marrying the young and pretty East End barmaid who had flirted with him as a dare in the local pub. Six months after they'd married Louise was born.

Racial prejudice was a part of everyday life for all of them. It was aimed at her mother for marrying a black man, at her father for marrying a white woman, and worst of all at Louise for being their daughter. She had been called it all over the years, but had learnt to rise above the playground taunts. She rarely responded but that didn't stop it hurting.

Her way of getting back at her harassers was to work hard at school, and she had her sights set high, thanks to her father's enduring encouragement. She knew he always regretted the lack of formal education that had led him to a life of poorly paid manual jobs. Now he wanted the best for his only child and her winning a place at grammar school had been the highlight of his life. Louise didn't want to let him down.

Now Fran's perfunctory knock on the bedroom door was followed instantly by her flinging it open.

'Your father's sodded off yet again and I've got to go out. I won't be long.'

Standing in the doorway dressed up to the nines, she smiled sarcastically at her daughter. Her shoulder-length red hair was backcombed and pinned up in a French pleat that emphasised her huge green eyes outlined in thick black eyeliner and edged with long false eyelashes. Her short, rounded body was poured into a tight white trouser suit two sizes too small, which showed every lump and bump born out of a constant diet of fish and chips.

'How do I look? Not quite up to the mark for a grammar school girl, I suppose . . .'

Louise acknowledged her cursorily, not wanting to get into a row. 'You look fine. I'll see you tomorrow.' She looked back down at her homework, waiting for the door to shut again.

'Tomorrow? What do you mean, tomorrow? I said I won't be long and I won't be long, you cheeky little cow. There's some money on the table – you can go down the chippie for your tea . . . Don't spend the change and take that bloody mongrel of yours for a walk. It's whining already.'

With that, she was gone. Louise didn't really care where so long as her mother left her alone to get on with her homework in peace.

The continuing encouragement from her father was always tempered by the sniping from her mother, who was openly embarrassed at having her daughter at grammar school. Louise tried to work it out but couldn't. Why did her parents hate each other so much? And more importantly, why did Fran dislike her so much?

They must have been happy together in the beginning, she thought. Why else would they have gone against both their families and got married? Fran was ostracised by all her family and had never been in contact since, despite living less than a mile away. Joshua had never been back to Barbados since the day he left and he had no family in England.

Her mother told Louise all this constantly: 'If you knew what I have sacrificed for you and your father . . . I gave up everything for him . . . Without you and him tied round my neck I could have made something of myself . . .'

Louise rarely responded to the outbursts, knowing that if she questioned any of it Fran would always say the same thing: 'Don't ask me, ask your father. It's all his fault . . .'

'Here, Gypsy.' Waving a leather lead, Louise called her dog in from the balcony.

Walking her to the chip shop at the end of the road she tied her up outside and went in. The fat little mongrel didn't take her eyes off her mistress the whole time she was queuing to be served. Gypsy was the girl's confidante and protector, and Louise took her everywhere she could. She knew the dog wouldn't normally hurt anyone, but she could growl and look fierce enough for the local kids to give them both a wide berth.

The taunts and catcalls had increased since Louise had gone to the grammar school. She could never make up her mind which was worse – the tormenting from the local kids or the pointedly polite aloofness of the girls at school. She refused to let either get to her. Her father always told her she was better than any of them and she was going to prove it.

As usual there had only been enough money on the table for a small bag of chips, and when Louise got back she put half of them between two slices of bread with a big dollop of ketchup, and gave the other half to Gypsy.

Just as she finished she heard the front door open.

'Lou? Are you in your bedroom?'

'I'm in the front room, Dad, just finishing my supper.'

She stood up as her father came into the room and, as always, he enveloped her in his huge arms. He was a big man, well over six foot and around seventeen stone. When he hugged her she almost disappeared.

'Mum's gone out. She said she won't be long.'

'I guessed she would have,' he responded carefully. 'Is there anything in the oven for me?'

Louise looked sheepish but didn't answer.

He laughed loudly. 'Not to worry, I wasn't expecting any. I've got enough fat to manage for an evening without fading away. Darling, I want to talk to you. Come over here and sit with me.'

Louise listened with increasing horror as her father explained gently that he was going away for a while. She couldn't take it in. Why did he suddenly want to go back to Barbados? He'd always said that England was his home now and that Barbados was in the past – what had happened to change that now?

'Baby, my parents are old now and I want to see them again. I haven't seen them for so long. I want to go now before it's too late.'

'Can I go with you?' she asked hopefully. 'They're my family as well. Can I get to know them?'

'The most important thing for you right now is your education. You have to make the most of the chances you have.' He smiled down at her, pulling her close. 'A good education is your escape from here, a better life in the future. That's what I want for you, that's what will make me the happiest man in the world.'

'How long are you going for? Weeks? Months? How long? When are you going?'

She didn't notice the shadow of sadness that crossed his face as he answered.

'I'm going tomorrow and I'll be gone for a while. I'm not sure how long right now but I'll keep in touch. We can write to each other, I know you love writing . . .'

His voice tailed off as his daughter cried silently into his chest. She couldn't imagine not having him around to talk to and laugh with; she could think of nothing worse than living there alone with her mother.

'Why didn't you tell me sooner? Is it because you and Mum have been fighting so much? Is that why? Is that why you're not taking us with you?' She was sobbing so much now she could barely get the words out.

'Darling, the way things are now isn't fair on any of us, is it? Mum is very unhappy, and a spell apart will help us all. I hate leaving you but I'll be back . . . just remember that. I love you and I'll be back.'

Louise was at school the next morning when her father left the flat and headed alone to the airport. He had insisted she wasn't to be there for his departure.

She had helped him pack the previous night, and had gone to bed before her mother came in. She'd taken Gypsy under the covers and cried herself to sleep, cuddling the dog tightly.

Her father had spent their last few hours together telling her stories of his life before he came to England. She had heard them all before but now savoured every detail. She needed to be able to picture where he was and what he was doing while he was away.

Joshua had walked with her to the bus stop. They'd left the flat early and had walked slowly but it had been a few short minutes before the unwelcome bus had appeared in the distance. He'd quickly pulled her to him in a bearhug and she'd clung so tightly he'd had to peel her off him and push her on board.

'Just remember, I love you . . . Now do your best at school for me.'

The last sight Louise had had of her tall, handsome father was him waving frantically as the bus sped round the corner. She'd thought he was crying but she'd been unable to focus enough to see.

Her mother hadn't even got out of bed.

'You OK, Louise? You're quiet today.'

Sharon Aberlone was the one friend that Louise had made at her new school. She was the perfect opposite of Louise. She was as fair as Louise was dark, and as tall and chunky as her friend was tiny and slight. Despite being poles apart in looks and background they had gravitated towards each other in the early weeks of the first term and forged quite a friendship.

The two girls stood close together in the corner of the netball courts to protect themselves from the wind creeping through the wire netting. A couple of drops of rain brought the possibility of being allowed indoors for lunch break and they looked expectantly at the sky.

'Not really, no. In fact, nothing's OK. My dad's just gone back home to Barbados for a while.' She glanced at the Timex on her wrist. 'Actually, he's leaving about now.'

'God, how exciting. Why didn't you go with him?' Sharon paused slightly to gather her thoughts and then continued quizzically, 'Whereabouts is Barbados exactly? I've read about it in the mags.'

'It's an island in the Caribbean, and Dad reckons it's the most beautiful place in the world, all golden beaches and palm trees. Lots of rich and famous people go there for holidays. It's the "in" place, he says. As soon as I leave school I'm going to go there and meet the rest of my family.'

'He's not going to be gone that long, is he?' Sharon looked at her friend in horror.

'Of course not, stupid. He's only going for a while.' As soon as she said it Louise realised he hadn't actually said how long he was going to be away, just that he would be back.

'Doesn't your mum mind? I mean, he'll be somewhere nice and hot and you'll both be here freezing in winter. Doesn't seem fair to me.'

Louise thought about confiding in Sharon about what had been going on but decided not to. They might be friends but their lives were so different she didn't know if she'd understand. Anyway it seemed disloyal to talk about her parents.

'Of course she doesn't mind. If she did, Dad wouldn't have gone, would he?'

'No, I suppose not . . . Fancy coming round to my house tonight? We can listen to some records. That'll cheer you up!'

Louise was tempted. She guessed her mother would be out as usual for the evening and the thought of the empty flat wasn't appealing at all.

'Thanks, Sharon, but won't your mum mind?'

'Oh, come on, you know my mum – she loves you, she loves everyone. The more people in the house the happier she is!'

'I'll have to go home first and leave a note for Mum or she'll wonder where I am.'

Louise knew this wasn't true but she wasn't going to admit that Fran was not the least bit interested in where she went or whom she went with just so long as it didn't interfere with her.

'I wish I had straight hair like you. I mean, look at it. I look like a lavatory brush. You could turn me upside down and use me to clean the school loos.'

Sharon laughed out loud. 'Yeah, yeah, and I wish I was dark-skinned like you. I only have to look at the sun and I turn lobster red and peel, so stop complaining. You can go to the hairdresser but I can't get a new skin. Just look at all these freckles creeping over my fat face, yuk, yuk, yuk.'

The two girls were sitting side by side looking at themselves in the dressing-table mirror in Sharon's bedroom.

'At least you don't get called wog or halfchat by every horrible kid in the street, do you?' Louise looked at herself thoughtfully.

'No, I don't, but I do get called thunder thighs and fatso, so what's the difference?'

'I hadn't thought of it like that. I suppose we're both different from most, but does that give everyone the right to insult us? Why can't they leave us alone?'

At that moment there was a gentle knocking and Sharon's mother put her head around the door.

'All right if I come in, girls? I've got some hot chocolate and biscuits for you – keep your strength up for all that homework you're not doing! Look at you both, gazing into the mirror at yourselves, I don't know . . .' She laughed loudly, making the girls giggle.

Mrs Aberlone was a larger-than-life character, a real earth mother. She always welcomed Louise as if she had known her all her life and treated her as one of the family. Although the Aberlones lived in a lovely house in a quiet neighbourhood, and seemed to have more than enough money, the one single thing that Louise envied her friend was her mother.

She loved Fran because she was her mother but she didn't like her. She felt ashamed for feeling embarrassed by her but couldn't help it. The neighbours laughed at Fran behind her back as she tottered down the road half pissed, and their kids tormented Louise because of it.

'Right, girls, I'll leave you to it. Louise, Sharon's dad will be in shortly and he'll give you a lift home. Can't have you out and about the streets in the dark, can we now? I'll shout when he's ready.'

She smiled at them both as she left the room. Louise felt like crying.

Later, she persuaded Mr Aberlone to drop her at the corner of the road as usual; it mortified her just to think of him seeing her mother all dolled up for a night on the town.

She needn't have worried. The flat was in darkness and freezing cold when she got in. Her note was still on the table where she'd left it, which meant Fran hadn't been home all evening.

Gypsy was going crazy, barking and jumping up at her; she knew she would have to take her round the block even if it was dark and cold.

Louise turned the tired old gas fire on in the lounge. She sat on the floor with her knees pulled up tight to her chin, trying to absorb some of the heat, and sobbed and sobbed at the unfairness of it all.

It was six weeks after Joshua Jermaine left for Barbados that Louise found out what his leaving was all about.

'Mum? Are you OK? . . . Mum, can you hear me?'

Louise was outside the bathroom door listening to her mother retching. She had heard it before but Fran had dismissed it as stomach flu. And then Louise had believed her.

'No, I'm not bloody all right, you daft cow. If I was I wouldn't be throwing up, would I?'

'Do you want me to do anything? Shall I call the doctor?'

The bathroom door opened and Fran glared defiantly at her daughter.

'I've already seen the doctor. I'm not ill, I'm pregnant.'

Louise was thunderstruck. 'But how? I mean . . . I thought . . .'

'How? What do you mean, how?' Fran started to laugh. 'For Christ's sake, Louise, I know you're a good little grammar school girl but this is ridiculous. How do you think?'

'That isn't what I meant . . . I mean . . . Oh, you know what I mean.' She stood in front of Fran, blushing and frantically trying to put into words the jumble of thoughts that were flashing through her head. 'Have you told Dad yet? Will he be coming home?'

Fran laughed again but this time without any humour. 'No, he won't be coming home and I don't want you telling him anything about this. In fact, I want you to keep your gob shut completely. I don't want anyone knowing yet, not before they have to.'

Louise looked at her mother in disbelief. 'But you must tell Dad, you must.'

'I said no one and I mean no one. You write and tell your father and I'll kick your arse all the way down the street, and that's before I skin you alive.'

Fran pushed past and went into the kitchen; Louise followed and watched from the doorway as she put the kettle on and lit a cigarette.

The carefully backcombed hair of the night before now stood out at all angles with the lacquered strands dull and sticky from days of coating with cheap spray. Her face was pasty from nausea, and globules of black mascara were caked down her cheeks. The faded red satin wrap and fluffy slippers may have looked good once but now they conspired together to make Fran look like a bad caricature.

Louise was ashamed of the distaste she felt for her mother and she wanted to get out into the fresh air. Picking up her satchel she turned to leave, but Fran called her back.

'Make me some toast before you go. I need something in me to get me going for work. I can't miss another session in the poxy pub, I'll get the sack. Not that I care really – it's a lousy job with lousy pay, but it's better than nothing now your father's left us to it.'

Louise refused to rise to the bait. She knew her mother enjoyed working in the pub. She enjoyed it so much she was rarely home.

14

Going back into the shabby kitchen, she lit the grill and cut two slices off the stale loaf that was just starting to mould around the edges.

'You'll have to have it dry. There's no marge left, in fact there's nothing left, as always.'

'Just shut up, you.' Fran pointed her finger close to the girl's face. 'When you get a job, and you bring some money in, then you can moan but until then you can make do, same as I bloody well have to now your father has pissed off.'

The tears started bubbling up but Louise was determined not to cry in front of her mother. Fran would only torment her more. She put the toast on a plate and slapped it down in front of her mother.

'I'll be late for school if I don't go now. I'll see you tonight.'

Louise ran down the road as fast as she could, not for fear of missing the bus but as a release. She ran as if her life depended on it, and could feel her lungs burning as she reached the bus stop in record time.

Everything was changing. Her father had gone and she didn't know when he would be back, and now her mother was having a baby. Fran – who made no secret of the fact that she didn't even like children and had always sworn 'never again' when Louise had innocently asked for a baby brother or sister. The same Fran who had opted out of motherhood as soon as her daughter could walk and talk and developed her own character, was going to have another child.

As if this wasn't all bad enough Louise couldn't even tell Sharon.

Chapter Two

Louise ran into her bedroom and shut the door quietly. She didn't want to disturb Fran, who was asleep on the sofa.

The letter had come in the morning post and she had put it straight in her blazer pocket. First, she hadn't wanted Fran to see it, and secondly, she had wanted to savour reading it slowly and carefully.

Instead of the usual flimsy blue airmail letter, this was a bulky white envelope with colourful exotic-looking stamps on the corner. She sliced it open gently with a kitchen knife to preserve the stamps, and pulled out the pages that were folded in half. Several black and white photographs fell out on to her lap. Putting them to one side she started reading.

PO Box 1374, Barbados

My darling Lou-Lou,

I was so happy to get your letter. You really are a very good letter writer, you know; you have such a good way with words I can picture everything you tell me. Perhaps you'll be a rich and famous writer one day. That's what I tell everyone.

The post to Barbados is not very good so it takes a while for your letters to reach me but you write so many that when I go to collect my mail the lady shouts, 'Another letter from daughter Louise for you, you lucky man!'

I am happy that you and Mum are doing OK. I feel guilty that I can't send you any money right now but there should still be enough in the bank account I set up before I left to help for another couple of months.

I'm sorry you had such a sad Christmas. I know you must think it's all my fault but one day maybe you will understand. Perhaps next Christmas will be happier. I hope so. That's all I really want – for you to be happy and of course successful. I know you will be – you're so clever already, darling.

17

I loved the photographs of you and your friend Sharon. You seem to have grown up so much in the past few months. I hope you thanked her parents for taking copies for me. Tell them I am very grateful.

This is only a short letter because I wanted to send you these photos. I have written on the back who everyone is – your grandparents, aunties and uncles, nephews and nieces. We gathered in as many as we could so that you can now picture all your family. One day I am sure you will meet them all. I know they all want to meet you.

I will write again soon but I must now take this into town to catch the post.

I love you and miss you very much.

Love from Dad

Studying the photographs carefully, Louise spent a long time matching faces to names and studying details of the background. These were the first ones Joshua had sent since leaving and it helped give her a picture of where he was and who he was with. It was strange that all these people were members of her family and yet she didn't recognise any of them.

The one good thing was that he must have made up with his family. They all looked so happy in the photos that they'd be aware were to be sent back to England.

After reading the letter again she slipped it back into the envelope with the photos and raced off to get the bus to Sharon's house.

'God, Louise, doesn't it look exciting? When I'm older I'm going to travel the world. I've decided I'm going to lose loads of weight and when I'm slim and beautiful I'm going to be an air hostess. Just imagine going to all those countries and getting paid for it!'

Sharon and her mother were passing the photos back and forth between them enthusiastically.

'It certainly looks interesting, dear. I could easily get used to that scenery, and the beach looks wonderful. Will you be able to get me a free flight when you're off jet-setting?'

Louise and Sharon both laughed.

'Still, back to reality. Are you going to have tea with us, Louise? I've made too many cakes as usual, so I could do with some help to get rid of them.'

Louise thought Nancy Aberlone was just being kind but she couldn't bring herself to refuse. She adored being involved in the

18

buzz of real family life and she loved Nancy – the motherly look on the big woman's open and kindly face, and the way she wafted about in her long baggy clothes with her light auburn hair halfway down her back and no make-up. Nancy was Louise's dream of a mother.

'Oh, I'd love to, thank you.'

As soon as Nancy left the lounge Sharon grabbed her friend's hand and pulled her upstairs.

'I need to talk to you now . . . in private.' Closing the bedroom door she perched on the corner of the bed.

'You know Susie Singleton, the girl in the fifth year who lives near you? Well, I heard her telling another girl that your mum is having a baby! Is that right? Why didn't you tell me?' Sharon watched Louise, waiting for an answer. 'Louise? Come on, we're best friends . . . I thought we told each other everything.'

Louise didn't reply. She just looked at her feet, suddenly feeling horribly embarrassed.

'Come on, tell me. I told Susie to stop spreading stupid rumours but she insisted it was true, said she'd seen her and that everyone in the street knew about it.'

'I'm sorry, Sharon, but Mum made me promise not to tell anyone, not even Dad.' Her bottom lip trembled dangerously as she looked at her best friend. 'This is just so awful. I'm really sorry . . . I wanted to tell you, honestly, but I couldn't. Tell me everything that bitch Susie is saying. God, I hate her.'

Taking Louise's hand again, Sharon gently pulled her down beside her.

'She said that she's having a baby and that the father is Barry from the pub near you.'

'That's rubbish,' Louise snapped angrily. 'It's my dad's and when he knows he'll come home. Anyway, Barry's married.'

'Yes, I know, and Susie said that Barry's wife has just found out and is going to go after her and beat her to a pulp. She said your mum's been sacked 'cos of it.'

Louise tried to take it all in. She didn't want to believe it but suddenly it made sense. Things had been different lately. Fran was spending more and more time at home, staying in bed till the afternoon and then slouching about not bothering to get dressed from one day to the next.

Thinking about it, she realised Barry had been a familiar face around the flat but he and Mum worked together so it hadn't seemed unusual at the time. Surely the gossip couldn't be true?

'That's crap, Sharon, I know it is. Dad's only been gone four

19

months and the baby's due in two months. It doesn't make sense. She was already pregnant when he left.'

Sharon looked sheepish. 'I know. Susie said that's why he left; not because she was pregnant – he didn't know that – but because he found out about Barry. I'm sorry, Lou, but she said she heard Barry's wife telling her mum all about it. She's going to divorce Barry and name your mum.'

Rising panic threatened to overwhelm Louise as she quickly stood up. She knew if she started crying now she wouldn't be able to stop.

'I have to go . . . I have to go home . . . I'm sorry, I have to see Mum and tell her.' She rushed from the room and down the stairs.

Nancy Aberlone watched in amazement as Louise ran past her, slamming the front door on her way out.

'Sharon?' Nancy put her head round the banister and shouted upstairs. 'Have you two had a row? What's going on? Why is Louise upset?'

Sharon went downstairs and told her mother all about it. The woman was shocked but didn't let it show. She had always thought of herself as open-minded but this was something else. Louise was certainly in need, they decided, but what could they do to help her?

On the way home on the bus Louise thought about what she had learnt. She decided it was obvious what was going on. No one liked her mother. She had married a West Indian and they despised her because of it. They were just trying to cause trouble to stop her father coming home. Yes, that was it, she decided, that was what it was about. She knew she would have to tell Fran about the rumours but she wouldn't admit to believing them. She would be cool and calm and just tell her and then her mother would deny it and tell her her father was coming home.

She watched the changing house fronts as the bus made its way through the streets. Woodford was only a short ride in distance but it was far removed from the drab combination of terraced houses and concrete blocks of flats of her street in Leytonstone. The Aberlones' home, with its pseudo-Tudor black and white front and flower-bordered garden, seemed like a mansion compared to the dingy council flat that was home to Louise.

Sharon had still not been invited to her home and she was fast running out of excuses. Deep down she knew that Sharon wouldn't mind, but Louise herself did. She minded very much. She sometimes wondered if Fran was right when she hurled abuse at her for being a little snob.

★ ★ ★

The flat was in darkness apart from the monochrome flickering of the worn out TV in the front room. She switched on the light as she went in.

'Switch that bloody thing off, will you? Can't you see I'm watching telly?'

Fran was still on the sofa, still in her stained red wrap that strained now to meet across her distended belly. The belt was tied tightly under her big breasts, emphasising her bump and pulling the wrap up shorter than ever, showing her white dimpled thighs. A cigarette hung from her hand as she flicked the ash in the direction of the overflowing ashtray at her feet. Beer bottles and glasses stood to attention on the worn rug that curled up at the corners.

Louise tried not to make comparisons with the home she had left barely half an hour ago.

'Mum, I really need to talk to you. Can I switch the telly off, please?'

'No you can't. You can talk to me when this has finished if you really must.'

Fran didn't take her eyes off the set until Louise determinedly walked over to it and clicked the switch.

'Oi, put that back on this minute . . . How dare you?' Fran was so incensed she jumped up from the sofa and lunged at Louise, trying to smack her round the head.

Louise ducked and moved quickly to one side as the next swipe whistled past her ears. 'Mum, this really is important, please listen . . . Susie at school has been saying horrible things about you. She said that the baby is Barry's, that you got the sack and that Barry's wife is going to name you in court in the divorce.'

This time the flat of Fran's hand connected sharply with Louise's cheek.

'Don't, Mum, please. I'm only telling you what she's saying. I don't believe it. It is Dad's baby, isn't it? She's lying, isn't she?' Louise was pleading with her mother to tell her what she wanted to hear.

Fran looked at her daughter and for a split second Louise could see fear in her eyes but this was quickly replaced by something close to loathing before she looked away. She moved purposefully back to the TV and pressed the button before settling back on to the sofa.

'It's none of your business. Now just piss off to your bedroom and don't come back in here.' She didn't take her eyes off the screen. 'Oh, and turn the light off as you go. This picture's really lousy.'

21

Louise was dreading her twelfth birthday. The baby was due in three weeks and Fran had virtually ignored her since the confrontation. Whenever she tried to bring up the subject of the baby Fran would either flounce out of the room or order her to her bedroom. Louise found herself spending more time at Sharon's house, even sleeping over on Saturday night sometimes.

She was aware that the gossips were having a field day about her mother but studiously ignored the barbs that she knew originated from Barry's wife. She couldn't have responded even if she had wanted to. She still didn't know the truth.

Her birthday dawned and to her surprise there was an envelope on the kitchen table. Inside was a flowery card signed just 'Mum' and a ten-shilling note.

Fran was still in bed. Louise rarely ventured into the musty bedroom that her parents used to share. She could still remember hurling herself in there on a Sunday morning and clambering in beside her father to be wrapped fiercely in his arms. Her mother always turned her back and went to sleep.

Now her mother was spread out across the whole bed, lying on her side snoring ferociously. The bedclothes were grubby and the floor was littered with dirty clothes and crockery.

Louise tapped her mother gently on the arm. 'Mum, wake up, Mum. I just wanted to say thank you for the card and the money . . . Mum?'

Fran stirred and rolled over on to her back, losing the blankets in the process but quickly resuming the snuffling and whistling of a hangover.

Disappointed, Louise pulled the covers back over her and went to school.

'Happy birthday to you, Happy birthday to you, Happy birthday, dear Louise . . . Happy birthday to you.'

Louise was embarrassed but pleased when Sharon led several of their classmates in a rousing chorus when she went into the cloakroom. At least things were better at school now.

She got more cards than she would ever have anticipated as well as a wonderful present from Sharon. She opened the daintily wrapped parcel to find a silver filigree cross and chain nestling in a tiny velvet box. She put it straight on despite the school rule of 'no jewellery' but tucked it inside her shirt.

'That's OK, that's OK,' laughed Sharon as Louise thanked her over and over again. 'It's from Mum as well, something for you to remember us by when you're off exploring Barbados. What did your dad send you?'

'The post hadn't been when I left home so I don't know yet.'

'Mum asked if you'd like to come over for the day on Saturday. Dad is taking my brothers to football so it'll just be us girls, as Mum puts it. Boys out . . . girls in.'

Louise was pleased out of all proportion. 'Us girls' was such an intimate description, she was thrilled it included her.

'Louise Jermaine to the office, please. Louise Jermaine, come straight to the office, please.' The Tannoy announcement echoed through the corridors of the sprawling old school building at lunchtime.

'God, Louise, what have you done? Why have you got to go to the office?' Sharon laughed at her friend's stricken expression. 'Only joking! Oh, come on, don't look so scared. You've got to go to the office, not the gas chamber. Perhaps the secretary wants to sing "Happy Birthday" as well. Go on, I'll see you in maths.' She shoved Louise in the direction of the door.

But the secretary had a rather different message from happy birthday wishes to convey.

'Louise, we've had a telephone call from the hospital. Your mother has been taken in by ambulance—'

'What's the matter with her? Has she had an accident?'

'Now, now, Louise, don't interrupt and you'll find out.'

Coming up to retirement, the secretary was a stereotypical severe old spinster. She had worked at the school for over thirty years and ruled as if she herself was headmistress.

'Your mother is expecting a baby, is she not?'

'Yes, miss.'

'Right, well, apparently she is in the process of having that baby quite shortly and it has been requested that in the absence of your father, who I understand is abroad, you be permitted to leave the school premises early in order to attend the hospital. I have discussed this with the Headmistress and permission is granted. Off you go.' Seeing Louise still hesitating in front of her she snapped, 'Well, go on, off you go . . . go on.'

'Please, miss, which hospital and how do I get there?'

Armed with explicit directions she found her way to the hospital and up to the maternity unit.

The sister in charge didn't want to admit her at all but eventually gave in after an impassioned plea from a friendly midwife.

'Not too long, mind. Mum's got a lot of work to do today.'

23

Louise couldn't remember the last time she'd seen her mother with no make-up, no hair lacquer and no nail varnish.

At just twelve she had no inkling of the basics of labour and the pre-birth rituals. She was just dumbstruck at how young and pretty Fran looked. The freshly washed red hair hanging loosely around her face and the splattering of freckles that were usually camouflaged in panstick conspired together to knock ten years off her.

'Hello, Mum. They sent for me from school but I'm not allowed to stay with you for long. How are you?'

Fran managed a watery smile. 'How am I? In pain, that's how I am. In sodding pain and pissed off. I had to have a bath, they gave me an enema and then shaved my privates as bald as a coot's head. What about dignity and shame, I said to them, and do you know what they said? The snotty tart actually said, "Babies have to have a nice clean entry into the world" so I said, what about babies in Africa? Do they get a nice clean entry into the world? No they don't. They tumble headfirst into a muddy puddle and are yanked out by their ankles!'

Despite herself Louise laughed out loud. 'Mum! You didn't really say that, did you?'

'Course I did . . . and not only that . . . ooooooohh . . .' Fran wailed loudly, making Louise jump backwards in panic.

'Nurse, nurse!' She shouted out of the door. 'There's something wrong.'

The midwife rushed in but quickly assessed the situation.

'Heavens above, Mrs Jermaine, there really is no need for that noise. You're frightening your daughter.'

She turned her attention to Louise. 'We've having a contraction, that's all, dear—'

Fran quickly interrupted. 'No we're not having a contraction, *I* am having a contraction – *me*, that is, not *you*.'

The nurse ignored the interruption. 'Everything is going nicely but it'll be a while yet before anything happens. Why don't you go on home and we'll ring you?'

'You're not sending her anywhere. I want her here with me. I've got no husband here. I'm not going through this on my own. Either she stays or I go and give birth in your frigging car park. Take your pick.'

Bewildered, Louise looked from one to the other, wondering who she should take notice of, but the decision was taken away from her.

'All right, Mrs Jermaine, she can stay for the time being but only if you stop the shouting. You're frightening our other mums-to-be.'

Her crisp white apron rustled as she turned on her heel and left the small side ward, closing the door behind her.

Fran smirked. 'Pompous bitch, that sorted her out, didn't it?'

Fran got worse and worse as the day wore on. She shouted, she screamed, she swore at everyone.

Louise sat nervously by the bed listening and trying her best to comfort her mother as well as any twelve-year-old in that position could. She felt completely helpless.

At eleven o'clock that night Fran was wheeled into the delivery room and Louise was told in no uncertain terms that she wasn't going in as well.

Her protestations were half-hearted. No way did she want to be part of the next bit.

The doors swung open at five to twelve and the midwife announced dramatically that Fran had given birth.

'Congratulations, my dear. You have a noisy baby brother. Come back tomorrow afternoon and you can see Mum and baby.'

It was only then that Louise remembered it was her birthday. Not only was she going to share her life with this baby she was also going to have to share her birthday.

She walked out into the smoke-filled waiting area in a daze and was suddenly swept up into the arms of Nancy Aberlone.

'Come along, birthday girl. You're coming home with us for the next few days. Dear, dear, your mum did make a fuss, didn't she? We could hear the kerfuffle out here.'

Louise was too tired and bewildered by her day to respond. She just let herself be led down to the car park and whisked off to the Aberlones' home.

Waking with a start Louise wasn't sure where she was for a second. Then it all came back. Looking up from the tiny camp bed in Sharon's bedroom she could just make out her friend creeping about getting ready for school.

'Sharon?'

'Sorry, Lou. I was trying not to wake you. Mum said to let you sleep in, but now you are awake tell me all about it. I want to know everything.'

Louise rubbed her eyes and glanced at the bedside clock. 'I'm going to be late for school . . .'

'No you're not. Mum said you're not going today, you lucky beggar. So tell me, what was it like? What's the baby like? Is he like you?' Sharon was firing questions so fast Louise could barely keep up.

'I don't know, they didn't let me see it. I've got to go back today, this afternoon . . . God, Sharon, it was awful. I'm never going to have kids, never ever in a million years.'

'Oh bugger, look at the time. Mum's waiting to drop Dad off at the station. I'll see you tonight and then I want all the gory details. Bye.' Sharon blew her a kiss as she flew out of the room.

Louise was now wide awake and alone. She was carefully turning over the last twenty-four hours when the thought hit her. Gypsy! Gypsy had been locked in the flat all night on her own with no food!

She was mortified but Nancy came to the rescue and insisted on driving Louise straight home. Louise tried her best to persuade her to stay in the car but the woman was adamant, though perceptive enough to realise that Louise was ashamed of her home. So she compromised. She was well aware that Sharon had never been invited there and there had to be a reason why Louise was always dropped off on the corner.

'Don't be silly, dear, the flat's been empty all night. You're not going in there on your own. I tell you what, I'll just come to the front door and wait for you there.'

Gypsy started barking as Louise put the key in the lock and as the door opened she flew out, nearly knocking them both over.

'Gypsy, I'm sorry, I'm sorry. How could I have forgotten about you?' Louise crouched down and cuddled the dog that was so excited her whole body was wagging along with the tail.

Nancy could feel the dreaded prickling sensation behind her eyes. She sighed. She knew she was too soft for her own good.

'Take Gypsy for a quick walk up the road and then put her in the car; she'll have to come home with us. She'll sleep in the kitchen, mind.'

While Louise was out with the dog Nancy took the opportunity to sneak a look inside the flat and found it much as she had anticipated. She was saddened by the state of the inside but the single thing that shocked her most was the daubing on the wall outside the flat. Someone had tried to scrub it off but the outline was still there of the words 'Go home wogs'. Beside it in a different hand was the single word 'whore'. Nancy felt sick. She knew she could figure out a way of passing on some furniture and curtains without offending the girl or her mother but the graffiti was something different, something poisonous she had never come across before.

They drove back in silence. Louise knew the woman had seen it all and Nancy knew that she knew, but neither knew what to say.

It wasn't so much butterflies in her stomach as a flock of hungry starlings flapping around. Nancy had dropped Louise at the hospital entrance and promised to wait in the canteen for her until she was ready to leave.

Nancy wanted to go in with her but she knew that Louise didn't want her to meet Fran so she didn't suggest it; she just wished her luck and kissed her on the cheek.

Pausing outside the swing doors to the maternity ward, Louise thought it was more nerve-racking than her first day at grammar school; she wanted to go in but felt strangely shy about facing her mother after the happenings of the day before. Forcing her feet to move she went up to the desk, clutching a heavy shopping bag of necessities that Nancy had suggested her mum would require. Louise had included Fran's make-up bag too.

'Can you tell me where Mrs Jermaine is, please? I'm her daughter.'

'Down the corridor, third bed on the left,' the nurse replied without looking up.

'Hello, Mum.' Louise stood uncomfortably beside the bed. She quickly noticed that all the other beds had Perspex cribs alongside them but the space beside Fran was empty.

'You took your time. Where have you been? Have you brought any of my things with you?'

'Where's the baby?' Louise looked around as if she expected the crib magically to appear next to her.

'He was a bit early so he's in special care. Where's my stuff? They said I've got to stay in here for ten days. Not content with all the other crap they put me through they've now stitched me up like a Christmas turkey and given me a bloody rubber ring to sit on. Never again, that's all I can say, never again. Why does it have to be us women? Why not the men, eh? Let them have the babies and sex would soon be a dying art.'

Louise waited impatiently for her to pause for breath.

'I've brought you a few things – nighties and underwear and a towel. What's wrong with the baby?'

'Nothing, he's just a bit premature . . . came too early.' Fran looked away as she spoke. Louise wondered if it had anything to do with her mother being drunk as a skunk the night before but didn't ask.

'Can I see him?'

'How do I know? Ask the nurse. Did you bring my make-up?'

Louise slapped the shopping bag down on the bed. 'Here's

27

everything I brought. If you want anything else I'll go back home tomorrow for it.'

'Be careful where you put that. I've just had a baby, in case you've forgotten . . .' Fran's protest faded as she realised what Louise had said. 'What do you mean, go back tomorrow? Why aren't you going back tonight?'

'I'm staying at Sharon's house while you're in here.' Louise paused for a second. 'So is Gypsy.'

'Oh, I bet you are! I know Leytonstone isn't good enough for you now you're a grammar school girl but now it's not even good enough for the dog—'

Louise interrupted her. 'I'm going to ask if I can see the baby.'

She walked unhappily away from the bed, wondering why her mother could never be nice to her.

The glassed room that housed incubators and cribs was steaming hot. Louise felt silly wearing the compulsory green mask, gown and overshoes that swamped her. She looked round in silent awe at the tiniest of babies, stark naked inside the incubators. There were wires and tubes everywhere and the room was silent apart from the beeping of the equipment.

There was one other woman in there, silently gazing at her baby. Louise noticed she had a gloved hand inside one of the portholes, gently stroking its head.

She looked away. 'Which one is he?' she whispered to the nurse, terrified of the answer.

'This one here. No need to whisper, just don't shout!' the nurse smiled sympathetically.

Louise felt a wave of relief rush over her; he was in a crib.

'I can't let you hold him today but at least you'll have seen him. He should go down to the ward in the next couple of days. He's doing fine.'

Louise gazed silently at her brother. He was covered with a blue blanket and a tiny muslin bonnet that looked as if it was about to engulf his head. All she could see was a cross little face with screwed-up eyes and tiny red lips.

Tied to the end of a crib was a pale blue name card. Louise picked it up. 'Baby Jermaine, 6lb 1oz' had been written in careful script. The word baby had been crossed out and replaced with 'Daniel'.

'He's quite sturdy for such a little mite, a good pair of lungs too. Do you want to wait while I feed him? You'll have to get used to this now, help your mum out.' Carefully lifting him out, the nurse tucked him in the crook of her arm and leant him towards Louise.

She was enthralled. She didn't know what she had expected. Babies were not new to her – there were several in the flats and she had even been enlisted to babysit on occasions – but this was different.

Watching in awe as the miniature mouth sucked eagerly on the teat of the bottle the nurse had given her, Louise fell in love for the first time.

She was there with Fran when, three days later, baby Daniel was transferred from the special unit to his mother's bedside.

Looking at him closely, for the first time removed from the swathes of muslin, Louise noticed that the postbirth redness had faded and his skin was pale pink. The downy hair on his head was sprouting red. He was beautiful.

'They were right, weren't they?' Louise spoke quietly without looking at Fran. 'He's not Dad's, is he? He's white.'

Fran's laugh was without humour. 'Of course he's white. After everything I've had to put up with, did you really think I'd have another black kid? You belong to your father, you always have – now this one is mine, a white baby for a white mother.'

The colour drained from Louise's face as she tried to take in the venomous words.

'How can you say that? Dad was black when you married him. He didn't suddenly change colour overnight—'

'That's right, but I didn't realise it would cost me everything – family, friends – and after you were born it got worse. I was a social outcast. It was OK for your father, he was used to it, but I hated every insult, every remark that was aimed at me for being with a black man.'

'I always thought you wanted me . . . loved me . . .' Louise looked Fran straight in the eye but the woman didn't glance up and her voice was flat when she spoke.

'I do, I suppose. I just wish you were white.'

The pain shot through Louise like a bullet and she stood stock-still for a few seconds before turning and walking straight out.

Louise didn't visit the hospital again.

The following days passed in a blur. Not even Sharon could get through to her. She was detached. All her energies went into her school work and walking Gypsy.

Nancy Aberlone tried her best but the brick wall was built that day on the hospital ward and there with no cracks to exploit.

Louise was polite and co-operative but the intimacy had gone; the hurt was too great to share with anyone. Her mother's rejection of her was complete, and to compound her misery there had been no letter or birthday card from her father.

The day Fran and Daniel were due home, Louise packed her belongings and asked to be dropped off on the corner.

After much discussion, and against her better judgement, Nancy concurred. She was at a loss to know what to do for the best other than to offer the girl as much love and support as she could.

She knew she would never be able to erase her image of the poor mite walking despondently down Albemarle Street, clutching a battered brown suitcase in one hand and Gypsy's lead in the other. Even the dog looked dejected as they turned the bend and slouched out of sight.

At least the flat was better than when she had left it. Old Mrs Anderson from downstairs, who had a spare key for emergencies, had gone in one day and busied herself cleaning right through. Louise had nearly had a heart attack when she'd gone to collect more of Fran's make-up and found her there.

'Bleedin' unhygienic, this is,' Mrs Anderson had greeted Louise. 'Don't know what your mother is thinking of, bringing a baby back here to this tip. Still, not to worry, eh? Soon be done. Well, don't just stand there gawping at me, girl. Get helping.'

The woman had an energy that belied her seventy-odd years. She loved cleaning and gossiping in that order, and knew everything about everyone and their homes. She also wasn't averse to sharing her titbits with the locals while she cleaned the pub. Nothing got past her; she knew exactly what was going on at number 3.

In the Jermaine flat she'd come into her own. Net curtains had been taken down and put up, beds had been changed, and the kitchen and bathroom disinfected from floor to ceiling. The rugs had been hung out of the windows that were flung open for the first time in months.

Louise had been packed off to the Launderette with two big bags of washing, and all the second-hand baby clothes that Fran had collected and dumped in a heap in the corner were washed and ironed, and, with a pile of white fluffy nappies, stacked in the carrycot in the bedroom.

Mrs Anderson had even found an old tin of white emulsion and slapped it over the obscenities on the wall outside.

By the time Louise had staggered back to Woodford the flat had looked almost homely.

Now Louise heard the key in the lock and went out into the dingy small hallway. The front door was open and she could see the outline of Fran, holding the baby.

She reached out for him but hesitated when she saw someone else standing behind her mother.

'I'll hold Danny, you help Barry with the bags. Christ, I could do with a decent cup of tea after all that gnat's piss, and a decent meal wouldn't go amiss either.'

Louise just stood there, frozen.

'Come on, girl. Move yourself and let us in.'

Fran pushed past, followed closely by a sheepish Barry, who was smiling nervously. Louise didn't look up as she reached out and took a carrier bag from him before turning back into the flat.

Fran flopped down on the sofa, still holding the baby. 'Pass my handbag, babe. I'm gasping for a fag.'

Louise automatically went to get the bag but she saw Barry holding it out to her mother.

Babe?

She glanced from one to the other silently.

Fran took a cigarette out of the packet and lit it. She inhaled deeply and looked straight at Louise.

'Barry's going to be living here now. He wants to be with me and his son.'

Louise opened her mouth to say something but Fran carried on.

'Don't look so shocked. If you'd bothered to get your lazy arse up the hospital you'd have known. At least Barry visited me.'

Chapter Three

Loyalty to her father meant she could never bring herself to admit it, but secretly Louise quite liked Barry. He had a sense of humour, made her laugh and sometimes slipped her his loose change when Fran wasn't looking.

In the beginning she'd ignored him and kept out of the way as much as she could but he persevered and finally won her over. What finally swung it was the way he talked to her and listened to her just like Joshua used to. The way her mother didn't.

Initially she nicknamed him 'the weasel'. At five foot five and stick thin he was not much bigger than Louise, and his thin greying hair was slicked back with Brylcreem. At first, she hated the way he looked, constantly comparing him to her father, whom she still thought was the most handsome man in the world, but gradually she had learnt to live with Barry in the flat. He even stuck up for her when Fran was at her most vitriolic, and often brought her home little treats.

Joshua had been gone a year now and it was coming up to Louise's second Christmas without him. The letters from him were now infrequent and she found it increasingly difficult to reply. She still felt guilty about this, despite being upset that he had forgotten her birthday, but what could she say without lying? She couldn't write about Daniel, she couldn't write about Barry, and she didn't want to write about her mother. So she put it off. The last letter from Joshua remained unopened; she just couldn't face the hurt she anticipated inside the envelope.

'What are you doing next weekend, Lou?' Barry asked one evening in November. He was sitting next to her on the new sofa that Nancy had cunningly given them under the guise of 'we really don't have room for it any more. You'll be doing us a good turn, you know.'

'I'm not sure. I'm going to Sharon's on Saturday but I'm not stopping over. They're going to a family do on Sunday. Why?'

'I'm not working at all on Sunday and I fancy taking Danny to the zoo. Do you want to come?'

Louise giggled. 'Barry, he's only six months old, why do you want to take him to the zoo? Anyway, it'll be freezing.'

'That's what dads do, isn't it, go to the zoo at the weekend?'

Barry took being a father seriously. He hadn't any other children and doted on Daniel. Fran was rapidly losing interest in the baby so he and Louise did most of the caring and loving between them.

The first night home from hospital Danny's carrycot had been quickly transferred into Louise's room and Fran had opted out of the night feeds. 'I need a good night's sleep to cope with him during the day' was her defence as Louise and Barry stumbled about bleary-eyed in the mornings. Then as soon as he was out of the night feeds she'd started delegating the daytime feeds and anything else she could get away with. Fran was not a natural-born mother and Louise made it all too easy for her to opt out.

Besotted with her baby brother, she didn't really mind. She spent hours with him; she fed him, changed him and sometimes even took him into bed with her. She loved mothering him but her schoolwork was suffering and it worried her. She didn't think she could ever face her father again if she failed.

The honeymoon was over in number 3 and tensions were mounting. Louise had a strange feeling of *déjà vu.*

'You coming as well, Fran?'

'What? To the zoo? In November? No way.'

Then Fran's tone suddenly changed to the wheedling whine that she had perfected for Barry's benefit. She went over to him and perched on his knee, pushing her breasts close to his face.

'I've got a better idea, babe. Louise can take Danny to the zoo and we can stay home on our own, like the old days, just you and me. Louise won't mind, will you?'

She turned and smiled encouragingly at Louise, looking for support, but as the girl hesitated Barry got in first, his voice quietly angry.

'I don't want Louise to take Danny to the zoo. I want to take him. Come on, Fran, it'll be fun. Let's all go together.'

'Please, Mum, come with us,' Louise joined in.

'Forget it. I'm not freezing to death in a bloody zoo surrounded by stinking animals, but no doubt you'll go without me . . . again . . . sod off and leave me on my own . . . again. Well, sod you all, I'm sure I can find something much more interesting to do all day without a baby in tow.' She looked sideways at Barry, waiting for a reaction.

34

He just looked at Louise and raised one eyebrow. 'You up for it?'

Louise didn't hesitate. She grabbed her little brother out of his playpen and danced round singing, '*We're going to the zoo, zoo, zoo. How about you, you, you? You can come too, too, too. We're going to the zoo.*'

'Pillocks, all of you.' The bedroom door slammed behind Fran.

They never did get to the zoo. The row that night was the worst ever between Fran and Barry, and Louise couldn't help but hear every word of it.

'You don't give a toss about me, do you? All you want is your precious son. Well, why don't you take your bastard son and piss off back to your barren, frigid wife . . . that's what you want, isn't it? Go and play happy families there.' Fran was screaming like a banshee at the top of her voice, totally oblivious to the banging on the wall from next door.

The thud of Barry's fist hitting the table echoed into Louise's bedroom.

'You're barking mad. I loved you – that's why I left Sally – but I love Daniel and I really don't think you do, any more than you love little Louise. You're a lousy mother, do you know that?'

'Yes I do know – you tell me often enough, but I'm good in bed, aren't I? That was enough for you once. Sodding kids, they spoil everything. One's a daddy's girl and now the other's turning into a daddy's boy. Two kids, both accidents – I can't win, can I? Why can't it be like it was?'

Fran was so hysterical she could hardly catch her breath but Barry wasn't going to give in.

'If you don't give love you don't get it back. You trample all over Louise and now you ignore Daniel. Either it changes or I will leave and I will take Daniel. You're not going to screw him up the same way you've screwed up your daughter.'

Three weeks later, Barry walked out with Daniel, and Louise thought her heart would break. She had expected Barry to give up on Fran but never for a moment had she thought he would take Daniel. She certainly never thought Fran would let him.

Fran was watching TV, even as Barry was packing his own and Daniel's things.

'Louise, I've promised you, you can see Daniel whenever you want. We'll only be two streets away. Are you sure you won't come with us? You can, you know—'

'No, she bloody well can't,' Fran shouted over her shoulder. 'You can take your little bastard but she stays with me. Louise . . . get in here now.'

'Mum, how can you let them go? Please stop them, please. It's not fair . . .' Louise was screaming in panic. 'Barry, please stay, please don't take Danny. I love him.'

'Sweetheart, I know you do, but so do I and that's why we have to go. Come and see him tomorrow after school, come for tea.'

He turned and went without looking back. He felt bad about Louise but he knew it was the only thing to do, for Danny's sake. He had discovered how destructive Fran could be to relationships.

Louise watched out of the window until the car was out of sight. She turned back to her mother.

'I hate you for this and I'll never forgive you. You're a selfish bitch.' She started to run out of the room.

'Louise?'

'What?'

'Don't slam the door on the way out.'

Nancy Aberlone and her daughter were open-mouthed in horror.

'I don't believe it. She just let him take the baby? Just like that? That is so horrible . . .'

'Now, Sharon, it's not for you to pass judgement. If Louise's mother thought that was best for Daniel then it was a very brave thing to do, let her baby go.'

'She didn't think it was best for Daniel, she just thought it was best for her,' Louise said. 'She's back behind the bar of another pub already, looking like the local slut.'

The bitterness in her voice and hatred in her eyes shook Nancy. She'd never heard the girl turn against her mother before.

'Why didn't you go with them then?' Sharon asked curiously. 'You like Barry – would it have been so bad?'

'I didn't have any choice. She'd have made me come back, wouldn't she?'

'Louise is right, dear, her mother would have the final say. Still, at least you can see him – he's not gone for good – and, after all, Barry sounds like a nice man. I'm sure it'll all be OK in the long run.'

Her confident approached belied her fears for Louise and her future. She wouldn't have dreamt of saying it to the girl but Nancy was horrified at the thought of a mother giving up her child so easily. It was something just too awful to contemplate.

'Louise darling, can I ask you something? What happened that day at the hospital after Daniel was born? I know something upset you dreadfully, isn't this a good time to get it all into the open?'

The anger at her mother was so intense that all Louise's

36

misplaced loyalty went out the window.

'She said that if Daniel had been black she wouldn't have had him. She didn't want another black kid. And she meant it. She must really hate me.'

For the first time in her life Nancy felt something closely akin to hatred herself. She was at a total loss for words at the wickedness of it.

Dry-eyed Louise looked at the mother and daughter and realised that no matter how hard she tried she would never have that relationship. She had nothing now and knew that it was time to accept that and start getting her own life together. Things couldn't get any worse so now the only way out was up.

Louise grew up that day. She went home and set out a life-plan for her future.

1. I will study hard and pass all my exams.
2. I will leave Leytonstone and never come back.
3. I will save enough money to go to Barbados.
4. I will never ever get married or have children.

Her father had always told her that a good education and hard work were the only way to get on and he was right. She knew for certain now she couldn't rely on her mother and she didn't want to rely on the Aberlones. They were so good to her it made her want to weep but they weren't family, no matter how much she would have liked it to be that way.

She took to doing her homework in the public library on the way home and was constantly searching the shelves for books to read in bed at night. Reading and writing became her escape from reality – the reality of life with Fran but without her father or Daniel.

The five-year diary with a lock and key that she bought with her birthday money had become a nightly ritual of penning her darkest thoughts and highest aspirations. She believed she would make it. She had to believe it.

'Louise, you must come round tonight, you really must. We've got a surprise for you.' It was a Monday morning at the end of the autumn term and Sharon was waiting at the school gates for her friend.

'What is it?'

'I can't tell you, silly. Mum'll kill me. You can come straight round if you want, come and have tea.'

Once Louise would have made a big pretence out of having to go home first but now she didn't bother.

'What about homework? We'll have loads.'

Sharon raised her eyes to the sky in mock exasperation and wagged her finger at Louise. 'No, we won't. We break up next week, in case you've forgotten, and that means holidays and no homework. Look at me, you swot . . . holidays mean no homework!'

Louise laughed. 'Yes, miss, anything you say, miss, sorry, miss.'

'That's better. Now don't let it happen again.'

They linked arms and strolled into school, laughing. They heard someone shout something about 'the odd couple' but that just made them laugh even more.

That afternoon Sharon opened the front door and shouted, 'Mum, we're home. Can I tell her now?'

Nancy walked down the hall to meet them.

'Heavens alive, let the poor girl get her coat off first and then I'll tell her, darling. You're too excited to get it straight.' Nancy knew a little tact and diplomacy was called for, and much as she loved her daughter she knew she wasn't too hot on that count. 'Come on into the kitchen and I'll put the kettle on.'

The two girls sat at the table, looking at her expectantly.

'Louise, how would you like to come on holiday with us in the summer?'

Louise was stunned. This was the last thing she had expected. 'Er, I don't know. I don't think Mum can afford it . . .'

'Money doesn't come into it. It won't cost you anything apart from your spending money. A friend of ours lives in Jersey, in the Channel Islands – well, he's coming to England for two weeks and we're going out there. We're swapping houses.'

'Louise, you must come. Can you imagine how boring it will be for me with two brothers? Please say you will. You'll be doing me a big favour.'

Nancy was sorry she'd doubted her daughter. She had said exactly the right thing to save Louise's pride.

'I'll have to ask Mum. I don't know what she'll say, but I'd love to . . . Jersey – I can't imagine it; I've only been to Southend.' She paused for a second. 'Where exactly are the Channel Islands?'

'I'll tell you in a minute. You don't know the best bit yet, Lou. We're going to fly.'

Louise's mouth dropped. 'Fly? In a plane?'

'Of course in a plane, how else do you think?' Sharon was laughing and Nancy tried hard to keep a straight face as she went to find an atlas. She was glad Louise hadn't thought about the air fare; that would be harder to explain away.

'Clothes!' Louise suddenly announced loudly. Sharon and her mother both looked at her. 'Clothes, I haven't got any. How can I go without clothes?'

'As in naked, do you mean? Too right, you're not coming on a plane with me if you're naked.'

'Sharon, I haven't got any holiday clothes. I'll show you all up . . . No, I can't go—'

Nancy interrupted her in mid-flow. 'You're getting ahead of yourself now. One thing at a time. We'll sort all that out nearer the holiday.'

Louise had been dreading Christmas but now there was something to look forward to. Too worried Fran might not agree, she decided not to discuss it with her yet. Louise told herself she'd do that after Christmas.

What Fran also didn't know was that she sometimes looked after Daniel while Barry was at work and he always paid her. It wasn't a chore and she would have willingly done it for nothing but Barry always insisted. He knew how difficult life was for her. She never spent the money, but put it into an old tea caddy and hid it under the mattress with her diary.

When she got home from the Aberlones that evening, she cut out a piece of paper and wrote 'Jersey Tin' in red letters and sellotaped it to the lid. Then she filled in her diary with her news.

Nancy was in a quandary. Three months later, Louise still hadn't discussed the holiday with Fran. 'After Christmas' had become 'after Easter', but that was cutting it fine. There were tickets to be bought. If they weren't arranged soon for Louise it would be too late and she wouldn't have the choice of going. Nancy decided to move things forward herself.

Parking her car on the main road she walked back to Albemarle Street. Usually loud and flamboyant in her choice of clothes and colours, she had dressed carefully in the most neutral outfit she could find in her colourful hippy wardrobe, a pair of light brown chainstore trousers teamed with a yellow blouse neatly tucked into the waistband. A rubber band pulling her long wild hair back into a ponytail at the nape of her neck just finished off the uncharacteristic look. On her way out she had looked in the mirror and thought: Yuk. She hated looking frumpy but the last thing she wanted to do was aggravate Louise's mother. She wanted to make sure Louise would be allowed to go on holiday and if that meant kowtowing to the dreadful Fran that was exactly what she would do.

Taking a deep breath, she knocked firmly on the door of number 3 and waited. It was 11 a.m., on a schoolday so she knew Louise wouldn't be there. There was no reply so she knocked again a bit louder. Nancy was just about to leave when the door opened a fraction and a bleary-eyed Fran peered out.

'Mrs Jermaine? Hello there. I'm Nancy Aberlone, Sharon's mother.'

There was not a flicker of recognition on Fran's face.

'Who?'

'Sharon's mother – you know, your daughter's school friend. I wondered if I might come in and have a chat. I thought it was about time we met – you know, mothers of best friends and all that.'

Fran opened her eyes wider and looked warily at the woman in front of her. 'You're sure you're not from the social?'

Nancy laughed nervously. 'No, of course not. I said, I'm Sharon Aberlone's mother.'

'I suppose you'd better come in then, but you'll have to take me as you find me. I don't make excuses to anyone.'

She turned away, leaving Nancy to close the door and follow her.

The lounge curtains were still closed, but they didn't meet in the middle and a solitary ray of sunshine beamed across the room, highlighting the dust. A mound of dirty washing was piled on the sofa but apart from that the room was quite tidy, nothing like the last time Nancy had peeked in.

Fran pulled open the curtains, blinking rapidly as the daylight hit her full on. Turning round to face Nancy she folded her arms across herself, pulling the edges of her wrap together at the same time.

'What exactly do you want, Mrs Woodford? Oops, sorry, I mean Mrs Aberlone.'

Nancy was a good nine inches taller than Fran so she sat down quickly, wriggling slightly to avoid the washing.

'Call me Nancy,' she smiled, ignoring the none-too-subtle dig. 'I wish I wasn't called Nancy but there's not much I can do about it really. Do you mind if I call you Fran?'

'Call me what you like. I'm going to put the kettle on – mouth like the bottom of a parrot's cage this morning . . .'

'What a wonderful expression. I must remember that, that's lovely . . .'

Nancy's raucous laugh took Fran by surprise; the woman was nothing like she'd imagined.

Tea made, they sat on opposite sides of the small room and sized each other while making small talk and sipping from stained mugs.

Mid-conversation Fran suddenly changed tack. 'Louise thinks I'm stupid . . . I know why she spends all her time at your house and I know why your daughter never comes round here. Louise is ashamed of me, and ashamed of her home . . . She'll be pig sick that you came here.'

'Oh, I don't think that's right at all. Your Louise is a lovely girl, a credit to you. She hasn't got a bad bone in her body.'

'Does she know you're here then?' Fran defiantly made direct eye contact for the first time.

Nancy hesitated, aware that what she said next was crucial. 'No, she doesn't, but neither does Sharon. Youngsters today think our generation are past it and have nothing better to do than talk about them. No, I just wanted to meet you and get to know you.'

'I'm sure you know all about me already. Married a black man, he left me, lived with a white one, he left me, I abandoned my son and my daughter hates me. There isn't much else, is there? I don't know why I carry on. I've got absolutely bugger all really.' Fran burst into tears. She put her face in her hands and her whole body shook with the ferocity of her torment.

This was the last thing Nancy had expected but suddenly it all became clear as day. Fran wasn't well. She was depressed. Nancy recognised the symptoms and was angry with herself for not piecing it together sooner. It wouldn't excuse everything but it would explain a lot – her treatment of Louise and Daniel, her mood swings, everything.

Nancy resisted the urge to wrap Fran in her arms and comfort her. It was too soon for that sort of intimacy.

Fran slowly calmed down and Nancy silently passed her some tissues from her handbag.

'Look at the state of me. I bet you think I'm a right pillock, bawling my eyes out in front of a stranger . . .'

'It's often easier to confide in strangers; family find it harder to understand. I'll make another pot of tea and we'll start again.'

Nancy spent over two hours with Fran Jermaine and came away feeling completely drained and helpless. The woman needed medical help. Nancy hoped she would take her advice and seek it, but somehow she doubted it. She feared she was more likely to self-destruct first.

The holiday hadn't been mentioned but Nancy knew she would visit again soon.

★ ★ ★

'What do you mean, you went round to see Mum? She never told me. What did you do that for?' Louise was angry and for once Nancy could feel herself losing patience with her.

'Now let's get something straight, young lady. You are thirteen years old and I really don't have to explain myself to you but I will. You're coming on holiday with us and your mother doesn't know us from Adam. I wouldn't dream of letting Sharon go on holiday with strangers and I'm sure your mother wouldn't either.' Nancy smiled to take some of the edge off her anger.

'She wouldn't care. She never takes any notice of me, she hates me . . .'

'In that case, why haven't you told her? She still doesn't know, does she?'

Louise lapsed into silence, kicking her feet deeply into the lawn to make the huge garden hammock swing gently. She was turning into such a pretty young woman. Still small for her age and dainty with it, she was going to be stunning, Nancy could see, but at that moment Louise looked quite sullen.

Sharon knew when to keep quiet. She just sat silently on the grass, throwing crumbs to the birds.

'Louise darling, I know you have every reason to resent your mother but have you ever thought that maybe she isn't very well, that maybe the way she is isn't all her fault?'

Louise didn't answer straight away. She kept looking down and kicking at the grass. Nancy waited. 'I don't care. You shouldn't have gone. Now you've done that everything's changed, you know.'

'You can't think much of me, or Sharon for that matter, if you thought that would change anything. Do you think I was born in this house? Do you think I've never gone outside of these four walls? Where do you think I was born and brought up?'

It all got too much for Sharon, 'I know, you come from Manchester.'

'That's dead right, I do come from Manchester – a little terraced house in Manchester with two bedrooms and four children. My parents were, and still are, poor as church mice but I love them and I'm not ashamed of them. I was lucky, that's all . . . lucky. I could easily be living where you do, and if I were, would you think any less of me?'

Louise looked embarrassed. 'What did she say about the holiday anyway? Can I go?'

'I didn't mention it. I'll ask her next time, unless of course you

42

do it first.' Nancy stood up. 'Right, enough lectures for one day. I'm off to do some very boring vacuuming. Anyone care to help?'

'Not likely . . .'

Both girls jumped up and ran off to Sharon's bedroom.

Louise and Sharon had taken Daniel to the park. He was a happy child, always giggling and easily amused. He loved the attention he got from both girls. They had no reservations about being silly with him, rolling round the grass and making daft noises.

His hair was now bright carrot red and he had freckles all over his nose and cheekbones. He was just starting to walk and he grasped their fingers tight as he tottered along between them.

Neither of them saw Fran as she walked across the grass towards them. She had a man with her and they were holding hands.

Daniel let go and sat down sharply on the grass. The girls flopped down beside him, laughing.

'All fall down, Danny, all fall down . . .' Louise was using a silly singsong voice to make the child laugh and then she glanced up and saw Fran just standing there, watching quietly.

Fran let go of the man's hand and bent down to the little boy. 'Come to Mummy, Danny, come and give Mummy a cuddle.' He crawled over to her and pulled himself up on her legs. She picked him up. 'Say hello to Uncle Tony, there's a good boy. Say hello.'

Louise looked at the man and her heart sank. He was tall and good-looking with shoulder-length blond hair. His skin-tight jeans and black tee shirt were moulded to him. He was a good ten years younger than Fran, and the woman was gazing at him like a besotted teenager.

'Tony, this is Danny and that's Louise, my daughter.'

The young man looked at Sharon and smiled. 'Hello, Louise.'

Fran laughed. 'No, not that one, that's her friend. This is Louise.'

His expression changed instantly as he looked deep into her eyes. Louise felt a shiver of fear.

'Well, well, well, Fran, you know how to keep a secret. Why didn't you tell me she was black?'

Chapter Four

The only good thing that Louise could see about her mother's latest boyfriend was that the woman was so happy she was on a permanent high. She was so completely besotted with Tony Willmott that everything else was forgotten, including Louise.

It also meant that her Jersey holiday was on. Louise had figured it would be a good time to ask and Fran had said yes without any hesitation, realising in a flash that it meant two weeks alone with Tony for herself. Two whole weeks to work on him and try to persuade him to move in.

Tony was popular with everyone. Even Mrs Anderson, who prided herself on being a good judge of character, thought he was OK. If they met in the street he would offer to carry her shopping and tell her how wonderful she was for her age. Normally sharp as a poison arrow, the old lady simpered like a teenager in love when the charming young man slipped his arm through hers and helped her along the road.

Louise overheard her one morning in the market, twittering about him.

'I can't understand it – a lovely young man like that knocking around with that old slapper. Old enough to be his mother, she is . . . I don't know. Mind, I did tell him when he gets pissed off with her I've got a pretty young granddaughter just up the road.'

Louise thought she knew better about Tony, but she wasn't giving him much thought. The only thing on her mind was Jersey. She went to the library and read everything she could find, and then lay awake at night trying to picture it. She just couldn't imagine boarding a plane and actually flying. It was pointless trying to talk to Fran about it, so Gypsy became the only dog in the world with a detailed knowledge of the Channel Islands and aeroplanes.

Sharon didn't share Louise's thirst for knowledge. She was busy savouring dreams of a holiday romance.

'Can't you just imagine it, Lou, strolling hand in hand along the beach with a gorgeous young fisherman, tanned and bleached blond from the—

Louise cut her off mid-flow. 'I can't think of anything worse. You've been reading too much romantic slush and playing too many soppy records. Your brain's addled.'

They were busy going through Sharon's wardrobe, choosing and discarding. The bigger girl had shot up and was now head and shoulders over the still petite Louise. It was a stroke of luck because Louise was now laden with enough holiday clothes for a month, even if they were all a bit on the baggy side. All she needed to buy was a swimsuit and a pair of sandals.

'Here, take this as well. I'm never going to get into it again. You don't mind, do you? Me giving you my stuff? I don't want you to be offended but most of it has hardly been worn – I got fat too quick – and it really is quite nice. It'll suit you a lot better than me . . .'

Nancy had drummed into Sharon that she must be tactful and not make Louise feel like a charity case so now the girl was into overkill.

'It's OK, really it is. Everything I ever have is second-hand. I'm used to it.' Sharon's face told Louise she'd said the wrong thing so she continued quickly, 'But these are all great. I'll have to buy a new swimsuit, though, 'cos you've got boobs and I haven't, you lucky cow.'

'Big boobs and a big arse to match. Just look at me from behind – King Kong in a cossie.' She turned round and wiggled her backside at Louise.

'I wish you'd stop going on about it. All the boys turn round and look at you. They don't even notice me. I'm still "Little Louise" to everyone. Sexy Sharon and Little Louise, the Odd Couple, friends to the end!'

They danced round the bedroom laughing happily.

The excitement was so much Louise couldn't sleep the night before the holiday started. She padded round the flat making endless cups of tea, with Gypsy, who sensed something was up, hot on her heels. Packing and unpacking her bag, checking endlessly, she made sure that the precious plane ticket was in the front pocket, and counted the money in her purse over and over again.

She had ten pounds – more than she'd ever had in her life. Barry had given her five, she had two left from her Jersey tin after she'd bought her swimsuit and sandals, and then, surprisingly, Fran had given her three.

Louise just knew it was going to be a good holiday.

The next morning, Louise was up early, looking out of the window, watching and waiting for the Aberlones' car to appear.

'For Christ's sake, girl, sit down. You're like a flea on a wet flannel. You're getting on my nerves.'

Fran had dragged herself out of bed for the occasion and was already dressed and made up. Louise didn't kid herself it was for her benefit; she knew it was because her mother wanted to impress Nancy.

'Mum! They're here, they're here.' She ran into the hallway and picked up her bag.

'Just you wait, girl. I'm coming out with you. I'm not having your fancy friends saying I don't care about my daughter. I'm going to wave goodbye properly.'

It was a squeeze with four of them in the back of the Rover but they managed. Laughing and waving, they pulled away, the car swaying under the weight of all the bags on the luggage rack.

'Your mother looked very smart, Louise, and so happy. Do you think she's better now?'

'I think smarmy Tony is probably walking into the flat right now. I bet he was waiting round the corner . . .'

'Now, now, Louise, forget all that and just enjoy your holiday.'

Sharon and her brothers, Paul and Simon, broke into song: . . . 'We're all going on a summer holiday . . .'

They were off.

Louise was right. Fran waved the car off down the road then rushed back into the flat.

The dress and cardigan were off en route to the bedroom, lobbed straight up the back of the wardrobe and quickly exchanged for the négligé set she had bought in anticipation. Looking in the mirror at herself admiringly, she decided that these two weeks were just what she needed to seduce Tony into living with her.

Low-cut and slashed to the thigh both sides, the black under-layer was sheer enough to show the black and red satin G-string that was her only concession to underwear. Wrapping the more demure full-length top layer tightly around her, she carefully did her hair and make-up, trying to look casually tousled.

Fran was on a high and so passionately in love with Tony she had no intention of losing him. The little niggle in her brain that questioned the young man's involvement with a woman of her age, a mother of two children, was deliberately silenced. He said he loved her and that was enough for her to want him there. She thought that was what he wanted as well; he was quite keen.

Quickly tidying the flat, Fran made her bed and then rumpled it up gently. Gone were the grime-laden blankets and threadbare sheets, and in their place was one of the new floral quilts that Joe from the pub was selling from the back of his estate car. Opening the wardrobe she piled in the dirty washing and forced the door closed, draped a silk scarf over the bedside lamp, and then stood back and critically surveyed the bedroom. She decided it, as well as she, looked good.

Fran opened the door to Tony, faking bewilderment.

'Tony! God, I'm sorry. I went back to bed after Louise left and must have overslept.' She stood aside to let him in. 'Just look at the state of me. I'm not even dressed . . . and my hair . . . Just sit down and I'll get myself together. You must be wondering what's going on . . .'

Tony knew exactly what was going on and was amused. He might be young but he certainly wasn't naïve. Still, he intended to play along with it for as long as it suited him.

'It's OK, sweetheart, you look gorgeous. Don't bother about getting dressed; that'll be a bit of a waste of time, won't it?'

He walked over to Fran and put his arms around her, gently kissing her on the neck. She took his hand and led him into the bedroom, not noticing the self-satisfied smirk that came over Tony's face as soon as her back was to him.

Louise was having the time of her life. The sun was shining and she was so happy she thought she would burst. All the traumatic events of the past couple of years had disappeared from her mind the moment she'd set off for the airport and the holiday was proving everything she had anticipated, plus a lot more.

When the Aberlones and Louise had all scrambled out of the hire car at the house that was to be home for two weeks even Sharon gasped.

'That poor man's in for a shock when he gets to our place. Just look at this.'

Set back on the side of a hill overlooking a sandy bay, the ultramodern L-shaped bungalow was discreetly tucked away in its own grounds behind two huge wrought-iron gates. The four youngsters abandoned Nancy and her husband instantly and headed off in two different directions to explore. Simon and Paul went one way, Sharon and Louise the other, and they all met up at the rear.

'Bloody hell, just look at that – our own pool. Come on, let's swim now . . .' At fifteen Paul thought he was in charge. 'Right everybody, back to the car for the cossies. Race you . . .'

Nancy didn't agree. 'Oh no you don't. We're going inside first to have a look around and allocate bedrooms, and then, I'm afraid, it's first things first, ground rules for the holiday. After that you can enjoy yourselves.'

Louise was completely overawed by the property in general and her and Sharon's room in particular. The bedroom was at the end of the building with sliding glass doors that opened out on to a small patio overlooking the sea.

'I bagsy this bed,' shouted Sharon, jumping on to one of them. 'Just look at these covers. They're just fab – real Hollywood white satin and Marilyn Monroe.' She looked around the room. 'I hate those wardrobes, though, with all those mirrors. I'll have to keep my eyes closed in here. She glanced at Louise. 'What's the matter? You haven't said a word. Aren't you impressed?'

Louise stood perfectly still in the doorway, gazing about her. 'I've never seen anything so beautiful. It's just like in the movies. Your friend must be a millionaire to have a place like this.' She tiptoed into the room, almost frightened to put her feet on to the floor, let alone jump on the bed like Sharon.

'Louise! Look! We've got our own bathroom even.'

Louise looked into the marble bathroom. 'One day I am going to have a place just like this. One day I'll get away from all the shit that I have to live with and have somewhere like this.'

'In your dreams! Come on, let's unpack and then we can get on with having a real ball. The odd couple go mad in Jersey.'

'Now then, everyone, ground rules. This is a family holiday and, believe it or not, mine and Dad's. All we're asking is that you clear up behind yourselves, and boys as well as girls help with the shopping and cooking. We want to know where you're going and when you'll be back and, most important of all, we want two weeks of NO FIGHTING.'

Nancy smiled at them all to take the edge off her words. She wanted them all to enjoy themselves, but especially she wanted Louise to be part of the family and to enjoy her first ever holiday.

'Right, let's see where we are and what's what. Mr Johnson has left all sorts of information and maps for us—'

Sharon interrupted her mother. 'I bet you didn't leave him a map of good old Woodford.'

'Actually, I did but he's over there on business so he'll be mostly

49

in London. But that's by the by, we're talking about us now.'

Nancy spread the maps out on the dining-room table and they figured out the shortest route to the beach and to the shops as well as all the usual holiday haunts. But Louise was distracted. She couldn't quite believe where she was – that this was actually happening.

By the end of the first week they had all found their way around. The girls had discovered a short cut to both the beach and the town, and their days were a combination of swimming, sunbathing and then wandering around looking in the shops and at boys. Sharon had set her heart on a holiday romance and was now starting to panic. Strolling through the twists and turns of the streets of St Helier, her eyes were everywhere.

'Seven days have gone, Lou, seven days, and all we've met are weedy little English boys who want water fights in the sea. Where's all the local talent?'

'Don't be boring, Sharon. I'm not interested and neither should you be. They're all trouble. I keep telling you.'

'What about those two then? They look quite cute . . .'

'Sharon!'

'Look, they're heading our way. Boobs out, bellies in. God, I wish I didn't look like a freckled prawn.'

The two young lads that were walking towards them paused as they drew alongside but then carried on by without so much as a second glance at the two girls.

Sharon groaned in disgust as Louise burst out laughing.

'Let's go for an ice cream. That's much more fun, isn't it?'

'No it's not, but it'll have to do.'

Louise was so happy she was almost frightened. Ever aware that this was just a pleasant interlude before having to go back to reality, she savoured every minute and every experience.

The first thing she did in the morning was to look around and absorb the feel of luxury. She would run her hands over the satiny quilt and then creep silently over to the window, gently stroking the fabric of the curtains before opening them to gaze out across the garden to the sea.

Watching the yachts out on the sea she imagined the feel and the smell of the salt water on the decks of the vast craft and added a boat to her imaginary list of things she intended to have 'one day'. Along, of course, with the private jet that had left her speechless at the airport. She couldn't believe it when Nancy had explained that it was probably privately owned. How could any one person need a plane to themselves? Walking through the shops, she picked out jewellery and clothes for 'one day'. She watched the open-topped sports cars that cruised the roads of the island and picked out the most expensive-looking models. Sharon couldn't understand how she could spend so much boy-hunting time peering through the gates of houses as they cut their way down to the beach.

The restaurants held a special fascination for Louise. She could picture herself wining and dining in them – no more fish and chips and ketchup, ever.

Sharon was looking for a blond suntanned young lad to pass the immediate time with. Louise was looking to her future away from Fran and Leytonstone. She now saw that success and money would be the only route out, but she also knew that for everything to be truly hers she had to earn it for herself. One day.

The two weeks ended and Sharon hadn't managed her holiday romance.

'Never mind, dear, there's always next year. You'll be older and wiser by then,' Nancy commiserated with her daughter as they were packing up to go home.

'Yeah, what you mean is, maybe I'll be thinner and prettier then and they might notice me.'

'That's not what I meant at all and you know it. You've got all your life to worry about those things. Just enjoy being young while you can.'

Nancy had watched Louise blossom during the holiday. She seemed more confident and certainly much more mature than her own children, and this aspect disturbed her. A firm believer that childhood was for childish pursuits, she was made uncomfortable finding a thirteen-year-old so absorbed with longing for material things. She even preferred Sharon's fixation with boys to Louise's financial calculations.

Fran couldn't believe how easy it had been to persuade her young man, as she liked to call him, to move in.

She had tentatively broached the idea the day Louise left, and was over the moon when he'd turned up the next day with a solitary holdall of clothes. It never entered her mind to question the lack of personal belongings and Tony had no intention of enlightening her about his past life. If the silly woman was daft enough to believe that he was there because he fancied her then he certainly wasn't going to disillusion her. The setup suited him down to the ground. No one would ever think of looking for him in a run-down council block in East London.

'When's that kid of yours due back?'

They were lying in bed. Tony was flat on his back with his hands under his head. The woman might be a bit of an old slapper but she knew her stuff in bed and at least then he didn't have to listen to her jabbering on about divorcing the old man and marrying him.

'Tomorrow evening sometime, the poncy Woodfords are dropping her back. She's going to be such a pain in the arse. Superior little cow at the best of times, but now . . .'

'She's got me to deal with now, sweetheart. I won't put up with her treating you like you say she does. You don't deserve it.'

Fran leant up on one elbow and smiled adoringly at him. She saw in Tony all she wanted to see: a young, single, good-looking fella to take care of her and support her. For once she was the envy of the street, and this alone was enough for her to be able to ignore the signposts.

Warning bells would occasionally ring in the back of her brain when she noticed his jaw tighten and the muscles in his neck twitch as he tried hard to keep a rein on his temper, but she ignored them. She reasoned any doubts away by convincing herself he was just sensitive.

'Tony, I love you so much. You're so good to me. No one's ever really looked after me before, not like you want to. I can't believe you're here and I can't understand what you see in me. I'm so much older than you . . .'

She was fishing for compliments and flattery was one of Tony's talents; he had had a lot of practice at it.

'Age doesn't come into it. You're beautiful and I love you, is that good enough for you? I'm sick of all the silly young girls that haven't a brain cell between them. You're sooooo mature and sooooo good in the sack.' With one eye on the bedside clock he reached down and lightly stroked her hair.

Fran giggled and pushed herself up before carefully swinging her leg over to sit astride him.

'Do you really think so?'

'I know so.'

Louise hadn't taken her key with her so when she arrived back she had to knock. The big black cloud had started to descend on the way home but as the car turned into Albemarle Street she wanted to get out and run in the opposite direction. The thought of returning to the flat made her feel physically sick, so sick that she almost wished she had never gone on holiday and had a taste of a better life. She felt like a little girl in the toy shop who was allowed to hold the big beautiful baby doll for a moment before being told to put it back on the shelf for some other child to have.

Fran opened the door slightly and it pulled against the chain. She looked through the gap.

'Oh, it's you, you're early.'

Shutting the door sharply, she unhooked it and walked away, leaving Louise to follow her into the flat with her suitcase and several carrier bags.

Louise wasn't in the least surprised to see Tony sitting casually on the sofa, looking perfectly at home.

'Tony's going to be living here now. I hope we'll all get on together.' Fran glared at Louise, defying her to say anything detrimental about the setup before continuing, 'It'll be nice to be a family again, won't it, Lou?'

Louise just looked disinterested. She had been expecting it and was past being shocked since the episode with Barry.

'Whatever.'

Fran looked across at Tony and raised her eyes to the ceiling as if to say, 'See what I have to put up with?'

'I've brought you a present from Jersey – it's in my case – and these are from Mrs Aberlone.' She handed her mother a duty-free carrier bag.

Fran snatched it and looked inside. It contained a carton of cigarettes.

'Your poncy friends trying to make a point here or something?'

'No, they just thought it would be a nice present for you, that's all. But if you don't want them I'll take them back. Perhaps they've got friends who will be more grateful . . .'

Tony jumped up from the sofa and hastily grabbed the bag. 'Give me them, and don't be so fucking rude to your mother. You need taking in hand, you do.'

'Oh yeah? By you and who else? You might be living here now but you are nothing to do with me.' She looked from one to the other. 'Oh, and thanks for asking about my holiday. Nice to know you're interested in me . . . I'm going to bed – if I've still got one, that is.'

With that she picked up her bag and slammed into her bedroom. Only a matter of seconds passed before she realised that there was no Gypsy behind her.

'Mum,' she called through, 'where's Gypsy?'

'She wasn't well so I took her to the PDSA and they had to put her down.'

53

Fran looked at Tony, who was smiling. Even she couldn't bring herself to tell Louise that Tony had given the old dog such a vicious kicking she had died cowering in the kitchen in agony. It had been heart-rending, even for the hardened Fran.

They had been out drinking all day and when they'd got home, fell straight into bed for the next twelve hours, neither of them bothering to take the dog out. When Tony walked in the puddle by the back door he had erupted. Dragging Gypsy across the kitchen by her collar into the corner, he'd held her in the air and lashed out with his booted feet at every inch of her body, pulling the collar tighter with every kick. When the yelping and squealing had finally stopped, he'd thrown her across the room and gone out.

Fran had covered her with her blanket, trying desperately not to meet the dog's pained gaze. She'd left her where she was, trying to convince herself that Tony had been justified in beating her; after all she had made a mess indoors.

When she'd returned to the kitchen Gypsy was dead.

Louise sobbed herself to sleep, and though she could hear the big rasping sobs well into the night, Fran didn't go near her. Tony told her to let the silly bitch get on with it.

When Fran finally got her divorce from Joshua finalised she was over the moon. Now she could get to work on Tony.

Joshua had agreed to sign the divorce papers, admitting unreasonable behaviour, as soon as she had written to him giving chapter and verse on Barry and Daniel. Fran had told him too that that was what Louise really wanted but didn't like to say, and that Barry was now her father figure.

Fran knew he still felt guilty about going back to Barbados so she had played on it, conveniently not mentioning that Barry and Daniel were long gone and Tony was now the number one fella in her life.

An expert on playing one off against the other, she was also getting experienced at blocking out anything unpleasant, so she crossed her fingers and continued intercepting all the mail from Barbados, telling Louise that Joshua had someone else and didn't want to hear from her any more.

Each thought the other had abandoned him or her, and each accepted it. Neither knew that Fran had opened the birthday card from father to daughter and purloined the pound note inside. Louise was hurt that he'd apparently forgotten and he was upset that Louise never responded.

Louise didn't question her mother's story that Joshua no longer wanted to be in touch. She was getting used to rejection and loss, and was hardening herself to it. The death of Gypsy was the final nail in the coffin of her emotions.

Two days before Christmas Fran awoke with a start, momentarily disorientated at finding herself alone in the bed. Then she remembered. Today was the day Tony was going to marry her. She was still completely besotted with him and no amount of pleas from Louise could persuade her to change her mind.

Louise just knew that this one was really bad and tried to talk her mother out of making the biggest mistake of her life but Fran was adamant. They loved each other and it was right. Tony could do no wrong in Fran's eyes but Louise knew different.

She had seen her mother change over the last few months into a submissive shell of her former self and she had soon realised that Tony was nothing but a controlling bully. Everything had to be done his way and on his terms, but he always tempered his behaviour with constant declarations of love, persuading Fran that it was because he loved her. 'Being cruel to be kind' was his favourite expression.

He chose her clothes, made her change her hairstyle, even dictated exactly what they would all eat and when they would eat it. He took complete control of Fran's life and she let him. The one person he couldn't control was Louise, although he tried constantly.

His bullying of Louise was subtle and psychological. Racist in the extreme, he made no bones about his hatred of anyone not pure white. He frequently called her 'Gollywog' but in such a way that Fran naïvely took it as a term of affection and couldn't understand why it upset Louise so much. When Fran wasn't around he constantly leered at the young teenager, calling her 'black meat', made obscene remarks about her sexuality and touched her at every opportunity.

She hated him with an intensity that frightened her.

'How do I look, Lou?'

Fran stood in front of the mirror, dressed and ready for the trip to the registry office.

'You look fine, Mum, but aren't you going to put any make-up on?'

'No. Tony says I don't need make-up, I'm pretty enough without it. Tony says that I look classier with the natural look. What about

55

the outfit? Isn't he clever to choose this? Men don't usually have a clue but Tony went off all on his own and picked it out, right size an' all.'

Louise looked at her mother. She bore no resemblance to the Fran of old. Her thick red hair was cut into a short bob and fixed back with two matching slides decorated with tiny rosebuds, emphasising the lack of make-up. The wedding outfit was a boring beige knee-length dress with a matching coat, and she wore strappy low-heeled sandals that did absolutely nothing for her short, rounded figure, and looked strangely out of place in December.

Louise regretted all the times she had complained about Fran being tarty; tarty was infinitely better than the new frumpy Fran, who waited on that bastard Tony hand foot and finger.

Louise had drawn the line at being a bridesmaid to her mother but had reluctantly agreed to be a witness.

With friends of Tony thin on the ground at the best of times, the wedding party was made up of friends of Fran from the local, plus Louise and Daniel. Barry had agreed to Daniel going for Louise's sake, on condition that he had as little to do with Tony as possible. Louise hadn't said anything to him about Tony but Barry had his own reservations about the match. He had also seen the Fran of old fade away, and wondered what it was all about, but now that he was back with his wife, and she had accepted Daniel as the child she could never have, he couldn't worry about Fran.

Louise thought she had never seen Tony looking quite as smug as he did after the ceremony. He headed over to Louise in the pub afterwards.

'You're gonna have to be nice to me, you little cow. I'm your father now—'

Louise interrupted angrily, 'You are not my father and you never will be. You're married to my mother, that's all, so just leave me alone and we'll be fine.'

Tony smiled and with one swift movement he had Louise tightly by the wrist and twisted her arm up her back.

'We'll be just fine so long as you do exactly as you're told and remember exactly what you are – Gollywog, a useless black gollywog who shouldn't even fucking look at me.'

He let go of her arm and patted her on the back gently as Fran looked across at them. Walking over to her, he put his arm around Fran's waist and pulled her towards him.

'Your little girl and I have just been having a chat about life together. I don't think she'll be a problem.'

'Great, Tony. I really want us to be a family. Maybe Danny might even come back, and then if we have one of our own—' She stopped mid-sentence when she saw the look on his face that she recognised. She knew from his expression that she had gone too far and upset him again. 'Take no notice of me, Tone. All I really want is just you. You're all I want, no one else.'

'I'm pleased to hear that, sweetheart, 'cos we're married now and it's what I say that counts.'

He looked at her and she saw in his face the same look that had come over him the night he had killed Gypsy. She shivered despite the warmth of the fire in the huge pub hearth.

Louise spent more and more time with the Aberlones. The house had been dramatically extended and now there was a large spare room over the garage that had somehow become Louise's. She could easily have moved in there – Nancy offered often enough – but despite everything that had happened the girl still felt a strong loyalty to her mother and couldn't bring herself to move out, tempting though it was.

Although top of the class in all her subjects at school, and fully expected by everyone to sail through her GCEs, she excelled especially in English. To Louise it was pure escapism, being able to weave and create pieces of work from the thoughts in her head. The five-year diary was full already and she had progressed to exercise books. Knowing Tony was not to be trusted, she changed hiding places, and the diaries and the Jersey Tin were now stowed safely away at the Aberlones'. She knew she could trust all of them not to pry.

Louise now had two lists, the original life-plan she'd drawn up and now the wish list for the future, following her taste of a different life on holiday. Both had expanded slightly but she was as focused as ever on the content. She would get out of the hellhole of a home one day and work her way to the top on her own merits. She was actually looking forward to her exams the next year and the thought of eventually making it away to university, the first step.

Fran was sitting at the dressing table, looking at herself in the mirror. The slowly developing black eye was nothing compared to the bruising down the full length of her spine and the lump the size of a golf ball in her groin. She ached all over from the kicking Tony had inflicted on her the night before.

She knew he didn't like her wearing make-up but there was no way she could go to work looking like that. She fumbled around in the drawer, searching for the panstick that used to be her best friend. Dabbing it carefully around her eyes and across the bridge of her swollen nose, she managed to disguise the purple and red tones seeping towards the surface of her skin.

She studied her reflection critically. Two stone lighter than a year ago, she should have looked good but with the dowdy clothes and ridiculous hairstyle she felt haggard and old. Since the wedding a year ago Tony had become more and more dominant. He ruled her totally and managed to confuse her so much that she always blamed herself for his outbursts. He always attacked her verbally afterwards for provoking him and she always apologised, convinced that he was right and she was in the wrong.

Louise knew that Tony bullied and manipulated her mother but didn't know that he beat her up. He usually only hit the places that weren't visible; the black eye had been a mistake when Fran had turned quickly and the blow had hit her face instead of her back. Louise tried to persuade her mother to stand up for herself but the reply was always the same. 'He only does it because he loves me, he really loves me.'

'Fran? Where are you? Fran?'

She jumped sharply away from the mirror, knocking over the stool in panic and put on a pair of sunglasses, quickly smoothing down her skirt and checking the length.

'Just getting ready for work,' she called. 'Be with you in a sec.'

The door opened and Tony came over to her, smiling. He put both muscular arms around her waist from behind, making her freeze with fear at his touch.

'I hate seeing you like this, sweetheart. Why do you make me do it? If you would just listen to me then it wouldn't happen . . . Learnt your lesson now, have you?'

'I'm sorry, Tone, I know I shouldn't upset you. It was stupid of me. Forgive me?'

'Of course I do. Now off you go to work, there's a good girl.'

He turned her round and kissed her on the cheek, and as soon as he looked at her she melted.

Fran had given up the pub on Tony's instructions and was now working long hours in the local supermarket. He didn't appear to do anything other than hang around the very pubs that Fran wasn't allowed in to – in fact he hadn't actually done a proper day's work in all the time she'd known him. She kept him and the Aberlones kept Louise – that was just the way that Tony liked it, although he was determined that one day he would deal with that superior little black bitch that had the cheek to look down on him.

He'd waited impatiently while it suited him to lie low and keep out of trouble, but he wasn't going to wait much longer.

Tony hammered on the bathroom door. 'Out now, bitch. I want the bathroom.'

Louise ignored him. She was lying in the bath and had no intention of hurrying for him.

'Unlock the fucking door and let me in now.'

She was sick to the back teeth of Tony Willmott. He spent more time in the bathroom than she and Fran put together, and for once Louise had got in there first; she had no intention of hurrying, especially for him.

She hated him but had long since decided that she wouldn't respond to him; that upset him a lot more. He tormented her constantly when she was there; he leered and made crude remarks about her to anyone who would listen. His Jack-the-lad attitude still made him popular with women, so there was always a pretty face and a ready ear to sympathise with him over getting caught up with Fran and her daughter.

Suddenly the door cracked open and flew off its hinges, splintering against the bath. Tony was in the bathroom with her. He stood in front of the bath as Louise scrambled to reach a towel off the rail to cover her naked body. His face was white with fury and his fists clenched and unclenched as he tried to resist beating her face to a pulp. He didn't like leaving visible marks.

Louise slipped as she stood up and grabbed for the nearest towel, though it was a hand towel and totally inadequate for the job. She scrambled out of the bath and tried to get past him and back to her bedroom.

He grabbed her wrist as she got to the door and whipped the towel away, leaving her naked and dripping wet in front of him. He grinned as he looked her up and down, holding so tightly that her hand started to go numb.

'Let go of me, you bastard. How dare you? LET GO.'

She tried to pull away but he grabbed the other hand and held her in front of him.

'Not too bad for a black bitch. I could fancy you in the dark.' He laughed. 'Dark? Darkie? Get it?'

He was still laughing as he dragged her into his and Fran's bedroom, aiming karate kicks at her body on the way as she struggled and wriggled, trying to get away from him.

'That's it, Gollywog, keep fighting – I like it that way – but shut

59

the fuck up or I'll not only smash your face, I'll smash in your mother's as well when she gets in.' He threw her face down on the bed with one hand on the back of her neck, pressing her face into the pillow.

She couldn't think. Her mind went blank, at the same time her body went limp and she stopped fighting and did exactly as he said.

Over an hour later he kicked her off the bed. Tony lay there on the blood-stained covers, stark naked, smoking a cigarette and grinning viciously as the battered and raped fourteen-year-old crawled silently out of the room on all fours.

'That's it, darlin', crawl like the dog you are . . . Woof woof, woof woof . . . Not so mouthy now you know who's boss, are you, slut?'

Tony was gone before Fran got in from work.

'What's happened to the bathroom door?' She looked at Louise, who was huddled in the corner of the sofa.

'Tony did it. Mum, he hurt me . . .' She looked pleadingly at her mother.

'Oh, Lou, you didn't wind him up again, did you? I've told you about that so many times.'

'No, Mum, Listen. He really hurt me.' She hesitated, unable to put into words the obscenities that Tony had put her through.

Fran's tone was sharp as she stood over Louise, pointing her finger in front of her face.

'I've got no sympathy for you, girl. You know how sensitive he is but you go on and on. You must really have gone over the top for him to do that to the door . . . Well, let that be a lesson to you! Don't wind him up.'

'Mum . . . he hurt me badly.' Louise was really sobbing. Great fat tears were rolling down her face unchecked as the impact of the afternoon hit her.

'ENOUGH. You're always so bleeding sorry for yourself. If he gave you a slap it's because you asked for it. Now I don't want to hear any more and I want you to apologise to Tony when he gets back.'

Louise didn't bother to pack anything; there was nothing that she wanted to remove from that flat. She just went round to Sharon's and asked if she could stay for good. But she couldn't begin to explain that Tony had raped her.

Nancy was delighted to get the child out of that flat and away from Fran and Tony at last.

60

Chapter Five

Sleep was a long time coming for Louise but as the tiredness washed over her and she closed her eyes, the nightmares started. Tony had threatened to send his friends round 'for more of the same' and she was terrified. She dreamt that they were in the room with her, that they were doing the same things to her; the feeling of relief when she woke to find it wasn't happening was quickly replaced by horror at what had happened.

Grateful that she wasn't sharing a room with Sharon, she just prayed that she didn't call out in her sleep. The ceiling light and the bedside lamp shone all night as she hugged the pillow close to her, imagining it was Gypsy she was cuddling. She knew Gypsy would have protected her from Tony and she imagined the dog ripping into him and pulling him off her. She imagined Gypsy lunging for his throat and tearing into the flesh, leaving him to bleed to death slowly and painfully. She didn't waste any energy imagining what Fran would have done.

Louise didn't want to get up for school – in fact she didn't ever want to get up again – but she knew she had no choice if she wanted to avoid the doctor Nancy had wanted to call the night before. She felt as if someone had turned on a blowtorch inside her and was gradually turning up the heat, the burning was so intense. The insides of her thighs were mottled purple, and when she looked in the mirror her back was bruised from top to bottom of her backbone but the skin wasn't broken and there wasn't a mark on her face.

She had given Sharon a blow-by-blow account of her fall down the stairs in Freeman's, knowing full well that she would tell Nancy. Sharon believed every word; Nancy didn't but decided that she would leave it for a while, certain that the truth would come out in the end.

The girls went to school as usual but Louise had a note from Nancy excusing her from PE because of her severe period pains.

Fran was unhappy. Tony was becoming increasingly violent and dominant and she now had to admit to herself that she was absolutely terrified of him. Nothing she did pleased him any more and she was at a loss to know what to do. He would batter her for the slightest thing.

Sometimes he disappeared for days at a time and she had no idea where he was. She no longer dared to question his movements; the fractured ribs last time had taught her how unwise that was. She often wondered why he had married her. It certainly wasn't the way she had thought it would be.

She even missed her daughter, although she would never dare admit it to Tony. Unable to understand why Louise had moved out completely, but guessing it was to do with him, she had tentatively asked about the incident with Louise. All he said was that she had been mouthy and had attacked him so he had 'to teach her who's boss'.

Fran decided to swallow her pride and phone Nancy Aberlone. In case Tony came back unexpectedly, she went to the phone box in the next street.

'Hello? It's Fran here, Louise's mum. Can I speak to her please?' She knew that Louise wouldn't be there in school time but she couldn't bring herself to phone Nancy without a pretext.

'I'm sorry, Fran, but she's at school. Do you want me to give her a message?'

'No, it's OK. I just wanted to talk to her. She's not been to see me for so long . . . I know we said it was OK for her to stay with you but I didn't expect her never to . . .' Despite being determined to hold it together, she started crying down the phone.

'Fran, whatever's the matter? Do you want me to come over?'

'No, you can't. Tony will go mad if you do.'

'OK, well, just get on the bus and come over here. You sound as if you need to talk.'

Fran had never been to the Aberlones' house before, despite the fact that Louise was living there. Nancy had contacted her when it became obvious that the girl was adamant she wasn't going to go back to Leytonstone, but Fran had readily agreed to her daughter staying there. A little too readily for Nancy's liking – she couldn't imagine letting her Sharon just move in with someone else in a million years.

Walking down the tree-lined road from the bus stop, Fran felt a tremendous depression sweeping over her. She had wanted Tony from the first moment she'd set eyes on him. He was so handsome and charming, and for once she could hold her head up. The vilification she had suffered because of her marriage to Joshua was still fresh in her mind, and she thought that Tony was the answer to her prayers: young and single, handsome and white, everything her parents had wanted for their only child the first time. But she had married Joshua and they had not spoken to her since. She didn't even know where they lived now.

Then Barry, for a while he had seemed to be the one but then he had been more interested in Daniel than in her.

Now Tony. She couldn't figure out why her relationships always had to change. All she really wanted was to be loved.

Walking up the path, she wanted to turn and run; the neatly mown front lawn edged with rose bushes summed up everything that she didn't have. But she didn't have time to ring the bell before Nancy flung the door open.

'I saw you coming. Come on in, Fran, and I'll put the kettle on. We can go and sit in the garden. It's a lovely day.'

Still tearful, Fran followed her through the house to the kitchen and perched on a stool as Nancy laid out a tray with a selection of cakes and biscuits. Fran felt irritated by the unintentional display of homeliness. No wonder Louise preferred to live here. The girl had got delusions of grandeur. Tony had planted the seed of that idea in Fran's head and she was only too willing to believe Louise's leaving wasn't her fault in any way. Ever on the lookout for a scapegoat for her own failings Fran had already decided her daughter's behaviour was all Joshua's fault for insisting she went to the grammar school.

They made small talk while Nancy brewed the tea, and then went out into the garden and sat side by side on the garden swing.

Fran made the first move away from the chitchat; she was getting impatient. 'Why doesn't Lou come home any more? I am her mother but she won't have anything to do with me . . .'

'Fran, Louise doesn't confide in me now. I guess it's something to do with your husband but she hasn't said.'

'They did have a falling out but Tone said it was only because Louise was just so rude to him. He said she swore at him and threatened him with a kitchen knife. He had no choice but to slap it out of her hand . . .'

'That doesn't sound like the Louise I know.' Nancy could feel the anger rising. 'I can't imagine her reacting like that even if she had a really good reason. What do you think?'

Nancy had no intention of voicing her dark suspicions about Tony Willmott to Fran. The day Louise had turned up there and asked if she could stay for good the girl had been walking carefully and was obviously in pain, but she told Sharon a long convoluted story about falling down the stairs in a shoe shop. Louise had denied so strongly that anyone had hurt her, Nancy had no choice but to accept her story, but she didn't believe it.

She looked at the woman sitting beside her and wondered at the transformation from over-the-top fashion disaster to middle-aged granny. Fran was stick thin. The former round and sexy woman was now completely sexless, bordering on androgynous. The jutting collarbone and hollow cheeks that were devoid of make-up added years to her age. The once-thick red hair was now dull and lifeless, cropped close to her head; the shapeless clothes that hung loosely disguised any femininity that may still have been underneath. Nancy guessed that the men who would once have wolf-whistled as Fran passed by would now not even notice her.

'If you really want my opinion, Fran – and you're not going to like what I say, I'm afraid – your Tony did a lot more than that, but Louise isn't saying anything about it to us, and frankly I'm worried about her.'

Fran didn't answer. She just looked at the ground. To admit that Tony had attacked Louise was to admit to her own secret fears and she couldn't do that. She had to believe that Tony had never touched the girl; the other option didn't bear thinking about.

Nancy reached over to Fran and gently touched her arm, sensing the turmoil that was churning away inside the woman beside her.

'Why don't you keep in touch with Louise, then? She is still your daughter and she's been through such a lot in the time we've known her. She really does love you and I know she misses you, but she won't go to the flat, presumably because of Tony. You could come here to tea sometimes—'

'Tony won't let me,' Fran interrupted quickly. 'I'm not allowed to see Louise. I'm not allowed to see anyone any more, not even Daniel. He'd go mad if he knew I was here today.'

'But, Fran, they're your children. He can't stop you, unless of course you're frightened of him?'

'How dare you? Of course I'm not frightened of him, but he's my husband I have to do what he wants, don't I?'

Nancy was almost pleased to hear the defiance in Fran's voice; at least there was still a bit of fight left in the woman. She decided to go for broke.

'He hits you, doesn't he? And he hit young Louise, I'm sure. The day she came here she could hardly walk, she was so bruised. Oh, I know she said she fell down the stairs but I wasn't born yesterday. I just wish I'd forced her to go to the doctor's and then we could have settled it. How can you let him get away with it?' Nancy was fired up now, totally incensed that Fran hadn't got the insight to see what Tony was up to. 'Domination is no basis for a relationship, is it? And that's what's going on. How can you let him stop you from seeing your children? Louise needs her mother and you should make the effort. It's not normal to lose touch with your kids.'

Fran stood up angrily. 'How do you know what's normal? You sit here in your bloody middle-class house with your bloody middle-class family and suck my daughter into it, giving her dreams about what she can never achieve. I bet you've never had a worry in your life, you stuck-up bitch. Just look at you, all poxy flowing skirts and "Love and Peace, Man", you haven't got a clue about real life – the life that I have to lead and the life that Louise will have to go back to one day.' She snatched up her handbag and headed across the lawn.

'Fran, I'm sorry. Come back. I only wanted to make you think. Please tell me what's wrong. Maybe I can help.'

'No one can help. You can keep Louise – she's more your daughter than mine now, anyway. Tell her I don't want to know. She's not to come near me when this cosy little setup all falls out of bed and she's got nowhere to go.'

Nancy knew she'd blown it. Fran had wanted to talk and she had dived in with both size eight feet. Damn, damn, damn, she thought.

Louise felt incredibly ill. She had felt bad ever since the attack but now, four months on, it was worse. The bleeding had stopped but the pain was still there physically and mentally, as were the nightmares. Just thinking about the rape made her want to throw up, and it was all she could think about. In the beginning, not confiding in Sharon had been difficult but Louise knew that to do that would open a whole can of worms. Sharon would tell Nancy, who would tell Fran – or, even worse, the police – and she couldn't have handled that. There was no way of putting into words the disgusting things that Tony had inflicted on her. Sharon was a good friend and Louise loved her dearly, but now even that was different. Louise had a secret, the worst secret imaginable, and there was no way she could share it. She had to bite her tongue and hide the irritation when Sharon went on and on about boys

65

and sex. They used to chat about what it would be like 'the first time' but now Louise knew first-hand what it was like and it wasn't how Sharon imagined it.

The day Tony had done what he did to her was the worst day of her life, she could not in her direst nightmares have imagined anything as terrible.

The second worst day was when she found out she was five months pregnant. She could have kicked herself for not figuring it out sooner. All the signs were there, the signs that she had seen when Fran was pregnant with Daniel. The daily nausea, the tight waistbands and the swollen breasts – they all pointed to it, but she had missed the clues until Sharon unwittingly pointed a couple of them out.

'Look, Lou, you've got boobs and a belly now. Where have they come from all of a sudden? You'll be catching me up soon.'

They were getting changed after swimming and were both crushed into one cubicle trying to dry themselves and get dressed without bending down. Louise glanced down at herself and nearly passed out: she was the same shape as Fran.

'It must be your mum's cooking. I wasn't used to three meals a day before I came to live with you. Come on, we'd better get a move on, there's a queue out there.'

Quickly pulling on her jeans, Louise realised that even they were tight round the waist. She was palpitating now; surely she couldn't be? She had to get out into the air, she felt sick and faint. How could it not have occurred to her? She knew sex made babies and that's what Tony had had with her . . . sex.

Fortunately the next day was Saturday and Sharon had a music lesson, so Louise went out on her own up to the High Street and headed for the chemist's with the remainder of her Jersey Tin money in her purse. After loitering and hesitating while she plucked up the courage to ask, she bought a pregnancy testing kit, pretending it was for her mother. The young assistant had looked at her knowingly. Teenagers always said it was for someone else.

It was far more complicated than she had imagined but the next morning she set it up in her wardrobe and waited for the hour that seemed for ever.

The brown circle that formed in the bottom of the test tube confirmed it. She was pregnant.

There was no doubt about the day it happened. It was etched in her diary in big red letters. She added up and knew that she was expecting a baby in December. She was only fifteen.

She decided exactly what she was going to do and planned it all with military precision. She would make sure Fran knew all about it, she would make Fran go with her to the doctor's and she would make sure Fran felt guilty as hell.

She knew Tony would not be going out that morning, but to make sure she got there early and went up to the top balcony of the flats opposite. He left on time with a sports bag and she guessed he was going to the gym. There was no sign of Fran leaving so Louise let herself in quietly, expecting to find her mother in bed but the flat was empty.

She was angry – all that wasted emotion, imagining what she was going to say and how.

Her old bedroom was now a junk room with all manner of stuff thrown in there, just dumped on top of her childhood things that had meant so much at the time. Some of her belongings were still there and she quickly checked through to see if there was anything she wanted to take.

Her battered old teddy bear that Joshua had given her as a baby and that they had called Fredbare, a small glass ornament and some photographs were all she could think of. Pulling carrier bags and boxes out from under the bed, looking for the bear, she found a heavy metal document box hidden right up the back. The lock was broken so she opened it and looked inside.

There was a plastic bag of white powder and a small set of scales at one end and at the other was a huge wad of notes. She only hesitated for a second before stuffing the money down her knickers.

Laughing to herself, she grabbed a pen and paper from the kitchen, wrote a quick note and put it in the tin before replacing everything as she had found it, minus, of course, the money.

Getting out of the flat as fast as her trembling legs would take her, she forgot all thoughts of confronting Fran.

She was still laughing on the bus on the way home, imagining Tony's face when he found the note.

TO TONY THE RAPIST.
    YOU OWE ME AND I'VE COLLECTED. TAKE IT OUT ON MUM AND I'LL GO TO THE POLICE.
    GOLLYWOG.

Behind the locked door of the bathroom Louise counted the notes. There was £1,725 and she suddenly knew without doubt what she was going to do. She very carefully sewed most of the money into the lining of her small suitcase, then packed a few belongings inside before hiding it in the garage. She then wrote another note.

Dear Sharon,
    I have to go away. There's things I can't tell and things I can't explain. I love you all for everything you have done for me but I can't stay here. I will be in touch so that you will know I'm all right. Tell your mum and dad I'm sorry.
    Fredbare is for you to remember me by. You'll always be my best friend in the world.
    Lots and lots of love always and forever. The odd couple to the end.
    Louise, xxxxxxxx

Next morning she crept out at the crack of dawn after leaving the bear and the note on her bed. Feeling quite light-headed she got the underground into London and across to Victoria station. Looking up at the departure boards she picked a destination at random. Brighton. The Aberlones had taken her there on a day trip so she knew roughly where it was.

Yes, she decided, Brighton would do.

On the journey down she planned exactly what she wanted to do. Get a flat, get a job, get an abortion, never go back. She was grown up now.

There was nothing in Leytonstone for her now: her father had abandoned her, her mother was married to a psychopathic drug dealer and Gypsy was dead. Daniel had his own family and Sharon had hers. Louise knew she was alone, and that was how she wanted it. She left her bag at the left-luggage counter at Brighton station and started looking around, not quite sure exactly what she was looking for but certain that the money she had would buy it.

Wandering aimlessly through the town she spotted a run-down accommodation agency and went in.

'Can I help you?' The young woman at the reception desk looked her up and down suspiciously.

'I'm looking for somewhere to live. Have you got anything small? It's just for me.'

'Fill in this form with all your details, then I'll check.'

Louise took the piece of paper and carefully completed it before handing it back. Her father had always told her she wrote wonderful stories and she took full advantage of her talents by reinventing herself and her circumstances. Louise Jermaine, pregnant schoolgirl, suddenly became Mrs Angela Kavanagh, the seventeen-year-old grieving army widow of a soldier killed in Northern Ireland.

The woman scrutinised it all carefully, glancing up at the girl in front of her sympathetically as she did so.

'We've got a self-contained furnished studio on our books. It's just off the seafront, slightly out of town, and is £20 a week, four weeks' in advance with £100 deposit up front plus £100 key money. That's £280 immediately. Can you afford that, Mrs Kavanagh?' She obviously thought she couldn't and smiled slightly as she passed her the details.

Louise put on her most charming smile. 'Yes, of course I can. I'll just pop up to the post office and withdraw the cash, if that's all right with you?'

'Don't you even want to see it first?'

'No, I'm sure I can trust you. I'll be back in half an hour.'

The studio turned out to be a glorified bedsit with a corner curtained off as a kitchen, and a small bathroom. Furniture was hardly the right description for the junk that filled the attic room but Louise didn't care. It was hers and it was private. It would serve her purpose nicely for the moment.

Unpacking her sparse belongings, she put them away in the huge rickety wardrobe. After carefully unpicking the lining of her case she took out the money and tucked most of it into a large envelope before hiding it well down the side of the old utility armchair. Next day she went out on a shopping spree. Never before had she been able to spend money on herself and she loved it. It lifted her spirits no end, especially when she let herself think about Tony and how he would be feeling following the discovery. She bought clothes and shoes, food and drink, as well as a few ornaments to liven up the attic. Despite everything she felt happy for the first time since Joshua had left.

She wasn't up to facing the practicalities of investigating having an abortion so she concentrated on getting a job. High season in the seaside town made it easy. There were several seasonal shops and cafés advertising 'Help wanted' in their windows, but Louise knew she had to find somewhere that wouldn't question her too closely. She needed anonymity just in case anyone came looking for her.

She had dressed in her carefully chosen new clothes that hung loosely over the now noticeable bump, and pulled her hair up on top of her head in an elastic band to make her look taller. A touch of make-up completed the image. Pleased with the overall picture, and sure that she looked the seventeen-year-old she claimed to be, she set off in her search for work.

Paolo's café and ice-cream parlour seemed just right. Tucked away up a pavemented lane off from the main holiday zone, it offered free food on shift, and although the pay was low it was cash-in-hand wages, no questions asked.

Paolo from Italy sounded more like Paul from London to Louise but he seemed pleasant enough so she took up the offer to start the next day.

Paolo didn't for a moment believe the 'young widow' story. He had seen too many runaways who thought Brighton was the modern equivalent of Dick Whittington's London. He guessed they all had good reasons for being on the run but he also knew that most of them gave up and went home eventually. And he didn't ask questions because he wasn't really interested in the answers. This one looked a bit of a hippy, so he launched into his 'no drugs, no alcohol, smoking only in the back yard' spiel before taking her on. He liked employing the pretty young girls; they were always good for business because they attracted other young-sters to the café.

Having found a home and a job, Louise decided the abortion issue could wait just a bit longer. She didn't need to see a doctor yet, she told herself.

Her first working day at the café was a nightmare. The other helper had left without warning and Louise was alone, with customers coming at her from all angles as Paolo struggled in the kitchen.

She was just considering walking out as well when a man appeared behind the counter.

'I'm sorry, you're not allowed behind here,' Louise explained. 'Take a seat and I'll serve you as soon as I can.'

The man laughed and grabbed an apron from off the hook. 'It's OK, Cinderella, I'm Gavin, your fairy godmother. I'm here to rescue you.'

Paolo stuck his head round the door. 'It's all right, Angie. He's a friend and he knows what he's doing. I rang for help.' At the end of the day Paolo handed all the tips to Louise.

'You did well for a young 'un. Will I see you tomorrow or have you had enough?'

Louise smiled. 'Of course I'll be back, but what about Gavin? Shouldn't he get half? He's worked really hard . . .'

Gavin put one arm round her shoulder and the other round the portly Paolo. 'Don't worry about me, little girl. I do it for love!' He smiled affectionately at the older man. 'Now, it's coffee and cake time, I think. For services rendered and in place of tips I bags the last iced bun . . .'

As they relaxed and chatted, Louise realised that the two men were more than just friends. With the occasional glance and touch, they were like a couple in love!

'So, little girl, tell me all about yourself . . .'

Louise looked up at Gavin as he spoke. He was smiling warmly and tousled her hair just like Joshua used to. She could feel the tears welling up.

'There's nothing to tell. I have to go now. I'll see you in the morning.'

Moving rapidly, Louise grabbed her jacket and bag, and was out of the door in a flash, leaving the two men open-mouthed.

Back in the attic room Louise cried her heart out as the reality of her situation hit her. She was alone completely for the first time and now the euphoria of her escape had passed it really hurt.

The following weeks rushed by in a blur of work and sleep. Blocking out all thoughts of her advancing pregnancy, she concentrated on each day as it came. The work was tiring, but not demanding in other ways, and soon her main aim was to take whatever opportunity there was to sit down out the back for five minutes.

'Wake up, Angie. There's customers want serving in here. Come on, chop chop.' Paolo's voice interrupted her thoughts.

She quickly dogged her cigarette in a flower pot and went inside.

'Sorry, Paolo. I was just having a quick break.'

'Well, now I want a break. I'm just going upstairs to do the books. Can you manage?'

Paolo was pulling his vast white apron over his head as he spoke. Louise guessed he must have weighed at least twenty stone and his face was permanently flushed. She had never come across openly gay men before and it still embarrassed her when he disappeared upstairs in the afternoons with Gavin, his young lover.

'No problem, Paolo. I'll give you a shout if I need you.'

She knew she wouldn't. There was no way she could bring herself to shout up the back stairs when Gavin was there; it was just too awful even to think about.

She had discovered Gavin worked behind the bar in a local night club and had a room there, but he spent most of his time with Paolo. They were an unlikely match – Gavin, young, dark-haired and handsome with humorous green eyes, Paolo considerably older, overweight and balding – but nevertheless they were a happy couple.

Once the season cooled down there was just Louise and Paolo, and she was only working a few hours a week although by then that suited her. She hadn't got round to arranging an abortion and she knew it was far too late now. The consequences didn't bear thinking about, so she didn't think; living from day to day was still her only priority.

As she became bigger she bought baggier clothes, and if anyone noticed her size they never mentioned it. Paolo occasionally commented that the free meals were doing her good, and she would laugh and compliment him on his cooking.

One day Paolo had been upstairs for a couple of hours, then came down looking even more flushed than usual.

'Make me a cup of coffee, pet, and have one yourself. We might as well close up now. I'm worn out. Praise the Lord for the coming of winter!'

Louise made the coffee and took the two mugs over to one of the tables as he locked the door and turned the sign round.

'You look a bit peaky, do you know that? Are you feeling OK?' Paolo looked intensely at her. He had become quite fond of her over the months; she was polite, hard-working and generally appeared happy. He guessed she'd been through a lot but she certainly wasn't confiding in him.

'I'm fine really, just a bit tired, and I haven't been sleeping too good. My flat's really cold at night. That stupid electric fire eats money so I can't have it on too long.'

'What are you doing for Christmas? It's not far off now, you know. Going home to the family?'

'Don't fish, Paolo,' she laughed gently. 'I told you before, I don't have any family now. No, I'll just stay here.'

'You can come to dinner with me and Gavin. We haven't got any family either – well, none that want to know us, that is. Come and keep us company.' Paolo laughed heartily but Louise sensed the hurt behind it. She knew all about the hurt of rejection.

'Thanks for the offer, Palo. You've been good to me and I love you for it, you and Gavin.' She leant across the table and planted a kiss on his forehead.

The big man was so moved he had to pull his cuff across his face quickly for fear of a tear falling down his cheek.

Louise had spent a lot of her spare time in the library, keeping warm, and had read up on childbirth and babies, so when she woke up in the middle of the night with raging stomach pains and a wet bed she knew she was in labour even though the baby wasn't due for another three weeks.

She had prepared herself for this day but she was still petrified. She should go to hospital, she had intended to, but an idea was forming as she paced the floor, chain-smoking and holding a hot-water bottle on her belly.

No one in the world knew she was pregnant. Her bump was so small and neat she convinced herself no one had even suspected. She hadn't signed on at a doctor's and she didn't talk to the neighbours. No one need know a thing.

Like someone possessed she started searching the flat for things she thought she needed. The pains got worse through the night and by the time daylight came she thought she was dying. She remembered how Fran had described childbirth – 'trying to push a cannonball out of your bum' – and hoped that this was normal. She knew she had to keep silent even though the urge was to scream the house down. The pains were searing through her entire body, turning her legs to jelly.

Having covered the bottom half of the bed in plastic carrier bags layered with newspaper, Louise slid out of her trousers and lay on top, sweating, and vomiting into the washing-up bowl. Just when she thought she couldn't hold out on her own any longer she raised her knees and pushed down. The baby popped out so forcefully it surprised her. She pulled it up from in between her legs, wrapping it in a towel just as the afterbirth appeared.

She began to panic. 'What next? What next? What the fuck do I do now?' she muttered, trying to remember everything she'd read. 'Cut the cord, cut the cord, I must cut the cord.' She got the string and scissors she'd gathered earlier and carefully tied two pieces tightly several inches apart on the cord.

'I can't do this. I can't cut it. What if I kill you?' She held the scissors open against the cord, trying to pluck up courage, her hands shaking. Suddenly she cut through the rubbery piece of cord that attached the afterbirth and it slipped away on to the floor.

She realised the baby was crying so she pulled it to her, still wrapped in the bloody towel. It stopped and she saw that it was looking straight at her face.

'What to do now?' She was talking to the baby. 'What have I done? Oh God, what am I going to do with you?'

She placed it carefully in the armchair and cleaned herself up before gently unwrapping the baby and wiping it with her face flannel.

It was a girl. Instantly Louise decided to name her Skye after the heroine in her favourite novel, a calm floaty name that suggested beauty and romance, all the things that she thought she herself would never be.

Louise got herself dressed as best she could; it was all she could do to get her clothes on she was shaking so much. She pulled her large totebag out of the wardrobe and laid a folded up sheet in the bottom. Taking out the snowy white crocheted shawl, the one solitary item of babywear she had bought, she carefully wrapped her daughter in it. She then got a sheet of paper and wrote a letter.

This is Skye. She was born on the 20th November 1973 at 2.00 p.m. Please find someone to love her as much as I would if I could keep her. She deserves far more than I can ever give her. Tell her I love her.

Willing the baby not to cry she crept quickly out of the flat and walked the short distance to the hospital. She knew she couldn't afford to make any mistakes now so she marched purposefully up the steps into the main building, looking for the toilets and praying they would be empty. One of the cubicles was engaged so she went into the other one and listened for the sound of the main door. She heard it close as someone went out and there was no sound of anyone else entering but she flushed the chain and opened the door a fraction just to check.

Without daring to look inside the bag again for fear of changing her mind, she walked out of the toilets and straight out of the hospital to a phone box nearby.

'There's a baby in a cubicle in the downstairs toilets. Please get to her quickly. She needs looking after.' She replaced the receiver sharply and headed for the next phone box.

'Paolo? It's Angie. I've got an upset stomach so I won't be in for a few days . . . No, I'll be OK. I just need to sleep it off . . .'

Walking back to the attic room she felt in a daze, unable to comprehend the enormity of what she had just done but grateful she hadn't been caught.

The state of the room took her by surprise even though it was exactly as she had left it. Realising she couldn't even get into the bed without clearing up first, she set to work on autopilot. She scrubbed and cleaned, she gathered up all the soiled sheets and towels and carefully wrapped them around the discarded placenta before placing it all in a large bag ready to go with the rubbish. She carried on in a frenzy until every trace of the birth of Skye was gone. Apart, that is, from a small piece of umbilical cord that she carefully placed in a small box and hid at the back of the wardrobe.

Lying down on the bed, she burst into tears.

Three days later she was back at work, all cried out.

BOOK TWO

Chapter Six

1980

Angie Kavanagh packed the last of her belongings that she was taking with her back to London. Looking round the flat, the same tiny flat that she had moved into seven years ago, she wondered again if she was doing the right thing. She had achieved all the things she had always wanted – a home to call her own, surrogate parents in the form of Paolo and Gavin, and a job that she enjoyed. Now she was leaving. Although she knew she wasn't going back literally – she never intended to set foot in Leytonstone again – she was going to London. Yet another chapter.

Although there was little left of the original furnishings and fittings, she could still picture the bedsit as she'd first seen it as clearly as if it was yesterday. She remembered the ineffectual one-bar electric fire and the Baby Belling cooker; she could still see the tatty grey net curtain that dipped in the middle on the overstretched wire, and the lumpy single bed that creaked at the slightest movement in the night.

The bed had been well past its use-by date when she moved in but the image of herself scrubbing the mattress with a ferocity she didn't even know she was capable of, following the traumatic events of November 1973, was engraved in her memory. Scrubbing and scrubbing until her arms ached in their sockets and her fingernails were ripped down to the quick. It had been her way of erasing the episode from her life, rubbing it out of her conscious mind. Only when the bed eventually went out with the rubbish did the nightmares stop.

The only concession she made to that day was to buy an identical totebag to the one she'd left at the hospital, and which now contained several volumes of diaries, an old flight boarding pass and the few photographs of her life before Brighton. In a biscuit tin were old newspaper cuttings that she had carefully read and clipped, and a dried and shrivelled piece of umbilical cord. Louise Jermaine's life was zipped up in one solitary bag.

Louise Jermaine herself no longer existed. Angie Kavanagh had formally taken her place, signed and sealed by deed poll.

She was brought sharply back by the sound of Paolo puffing up the narrow stairs to the attic.

'Get a move on, girl. We're just about ready to go, thank God. These stairs are going to see me off; one more trip up them and I'll expire at your feet. Give us the bag . . .'

'No, it's OK, I'll carry this one.' She hugged the zippered bag tight to her chest. 'It's only got papers in it; it's not heavy.'

After taking one last look she shut the door firmly behind her and followed Paolo down the stairs to the car where Gavin was waiting patiently at the wheel without a care for the yellow lines and the grim-faced warden who stood, pen poised.

The two men had insisted on driving Angie to London. Not only that, they had searched carefully for what they thought was a suitable flat for 'their daughter' after she had been offered a job on a magazine.

She was embarrassed now to remember how horrified she'd first been when confronted by their homosexuality. But the older overweight Paolo and the younger handsome Gavin had happily taken her under their wing and encouraged her to grow up safely and securely over the past few years. She climbed in the back, still clutching the bag, and wedged herself among the boxes and bags that overflowed from the boot of the estate car.

'Right now, Angie baby, we're off to the big city. You just be careful, young lady, there's a dangerous world out there.' Paolo smiled over his shoulder at her.

'Yes, you be careful. Any problems and we'll be straight up to sort it. No one messes with our girl and gets away with it.'

They all laughed together and Angie felt an intense wave of affection for the two men she had nicknamed the odd couple in memory of her own friendship long ago.

Driving away from the flat, she remembered a trip to Jersey many moons ago with the Aberlones. She thought about the dreams that she had had then of university and becoming a rich and independent career woman with all the trappings that money could buy . . . Maybe she was just taking a different path to the same goal.

Gavin weaved the car through the traffic-clogged summer roads. 'Bloody holidaymakers, should be banned from the roads.'

'Oh yes, Gav,' Paolo retorted, 'let's get them all off the roads, let's stop them all from heading to the sea, let's trash our livelihood in one hit. No holidaymakers equals no business for us, you silly sod.'

Gavin laughed and glanced quickly at Angie. 'He does get his trousers in a tussle sometimes, doesn't he?'

The friendly bickering continued all the way to South London. Angie knew a lot of it was for her benefit, to ease the nervousness of moving on to a new life.

It was all thanks to Gavin that she had got her first job of general dogsbody in the office of the local newspaper.

'You've always either got a pen in your hand, your nose in a book or your body in the library, why don't you get yourself signed up for college? Your talents are wasted in this café . . .'

'Oh, thank you very much, Gavin.' Paolo had stood, hands on hips, pretending to glare at the man he shared his life with. 'Trying to get rid of my staff—'

Angie had interrupted quickly. 'It's OK, Paolo, I'm not going anywhere. I love it here.'

'Angie baby, I'm only joking. Gavin is right; you should be making the best of your talents and even I have to admit Paolo's Café is hardly providing a career for a bright girl like you. We'll go down there tomorrow and make some enquiries.'

True to his word they'd gone to the college and Angie had enrolled for all the exams she had missed.

She had still worked hard in the café and had been gradually paying money into her Post Office account to replace the cash she had taken from Tony. Blood money. She knew she wouldn't be able to block out the past completely until there was £1,725 in the account – not to return to Tony, but to ease her own conscience. She had even thought about giving it to charity.

She had passed her exams with flying colours and Gavin had persuaded a friend of his to put a word in for her at the newspaper. Her career in journalism had begun, even if it was only filing, tea-making and running errands for anyone who snapped their fingers.

It had been a long and frustrating time before she'd been allowed out to cover local events and minor hearings in the magistrates' courts but it had been eventually acknowledged that she was keen and eager and, more importantly, didn't have a social life. This meant that it had always been, 'Angie, can you just . . .', 'Angie, do me a favour . . .', 'Angie, I've got a hot date tonight, can you cover me . . .' She'd never said no; it had all been good experience and a bit extra on the CV that had eventually contributed to the offer of a job on *Woman's Life*, based in London.

The car rolled to a stop outside the old Victorian house, converted into four flats, that was to be home. Angie's was on the ground floor at the rear and was only minimally larger than the attic in Brighton but so light and bright that she had fallen in love with it immediately. There was even a tiny patio outside the French windows.

'First things first, Angie baby. I'll put the kettle on, you find the tea and coffee.' Gavin looked at all the boxes in the middle of the floor. 'Shall we get some of this lot put away before we go, Paolo, give the girl a head start? She starts work tomorrow and needs to be bright-eyed and bushy-tailed at the crack of dawn.'

Before the kettle boiled the boxes were all in their right rooms, the lampshades were up and ornaments on the mantelpiece. Already the place looked like home.

'I know what I've forgotten.' Gavin jumped up and went out to the car, returning a couple of minutes later and handing Angie a gift-wrapped box. She opened it carefully, peeling the tape slowly to avoid tearing the silver paper. Inside the long red box was a gold charm bracelet with a small padlock for a clasp and three small charms, a St Christopher medal, a tiny book and a round disc engraved 'Angie Baby, love P&G'.

'You can keep adding to them . . . What's the matter? Don't you like it?' He looked at her face.

She burst into tears. She was suddenly aware of the silver cross that she still wore around her neck, her present from Sharon in her other life; she vowed never to take either of them off.

She flung her arms round Paolo and Gavin in turn, and it took all her willpower not to chase after the car and go back with them as they left.

They had only been gone a short while when there was a knock on the door. Angie opened it a fraction and peered out over the chain that Paolo had insisted on fitting.

'Hi, I just thought I'd introduce myself. I'm Sue, I live upstairs. I know how awful it is the first night somewhere new . . .'

Angie unchained the door and opened it wide. The girl in front of her smiled broadly and held out her hand. Angie took it.

'My name's Angie, and yes, you're right, it does feel a bit strange. I only came up from Brighton today. I'd ask you in but it's still a mess—'

The girl walked straight past. 'Don't worry about that. I'm still

82

in a mess and I've lived here for two years. There's stuff in boxes that I've forgotten about . . . Still, I can't need it or I'd have missed it, wouldn't I?'

Angie followed her through, slightly discomfited at the invasion of her space. She had never invited anyone into the attic.

'Heavens, darling, call this a mess? It's tidier than mine already and a bloody sight better than when Pete lived here. He was such a slob, they probably had to fumigate it after he went back to Oz.'

She sank gracefully on to the sofa and crossed her long slender legs dramatically. 'Well, Angie, what do you do for a living?'

'I'm a journalist. I start work tomorrow on *Woman's Life*. I don't know if you know it; it's a weekly magazine—'

'Ooh, that's interesting. If you want any hot goss I'm your girl. I'm a model – well, I'm trying to be a model. At the moment I'm working in The Pig and Whistle on the corner – you must have seen it when you turned into the street – but I have had a few shoots. In fact I'm going up west tomorrow for a cattle call. Wish me luck.'

Angie looked at the girl in front of her, who was oozing personality and self-confidence. She looked every inch a model and spoke with the most impressive cut-glass accent that Angie had ever heard. The skin-tight jeans were welded to her seemingly endless legs and her ink-black hair hung straight as curtains down to her shoulders. She was stunning, and Angie felt small and dowdy beside her. The girl looked a good five foot ten in her bare feet.

Angie was at a loss, as Sue obviously wasn't planning on leaving. 'Would you like a drink?' she offered tentatively.

'I'd kill for a vodka tonic. It's been stinking hot today.'

'Sorry, I haven't any alcohol. I've got tea or coffee or lemonade, that's about it.' Angie smiled apologetically. She felt like a country bumpkin and mentally added booze to her shopping list.

Sue chuckled loudly. 'It was worth a try. I'll have a coffee, please, black, no sugar. I've got to lose half a stone, my agent's told me.' She slapped her slender thighs and looked at Angie. 'Half a stone, can you imagine? The man's barking mad.'

Angie made the coffee as Sue pulled a crumpled pack of cigarettes out of her pocket. She offered the pack to Angie as she brought the mugs over.

'Now, are you sitting comfortably? Right, I'll fill you in on everyone else in the flats . . .'

By the time she left, Angie's head was reeling. Sue didn't seem to take breath until the phone rang. She jumped up.

'I'll leave you to it. I bet it's the boyfriend checking up on you. I saw him this morning when he and your dad moved you in. A bit of all right, I thought. Byeeee.'

Before Angie could put her right she was gone, leaving clouds of expensive perfume in her wake.

It was Paolo on the phone, checking Angie was OK.

Angie loved her job from the minute she set foot in the glass tower block where the magazine was based.

On the first day she was introduced to everyone, shown her desk that already had a mound of paper waiting for her on it, and pretty much left to get on with it. From then on she picked the job up as she went along and after a few weeks felt she had been there for ever.

Ambitious and conscientious, she thrived on the pressure and responsibility that was given to her and got on with all her new colleagues bar one: her immediate boss, Felicity O'Malley, the bad-tempered, hard-faced features editor and number-one bitch. It hadn't been long before the other girls in the office warned Angie about Felicity. No one liked her and they were all wary of her. She had worked for the company for so long that she was unlikely to move on now, and everyone felt it would be foolish to cross swords with her openly.

Sue was on one of her regular sorties down to Angie's flat. Now Angie had got to know her she appreciated her company and was fascinated to hear about all her escapades.

'Darling, I was just so off my face I couldn't stand up. Giles and Gabby had to almost carry me up the steps and then march me past the dreaded doormen. I don't even remember getting home but I must have done or I wouldn't be here, would I?'

Her throaty laugh never failed to make Angie smile. The girl was always so happy.

'I don't know how you do it, you're out every night, pissed most of the time, but you still look fantastic. One late night and I'm dead for a week.'

'Practice, darling, practice. You don't get enough of it; you spend far too long in that greenhouse thing they call an office block and not enough time enjoying yourself. The invitation still stands, you know. You're welcome to come out with us any time.'

Sue had taken Angie under her wing. She decided her neighbour was a mouse with potential who just needed bringing out of herself. She wasn't called Sunny Sue for nothing. Both were twenty-two but light years apart in the experience of life – or so Sue thought.

It had passed fleetingly through her mind that Angie rarely spoke about herself but she decided it was because she hadn't ever done anything worth talking about. She assumed she was born and brought up in Brighton and Angie was happy to let her think it.

'I've made up my mind; tonight's the night, no excuses. We're all going to Ciro's and you're coming. It's Friday, you haven't got work tomorrow—'

Angie panicked. 'I can't, Sue, I really can't. I've brought a load of features home that I have to go through by Monday. Another time, perhaps.'

'Another time, always another time . . . No, no, no, darling, *this* time. I'll knock for you at nine on the dot. Giles is picking me up en route and you're coming. Dust off the trendy gear, tonight we're going to party. Subject closed now. Tell me what the wicked witch of the west has been up to this week.'

Angie giggled. She enjoyed telling Sue about the dreaded Felicity. She could never take the advice Sue offered, such as Tippex in her tea, Paraquat in her pudding or a sharp smack in the mouth, but it always cheered her up.

'That woman is such a cow. I found out I'm the third assistant she's had in a year. She called me a fucking moron today because I didn't pick up one of HER mistakes. Actually, I had noticed it but didn't dare point it out to her. She only went and told Hilary that I had screwed up. She's like a truculent five-year-old when she kicks off and everyone keeps their head down. Cow!'

Sue smiled encouragingly. 'You go for it, sweetie. Sound off, it'll make you feel a whole lot better!'

'Annabelle told me she's been having an affair with one of the top cheeses for years, thought it would buy her promotion but all that's happened is she's stayed where she is, getting more frustrated. She's all shoulder pads and make-up, looks like a refugee from *Dallas*. I'd love to get one over on her.'

'How about . . .' Sue put her forefinger under her chin and pretended to be thinking, 'how about . . . taking in a cannabis cake? Lighten her up a bit, or . . . clingfilm on the lav so that she pees all over her Janet Reger knickers?'

Angie was falling about. 'I can tell you went to boarding school, you're quite mad.'

'I know, I know, but at least I'm happily mad.' Sue stood up. 'I'm off to beautify myself. See you at nine. If you don't answer I'll kick the door in.'

Ciro's, the supertrendy nightclub, was a revelation to Angie. She hadn't expected a chandelier-lit ballroom but equally she hadn't anticipated the dungeonlike room with a handkerchief-sized dance floor.

Sue seemed to know everyone, flitting from table to table, air-kissing and hugging male and female alike, dragging Angie behind her.

'This is Angie, my new neighbour. She's from Brighton. I'm introducing her to Ciro's and the wicked ways of London. Be nice to her, won't you?'

Angie was embarrassed, feeling out of her depth, but the place was so dimly lit and smoky no one noticed. There was a cross section of ages in the club but, even so, it was like a fashion show. She had thought she looked quite good in her new calf-length suede gypsy skirt and tight black top, but she felt out of place now amid all the top fashion statements.

'You OK there? You look a bit pissed off.' Giles came up behind her as she was sitting at a table on her own, watching the dancing.

'I'm OK. It's all just a bit strange and I don't know anyone.'

'You know me. Come on, let's dance, and then I'll get you a drink.' He took her hand and led her into the middle of the already overcrowded dance floor.

Sue waved over the top of the crowd and winked at her. Angie guessed she had told Giles to dance with her but she enjoyed it just the same; he was a good mover.

By the end of the night she was quite light-headed. She didn't think she had drunk that much but her legs were wobbly and she was having trouble focusing on the way home. There were eight of them in two taxis, and when they got to the house they all piled into Sue's flat.

Giles eyed the room in disgust. 'Look at the state of this place, Sue. You're such a slut.'

She laughed as she bundled everything off the chairs into a heap in the corner and got out some glasses.

'Giles, you have to stop thinking you're my mother. Wine? All I've got is wine. Help yourselves.'

Angie knew that just one glass on top of everything else would make her ill, but she had reckoned without the big fat joint that Giles rolled and passed round the room.

She woke up next morning, curled up on Sue's sofa with a coat thrown over her. Her head hurt, her back hurt and her feet hurt. She felt like death.

Much later, as she lay in the bath trying to soak all the pain away, she told herself 'never again'.

'Angela, haven't you got a brain tucked away anywhere? I told you we're not using any more features from that goddamned pain in the arse and yet here one is, on my desk.' Felicity held the offending feature in her beautifully manicured hand and flapped it in front of Angie's face as if it was something obscene. 'Now you can phone her and tell her we don't want any more of her shite in this office.'

'But, Felicity, you commissioned that feature; you said you wanted it urgently . . .'

'That was before she had the sauce to try and up her rates. Who does she think she is? Freelancers? Who needs them?'

Angie knew they did, but thought better of saying it. The fact that the feature was well-written and that Julie Jones was well known and respected would be irrelevant to Felicity in this mood.

'How are you going to fill the space in the four-page pull-out then?' Angie asked the older woman, who was standing close to her desk and deliberately invading her body space, the strong heavy perfume that Felicity always wore making Angie feel quite nauseous.

'That's your problem. I want something on the subject in front of me by nine tomorrow morning. Find one in the files or something.'

She flounced back into her office, slamming the glass door behind her. There was a lot of sniggering behind hands; Felicity didn't realise she was the office joke.

Angie went through the files frantically, knowing that it wouldn't be likely she would find a thousand words on transvestites with an accompanying interview tucked away. By the end of the day she knew that if she were to have anything for Felicity by the next morning there was only one course of action. That night she knuckled down and wrote the feature herself with a bit of verbal help from Sue, who seemed to know everything about everything. Next morning on the dot of nine Angie handed it to Felicity under a pen name, inferring it had been in the office all along.

On publication day, the excitement of seeing her first full-length feature in print sent Angie racing up to Sue's flat the minute she got in.

'Are we out tonight? I feel like celebrating and it's my treat. I couldn't have done it without you.'

'Angela Kavanagh, you're worse than me, do you know that? Little did I know when I dragged you to Ciro's last year that I was opening the cage door and releasing the beast.'

Angie laughed loudly. 'Yes, well, it is all your fault but it's done now and you have to pay the price. See you later, yeah?'

Angie was quietly happy. She thought her first year in London had been good to her; she felt more confident and enjoyed her social life more than she could ever have imagined. Not only that, she had a good friend in Sue, something she had missed very much after Sharon.

And there was Giles.

'Sue, can I ask you something? Something personal?'

'Natch, darling, fire away. Aunty Marge is always on hand for you.' She leant forward across the bar and patted Angie's hand. 'I've always fancied having a go on your problem page. I can see it now: "Sue's Solutions to Sex" . . . a nice ring, methinks.'

'Seriously, it's about Giles. Is there anything between you two? I mean, have you ever . . . you know, been a couple?'

Sue shrieked so loudly the other two customers in The Pig and Whistle jumped. 'Me and Giles? You're kidding. I've known him since he was a snotty little boy. Our parents lived next door to each other . . . Never in a million years. I want a Clint Eastwood lookalike with pots of money who will whisk me off to the Caribbean and make made passionate love to me under the waving palms, why?' She looked at Angie and suddenly realised what she meant.

'Oh, no, don't tell me you fancy him, not good old Giles?'

'Shut up, Sue. Everyone's looking at us. But actually, yes. I do quite like him and he has asked me out but I didn't want to tread on your toes. You've been a good friend. Without you—'

'OK, I know, without me you wouldn't be out getting pissed every night, smoking dope like it's going on rations and partying like a mad woman on speed.'

Sue looked carefully at the young woman standing on the opposite side of the bar. She bore little resemblance to the mouse she had dragged kicking and screaming into London nightlife. She knew if Angie had been six inches taller she'd have been fierce competition for her in the modelling world. She had a perfect size 10 figure and had quickly learnt the art of shopping. She dressed to maximise her height and the thick black curly hair was always dragged back up on to the top of her head, emphasising her exotic features and colouring. When she walked into a club everyone

88

looked but no one touched. The barrier Angie had built was almost tangible, the signals easily read.

Angie still mistook admiration for criticism and thought Sue was laughing at her.

'Forget I said anything, Sue. He probably only feels sorry for me. I won't go—'

'For someone so intelligent you can actually be quite dumb sometimes. You are beautiful and funny and kind – of course he fancies you, he always has done, Dumbo. He's quite mad about you, only don't tell him I said that, will you?' She hesitated for a second. 'The only advice I would give you, though, is beware of Gabby. She's definitely got the hots for Giles – sees him as suitable husband material and he's just too naïve to realise – so if you fancy him go for it before she does!'

She looked over Angie's shoulder. 'Well, bugger me, talk of the devil and so he shall appear . . . Hi, Giles. Here to boost the takings again?'

Angie could feel herself blushing right down to her boots. Sue looked at her and winked.

'Why don't you two take your drinks over there? Customers are calling, and I'll be in trouble again. I'll come over for a ciggie in my break.'

No one knew that at twenty-three Angie had never had a date, let alone a relationship. Her sole experience of sex had been one of violence and pain, and she had no intentions of repeating it. She had always, without fail, said a firm no.

She did, however, fancy Giles, and it frightened her.

'You going to the party on Saturday? It should be good – all Sue's modelling friends are going . . .'

Angie cursed inwardly. She had promised to go to see Paolo and Gavin for the weekend.

'I can't, not this Saturday. I'm going down to Brighton on Friday and staying till Sunday.'

'Can't you put it off? Go next weekend instead?'

She hesitated but her conscience got the better of her. 'I can't. I haven't been down for weeks. I have to go, they're expecting me.'

'Fancy a meal on Sunday night then? We could go to the Spaghetti House.'

'That'd be great. I'm sorry I'm going to miss the party. That's the problem here – it's all spur-of-the-moment. Mind you, I never knew there could be so many parties. Sue knows half of London, doesn't she?'

They chatted together for most of the evening and apart from one break Sue kept a discreet distance from their table. When she'd finished work they all walked back together to Sue's and made light work of a bottle of vodka.

When Giles eventually left he pecked them each on the cheek.

'See you at the party, Sue. See you on Sunday, Ange.'

Sue raised one eyebrow as he shut the front door.

'See you on Sunday, Ange? What are you doing on Sunday, Ange?'

'We're going to the Spaghetti House after I get back from Brighton. OK with you?' Angie smiled at her friend.

'OK! Now, tell me again about Paolo and Gavin. God, that is just so romantic!'

'Angie baby, we thought you'd deserted us.' Gavin took hold of her by the arms and looked her up and down. 'Just look at you, a proper little fashion plate. Who'd have thought?'

She laughed and threw her arms round his neck. 'It's so good to see you, Gav. Is Paolo any better?'

Suddenly Gavin was serious. 'Not really. He's such a stubborn git. He knows he has to lose weight and start looking after himself but he takes absolutely no notice of the doctors. Five stone, they said, and he just laughed at them; said if he was going to go he wanted to go happy with a good meal and a bottle of wine in his belly. Anyway, come on up, he's desperate to see you. Needless to say he's killed the fatted calf especially!'

Paolo looked awful and Angie felt the familiar black cloud of old settling over her head. He shuffled back and forth to the kitchen, sweating and breathing heavily, but neither of them could persuade him to sit down. Suddenly he was looking like an old man, and she was frightened for all of them.

'Come on now, you two, the grim reaper isn't here yet, and I don't need you sitting there like a couple of pallbearers looking for customers. Let's eat, and you, young lady, can tell us everything that's been happening in your life. For a journalist you're totally useless at writing letters.'

On Saturday morning Angie went into town, leaving Gavin to keep an eye on Paolo. It was time for her annual visit.

She walked into the hospital and looked around. Nothing had changed; the paint was new but the same colour and smell . . . She knew she would never forget that smell, a mixture of disinfectant, scouring powder and anaesthetic. She savoured it as she walked through to the toilets. It was visiting time and there was a queue so she waited outside until there was a lull.

In the cubicle she half expected to see the familiar bag on the floor with a swaddled baby inside. She could picture the tiny face silently looking up at her as clearly as if it was yesterday.

There was a banging on the door. 'Are you all right in there?'

She flushed the chain quickly and carefully placed a single pink rosebud on the floor behind the bowl. She knew it would either be trodden on or swept up but she had to do it every year. It was a pilgrimage that she had to make.

She sat on the wall outside for a long time lost in her memories and nightmares.

Gavin walked her to the station on Sunday afternoon while Paolo took a nap at their insistence.

'Gav, I'm so worried for him, he looks so ill.'

'I know, my darling, but don't worry, I'll look after him and the café. We'll sort him out.'

But they couldn't. On Monday morning Angie was on her way back to Brighton to console Gavin and help with the funeral arrangements. Paolo had suffered a massive heart attack on the Sunday night while Angie was at the Spaghetti House with Giles.

The church was full to overflowing for the funeral. Paolo was popular and all his friends turned out in force but none of his family showed up. The day he had confessed to his homosexuality and admitted his love for Gavin was the day they had closed the door on him.

The relationship had cost him his marriage, his house and most of his money, but he had been happy with Gavin, the love of his life, and later with Angie as well, the daughter he never had.

Gavin was inconsolable and Angie worried about leaving him and going back to London, but she had to. Compassionate leave didn't take into account surrogate fathers. She tried to persuade him to go to London with her but he was insistent that Paolo would have wanted him to keep the café open.

'Angie baby, it has to be business as usual for both of us, for Paolo's sake. I'll come and visit you really soon. Don't forget me, will you?'

'As if I ever could.'

Angie sat in Sue's flat, sobbing and drinking herself into oblivion.

'I should have stayed. I knew he was ill. I should have been with him instead of rushing back for a bloody date . . .'

'Sweetie, you couldn't have known. Anyway, Gavin was with him; that's what he would have wanted, isn't it? You can't blame yourself for everything.' She put her arms round Angie and hugged her close. 'Listen to me, it's not your fault. Anyone else would have gone on a hot date and cancelled going home, but you didn't. You spent the last weekend of his life with him, didn't you?'

Angie didn't agree. She was racked with guilt.

Chapter Seven

They were all in the pub to celebrate Sue's last night working there. Her modelling career was on the up and she was off to the States for a week for a calendar shoot, and had regular work in the pipeline for the first time. Giles was perched on a bar stool talking to her.

'You know, I'm really worried about Angie. She's smashed most of the time and so high sometimes it's getting really dodgy,' Giles was looking around as he spoke, making sure she wasn't in earshot. 'She frightens me, she can be so manic. It's almost a death wish. I don't know how she manages at work.'

'You're overreacting, darling. She's just making up for lost time, and as far as I know it's onwards and upwards on the work front. Didn't she tell you she's had the offer of features editor on one of the glossies? That wouldn't happen if she couldn't hack it. What about all those features she's written at home? It's like doing two jobs . . . Ssshh, she's coming over.'

Angie worked her way through the crowd, waving a glass high in the air. She flashed a smile at Giles and put her arms around his waist. 'Any chance of a top-up?'

'Coming right up.' Sue turned away to get the drinks. 'They're on me tonight and come closing time it's off to Ciro's. Let's really push the boat out. I want to celebrate.'

Giles put his arm around Angie's waist, and as they stood entwined at the bar he could feel her swaying slightly.

'Hadn't you better slow down? We've got a long night ahead of us. Sue's intent on partying till dawn.'

'You're turning into a right old party pooper, Giles, do you know that? I'm as sober as that pot plant in the corner.'

She looked at him affectionately. She thought she might be in love with him. He was tall and good-looking in an old-fashioned kind of way. She loved the way his thick mousy hair was slightly bleached at the ends by the sun and fell forward over his forehead.

His dark brown eyes and smiley mouth attracted women wherever he went but he remained innocently unaware of his attraction. He doesn't look like a city banker, she thought, and started giggling.

'What's the joke, Ange? I'm not trying to tell you what to do, I just don't want you to be ill again.'

'No joke. I was just thinking I may be just a teeny bit in love with you, Mr Giles Boughton-Jones.'

Giles looked uncomfortable. 'Tell me that in the cold light of day when you're sober, eh?'

He felt passionately about her, he adored her, but she was only responsive when she'd had a few drinks; stone-cold sober and there was an emotional barrier as high as the Berlin Wall between them.

The first time they had made love, Angie had been drunk – and off her face every time since. They had not once made love when she was sober. Giles thought back to that first time, wondering if it was something he had done wrong – whether he had freaked her somehow and put her off . . .

The lovely summer's day had been spent lazily in the tiny garden, drinking wine and sunbathing, with a steady stream of friends, including Gabby, going in and out of both flats. Giles could sense the bad vibes between her and Angie but couldn't understand why. Then as Gabby wandered back to Sue's flat to get some more wine, Angie jumped up and locked the door behind her.

'I'm getting a wee bit pissed off with her,' she laughed as she went over and sat on Giles's lap. 'She fancies you, you know, she really, really fancies you . . .'

'Don't be a dope, Ange. She's just a friend, same as Sue. Anyway, I really, really fancy you . . .'

He pulled her to him and kissed her, gently at first but more passionately when she responded. As he undid the clasp of her bikini top she pulled away, and he thought she was backing off again, but instead she got up and led him into the tiny bedroom and they fell on the single bed, clumsily undressing at the same time.

Afterwards he lay crunched up against the wall, looking at her as she lay there smiling. He thought she was smiling because she had enjoyed making love with him.

Angie just felt a wave of relief that she had done it for the first time without violence and pain. She had actually hated every minute of it but she had been determined to get it over and done with, and try to lay the ghost.

She had another drink to help put the past behind her – and to celebrate privately a milestone passed.

Aware that his parents would disapprove of his girlfriend, Giles kept her under wraps, waiting for the right time. The way she was now made it look as if there would never be a right time. He knew that both sets of parents hoped that he and Sue would get it together. They saw it as a match made in heaven – same income bracket, same class, same childhood friends, and parents who were close neighbours and friends – but though he loved Sue dearly it was more brother-and-sister love.

With Angie it was different, but as he watched her spiralling out of control Giles wasn't sure if he could handle it, and he knew for certain his parents wouldn't be able to.

Many vodkas and several joints later, Giles managed to get Angie home and tucked up in bed. She tried to pull him in with her but he just pecked her on the forehead and took up his usual sentry-like position on the sofa; as usual sleep eluded him. He was always terrified she would choke to death on her vomit one night when no one was around.

He knew what he had to do, he didn't want to do it, but someone had to stop Angie Kavanagh before it was too late – before she cracked completely. He opened her bureau and flicked silently through her organiser for the number of the only person he thought she might listen to.

'Hi, Angie baby, how are you today?' Gavin had been quick to respond and had reassured a nervous Giles he wouldn't let on about the phone call. 'I'm completely bushed, sweetie, so I'm putting the café in Selina's capable hands for a fortnight and coming to London to catch up with you. Can I kip on your floor?'

Angie was delighted at the prospect of his visiting. Apart from the occasional day trip she hadn't seen much of Gavin since Paolo's death.

'Of course you can. A whole fortnight? Business must be booming if you can spare that long.'

It wasn't and he couldn't, but he wasn't going to tell Angie that. She was, to all intents and purposes, his and Paolo's daughter, and if she needed help then so be it.

'I'll be up tomorrow, about tea-time.'

They chatted for a while and Angie seemed fine to Gavin, but he knew Giles wouldn't have phoned on a whim. Whatever the problem, it had to be serious. He planned to catch the early train up and meet Giles in the city for lunch to get the lowdown, before going on to Angie's.

For the first time in her life Angie took a sickie from work. The flat was a mess, she was a mess and she didn't want Gavin to see her like it. She knew she wasn't coping but there was no way she would admit it to anyone else.

She took a quick shower and set to work cleaning the flat through. As she changed the grubby sheets on the bed she had a flashback to the flat in Albemarle Street. She could see Fran, pissed and dishevelled, sprawled across the filthy double bed, and for a split second she pictured herself there. Pausing for a moment, she wondered if she was going down the same road after all. Was it hereditary?

She needed a drink to clear her head, she decided. Just one, and then she could carry on getting ready for Gavin. When it didn't work she quickly rolled a joint and inhaled so deeply she was dizzy. But soon that made her feel better, the images of Albemarle Street faded and she could get on.

Giles and Gavin had arranged to meet in a little restaurant just off Threadneedle Street. 'Gavin, I'm so sorry, I should never have called you in the early hours like that, but I really don't know what to do. She won't listen to me . . . insists there's no problem and so does Sue. They both think I'm being a spoilsport.'

'You did right to phone me. Angie is very important to me and I promised Paolo I would take care of her. I'd die if anything happened to her.'

Giles looked hard at the man sitting opposite him, toying half-heartedly with a salad. He was the epitome of a romantic hero in a novel. Ruggedly good-looking, he was dressed immaculately, with knife-edge creases in his slacks and a white polo shirt that would have passed any soap powder test. The precisely cut collar-length black hair that was slightly speckled with grey around the temples gave him an air of distinction that had all the women in the restaurant looking his way. Giles guessed he was in his mid-forties, a good twenty years younger than the late Paolo had been.

Giles had found it all very strange in the beginning – two gay men caring paternally for a young girl with no family of her own. It was all so alien to the life that he had been brought up to: a mother and father, three siblings and pots of money. He and Sue had led parallel lives from birth: comfortable houses in the country and holidays abroad, prep school, boarding school and a choice of career. He chose banking, she modelling, both with their salaries topped up by trust funds at twenty-one. Both happy and loved. Giles found it impossible to get a handle on Angie's life, let alone Paolo and Gavin's.

'You don't feel uncomfortable with me, do you, Giles? I may be gay but I'm not going to jump any man who passes by, same as I assume you're not going to jump every woman in the restaurant?'

Giles blushed so deeply he could feel himself burning up under Gavin's intense gaze.

'Of course I don't, I'm just worried about Angie.' He knew he sounded defensive and guilty. Normally laid back and liberal, he felt he had let himself down both by stereotyping Gavin and by letting him see it.

'OK,' Gavin smiled, 'now that's out of the way let's talk about Angie. What's been going on that I need to know about? I won't say anything, I just need the background.'

Giles told him everything – the drinking, the drugs, the mood swings and the irrational behaviour, no holds barred.

Gavin knew Angie had taken a sickie – he had tried to phone her at work – but he left it until she would have been home anyway before walking to the flat and ringing the bell.

She threw the door open and flung her arms around his neck.

'Angie baby . . . it's good to see you.' He hugged her closely.

'And it's so good to see you. I've missed you so much . . .'

'Careful, you're strangling me.' Gavin peeled her arms from around him and took her hands. 'Let's have a cuppa and catch up. I want to hear all your news.' Gavin knew he had to tread carefully. He had to respect Giles's confidences and try to get Angie to open up of her own free will. 'You look a bit peaky to me, are you eating properly? I've seen more fat on the café floor – and you know how spotless I am.'

He laughed to take the edge off his remarks but there was no doubt about it, she was positively waiflike. The neat size ten figure was now a scrawny eight and descending.

'Thin is in. I thought you knew that, Mr Fashionable. Evidently one can never be too thin or too rich, according to either Jackie Onassis or the Duchess of Windsor – I can never remember which. I can relate to that.'

'Well, don't relate to it much more or you'll be too ill to make your fortune. Talking of making a fortune, tell me all about the new job.'

Angie gave Gavin chapter and verse on the dreadful Felicity and the job offer that she was considering that would take her away from it all. As he listened he grew to feel that she wasn't being completely honest, that this career move was the last thing she wanted at the moment.

'Sure you're not running away, babe? Frying pan into fire sort of thing? If you're unhappy you need to deal with why you feel like it. Running away won't help.'

She turned on him. 'I'm not running away. It's an opportunity, a bloody good opportunity, and I'm going to take it. I'm not running away!'

Gavin was stunned by the venom of her outburst, and realised straight away there was more to it all.

'Hey, don't blast me out of the water. I'm just interested, that's all. I don't want you making a mistake, but if that's what you really want then go for it.'

Angie's eyes filled up. She needed a drink but didn't want to have one in front of Gavin. She lit a cigarette and dragged hard but the effect wasn't the same.

'I'll put the kettle on.' She jumped up and went into the kitchen. Quietly opening the cupboard she pulled out a nearly empty bottle of vodka and drank the remains straight from the bottle.

'What's all this then, Angie baby? Swigging from the bottle like an old soak?'

She jumped so high she nearly choked.

'What do you think you're doing, creeping up on me? You nearly gave me a heart attack.'

Gavin looked her directly in the eye. 'I came to help you make the tea. I wasn't creeping up on you, Angie. Is there something you're not telling me? I thought we always confided in each other.'

'No, we don't, Gavin. You actually know nothing about me – no one really does. I reinvented myself at fifteen and that's who you know. You don't know ME, do you? Not really, not the real me.'

Gavin leaned back against the sink and crossed his arms.

'Don't you think it's time we talked – really talked? Let's get the memories out and give them an airing, good and bad, both of us. If you think you need a drink to do that then so be it. I'll nip down the offie and get us a bottle.'

Angie was a rabbit caught in the headlights. She knew something had to give but she had become accustomed to secrecy. Her whole life was shrouded in it so she didn't know if she could be selective about what she revealed.

'OK, let's talk, but I can't guarantee telling you everything, and I certainly can't guarantee you'll like it.'

They talked into the night and it was a revelation for both of them. Angie discovered the nightmare that Gavin had endured before finding the courage to come out into the open about his sexuality – the teasing from the schoolboys who sensed he was different, and the pressure to find a nice girlfriend, followed finally by the exclusion from his family.

'Can you imagine the shame my father felt? A Welsh miner who had worked all his life down the pits and lived on their doorstep, a macho man who drank with the best of them on Saturdays and went to chapel on Sundays? He was master in the house and my mother and sisters were ordered never to have contact with me again. He actually said he wished I'd never been born. I left Wales that night and have never been back, never seen nor heard from any of them.'

Suddenly Angie felt she had someone to relate to. Gavin had never spoken until now of his life before Brighton, and neither had she. The barriers came down and she told him everything, leaving out only the rape, her pregnancy and the birth of Skye. That was just too awful to put into words. They were soulmates, both different from the rest and both excluded by virtue of birth rather than any deliberate wrongdoings.

After just two hours' sleep Angie dragged herself from her bed into the bathroom; she looked in the mirror and didn't like what she saw. Her eyes were red-rimmed slits in a sallow and drawn face that she decided closely resembled a death mask. She could see Fran looking back at her.

She didn't want to go to work, not looking like an old meths drinker. She decided to phone in sick again, pleading the same stomach bug and spend the day sobering up: no vodka, no dope, no pill-popping, nothing.

It wasn't as easy as she'd imagined. Without her lunchtime booster she was a wreck and was making Gavin's life hell.

He recognised the symptoms. With no props she had to face up to realism and it was too much to cope with. Admitting a habit was harder still and she wasn't up to that just yet.

Gavin persuaded Angie to see her doctor and get signed off. She put up a token resistance but deep down she knew she wasn't up to work. Confession may be good for the soul, she thought grimly, but it's draining on the brain.

While she was out Gavin phoned Giles and updated him without betraying any of Angie's secrets. They arranged to take her for a meal that evening with strictly no alcohol and no clubbing afterwards. Healthy was going to be the new word.

Giles knew it wouldn't do him any harm to abstain for the time being either, at least in front of Angie.

★ ★ ★

Angie was prescribed some tranquillisers and told to come back in a fortnight. During that time the feeling of being locked up and supervised was claustrophobic. No one put up any fences and no one said anything but she felt the eyes on her. Paranoia was setting in.

Sue was still away in the States so her flat was empty, the other upstairs flat was vacant, and no one ever saw hide nor hair of the mysterious Mr Smith who rented the flat at the front but was rarely there. That left just Gavin and sometimes Giles watching her every move.

The third day of her sick leave, Gavin went out to get some fresh bread, leaving Angie alone for the first time.

She needed a drink, she needed a joint, in fact she needed anything that would dissolve the all-too-familiar black cloud. There was half a bottle of vodka in her wardrobe and a piece of cannabis wrapped carefully in tin foil stuffed in the toe of one of her old shoes. It tormented her knowing they were there, but at the same time they gave her security. There was no way she could bring herself to throw them out – not her security blanket, not with Gavin and Giles hanging around her like angels of mercy crossed with prison warders.

She opened the wardrobe and took out the bottle.

The doorbell rang and her stomach sank. She'd only just managed a mouthful of vodka and it wasn't enough. Trying to ignore the insistent ringing she flattened herself against the bedroom wall and stood silently, praying whoever it was would go away. The letterbox rattled.

'Angie? Are you there? It's me, Giles. Come on, open up. I haven't got long, I'm on my lunch hour.'

'Piss off, Giles. I don't need minding every second of the day. I bet Gavin phoned you, didn't he? You're like a couple of old women, the pair of you.'

Giles wasn't going to be deterred. 'Don't be so bloody awkward, just open the door.'

She hid the bottle, glanced in the mirror to straighten her face and went to the door.

'How are you doing then? Feeling OK?' Giles hugged her to him affectionately.

A thought flashed through Angie's mind. 'Did you talk to Gavin about me? Did you drag him up from Brighton to child-mind me? Tell me. I need to know.' She was screaming at him, her face screwed up with rage.

He didn't want to upset Angie but he couldn't lie to her outright, so he settled on a half-truth.

'I did speak to him, yes, but only because I was worried about you, and so was he once he saw you. I knew he was here for two weeks so it seemed as good a time as any for him to help you.'

Angie was incensed. How dare he interfere?

'Arsehole, I am a grown-up woman. I've lived on my own since I was fifteen. Do you really think I need you or any other man to watch over me like the bloody prophet of doom? All you've done is frighten the shit out of Gavin; he doesn't need it.'

She glared at him wildly. She wanted to hit him but was shocked when he answered back.

'You can hurl insults at me till the cows come home but you need help. You might not want it but you need it, and I wouldn't be much of a friend if I ignored it. You have a problem with booze and drugs, and you have to stop now before you end up in the gutter.'

'Giles darling,' she sneered sarcastically, 'I came from the gutter. There's nothing you can tell me about it. Now fuck off.'

'Like it or lump it, I'm waiting till Gavin gets back.'

Defiantly Giles sat down rigidly at the small dining table, pretending an interest in the birds on the patio.

Angie was suddenly unsure of herself. She wanted him out so that she could get back to her bottle in the wardrobe; she couldn't think of anything else. She lit a cigarette and paced the floor in silence.

How had it all fallen apart so quickly? A few social drinks and the occasional joint had turned into nearly a bottle a day to function and several joints at night, often topped up with a line of coke.

It had all started when she discovered the feeling of elation and the ability to forget the horrors of the past that the odd indulgence gave her. She could forget the tiny wrinkled face looking up from the totebag in the toilets; she could forget Tony forcing himself inside her the same way she had seen a stray dog mount Gypsy in the park; she could forget everything and be happy for a short while. She could also let Giles make love to her without feeling physically sick at the thought of a man's touch on her body.

Oh yes, being high as a kite certainly had its advantages in the beginning, but now she couldn't even go to work without a small bottle in her bag to get her through the long working day.

She was dependent, and deep down she knew it, but that still didn't stop her needing something right now.

The bell rang again and Giles jumped up and legged it to the door.

'Whose flat is this?' Angie shouted sarcastically after him.

Gavin came in carrying a bag of shopping in one hand and a bunch of flowers in the others. He handed the flowers to her and she took them ungraciously, went into the kitchen and put them in the sink.

She knew the men would be exchanging knowing looks behind her back and again, she reminded herself of Fran the ever ungrateful.

'I'm going to lie down, if it's all right with you. You can come and sit by my bed, if you wish, hold vigil over the sick, make sure I don't do anything naughty.' She looked from one to the other, waiting for a response. She didn't get the answer she wanted.

'Sounds good to me. You have a nap and I'll go out on the patio and sunbathe after Giles has gone back to work. Got any ciggies, Angie baby? I'm gasping; forgot to get any up the road.'

He smiled at her as she threw the packet across the room at him.

'Right then, I'm off back to the daily grind, earning a crust, and all that crap. I'll speak to you soon.' Giles looked expectantly at her but no response was forthcoming. She went into her bedroom and slammed the door.

She was screwing up and she knew it. She knew that she had blown her chances of the new job and was pushing her luck at *Woman's Life*. Felicity was on her case all the time, and now with sick leave . . . She also knew it was probably over with Giles. So close yet so far, she thought, lying on her bed behind the locked door with a bottle in one hand and a joint in the other.

She thought about Daniel and Sharon, Joshua and Nancy, all tucked away in the past. She thought about Skye and tried to imagine where she was and how she looked. She had phoned Sharon a few times in the beginning but the pressure to go back was too much. She had known she could never go back. She had wanted a new start and had got it, worked hard for it and was about to achieve everything she had dreamt of, everything Joshua had wanted for her . . . except it was all soiled by nightmares from the past . . .

The vodka and cannabis were taking effect; a few days without had heightened their impact. The bottle of tranquillisers beside her bed were beckoning her. Oblivion, that was all she wanted, just a little peace, a chance to get rid of all the pain . . .

She tipped them into her hand and almost instantly put them all in her mouth at once. She washed them down with the last of the vodka and turned over, cuddling the pillow to her, pretending it was Gypsy.

102

★ ★ ★

Angie had no recollection of Gavin kicking the door in and the ambulance taking her to hospital with sirens blaring and lights flashing. She also had no recollection of the indignity of the stomach pump that unceremoniously washed her stomach contents into the bucket beside the bed.

She did remember waking up in a hospital bed and being told she was being transferred to the psychiatric hospital for observation, Gavin watching over her anxiously.

As the ambulance pulled up outside the specialist hospital, the first thing that struck Gavin was what a dump it looked – a run-down, old-fashioned general hospital that had been designated for the mentally ill while the physically ill were admitted, pride intact, to the shiny new building a few roads away.

He followed the wheelchair in despair as Angie was taken to the long narrow ground-floor ward, lined with beds, where the only concession to privacy was the inadequate faded curtains that blocked out sights but not sounds. Gavin wanted to snatch her up and take her home with him, she looked so small and sad but deep down he knew she needed more help than he could give her. The doctors didn't use the term, but Gavin was aware Angie had suffered a nervous breakdown.

For over a week they tried everything to get through to her. Gavin was there all the time and brought her supplies of cigarettes, soft drinks, books and magazines, but she refused to respond and she refused to allow Giles or Sue, who was now home from the States, to come and visit.

Angie was angry. She took it out on everyone else but she was actually angry with herself – angry at her own weakness, angry at letting herself down. She found it hard to believe that just when things were going right, she had let this happen.

Gavin was sitting beside her, at his wits' end.

'Angie baby, please talk to me – please. I want you to get better and get out of here. You can come back to Brighton with me and I'll look after you. Please co-operate. It's the only way you can get out of here soon.'

Angie looked out of the window without making any eye contact.

'I don't know if I want to get out of here. They think I'm mad so I'm better off in here. In here I can't fuck up my life any more, can I?'

'They don't think you're mad at all, just confused. You've had a breakdown. It's been coming on for a while; I just wish I'd noticed.

103

The psychiatrist is coming to see you today. Please talk to him, tell him what's wrong, let him help you get better . . .'

'I don't want to get better and I don't want to get out. I belong here, I like it here.'

Gavin raised his hands in defeat. He just couldn't get through to her.

Caro had been admitted to the same ward just after Angie. She was brought in kicking and screaming, and fighting anyone who came near her. It was hard to work out the age of the punk girl with bright yellow and orange striped spiky hair, who was spitting like a wildcat at the nurses trying hard to restrain her.

The amateur tattoos up both arms were so infected it was impossible to make out what they were supposed to be, and everyone stopped to watch as she brought chaos to the ward before she was sedated and her arms bandaged.

Angie had looked on with interest. She almost wished that she had been able to put up a fight, to shout and swear at everyone instead of constantly seeking approval.

'What are you looking at?'

Caro was on the move as usual one morning, marching down the ward, her boots clacking loudly as she came towards Angie. She stopped aggressively in front of her, nearly nose to nose.

'I was looking at your hair actually, just wondering what I'd look like with mine striped.' Angie smiled cautiously.

'You taking the piss?'

'No, of course I'm not. I'm just . . . Oh, never mind, excuse me.'

Caro didn't move. For a moment Angie thought the girl was going to attack her so she moved around her and headed for the safety of the dayroom, but Caro followed.

'Why are you in this loony bin? What did you do?'

Angie thought for a second before replying, 'I took an overdose, what about you?'

'They found me pissed as a fart in the middle of the motorway, trying to hitch a lift to Newcastle and 'cos I've got a history they brought me here . . . again. Stupid bastards, this place is as much use to me as a chocolate dick.'

Angie laughed for the first time. 'I'm Angie; I know you're Caro. I'm going out for a smoke, do you want to come?'

'What are you after? I haven't got anything on me.'

'I'm not after anything, only some like-minded company. You sound as messed up as I am!'

Angie found out that Caro was seventeen and had been living in a squat in London for three years after running away from a children's home in Newcastle.

'I never knew me mum or dad. Fostered from three, I was, but none of them could handle me so after five chances they put me in a home. I hated it. I got beat up there more often than a pudding mix. Ran away when I was fourteen and been here ever since. What about you?'

The empty, expressionless eyes told Angie far more than the words the girl spoke.

'Much the same really . . . but I didn't have it as bad as you, nowhere near. Makes me feel a bit of a fraud . . .'

'Bloody hell, you've done all right for yourself then – nice clothes, nice fella. Why'd you try and top yourself?'

Caro looked her up and down and suddenly Angie felt very conservative in front of her.

'I didn't. Well, I don't think I did. Everything was getting me down. Things had happened. I was drinking too much, doing drugs and I just wanted a rest from it all . . . I was just a bit muddled but no one believed me so here I am, cold turkey. Oh, and Gavin's not my fella, he's my sort of foster father.'

'Yeah, right, sugar daddy, you mean . . .'

Angie went bright red with embarrassment. 'No, I don't mean that. I haven't got any family and he and his partner, Paolo, were really good to me!'

Caro laughed loudly. 'You mean he's gay? What a fucking shame. Waste of a good-looking fella; he's a bit of all right. Do you think he'd like to foster me?'

Angie smiled and felt the cloud lift a fraction.

During the six weeks that Angie and Caro were together in the hospital they formed an unlikely friendship that made Angie rethink her life. She knew that without Paolo and Gavin she could easily have become like Caro, and the guilt from letting them down was almost too painful to bear. Caro had nothing and she had everything by comparison, thanks to them, and she knew the only way to repay them was to get her act together and pick up the pieces.

When she asked Gavin to bring in her notepads and pens, and the new camera, still unopened in its box, that she'd bought in anticipation of taking up her recently offered job, he knew that she was on the mend.

Angie had explained her job to Caro, and the girl was a more-than-willing interviewee. They spent hours walking round the grounds, and chatting and drinking muddy coffee in the cafeteria between the regular therapy sessions.

Angie secretly felt that Caro did her more good than any of the professionals, but she co-operated with everyone and bared her soul, apart from anything about Skye, who was to be her secret for ever. She hoped desperately that she was doing Caro some good as well.

The day she was discharged Angie had a sick feeling in the pit of her stomach. She feared she wouldn't see Caro again. She made the young girl promise to keep in touch and contact her once she was discharged but she wasn't optimistic. Caro was a lost soul through no fault of her own.

'Well, Angie baby, are you all set? Let's go.'

As they drove away from the hospital Caro waved from the steps for an instant and then quickly turned back into the building. Angie alone knew it was because it didn't fit her image to be seen crying.

'Are you really sure you won't come back to Brighton with me? I worry about you . . .'

'I know you do, Gavin, and I really, really appreciate everything, but I feel tons better and I have to get back to reality now. Don't worry, I'll be fine, I promise. No more dubious substances ever, and I'll keep taking the medication!'

The banner waiting for her outside her flat took Angie by surprise. The 'WELCOME HOME' sign was bordered by a mass of multicoloured balloons, and Angie and Gavin had to duck to get through the door. Sue and Giles were in there waiting for her, and they threw their arms around her, greeting her like a returning hero.

'It is so good to have you home, sweetie. I've missed having you around to offload on. Just wait till I tell you about the States. God, it was just so exciting. I'm off to the Caribbean soon as well—'

'Hang on, Sue,' Giles interrupted her mid-flow, 'give the girl a chance to get inside.'

Angie looked at him shyly as he spoke. 'I thought you might not want to know me now I'm a fully paid-up member of the nuthouse . . .'

Giles looked indignant. 'Is that the sort of friends you thought we were? I'm disappointed you could even consider it, Angie Kavanagh!'

Angie picked up on his use of the word 'friend'. She knew then there was no future for her and Giles as a couple. She was surprised that the realisation didn't hurt.

'Right everyone,' Gavin laughed, 'enough of the bickering. Let's all just quieten down and relax and give Angie time to get used to being home. Where's the food?'

Sue and Giles disappeared into the kitchen and returned with plates of dainty sandwiches and scones and a big wooden tray on which were cups and saucers, sideplates, and a huge pot of tea all laid out on an embroidered traycloth.

'Afternoon tea, anyone . . .?'

Later, when Sue had drifted off, Gavin sensed it was the right time for a tactful exit, leaving Giles alone with Angie.

'I'm just off to fill the car up with petrol for tomorrow. I'll see you both later.'

Giles and Angie sat side by side on the sofa.

'It's over between us, isn't it, Angie?' Giles looked at her sadly.

'I think so.' She took his hand as she spoke. 'I love you dearly and I'm so grateful to you but I think too much has happened . . . We will still be friends, though, won't we?'

'Always, I promise.'

By the time Gavin came back Giles had gone. Gavin guessed what had happened and hugged her.

'You sure you'll be OK?'

'I'm sure,' Angie replied. 'It's onwards and upwards now!'

When Angie heard that Caro had died from a heroin overdose the day after leaving hospital she was overwhelmingly sad but not surprised. She also knew she wasn't going to have a drink to console herself, she was going to do something positive.

Caro had no one really close, and Angie was determined the death of a seventeen-year-old was not going to go unnoticed. She would have a good sendoff. Tony's blood money that she'd taken all those years ago was used to pay for the funeral and the wake that were attended by all the people Angie could recruit, along with Caro's friends from the squat. As the coffin slid silently through the purple curtains at the crematorium, Angie said a silent thank you to the girl who had unwittingly rescued her.

Angie felt there was some retribution in using the drug dealer's money to pay for the drug addict's funeral. She had signed the card on the wreath, 'I will survive in your memory,' and after the funeral she felt cleansed and ready to start her life again.

Angie worked hard on the feature about Caro, determined to do justice to the girl's memory and to make people sit up and think about all the other Caros out there.

When she sold it, along with the photographs of the girl and her funeral, to a Sunday newspaper for a large sum, she decided it was enough money to make her career change. Looking at the cheque Angie resolved to try to make it on her own as a freelance – no more office, no more Felicity.

The feature was such a success and raised such a lot of interest Angie was suddenly in demand, and there were spin-offs in most of the magazines. Drugs were big news and Angie had touched a nerve in everyone with her hard-hitting story about the life and death of young Caro, a child in care with no one to care.

It had taken a long time but Angie was back in control of her life.

Chapter Eight

1990

Angie dumped her suitcase in the spacious hall and threw herself straight into the kitchen.

'Hi, I'm home,' she shouted, en route. 'I must, must, must have a decent cup of tea and a Marmite sandwich. I've been dreaming of it . . .'

As she put the kettle on Sue came through and flung her arms round her, smiling widely.

'It's good to see you back. How was Cannes, you lucky cow?'

'Hectic but I got the interview *and* I got an exclusive. Christ, that Jed Warman is a slimeball. Why are so many so-called superstars completely up themselves? Still, everyone gets what they want out of it; he gets his publicity and I get to pay the mortgage.'

'And you got to go to Cannes. That must be just a teensy bonus for you, sweetie, um?'

Angie laughed. 'Yes, all right, I have to admit I had a ball really, but now the proper work starts – well, tomorrow anyway. Any calls?'

'Loads on the answerphone.'

'I'll check them tomorrow. Tonight I just want to crash. It's been a hectic week, party after party. It's a dirty job but someone's got to do it!' She looked at her friend and raised her eyes upwards in mock despair. 'Anyway, you're looking a bit smug, and ultraglamorous, where are you off to? Or, more to the point, who with?'

Angie thought wryly how Sue always looked fabulous and certainly not her age despite the years of alcohol, junk food and going to bed with her make-up on. The hair was shorter but still shoulder length, and the hips a tiny bit wider, but that was all. They were both, however, moving too quickly away from thirty for comfort.

'Oh God, no one special, only Giles. But we're going to a do at the Carlton. It's the annual bash to find the new face of the year so there's no way I'm going to be overshadowed by a litter of skinny pubescent wannabee models searching for fame and fortune. Giles is coming to give me his male opinion and keep an eye on my bank balance. He's terrified I'll promise one of the nymphettes vast amounts of money!'

'Bitch, bitch, bitch!' Angie grinned. 'You used to be one of them, remember?'

'Oh, I do remember. God, I was so naïve, wasn't I?'

Angie laughed. 'Weren't we all?'

She thought about perhaps why Sue had never quite made it. She had the figure, the height and the looks but not the drive. Angie had always wondered whether the private income had hindered more than helped. Sue might have been more motivated to stay the course if what she earned modelling had been her only income. Instead she opted to invest in starting up her own agency, Wondermodels.

'So, are you hoping to pick out a few for yourself?'

'Let's just say I'm on the prowl. I need one really good find. I've got the bread and butter but now I need the jam to sweeten it up for me. Still, must dash. Giles is picking me up outside to save the parking nightmare. We can catch up in the morning.'

Despite the tiredness Angie found it hard to sleep that night. Her brain was in overdrive, causing the feeling of a tight band around her temples. It was always the same after a trip; it took a couple of days to settle back. Grimacing, she glanced at the digital 3 a.m. on the bedside clock and decided to make the best of it and start some work.

Without getting dressed she made a drink and then padded quietly into her office, trying not to disturb Sue, who had not long fallen in the front door, muttering crossly as she tripped over one of the cats. Angie knew by instinct that Sue had someone with her but the lights were all out so she guessed they were in Sue's bedroom. She also knew it was no good trying to guess who it might be; the standing joke between them was that Sue the eternal romantic had been blessed with Angie the celibate's share of sexual appetite.

Sue's whirlwind marriage on a Caribbean beach to a male model who loved himself more than anything else, had been short-lived. Now Sue and Angie were single, and happy sharing the far-too-expensive Fulham house with each other and two demanding Siamese cats.

110

Turning down the volume on the phone, Angie played her messages back: nothing too urgent but one more interesting than the other.

'Hi, Angie. It's Dave Oliver here, returning your call. I am free for the photos of Michael MacGregor week after next. Can we meet to discuss it? Call me back.'

She rewound and played the message again.

The freelance photographer was the first man since her relationship with Giles that she actually wanted to get to know better. They had been on a few assignments together and worked well with each other. A big gentle man with no interest in his appearance – she had never seen him in anything other than jeans and desert boots – he loved his work and was the best as far as she was concerned. The thought of working with Dave again was a welcome one to come home to.

The coffee was on and the orange juice squeezed when Sue surfaced next morning, swathed in a vast multicoloured beach towel.

'Bloody hell, Sue, it must have been a good night. You look like Minnehaha after she'd been staked out for a week. I wasn't expecting to see you till this afternoon at least. Have a caffeine fix, quick, and tell me all about it. Good job it's Sunday!'

Sue slumped on to the rattan highstool and buried her head in her hands. 'You won't believe what I've done. Oh God, I can't believe it. I have to give up alcohol right this minute. Don't let me ever have another drop.'

'Right,' Angie smiled at her knowingly, 'you always say that. Go on then, what have you done now?'

'Promise you won't hold it against me for ever and a day?'

'I promise, now tell me.'

'Giles came back with me and we sort of ended up in bed . . .'

Angie stood stock-still for a moment while she digested just exactly what her friend had said. She was horrified. 'Oh, Sue, how could you? After all these years . . . How could you do that to your friend, for Christ's sake?'

Sue groaned again. 'I know, I know. I feel so guilty . . .'

'Well, I bloody well hope he does too. You're both barking mad, if you ask me. HOW COULD YOU?' she repeated emphatically before swinging on her heel and heading for the door, taking her coffee with her. 'I'm going to get dressed and cool down before I say the wrong thing.'

She was so angry she was shaking when she got to the bedroom. She lay back on her bed and lit a cigarette, inhaling deeply.

After Angie, everyone had thought Sue and Giles would become an item, they were so close, but it had never happened. Sue was forever flying off around the world on fashion shoots while Giles stayed put and carved a successful career in banking.

The announcement that Giles and Gabby were getting married took nearly everyone by surprise but they seemed the perfect match. Gabby had never had any high ambition other than to get married and have babies, and Giles had always been more of a homebody than he cared to let on.

Angie lay looking at the ceiling and thinking back to the wedding five years ago. Sue and Angie had both been bridesmaids, and both sets of parents pushed the boat out with an extravagant do followed by a honeymoon on safari in Kenya. Giles and Gabby had seemed so happy, with two children following quickly. Sue and Angie were godmothers to Harry, their first born.

Giles was a wonderful money man and he helped Sue and Angie with their accounts and also had a stake in the model agency. They even all socialised together successfully, just like in the old days – up to now. Angie could see that being a problem if Sue and Giles were going to be bonking like rabbits.

There was a tentative knock on the door but when she ignored it the door opened just a fraction.

'Talk to me, Angie. I hate to fall out with you . . . Come on, I could have not told you and you wouldn't be any the wiser.' The door opened a bit more and Sue stood in the doorway. She had obviously been crying. 'I didn't mean it to happen. I wish it hadn't – I bloody well wish it hadn't – but at the time . . . Please don't tell Giles I told you. He'll be mortified . . .' The words trailed off as she looked at Angie apologetically.

'Good. He deserves to be. I suppose it's none of my business. You're both big grown-up people . . . allegedly. But how did it happen? I really thought you two were the most platonic of platonics.'

'So did I, but something just clicked – fuelled, of course, by too much champagne on my part maybe, but Giles was stone-cold sober so I don't know . . . How on earth am I going to face them?'

Angie had no answer to that.

Angie couldn't concentrate on her word processor. She kept thinking about men and marriage, and it started her back to the past: her mother and father, her mother and Barry, her mother and Tony and who knows since?

Sue obviously hadn't a clue about the misery she could cause to Giles and Gabby's children. It was always the children Angie felt for; she knew the suffering from personal experience.

On a sudden impulse she picked up the phone as she had nearly done so many times in the past but this time she dialled the number and let it ring.

A woman answered. 'Hello?'

Angie put the receiver down. How could she possibly explain everything to Nancy after all this time? That was another life, another person. Louise Jermaine was dead and buried in the past. She sent Christmas and birthday cards to Nancy and Sharon without fail, and signed them Louise, but she never gave a forwarding address. Angie Kavanagh had now been around longer than little Louise had.

Angie wandered into the hall and looked at herself in the full-length mirror. The thick hair pulled up on top of her head had been replaced by a close crop, and there were definitely a few lines around the mouth and eyes, but she was still only just over five foot in bare feet and still a perfect size ten. More confident maybe but the self-protective barriers were still there.

Why were all men such shits? she wondered sadly. Sue shouldn't have done it but at least she was single and drunk. Giles was married and, according to Sue, stone-cold sober. Whatever possessed him to do something so stupid, so wrong to Gabby and the two children, tucked safely away in Sussex?

The more she thought about it the more Angie realised it was really none of her business. They were both adults, and even though she was so upset there was not a lot she could do to change the situation so she decided to distance herself from it. So when Sue tried to discuss it later Angie simply said, 'Subject closed. I don't want to know so don't tell me any more otherwise I'll never be able to look either Giles or Gabby in the eye again.'

One of the many things she was good at was blocking out the bad things. She had had lots of practice.

On the dot of nine on Monday morning she returned Dave Oliver's call. It was the answerphone but as she gave her name the call was intercepted.

'Angie? Hang on, I'm here, just fielding calls, you know how it is . . .'

Angie laughed. 'Oh yes, I do know. Monday morning trivia and all that. Anyway, I got your message. I was in Cannes for the film festival and didn't get back till Saturday evening.'

'How was the lovely Cannes? Still a seething mass of eager young hopefuls?'

'Yep, but I have to say it was fun. I'm glad I'm not an actor, though. Anyway, back to Michael MacGregor. This is an in-depth political interview so I'm going to need the usual serious shots, in his study, et cetera, as well as some casual ones – playing with the pets, stroking the children or vice versa, you know the sort of thing – all to be vetted by his office before publication.'

'You don't mean cosmetic surgery, do you?' The voice at the other end laughed, a deep gutsy laugh. 'A sanitised politician at play kissing babies?'

'Not at all. I'm not a celebrity crawler . . .' She knew she sounded pompous as soon as she'd said it.

'Only joking, only joking. Come down from the ceiling . . .' He was still laughing and she couldn't help but join in. His voice was just so sexy!

'Sorry. Can we meet beforehand to discuss it? I really need this to be spot-on to avoid it being axed by his office. Do you want to come here or shall I come to you?'

'I've got a better idea. How about thrashing it out over dinner? Say Friday? I've got a meeting at Blackfriars in the afternoon . . .'

Angie only hesitated for a second. 'Sounds good to me. Shall we talk later in the week to confirm?'

'Great, I'll see you then. I'm looking forward to it.'

She put the phone down and sat thinking about Dave Oliver for a while. She had known him superficially for a few years, and their paths occasionally crossed in the course of work, but this was the first time just the two of them were going to be working together formally; she found herself looking forward to it.

'Angie,' she heard Sue shouting, 'have you got a minute? I need urgent help . . .'

As she stood up she thought wryly that that was one of the disadvantages of working at home – the interruptions.

'What's the problem? I'm a bit buried at the moment, trying to catch up . . .'

'Sorry, sweetie, but I have to get to Greece a.s.a.p. That new model Rebekah Alari is playing up and disrupting the shoot. I wish I could fire the little bitch but she's so bloody photogenic they all want her. Can you give me a hand to throw a few things in the case? I've got a cab coming in half an hour.'

Angie went into Sue's bedroom, which closely resembled a devastation zone with clothes and shoes all over the place. Angie bordered on obsessively tidy but Sue was a one-woman walking disaster. It never failed to amaze Angie that this unbearably disorganised woman could present herself beautifully ready for a party after digging around under the bed for ten minutes trying to find something clean to wear.

'How long are you going for?'

'Only a couple of days. I can't really afford to leave the agency for even that long but I also can't afford to lose this contract. I'd like to slap the brat. The young ones are a nightmare to me. They don't know the meaning of the word professional.'

'OK, calm down.'

As Angie started to make some order out of the chaos she was silently offering up a little prayer for a couple of days' peace to get on with some work. With Sue out of the way she could settle down to serious catching-up.

'Now you only need an overnight bag and two changes of clothes, underwear and cosmetics. Anything you don't take you have to borrow or do without.'

The packing was sorted out in record time and Angie heaved a sigh of relief as she waved at the departing taxi. She loved Sue dearly but she was inclined regularly to lurch hyperactively from crisis to crisis, whereas she herself would plan carefully and avoid high drama at all costs. She had had enough traumas to last a lifetime without looking for any more.

She made a cup of tea, then went back to work in her office.

The three-storey terraced house was spacious, with four bedrooms and three reception rooms. Each of the women had her own bedroom, and Angie also had an office tucked away on the top floor as she worked from home. Everything else was shared, including the mortgage, although it was Angie's house.

The house was Angie's pride and joy. She loved the feeling of space, and spent her spare time decorating, and scouring the second-hand shops for Victoriana that suited the age of the house. For the first time in her life she felt settled and couldn't imagine ever moving. She often smiled to herself as she remembered the holiday in Jersey and how she had dreamed of one day owning an ultramodern mansion with swathes of white satin and enormous picture windows overlooking the sea.

This was the complete opposite but it was hers.

When Friday came, Angie still couldn't decide what to wear. She and Dave were only going to the Chinese restaurant round the corner from the house but her long-standing insecurity made her indecisive when it came to men. She dismissed a dress as too formal and jeans as too casual before finally deciding on tight black ski-pants, a white polo shirt topped with a fitted leather jacket and cuban-heeled ankle boots. She carefully applied a touch of make-up and ran a pick through her hair.

'Oh, very smartly casual. I'm sure he'll be impressed! Who is he, did you say?'

'Just shut up, Sue. I told you it's business. I'm meeting the photographer who's coming to Scotland with me for the interview with Michael MacGregor, that's all.'

Sue looked her up and down. 'Why is it that I don't believe you? Could it be because this so-called meeting is taking place in a restaurant in the evening? Or is it because you've just spent hours getting ready as opposed to the usual ten minutes?'

'Why don't you piss off back to Greece and play with your child models? It was so peaceful without you.'

They were both laughing as they bickered amiably.

'What are you doing tonight, Sue? Surely not an early night?'

'I'm not sure yet. I may just stay in and destress – I don't know, I haven't decided. What time do you think you'll be back?'

'You know me – Cinderella, back before midnight usually! Will you be around tomorrow?'

Sue looked uncomfortable. 'Actually, I'm going to see Gabby. It's a long-standing arrangement and there's no way I can get out of it. She's cooking lunch. You can come as well . . .'

Angie's jaw dropped. 'You've got more front than Harrods. How can you just swan off down there as if nothing's happened? I certainly couldn't.'

'Yes, well, I am so there you go . . . It'd look far worse if I didn't. Anyway, Giles won't be there; he's at the flat this weekend.'

'Oh well, it's your funeral – or it will be if Gabby ever finds out. I'm off. I'll see you whenever.'

'Have a good time with whatshisname, won't you? It's time you got out more!'

Dave Oliver was already waiting outside when Angie got to the restaurant. He kissed her on both cheeks.

'Angie! Good to see you again. You look well.'

'Thank you, so do you. Shall we go in?'

They settled at a table for two tucked away at the back, and Angie quickly produced her notes and itinerary, anxious to start off on a professional footing. They ordered their meal and then went through the details but she sensed that Dave wasn't taking it quite as seriously as she was. As soon as the first course arrived he snapped her folder shut and handed it back to her.

'Enough business for now. Let's eat and talk. We can tie up the loose ends over coffee. Now tell me all about yourself, Angie

116

Kavanagh, journo extraordinaire.'

She didn't know what to say; most of the men she knew only wanted to talk about themselves.

'My name is Angie Kavanagh, I am a thirtysomething-year-old journalist. I specialise in celebrity interviews and I live in Fulham. Oh, and I have two Siamese cats. Is that good enough?'

'Involved? Engaged? Married?' He looked at her quizzically. 'I didn't want a CV, I want to know about the person.'

She laughed, suddenly feeling relaxed. 'There is no one special. I've never been married or engaged and I share a house with my friend Sue, who runs a model agency. Oh, and I'm addicted to work. So what about you? Fair's fair; tell me all.'

'My name is David Oliver, I am fortysomething – well, forty to be precise. I'm a photographer and I live in a little village in Kent, no pets.'

'Involved? Engaged? Married?' She laughed, hoping he wouldn't realise she was really interested.

'Touché, Madame! Divorced actually, five years ago; one daughter, Jemima, aged seventeen.'

Angie felt her heart lurch. Seventeen, she thought, that's how old Skye would be now. 'Does she live with you, your daughter?'

'No, she lives with her mother. It's all quite civilised. Jemima spends time with me when I'm at home but she's more independent now and has her own life and boyfriends. My ex-wife has remarried and Jemima gets on well with her stepfather. I'm very lucky – there's never been a problem.'

'Why did you divorce then?' Angie was puzzled.

'I was away a lot and she met someone else, simple as that. I have to admire you, you've turned it around very quickly; I was asking about you, remember?'

He smiled across the table at her and she felt a shiver. This was dangerous territory. She suddenly realised she fancied him! Dave was notorious for being denim man, and this evening was no exception. Clad in worn jeans, a faded denim shirt and his statutory Doc Martins, he could have looked scruffy, but everything was spotlessly clean. His long blond hair was pulled back into a ponytail at the nape of his neck, emphasising the strong and incredibly sexy jawline, and fair skin that she could see would go brown in the sun.

Angie pulled herself up sharply.

'There's not really a lot to tell.' She crossed her fingers as she spoke. 'I came to London from Brighton to work on a magazine and then went freelance. I've got no family, no ties, in fact I'm free

117

as a bird. Good thing, really, in this job. I can be off at the drop of a hat . . .' She could feel the sapphire-blue eyes looking deep into her soul and kept her fingers firmly crossed. She wondered if it was the photographer in him that was making him study her so closely. Angie tried hard to keep the conversation light-hearted, but found Dave's eyes more and more distracting. She knew she was talking too much about nothing in particular, like a besotted teenager, but couldn't help herself.

'How long are you going to spend in Scotland? Just overnight?' Dave suddenly asked.

'No, I'm intending to go on Thursday and come back Saturday. I fancy some shopping in Edinburgh. What about you?'

'That depends on you.' The eyes pierced again. 'How about we stay at the same hotel and have a look round together? Please say no if you'd sooner not. I won't be offended but I will be disappointed.'

She thought for only a split second. 'I'd like that.'

As they left the restaurant she felt uncomfortable. He knew she lived only round the corner and it seemed churlish not to invite him back as she would have done any other friend, but this was different and she knew it. She decided to go for broke.

'Would you like a coffee before you drive back?'

'No, I'd better not. Jemima is at the cottage so I ought to get going. I will walk you home, though, make sure you get there safe and sound.'

She felt unreasonably disappointed as they strolled back. Well over six foot, he stood head and shoulders taller than her, and when he draped his arm casually round her shoulder she felt comfortable about the close contact.

At the door he kissed her on both cheeks. 'Thank you for a most enjoyable evening, Angie. I look forward to Scotland.'

She shut the front door behind her and went through to the kitchen. Sue was sitting there nose to nose with Giles.

'For Christ's sake, you two, haven't either of you got any brains other than those in your pants?'

Giles jumped up quickly. 'It's not like that, Angie. We're just talking business. I do have an interest in the agency, in case you've forgotten . . .'

'Yeah right. So does her goddamned bank manager but I don't find him talking about it at home at midnight. Still, it's your life. I'm off to bed.'

She heard the front door shut shortly after she'd settled in bed. At least he hadn't stayed the night, she thought, and wondered if she'd been a bit too sharp.

She got up again and went downstairs to find Sue crying buckets. She looked up as Angie came in and hurled herself across the kitchen into her arms.

'We love each other, we really love each other. What am I going to do?'

All Angie could think to say was, 'Oh fuck!'

Angie spoke with Dave during the week to finalise the arrangements for Scotland. They were going to fly up on Thursday afternoon and return Saturday evening, and arranged to meet at Heathrow Airport.

Angie was there first and felt a surge of excitement as she spotted Dave striding through the crowds, lugging a mountain of equipment with ease. She waved to him and he smiled broadly as he made his way over.

Angie laughed as he leaned forward to kiss her on the cheek. 'Good job I never decided to be a photographer; my shoulders aren't broad enough for all that.'

'You get used to it. How are you today? All fit and raring to go and talk to the Right Honourable Mr MacGregor?'

'As fit as I'll ever be. Let's check in and then get a coffee. There's just about enough time . . .'

The flight passed smoothly. Angie buried her head in her notes and checked the revised questions that had been returned by the MP's press agent, along with a note of topics that were off limits. She showed it to Dave and laughed, 'Off limits usually means interesting. I'll find a way to slip a few extras in.'

'You really enjoy your job, don't you?' He looked sideways at her.

'I do. I'm quite passionate about it. I've worked hard to get to where I am and I'm proud of myself. I did it for my father.' As soon as she'd said it she regretted it; the guard had momentarily come down and it startled her.

'Tell me about him . . .'

'Sorry, as the political press officer said to the journalist, it's off limits. Comes under the category of sensitive information.' She smiled as she said it to take the edge off the words, but she wasn't ready for anything personal about her past.

The small but tasteful hotel was tucked away in a relatively quiet side street in the centre of Edinburgh. They booked in and arranged to meet in the bar for dinner.

Angie soaked in her bath and thought about Dave, and then wondered at that. Usually it was only work that she contemplated in a hot bubbly bath.

She had first met him at a PR function, and over the years they had bumped into each other at various promos and shoots. There'd always been an attraction between them but the opportunity to work one to one and get to know each other hadn't presented itself until now. Men had been a no-go area of her life for so long she wasn't sure what she wanted. She was just aware that Dave interested her and she wanted to get to know him better now she knew he was unattached.

Just twenty-four hours later they were gathering up all the equipment and leaving Mike MacGregor's Edinburgh mansion. They had been there for hours, getting ready and waiting for him to arrive, but were allocated only one hour for the interview and photographs. Time was tight but they did it.

'That went quite well, didn't it? No major upsets but nothing too controversial either. Do you think you've got enough?' Dave asked.

'Oh yes,' Angie replied confidently. 'This plus all the background information will make a good feature. I'm happy with it; I'll put it all together next week.'

'Good, then let's forget about it until then. Tomorrow we're free to be tourists.'

Later, Angie looked back on that second day in Edinburgh as one of the best she'd spent. After an early breakfast they left their luggage packed up and ready to collect later before heading out to see the city.

They walked their legs off through the old part, took photos of each other outside Edinburgh Castle and shopped in Princes Street. Angie gave Dave a cheap plastic tartan keyring that said 'Souvenir of Scotland', and he bought her a doll, complete with kilt, with a sash on it that said the same.

When he took her hand as they strolled through the castle grounds it felt the most natural thing in the world, and when Dave waylaid a passing tourist and asked him to take a photograph of them together Angie laughed for the camera as Dave put his arm tightly round her waist and pulled her close.

As they moved apart he gently kissed the top of her head.

'Do you have to go back today? Shall we stay another night and really get to know each other?'

'I think I'd like that,' she replied without any hesitation.

They walked back to the hotel, arms around each other, and then Angie waited in the bar as Dave booked them back in. He came back laughing.

'Our reputations are intact. There are no single rooms left so I grudgingly accepted that we would have to share. They were most apologetic! Let's dump our stuff and go and eat. I'm starving. All that walking has given me an appetite!'

Angie went into the room first and Dave followed. As he closed the door she turned round and looked at him, they dropped their bags simultaneously and fell straight into each other's arms. She felt the goosebumps rising as he gently kissed her properly for the first time. He wasn't rough and aggressive like some of those who had pounced over the years, but soft and tender.

Suddenly he stopped and stepped back, taking hold of both her hands. 'Are you sure this is what you want, Angie? I don't want to push you into anything . . .'

'Oh God, yes, this is exactly what I want . . .'

She started to take off her clothes but he stopped her. 'No, let me do that for you. Tonight is going to be the start of something very special, I just know it.'

They never did get down to dinner . . . or breakfast the next morning.

Chapter Nine

The Wondermodels birthday party was in full swing when Angie and Dave arrived. Neither really wanted to be there but it was an important event for Sue. All her models were under orders to attend and the guest list was quite impressive.

Sue had perfected the art of sending out only a limited number of high-profile invitations and giving the event an air of exclusivity. It worked, and the phone lines were hot for weeks before with requests for invites from a lot of the celebrities of the moment who Sue wanted to be there anyway. It was a good ploy that she had learnt from her businessman father.

Angie and Dave entered the huge marquee that had been erected in the grounds of the Autumn Garden Hotel in the heart of the West End. It was carefully designed as a Caribbean tiki hut with little hint of the boring white marquee. The theme for the evening was 'Totally Caribbean', with waiters in loud floral shirts and white trousers serving huge colourful rum punches alongside the statutory mineral water. A steel band played calypso in the corner, surrounded by enormous palm trees in pots, and a trio of beautiful young Wondermodels wore the smallest of grass skirts and minuscule bikini bandanas that barely covered their breasts.

'Sue's really pushed the boat out this year, hasn't she, Dave? I'm impressed.'

Angie had managed to persuade Dave into a rather loud shirt with a full-sized parrot printed on the back and palm fronds all over the front, but that was the limit of his compliance; the jeans and boots stayed.

'Hmm,' Dave looked around in amazement, 'a bit over the top if you ask me. See what you've done to me, woman? Not so long ago I wouldn't have been seen dead at one of these shenanigans, and now here I am wearing a parrot.'

She laughed. 'You look the part from the waist up, I'll give you that, Mr Oliver.'

Sue appeared beside them, wearing a tight floral blouse tied under the bust and a pair of royal-blue pedal pushers. She kissed them both excitedly. 'It is going sooo well. Anyone who is anyone is here – it's bound to get in the papers tomorrow. There are two gossip columnists who actually believe they've wheedled their way in, dumb buggers. I'd have paid them to come if I'd had to!' She stood back and looked them up and down. 'Angie, you look absolutely bloodly gorgeous. Those colours suit you down to the ground. How come I've spent a fortune on my outfit and you look a million dollars in some old thing out of your wardrobe . . .? Yes, that's right, I recognise it all.'

Angie was wearing a short emerald-green and blue silk sarong that was wrapped tightly around her hips and knotted at the side, showing one leg up to the top of her thigh. The plain black bikini top had a flower placed strategically in her cleavage that matched the one behind her ear, and loads of chunky wooden bracelets, anklets and necklaces finished off the outfit. Angie was pleased with the effect.

'You look good yourself. I love the earrings, a rare old fruit salad.' Glancing around, she gave an appreciative whistle. 'The decorations are really authentic! I could almost think myself into the Caribbean if it wasn't for the pissing rain outside!'

'Don't think of it as London rain, consider it a tropical storm arranged especially by moi! Anyway, I have to go and network, sweetie. You two go and circulate and enjoy. I'll see you later.'

Dave smiled. 'She is just so hyperactive, that woman. I don't know how she keeps functioning at that level.'

Angie watched Sue affectionately as she sashayed around the throng of rich and famous celebrities who were forming into their usual territorial groups that silently excluded all but the bravest – supermodels and pop singers, PR girls and wealthy businessmen, actors and actresses. It was always so predictable, Angie thought as she surveyed the crowd, but it was always fun and a good arena for spotting her next interviewee.

'Come on, Dave, let's make our way to the bar for something we can both actually drink. Oh look, there's Giles and Gabby. Let's join them.'

As Angie and Dave got closer it was apparent that a whispered row was in progress, but by then it was too late to change direction.

'Hello, Giles, Gabby, isn't it just great?' Angie flashed a happy smile at them as they all air-kissed fleetingly. 'Gabby, you haven't met Dave, have you? It's so long since you've been to London. How are the children?'

Angie knew she was waffling but the atmosphere was so tense between the couple; Giles had a face like thunder and Gabby looked a mere whisper away from tears.

'Dave, why don't you and Giles go and find us some drinks? I'm gasping for an ice-cold soda.' Angie looked at both of them in a way that brooked no argument, and they quickly disappeared.

'I know it's none of my business, Gabby, but you look really unhappy. Didn't you want to come?'

'Of course I didn't want to fucking come. Look at me . . . I can disguise an extra two stone with green wellies and a Barbour but Caribbean? Come on, I look like the whale that got beached. I'm on tenterhooks waiting for Greenpeace to burst through the doors and drag me off back to the sea. I hate it at these dos, surrounded by seven-foot-tall, six-stone models who are half my age.'

Angie laughed out loud. 'You and me both. How do you think I feel at five foot nothing? Trust me, Gabby, you look good. Don't be so neurotic. Forget the models and enjoy yourself like you used to.'

Gabby looked Angie straight in the eye. 'Is Giles having an affair?'

Angie could feel the blood rising to her face. She played for time to find out how much Gabby knew. 'Good God, Gabby, whatever makes you think that? You and Giles are made for each other.'

'Maybe once we were, now I'm not so sure. I think he's shagging one or all of the Wondermodels. He spends a lot of time in London now, and he only ever comes home at weekends, and sometimes not even then if he's allegedly working.'

Angie felt on surer ground. At least Sue wasn't in the frame. 'Gabby, I'm sure Giles wouldn't go within a mile of any of those young girls. He loves you and he loves the children. He's probably overseeing his investment. He does have an interest in Wondermodels, doesn't he?'

Dave and Giles arrived back and the conversation stopped abruptly. Angie heaved a sigh of relief. She hadn't had to lie exactly, but she knew that if Gabby found out about Giles and Sue, it would be the ultimate betrayal, far more unforgivable than a quickie with a model. She looked furtively at Gabby. The woman had put on a lot of weight and was now looking positively sullen as she looked around the room distastefully, as if she had suddenly found herself in the middle of an orgy in a brothel. Angie wondered what had happened to the Gabby she had known, the one who Giles had married.

The music stopped and a hush descended on the room as Sue moved on to a small podium, where a microphone was ready and waiting for her speech.

Angie didn't hear much of what she said. She was too busy watching Giles, who was staring openly in admiration at Sue while Gabby glared daggers at his back. Angie knew it was all going to end in tears before long.

The applause was still ringing when Angie moved close to Giles and, without changing her expression, whispered sideways at him, 'I need to talk to you, you bastard, outside NOW.'

As the music started up again and Sue moved back among the guests Angie smiled at Dave, and said, 'I'll be back in a sec, I just want to introduce Giles to someone. Do you mind keeping Gabby company for a while? She's a bit pissed off with being here.'

Dave raised his eyes to the ceiling. 'I can relate to that.' He leant down and kissed her gently on the lips. 'Off you go, darling. We're not joined at the hip!'

Angie ducked out under the palm fronts to find Giles already waiting for her, looking worried but defiant.

'What's up with you, Ange? Gabby been shooting off at the mouth again? Whingeing about my inadequacies as both husband and father?'

'Shut up, Giles. Don't forget I know about you and Sue. What are you playing at?'

'Tempting though it is to say it's none of your business, I respect that we've been friends for a long time so I'll try and explain briefly before she comes looking for me, expecting to find me in the pot plant with Rebekah Alari et al. What's happening with Sue shouldn't be, I give you that, but if you get accused of it all day every day it doesn't seem such a big deal to actually do it.'

'But I thought you two were happy . . .' Angie was puzzled. She hadn't expected an outburst from Giles – good, kind Giles, who had supported her through thick and thin, and played as big a part in her life as Sue.

'I thought we would be but we're not and I don't know what to do. I really love Sue, though it took me a long time to realise it. All Gabby wants is the house in the country a bevy of servants, loads of money and a lapdog . . . ME. She questions my every movement and thinks I'm at it with every female that I have a passing word with, including you, of course! I really don't know how much longer I can take it.'

'I'm so sorry, Giles, I had no idea – I don't think anyone did . . .'

'Oh, oh, here she comes . . .'

Gabby appeared through the foliage, glaring at Giles. 'Oh, you're with Angie . . . I just wondered where you were . . .'

'Just getting a bit of fresh air, Gabby. I'd better get back to Dave. Give me a ring soon, Giles. We need to discuss my accounts; they're up the wall as usual.'

Laughing nervously, Angie quickly turned and went back inside, leaving the couple to slug it out in private.

They didn't appear again.

'Sue, which one is Rebekah Alari? I keep hearing her name . . .'

'Over there, Dave, in the Gucci bra, the one with the legs up to her armpits. She is just so gorgeous and photogenic, but such a drama queen and so up herself you wouldn't believe. Just look at those men hanging on her every word.' Sue put her fingers to her throat on her usual gesture of disgust. 'She treats them all like shit and they keep coming back for more, *and*, to make it worse she's only seventeen. She is my own personal nightmare but she's going to make it big and earn me sooooo much money I have to deal with it other than by slapping her face and grounding her!'

Dave looked over at Rebekah with a photographer's eye. 'Up herself or not I'd love to do a shoot. She's stunning – is she Mediterranean?'

'Not really. I think her father is of Italian or Spanish origin but she was born and brought up in leafy Surrey. He is a multimillionaire who gives Rebekah everything she wants – apartment, cars, free run of all his various homes and a fucking great allowance to boot. She doesn't need the money from this, but she loves the attention. That can be a problem to me; she could walk any time and Daddy would buy her out of her contract with me and into a new one with someone else. It's a bit like walking on eggshells, trying to keep her in line and happy at the same time.'

They all looked at the girl holding court centre stage. She laughed loudly, touched her companion gently and flicked her hair seductively. Angie was completely enthralled by Rebekah's looks but the thing that most impressed her was the air of complete confidence. She could see that the girl was destined for fame and fortune.

She was over six foot tall, with thick, brownish black hair that hung sleekly over her shiny tanned shoulders. The tiniest white bikini top neatly enclosed her small breasts, and her boyish bottom was encased in a pair of white cut-off hipster shorts that almost disappeared up her backside, exaggerating her outrageously long slim legs. The finishing touch was a simple gold chain strung loosely around her tiny waist. There was no question, the girl was stunning and classy and she knew it. Self-confidence oozed from every pore of the teenager as her audience hung on her every word. She certainly had it.

Angie smiled at Dave. 'To quote a well-worn phrase, I'll have what she's having. She's charismatic all right.'

'Don't knock yourself, woman, you're as beautiful as her any day of the week. You're just not aware of it.'

Angie laughed. Dave was such a great guy 'I wish,' she said.

Dave stayed over with Angie after the party but left at seven the next morning for the airport and three weeks on assignment in Borneo. They both acknowledged that their lives worked in that way, but Angie knew this time she would really miss him, a first for her.

The cab wasn't even out of sight when Sue arrived home in another one.

'I'm totally wiped.' She fell on to the huge sofa dramatically. 'You couldn't possibly make a poor hard-working old woman a good strong cup of caffeine, could you, sweetie?'

Angie didn't feel a lot better herself. She and Dave may have left the party early but they certainly hadn't had any sleep, it being their last night together for three weeks.

'You poor old love, sure you wouldn't sooner have a nice cup of cocoa and a pair of furry slippers?' She leant over Sue and patted her hand. 'There, there, I know how hard it is for you, partying all night. Of course I'll wait on you hand, foot and finger.'

She made the coffee good and strong, and brought the cafetiere into the lounge with two oversized mugs and a plate of chocolate digestives.

'I had a chat with Giles last night, and Gabby. It was quite interesting. Why didn't you tell me what was going on?'

'I couldn't, could I? You were so angry with me that if I had told you it would have sounded as if I was justifying what I had done. Anyway, you wouldn't have believed me, would you?'

Angie looked thoughtful. 'No, I don't suppose I would. So where is it at now? I know I said I didn't want to know but I did sense that Giles is really unhappy and I do love him dearly – in a friendship way, of course.'

Sue hesitated for a second and then launched. 'Gabby is a first-rate cow. With hindsight I don't think she ever loved Giles, just his prospects. She's a chameleon, that woman – she can pretend to be whatever she thinks is right for the circumstances – and once they were married she eventually changed back into herself.' Now Sue was in full flow there was no stopping her. 'She's a money-grabbing, blood-sucking leech. I suppose I wasn't totally convinced of all Giles said and that was why I went down to lunch with her. Because she didn't know how close we had become it gave her free rein, and the things she told me about him were unbelievable – all said in the nicest possible way, of course . . .'

Angie was shocked. 'But you and Gabby were friends for so long . . .'

'Gabby was only friends with me with a view to getting Giles, I can see that now. The coy, shy, looking up through the eyelashes, friend in need, mother earth persona was all total crap, manipulation pure and simple, and it worked. She got Giles in the end and we all thought she would be good for him.'

They sat quietly for a few moments before Sue continued, 'Makes you admire her in a funny sort of way, doesn't it? She took us all in and now she'll take him straight to the cleaners, you mark my words, and she'll have no qualms about using the kids to get at him either.'

Angie didn't respond. She just thought about it all and decided, with hindsight, maybe what Sue had said did all ring true. Gabby had never been a person in her own right; she was always hanging on someone's shirt-tails and being a helpless little girlie.

Angie was just about to ask more when she realised Sue was fast asleep. Grabbing the duvet from Sue's bed, she gently put it over her before going back to bed herself. She was beginning to wonder if any relationship ever really worked out, and whether she and Dave could make a go of it.

She desperately wanted this relationship to work. She was deeply in love for the first time, but the big black cloud hovered overhead, and when she slept it was fitfully, and her dreams were speckled with images from the past that she wanted to forget.

The ringing of the telephone woke her. She glanced at the clock. It was only 9 a.m.

'Good morning, Miss Kavanagh.' It was Dave's voice. 'This is your early morning alarm call. Will you marry me?'

'What did you say?'

'I said, will you marry me? I love you and I want to marry you . . . how about it?'

Angie didn't answer for a few seconds. She couldn't get her head round what Dave was saying. 'Have you been drinking?' was the best she could think of.

'You're mad, woman. It's nine o'clock in the morning, I haven't had any sleep, thanks to you and your wild urges, and I'm about to sit on a plane for hours and hours and hours, to the other side of the world almost, and without even the luxury of business class.

The last thing I need is a drink. I need to sleep and I need you to marry me.'

Angie took a slug of cold coffee from the mug beside her bed. 'Isn't this a bit sudden?'

'Do you love me?'

'Yes I do.'

'Well, marry me then. It's simple.'

'Dave, we have to talk – talk properly, I mean, as in, the past, the future, even the present. Can we discuss this when you get back?'

'So it's not no, then?'

'No, I just need—'

'At least it's not no. I've gotta go. Love you . . .'

The phone went down and Angie was left holding the receiver in her hand, not knowing whether to laugh or cry, and with no way of contacting Dave until the next day at the very least.

Trying to sleep really was a waste of time so she got up and headed for the kitchen. When in doubt, eat, was her motto, so she popped some bread in the toaster and quickly scrambled some eggs in the microwave.

Sue staggered in.

'Can I smell food? What time is it?'

'It's nine o'clock and I'm having scrambled eggs. Dave's just phoned. He asked me to marry him.'

'Sounds good to me, have we got any Worcester sauce?' She spun round, eyes wide open for the first time. 'What did you just say?' she shrieked at the top of her voice. 'He wants to marry you? Did you agree?'

'I didn't have time. He had to hang up, he's at the airport on the way to Borneo. He won't be back for three weeks.'

'Oh God, Angie, this is so exciting. I wish you could phone Giles but he's at home and old iron drawers will decide we're all after shagging him. Will you? Won't you? Do tell . . .'

Angie laughed. 'I haven't even thought about it yet. It was only five minutes ago. Now do you want scrambled eggs even though we're out of Worcester sauce?'

'Angie Kavanagh, sometimes I could beat you around the head until your brains rattle. Aren't you even remotely excited about a proposal from a really hunky man who's kind and caring and loves you to bits?'

'Seriously, Sue, to tell you the truth I'm shit scared. I don't ever want to get married – it changes people and causes so much unhappiness – but I do love Dave and I want to be with him. Do you think he'll be happy with that or will I blow it?'

Angie had a lot of work on over the three weeks Dave was away, but it didn't stop her churning his proposal over and over in her mind and losing a lot of sleep into the bargain. By the time he got back she was ready with her answer.

She met him at the airport and they drove back to Fulham, making small talk and chatting about his trip, both trying to avoid anything too personal as they wove in and out of the traffic-clogged streets. He kept looking at her but she just kept concentrating with all the intensity of a racing driver trying to negotiate a hairpin bend at a hundred miles an hour.

Before she'd left for the airport she had prepared a few sandwiches and snacks and put them in the fridge so all she had to do now they were back was put the kettle on.

'I've missed you,' Dave suddenly said.

'It's so good to see you, Dave. I've really missed you too. To think just a few months ago I didn't give a toss about who was where. It's a strange feeling, you know.'

He put his arms round her in a bear hug and pulled her close. 'I've missed you far more than you'll ever know. Now is it good news or bad news? I can't wait any longer.'

Angie snuggled closely into his chest, savouring the familiar smell of his afterhsave. 'A bit of both. I know that I love you and I know that I want to be with you, but I can't marry you – or not at the moment, anyway. It's too soon.'

He looked at her silently but she couldn't bring herself to meet his gaze.

'I'm sorry, Dave. It's not you, it's me and the demons from my past. Perhaps I need a bit of good old exorcism.'

She moved away from him, nervously waiting for his response. He was deep in thought as he looked at her and she felt her stomach leap. His expressive eyes bored deep into her and she wondered anew at the phrase, 'the look of love'. Not so long ago she would have stuck her fingers in her mouth, feigning throwing up at the cliché, but suddenly she understood. No one had ever looked at her that way before.

'I'll settle for that for the moment then, but I'm not going to let it go. Now I've found you I'm not giving up easily, and when you're ready we'll talk – really talk – about both our demons. Now how about a cuppa? Borneo has the most exquisite wildlife but the tea is absolute crap!'

Angie was so happy she burst into tears, then started laughing at yet another romantic cliché she had acted out.

They didn't actually set up home together but divided their time between his cottage in Kent and her house in Fulham and then went their separate ways when they were working. The arrangement worked well for Angie and was temporarily acceptable to Dave.

As time went on they spent more time working together, as Angie often requested Dave for the photography if an in-house photographer wasn't part of the package. It all worked nicely and they never rowed, just bickered occasionally. Sometimes she thought it was all too good to be true but Dave just philosophically accepted that they were soulmates destined to meet and be together for ever.

There was an added bonus to the relationship in Jemima, Dave's daughter. She and Angie hit it off from the start and got on so well Angie was nearly swayed to Dave's views on predestination. She may have lost Skye but now she had an almost daughter in Jemima, the sunny, easygoing young woman who was a clone for her father in temperament and virtually the same age as Skye.

After all the trauma of the past Angie now had a man she loved and who loved her, a daughter in all but name and a continually rising career. They even accepted Gavin as part of the family. Life was good.

'Angie, I've got some news for you but I don't know how you're going to take it.' Sue had come into the bathroom as usual as Angie was soaking herself in a tub full of the far-too-expensive bubbles that Jemima had bought her for Christmas.

Sue sat on the edge of the bath and picked up a handful of the foam, gently rubbing it into her hands.

'Come on, then, out with it, but it had better be good to justify putting your hands in my thirty-quid bathwater.'

'Giles is leaving Gabby. He's going to live in his London flat permanently. The solicitors are talking already.' Sue looked at her friend apprehensively, waiting for her reaction.

Angie sat up sharply. 'So the shit has finally hit the fan then. How's she taking it? What about Harry and Emily? Are they going to be OK? Giles must put them first . . .'

'Well, he hasn't told her about us but, let's face it, that's not even the real reason. He's totally pissed off with her obsession with one and all of the Wondermodels, or rather the obsession she pretends to have. If you ask me, when she couldn't find a viable means of dumping him she made one up, and a good one!' She leant forward and lit a long slim cigarette from one of the many flickering candles that gently lit the bathroom. 'As for the kids, if she had her way she'd closet them away and not let Giles near them, but his legal eagle is very sharp and very expensive. It'll get dealt with along with all the other issues.'

'Come on now, Sue, you're just being dramatic. I'm sure it's not like that—'

Sue interrupted sharply. 'Think about it. By forcing him to leave instead of throwing him out she is the victim, the poor deserted wife. Now everyone feels sorry for her, and when she rips him off in court they'll all think it serves him right . . . The bastard deserted his wife and children, he's screwing around with young girls while she patiently waits at home . . . Well, I just hope she doesn't think she's going to get a finger in Wondermodels by default.'

Angie looked closely at Sue, and much as she hated even to think it of Gabby she did wonder whether Sue had hit the nail on the head.

'Are you going to move in with him?'

'Christ no. Well, not yet – not until his life is sorted and he's shot of her. Just imagine the meal she would make of that. The gossip columns would have a field day if she even breathed the name Rebekah Alari. No, for the moment it's heads down and pay her off when the time is right. She'll soon have some other poor bastard in tow.' Sue paused for a second, looking thoughtful. 'That isn't a hint for me to move out and leave the way clear for Dave, is it? It's your house; you only have to say the word you know . . .'

Angie stood up quickly, stark naked and dripping wet, and threw her arms around Sue's neck, planting a big wet kiss on her cheek. 'You daft bitch, as if . . . I'm happy with the arrangement as it is and Dave accepts it. If things change you'll be the first to know.'

'OK, OK, now put me down. This dress cost nearly a grand, you know, so I don't want it splashed. Don't you just love it? Understated chic is how it's described.' She placed a hand on a pushed-out hip and mimicked the catwalk glide around the bathroom before perching daintily on the toilet seat, grinning from ear to ear.

Angie slid back into the bath, feeling guilty. She knew things might just be about to change but she wasn't quite sure how.

'Do you think I'm being unfair to Dave – you know, not living with him permanently and all that?'

'It's not for me to say, sweetie. I think he's a terrific guy and just the one for you . . . I'm sure you'll stay with him and probably marry him when the time is right. Just don't leave it too long is all I'd say on the subject.'

Angie looked thoughtfully into the flickering candles.

'If I tell you something do you promise faithfully not to say a word to anyone? I mean not a soul, not even Giles?'

Sue leant forward in anticipation; she loved a good secret.

'Of course, sweetie. I can keep quiet if I have to.'

'I think I'm pregnant. Well, I don't just think I am, I know I am, eight weeks.'

Sue jumped up and clapped her hands to her mouth.

'Oh shit . . . a bombshell or what? What does Dave think? Or, more to the point, what do you think?'

'I haven't told him yet. I'm still so confused. A part of me is delighted, another part is horrified and the third part is terrified that Dave might disappear off into the great unknown when he finds out. We've never discussed children.'

Angie had suspected her pregnancy as soon as her period was late. She could remember clear as a bell the night the condom had split, the only time it had happened. It had been hard to go into the chemist's and buy a DIY testing kit. It brought the past flooding back, and when it read positive the palpitations had been so fierce she had thought she was actually having a heart attack. The panic surged through her veins and for the first time in years she would have killed for a big juicy joint or a slug of neat alcohol, or even both.

Her first thoughts weren't for Dave, or her career, it was the totally irrational fear of going to the doctor's and having to admit for the first time to anyone that she had given birth before. Not a soul knew about Skye, not one single solitary person, and the thought of owning up to having already had a baby was just too scary. She didn't know how she could bring herself to say the words, certainly not after so long.

She realised that Sue was speaking to her and she had no idea what she had said.

'You're not listening to me, are you, sweetie? The man adores you, he wants to marry you. I'm sure he'll be breaking open the Moët and dancing with the pixies in the garden when he finds out.' Sue smiled sympathetically at the woman who had become her closest friend.

'Don't you breathe a word to anyone or I'll break your legs, I really will. I have to deal with this in my own way. Now piss off and let me get dressed. I have a plane to catch.'

'Your manners underwhelm me, Miss Kavanagh, but I'll make allowances for a woman in your condition just this once.'

Angie splashed water at her as she got out of the bath and they both giggled like schoolgirls as Sue ran off down the landing with Angie in hot pursuit, flicking dripping wet hands at her disappearing back.

Jemima was going to Los Angeles with Angie. The girl had a good brain, was a quick thinker, and was about to start a media studies course so the trip would give her a head start. It was also a good way for both of them to really get to know each other.

Focused on the task ahead of her, Angie already had her notes spread out in front of her before the plane was cruising. She was going to interview Ellie MacNamara, the British pop singer turned actress who had just gone down a bomb in a Hollywood blockbuster and was suddenly a hot property. Having been sympathetically interviewed by Angie a couple of years before when she was struggling to make the changeover and was being given a hard time by the press, the budding superstar had agreed instantly to Angie's request for an exclusive.

This was going to be a big one for Angie and for the first time a TV camera crew was going to be there with her. She couldn't afford any mistakes. She had set her sights on a television career next, and this was the chance to prove herself.

'How can you sit there working at a time like this?' Jemima asked. 'God, this just so not real – business class to LA. The best I've ever managed is a cheapo charter flight to Spain with my knees up round my chin and elbows locked with the drunk beside me.' Her eyes were alight with excitement.

Angie thought she was an exceptionally sexy young woman. Only minimally taller than herself, Jemima was bubbly and rounded, with a mass of unruly auburn curls and sharp emerald-green eyes that betrayed her every emotion. She was the opposite of all the tall, stick-thin, leggy young girls that were so much in demand in the model industry but no way did the girl have a complex about it. Her grungy dress sense was as individual as her father's was uniform, and her self-confidence shone through.

Angie often wished she could have been like that at Jemima's age instead of forever trying to blend into the background and not be noticed.

'I must admit I take it all a bit for granted now but I well

135

remember the cattle truck flights. If there's one thing I'm grateful for it's comfortable travel, but only when I'm working, of course. If it's a holiday then it's still good old economy.'

Bouncing about excitedly, Jemima checked out the freebie potions and lotions in the washbag and then carefully tucked them all away unopened as a souvenir. Angie smiled; she remembered doing that herself several years ago.

'I wish I didn't have such chunky thighs and was a few inches taller. I'd love to be a flight attendant and travel the world for free, such a cool job.'

Angie laughed out loud; she was suddenly reminded of her childhood best friend, Sharon Aberlone, wanting exactly the same thing. She wondered if Sharon had ever made it. Without thinking, she fingered the silver cross that she still wore around her neck, her birthday present from Sharon the day Daniel was born.

Dave had been disappointed but philosophical about not getting the photo commission for the Ellie MacNamara interview.

'That's the way it goes, darling,' he'd told her when they'd gone out for dinner the day before Angie's departure. 'If she wants her own photographer then there's not a lot I can do about it. Just make sure you don't go falling for any pretty boy actors while you're there. A predatory place is Hollywood, you know.'

'Yeah right. How could I possibly pull when I'm going to be accompanied by your gorgeous daughter? All eyes will be on her, not an old woman like me!'

Dave had looked at Angie and stroked her cheek gently in the way that made her legs tingle. It was hard to keep her hands off him when he did that. She'd wanted to rip his clothes off there and then in the middle of the restaurant.

'I love you just the way you are, old woman, and I can't imagine them not falling all over you.'

They'd smiled affectionately at each other, gently linking fingers.

'Jem is ecstatic, you know. She just can't believe her luck. I think it's an omen that we all get on so well, don't you?'

'You and your omens and destinies, you're quite a philosopher at heart, aren't you?'

'Yep, unlike you, the pessimistic cynic. You don't seem to be able to trust anything to be right. You should just go with the flow now and again.'

Angie had sensed a slight undertone in his voice although he'd smiled warmly as he'd spoken. She'd decided to tell him about the baby when she got back. By then she would have to.

★ ★ ★

136

Angie and Jemima had a great time fitting in all the touristy and girlie things that Angie normally avoided like the plague. Jemima squealed with delight as they peered into the shops in Rodeo Drive that they had no chance of entering without an appointment and a platinum card at the very least. They took the bus trip that toured Beverly Hills, gasping at the palatial mansions of the rich and famous, and walked down Sunset Boulevard, celebrity spotting. As a surprise Angie hired a black stretch limo, complete with chauffeur and blacked out windows, to drive them to the coast for the day.

They rode the carousel in Palisades Park and laughed at every footprint they left on Malibu Beach, wondering who was going to follow in their footsteps before the tide washed the prints away.

The interview went exactly as planned, although not as comfortably as the last time. Ellie MacNamara was big now and that meant the accompanying PR people and publicists, the top photographer, hairstylist and make-up artist, and an assortment of gofers.

Still down to earth, Ellie had waved her hands around the room and whispered to Angie, 'Not quite the same as last time when I was a social outcast and only one step removed from a leper, is it? As we speak I can do no wrong. Suddenly I'm God's most precious gift to the movie world . . . for the moment. That's off the record, of course, darling!'

Angie was nervous about being filmed but once she got into the swing of doing the job she'd come for, the job she loved, the technicians all faded into the background.

'You were just so cool, Angie,' Jemima enthused. 'I watched you on the monitor and you looked so top dollar, I can't wait to see it on TV. You're going to be famous.'

Angie blushed at the praise and wondered yet again at the good relationship she had with Jemima. Like father, like daughter, she thought to herself. The girl had absolutely no side to her.

She knew she had to tell Dave about the baby as soon as she got home.

He was there to meet them at the airport and they drove straight to Kent to drop Jemima off at her mother's before heading back to Fulham. The excited girl talked nonstop all the way, for which Angie was grateful; it gave her time to think about what she was going to say.

The house was in darkness when they got to Fulham and Angie felt guilty as she heaved a sigh of relief that Sue wasn't there. Jet lag was setting in and she felt totally bushed after the hectic schedule of the week but she had decided to tell Dave about the baby as soon as possible. There was no putting it off any longer. The other bridges she could cross later.

'Jem seems to have had the time of her life. It's all going to be a bit of an anticlimax now, going to uni and living the life of an impoverished student temping in Woolies. But I noticed you were unusually quiet driving back. Is everything OK?'

Angie took a deep breath.

'I don't know if it's OK or not. You'll have to tell me.' She paused and looked him straight in the eye. This was it. 'I'm pregnant.'

The silence for a split second was deafening.

'Pregnant? You mean we're going to have a baby? How did it happen? When?'

She laughed nervously. 'Well, I hope that's what it's going to be, a baby, in about six and a half months' time, and as for how it happened, if you need to ask then you should be going back to college and studying anatomy.'

Dave flew across the room and swept her up in his arms. He was nearly in tears.

'A baby! Well, I never! A father again at the bloody old age of forty something or other!' He hesitated for a second and looked at her. 'How do you feel about it?'

In that moment it all became crystal clear to Angie. 'I'm happy and I'm glad you are too. As you yourself would say, I guess it's meant to be.'

Chapter Ten

Angie, Dave, Jemima, Sue, Giles and Gavin were bunched together around the television waiting expectantly for breakfast-time TV to broadcast Angie's interview with Ellie MacNamara.

It had been drastically cut to five minutes and was being interspersed with clips of the new movie but Angie was still over the moon. Three pages in a Sunday supplement, one page in a woman's glossy and five minutes on TV had topped up the bank balance no end, and the publicity would ensure more good commissions.

The viewing had turned into an early morning smorgasbord courtesy of Gavin, who was so delighted at the prospect of being a surrogate granddad he had spent two days preparing the feast. Hotfooting it excitedly from Brighton, he had arrived on the doorstep with masses of flowers, a four-foot white teddy bear, six bottles of champagne and enough food in his car boot to feed twenty people.

'A television star and a mother – I always knew you'd make it to the top and be happy one day, Angie baby.' He turned to Dave. 'And what about you, me old son? How does it feel to have a nearly father-in-law who's just a smidgen your senior and an old queen to boot? Whatever are your friends going to say to that, eh?'

Everyone laughed. Gavin was not overtly gay but he could camp it up and laugh at himself in the right company of friends whom he knew would laugh with him rather than at him.

They all watched in silence as the television interview started, and then suddenly it was over, but the video recorder saved Angie's first TV appearance for analysis and posterity. A copy of which Angie knew would have to go in the tote bag to join her first published features and all the other good and bad souvenirs of her life.

It was Gavin who broke the silence as it finished. 'Wow, Angie babe, you were just so great – all polished and professional – and isn't that Ellie a cutie? A face and figure to die for, wouldn't you say!'

Suddenly they were all jumping about kissing and congratulating Angie, and the early morning party went on into the afternoon as they toasted the interview, the baby and everything else they could think of – even the weather towards the end.

Although deliriously happy to be surrounded by her closest friends, and pleased with the finished programme herself, Angie saw a cloud looming on the horizon. The ante-natal appointment was the next day. Her conscience twitched at not having told Dave but she didn't want him there when all the questions were asked. She had already plotted her answers but there was no way she could talk about a previous baby in front of him. It had to be cleared away and filed under confidential information before he could be part of it all.

'Ms Angie Kavanagh?'

The stomach churning and waves of nervous nausea took a took for the worse as the nurse called out her name. Ironic really, Angie thought, as she had suffered no morning sickness at all. In fact generally she felt better than ever.

She went into the small room with the nurse, who started through the list of routine questions. The first few were easy but suddenly it was there, the big one.

'First baby?'

'No, second. I had one nearly eighteen years ago.' Breathing deeply to ward off the panic attack that was hovering Angie answered confidently. The words were out. For the first time ever she had spoken about Skye.

'Any problems with the birth?'

'No.'

'Still fit and healthy? Any illnesses?'

'I don't know. She was adopted.'

'Where did the birth take place? We could do with the records.'

'I don't have any. She was born and adopted in Spain . . .' She hesitated and looked warily at the nurse who was probably not much older than Skye herself. 'Is this information confidential? I don't want anyone to know, you see. It was all a long time ago . . .'

'Yes, of course it is, but it would be helpful to know anything you feel you can share with us about the birth – for medical reasons.' The sympathetic smile of the nurse caused Angie to hesitate for a moment before deciding it was too risky.

'The baby was born in a small clinic in Spain. I can't even remember where it was now exactly, and was taken for adoption almost straight away. I don't know anything else. I didn't speak

140

Spanish and they didn't speak much English. I just came back to England afterwards and got on with my life.'

She frightened herself with her ability to lie so easily. Previously it had always been by omission, letting people make assumptions that were wrong and not correcting them. This was lying, but she could see no alternative.

'After you've been examined by a doctor and we've done the blood tests, you'll be given an appointment for a scan to check dates. I know you're about ten weeks pregnant by your reckoning but the scan will confirm it.'

The rest of the interview wasn't so difficult. The lie was told and now had to be consolidated. There was no option of going back. The next lie would be for Dave. Best to tell him that evening.

'I called into the clinic today to make an ante-natal appointment and they had a cancellation so they saw me then and there. I have to go for a scan next week, would you like to come?'

There, she thought, it's over. Now there should be no need for any more lies. Back to the straight and narrow.

The scan the following week was straightforward, and Angie and Dave went straight home to give the good news and a copy of the fuzzy picture to Gavin, who was eager to head back to Brighton and the café.

'Well, goodbye again, Angie baby, and well done! You've worked hard and you should be pleased with yourself. Posh house, nice man, a baby on the way and all your own work – apart from the baby, of course! I am so proud of you and so is Paolo. I'm sure he's up there looking down and wishing you well.' Hugging her tight he looked over her shoulder at Dave. 'You look after her, won't you? She's special.'

Leaning forward to shake Gavin's hand, Dave grinned. 'You don't need to tell me. I'd even go so far as to make an honest woman of her but she won't have it!'

'Give her time, just give her time. She needs to be one hundred and fifty per cent sure of everything, does our Angie, but she'll get there in the end.'

Two weeks later Angie went from the heights of happiness to the depths of despair in one hit. Everything in her life came crashing down around her ears and she could see all she'd strived for crumbling away.

It had started as a perfectly routine day. Dave was away on a fashion shoot in Paris, and Angie and Sue were having a leisurely Saturday breakfast out on the patio in their dressing gowns, lying

141

on sunloungers, eating chocolate muffins and being sluttish.

The fiercely sprung letter box clattered, the sound echoing down the hall and through the open French windows.

'Are you going to get the post, sweetie? I can't be bothered to get up.' Sue tried to sound persuasive.

'Well, I'm pregnant. Why should I go?'

'It might be a huge cheque for you . . .'

'It might be one for you . . .'

'Perhaps your premium bond's come up . . .'

'That'd be a miracle. I haven't got any . . .'

The banter batted back and forth until eventually Sue got up from the lounger. 'I'll go this week if you go next week.'

'It's a deal.' Angie smiled to herself. Sue's curiosity always got the better of her in the end.

'A couple for me and a bundle for you. The silly bastard postman just knocked and left them on the doorstep . . . There's a big one for you here. Looks like it's from your agent.'

Angie laughed and snatched the package. 'How do you know that, you nosy hag?'

'You're forgetting what business I'm in, sweetie. I can sniff out an agent at two miles. Do you want a coffee or some more of that obnoxious camomile?'

'Camomile, please. I'm a caffeine- and nicotine-free zone now.'

She opened the package. It was from her agent.

'You were a bit hit on TV. You've got some fan mail . . . congratulations.'

There were about a dozen letters inside. All except one were the normal run-of-the-mill letters from the public at large: a few general complimentary letters; a couple from young men wanting an introduction to Ellie MacNamara; a gruesome one from a pervert wanting to shag Angie; a woman who was angry because her husband wanted to shag Angie; and a little old lady who thought Angie needed mothering and feeding up. And one other, marked 'Private and confidential' in bright red felt tip.

As she read the single handwritten page Angie thought she was going to pass out. Her heart pounded in her chest and the familiar big black cloud engulfed her in a direct hit.

Hi, Gollywog, remember me? I remember you only too well. I'd know you anywhere, you black bitch. Now this time you owe me, by return, plus interest. If I don't hear I shall track you down and carry on where I left off but this time I'll do it properly. No one gets away with what you did to me.

REMEMBER – BY RETURN. TO THE ABOVE BOX NO.

£25,000 IN CASH. REGISTERED MAIL.

PS. Just in case you think the police are an option I'm sure the *Screws of the World* would be interested to know that the whiter-than-white Angie Kavanagh is a whore called Louise Jermaine, who fucked her stepfather and stole his life savings before disappearing off the face of the earth and breaking her mother's heart.

DON'T FORGET, BY RETURN.

Love from Tony.

'Here's your cup of gnat's piss – sorry, I mean camomile. Hey, are you OK?' Sue suddenly noticed Angie was as white as the sheet of paper she was holding. 'Not bad news, is it?'

Angie pulled herself together as best she could. No one must know, she thought. I have to deal with this myself.

'I'm fine, just feeling a bit sick, that's all. I'm just going to dump this lot in my office and deal with it on Monday. I'll be back in a sec.'

She managed to stay silent long enough to get behind the closed office door, then she disintegrated and buried her face in a cushion, howling like an animal with its leg clamped in a gin trap. Never in her worst nightmares had she anticipated something like this.

She could hear Fran as clearly as if she was in the room beside her: '. . . Serves you right, you stuck-up grammar school bitch . . . pride comes before a fall . . . you'll get your comeuppance one day . . . I'd never have another half-caste kid . . .'

How her mother must be laughing now, she thought. She could just imagine them plotting together, sniggering at the thought of bringing her down and making some money in the bargain. The memories came rushing back to hit her full on.

Angry at herself for being stupid enough to raise her head over the parapet and appear on national television, she picked up the video tape in her desk and, ripping the tape out of the cassette, systematically cut it to shreds with a pair of scissors.

She wondered how she could possibly have thought her life could be good. Now everything she had fought for and worked for was about to fall apart and she had no idea what to do about it.

Fumbling in her desk drawer, she found a packet of cigarettes and quickly lit one, inhaling deeply to try to calm the rising panic that threatened to engulf her.

'Is that aroma of nicotine that I can smell seeping out from under your door?' Sue tried the handle but it was locked. 'You don't have to lock yourself in for a quick puff, you know. I'm hardly up for Puritan of the Year. Come on, open up. I've got some totally delicious photographs I want to show you.'

Angie tried to get herself together, and when she called back through the door she amazed herself at her ability to sound normal. 'I'll be down in two minutes. I'd forgotten that I had a call to make.'

Her survival instinct started to seep through. She knew the letter had to be dealt with somehow, but not in haste and not without a lot of thought. Over the years she had learnt from necessity how to deposit the truly unpleasant to the back compartment of her brain to be retrieved later.

That is what I'll do, she decided, put it away until my head is in the right frame of mind for a game plan.

One way or another she knew she had to figure out a way to deal with Tony once and for all. He'd fucked up her life once; he couldn't do it again. She wouldn't let him.

She went into the bathroom, washed and straightened her face, then walked back down the stairs, for all the world still happy.

'Feeling better now, sweetie? It was the body cleansing that got to you, I'm sure. Too much healthy living isn't good for you. Now just have a look at these . . .'

Angie looked at the big shiny photographs spread out over the breakfast bar. Sue leant over her shoulder as she studied them.

'Isn't she just the greatest? No one would guess this gorgeous creature is the most vicious spoilt mare this side of the Khyber Pass.'

The photos of Rebekah Alari were stunning. Pouting and smiling, seductive and innocent, hair up and hair down – there was not one that didn't stand out. The midnight-dark hair glinted in the flashlight reflection as she stared self-confidently into the lens, emphasising the most wonderful facial bone structure. The images were all endless legs and hair and deep brown, provocative eyes.

'She is incredible. When I saw her at your party it sent shivers down my spine. How old did you say she was?'

Sue raised her eyes to the ceiling and banged her hand on the counter in mock exasperation. 'Seventeen, she's only fucking seventeen. I'm old enough to be her mother and she talks to me like shit. She has a real nasty streak in her, that girl. When she stares at you in contempt there's something about her that's quite scary, but, having said that, she's going to be huge, a catwalk

144

queen. Providing, of course, she stays the pace. You know how it is with the trust-fund cokeheads: they don't have the hunger; it's just a game to them.'

Despite everything that was going on Angie couldn't help but laugh.

'Excuse me? Who is this woman talking to me? It couldn't possibly be my friend with a trust fund, could it?'

Sue looked quite affronted.

'You know what I mean. I've never made a big song and dance about it and it wasn't really that much in the scheme of things. Giles had heaps more than me . . . mind you, not for much longer, once Gabby's finished with him.'

'Sue darling, I was only teasing. Where's your sense of humour?'

'OK, I get your drift, but Rebekah has Daddy's millions to fall back on. Her earning potential would be a fortune to you or me but to her it's just pocket money. I really think her parents have done her no favours at all – except, of course, in the genes department.' She looked thoughtful. 'It's strange really, you know, because her brother, Lewis, who follows her around like a protective great Labrador, is such a cutie – all blond hair and loving. He spends half his time apologising and making excuses for her. He's so gentle and sweet, you'd never think they were siblings.'

Angie's mind was drifting. Usually she loved to hear all the gossip from the modelling world but now she couldn't concentrate. She wondered how Sue and Giles would feel if they knew her real past but, more to the point, she wondered about Dave and Jemima . . . Would that be the end of it all? She knew she couldn't take the chance that Tony might be bluffing. The only person she knew she could trust to love her regardless was Gavin. She would have to tell him.

'Fucking hell, Angie, I can't believe it. I just can't take this on board.'

Gavin was thunderstruck when she launched without warning into the whole story. She had left London early to drive to Brighton in record time and had just turned up. He had been surprised to see her, and guessed something was wrong, but never in his wildest dreams could he have known what was about to hit him.

Thinking about it during the journey Angie had decided the only way she could tell him was directly and as soon as she got there – before her courage failed her.

'I know. I find it hard to believe myself sometimes. When I think about it it's almost as if it happened to someone I once knew, not me personally. Apart from the odd moment I had detached myself from it.'

She was huddled on the sofa, her face pallid and her expression unbearably sad.

'But you were just a kid. I don't know how you handled it. Why didn't you tell us? We'd have helped you.'

The globules of tears dissolved on Angie's cheeks as she told Gavin the whole story, no holds barred.

'I know that now but I didn't then. Paolo was just my employer and you were his friend. I didn't really know either of you. That came after.'

Gavin could feel the anger welling up in him, an anger that he'd never experienced before, even in his own darkest days.

'Christ, I remember us all discussing it at the time. "The baby in the bag" was the headline, if I remember rightly.'

'Yes,' she replied with a grim smile, 'plus a lot of other things; "How could any mother do this?" . . . "What kind of person . . ." et cetera, et cetera. I've still got them all at home. The worst thing was the photos of the baby in the arms of a smiling nurse, emotional blackmail to get me to come forward. I really did think about it but I knew they'd never let me keep her anyway. With hindsight I might have done things differently but I was only fifteen . . .'

He sat beside her, holding both her hands in his. 'I'm not criticising you, sweetheart. I'd just like to get my hands on the animal who did it to you. But why are you telling me now? Are you preparing to tell Dave or what?'

Silently Angie dipped into her handbag and handed over the note from Tony.

Gavin's face went white and she could see the muscles moving angrily in his clean-cut jaw.

'Fucking bastard, I'll break his filthy little neck and rip his balls off one by one. Just leave it to me. I'll see the little shit never gets his hands on you again. Twenty-five grand? Scavenging arsehole . . .'

Angie was shocked at his response. Gavin was the least violent man she knew, apart from Dave.

'No, Gavin, that's the last thing I want. You locked up for good – that'd be even worse. No, what I want is for us to discuss it and decide the best way forward for everyone.'

'The best way forward is for him to be dead – slowly and painfully preferably, but dead as a doornail.'

Suddenly Angie was in charge of the situation. She felt better knowing there was someone she could talk to about the blackmail, someone she knew for certain was unquestionably on her side, but she knew whatever she decided to do could all too easily get out of hand.

'There are other people to consider in this. If the press got hold of my past they would soon add up two and two and realise I'd abandoned the baby, and her parents would know who I was. I've got a half-brother out there somewhere – maybe more by now – and there's Dave and Jemima to consider. There has to be a way out; we've just got to find it.'

'Are you going to tell Dave? He should know. After all, you're having his baby and going to live with the guy . . .'

She was adamant. 'No way. I don't want him to know a thing. Promise me you'll not breathe a word.'

He pulled her to him. 'Not if you don't want me to but, for what it's worth, I think you're wrong and this all might just backfire on you.'

Angie moved away and sat ramrod straight on the small sofa. 'I'm not telling him. I'm not telling anyone. This is between you and me.'

Gavin shook his head as he looked at the woman who had come to mean so much to him. She had changed little over the years but now, as she sat there crumpled and distraught, he could see the young girl she had been when they first met – a child really, with more to deal with than most people have in a whole lifetime . . . and she'd gone through it all alone.

'If that's the way you want it . . .'

'It is. I feel better already just having you to talk to.' A watery smile broke through. 'Now tell me about your fella. I didn't give you enough time to hide the evidence, did I?'

She glanced knowingly at the framed photo on the side of Gavin and another man standing close, too close to be just friends. He looked as much younger than Gavin as Paolo had been older – a very ordinary young man with cropped hair and wire-rimmed glasses. His eyes were on Gavin alone and Angie felt reassured by the look.

'I wasn't sure how to tell you,' he smiled guiltily at her. 'I know how fond you were of Paolo, the main man in your life.'

'You were both main men in my life – you still are – but Paolo is gone and I'd love you to be happy with someone. You're not suited to the single life.'

'His name's Simon. He's younger than me and yes, we are happy. You will get to meet him but not today. He lives and works in London, but I hope that will change soon. Sure you don't mind, Angie baby?'

147

She kissed him on the cheek. 'How could I possibly mind if you're happy, you silly old fool.'

'Not so much of the old, thank you!'

They laughed together but both their minds were on the main topic. What to do about Tony Willmott?

There was no way Angie wanted to get caught up in a web of her own lies so when Dave phoned she told him she had been to see Gavin and that he had told her about the new man in his life. All true, just a few omissions.

'Do you know yet when you'll be back? I miss you.'

She desperately needed him. More than ever she needed to know he loved her.

'And I miss you too, more than you can guess. It should only be a few more days. It's all going to plan so far. Not bored without me, are you?' He was teasing and she knew it.

'No, I've got plenty of work, boring writing-up-type work; stay-in-the-office-and-get-on-with-it-type work, but what I really want is you in my bed now.'

'Oh Christ, no, not phone sex again. I've done six already today . . .'

'Only six? You're slipping, Mr Sex-on-legs. Anyway, not tonight, I've got a headache.'

They snapped the humour back and forth, affectionately comfortable with each other.

The thought of that changing upset Angie. She knew she couldn't afford to lose Dave. She would find a solution that saved everyone, including herself and her self-respect that had been earned the hard way.

The griping pains that woke her during the night were vaguely familiar but it took her a while to realise. Then she discovered the bleeding.

She padded down the hall to Sue's room and knocked on the door. Giles was in there, she had heard them earlier, but there wasn't time for niceties.

'Sue? Are you there, Sue? I'm sorry but I think I need to go to hospital. I'm bleeding – I think I'm losing the baby.'

The door flew open. Sue was naked bar a pillow and Giles was sitting bolt upright in the bed, looking bewildered.

'Do you want an ambulance or shall we take you? Is Dave back yet?'

'Not for a few days.' Angie was now in tears. 'Can you take me?'

In almost no time at all they were dressed and on their way to the nearest A&E department, where, after a quick examination, Angie was whisked away to a ward to await a scan the next morning.

The doctor was sympathetic. 'Thirteen weeks is a dangerous time in pregnancy. This may just be a little hiccup but pains and bleeding can indicate a miscarriage. The scan tomorrow will tell us more but, chin up, the cervix is still closed so there is hope, Mrs Kavanagh. Just hang on in there.'

Sleep was an impossibility. Common sense told Angie that these things happened, but her demons told her that this was a punishment. She had not wanted Skye so she wasn't entitled to have another one. You can't pick and choose, she told herself. Babies aren't disposable. You can't just give away the one you don't want and keep the one you do. The morning was a long time coming.

Sue and Giles had been packed off home but Sue had promised to come back in the morning with a nightie and some bits and pieces that no one had thought of in the panic.

'How's it going, sweetie?' Sue asked anxiously, clutching the necessities she'd brought. 'Have they told you anything yet?'

'I'm going for the scan in a few minutes. Will you come with me? I think I'm going to need some moral support.' Angie hadn't broken down but was dangerously close.

'Of course I will. Maybe it'll all be OK. You've got through the night with nothing happening. Do you want me to phone Dave? I couldn't last night; I wasn't sure where he was . . .'

'No!' Angie cried out. 'I don't want to worry him. There's no point in him rushing back at the moment. I'll see after the scan.'

The technician was silent to start with as he ran the handheld sensor over her gel-covered belly. Angie remembered the last scan that had been such an exciting event with Dave beside her as they carefully studied the screen. This time the suspense in the room was almost tangible. Neither Angie nor Sue said a word. They just watched the screen, and Sue had her fingers crossed behind her back.

'Right,' he suddenly said, 'there's the heartbeat. The little mite appears to be OK at the moment. It all looks good. If you'd like to get dressed I'll take you along to the doctor.'

'Are you sure there's nothing wrong? I'm not going to lose my baby?'

The man smiled sympathetically. 'As I said, it looks good but the doctor will explain to you.'

Sue waited outside the small room, pacing up and down the corridor like a stereotypical expectant father while Angie was in with the consultant. Then the door opened and Angie was wheeled out, a tremulous smile on her lips.

'He thinks it's going to be OK as well. I've got to rest for a while but he thinks the baby is safe.'

'Thank fuck for that.'

The elderly nurse pushing the wheelchair pursed her lips, putting her own interpretation on the two women hugging and crying at the news.

'Why didn't you tell me? Don't you think I have a right to know?'

For the first time in the relationship Dave was angry, really angry. He had arrived home to find Angie in bed and to be confronted by the news that she had been in hospital and had nearly lost the baby.

'I didn't think it was fair to worry you. You were working and, anyway, we're both all right now . . . I hope. I've just got to take it easy.'

He shook his head. 'You don't get it, do you? We're meant to be in a relationship, we're having a baby – didn't it occur to you I'd want to know what was happening?'

'But you were working—'

'Fuck work. We're not all like you: work does not come first – or not for me at any rate. You come first, you and the baby. I had thought I came first with you—'

He stopped in his tracks when he saw her face. Suddenly he was kneeling beside the bed, reaching across to hug her.

'I'm sorry. Please don't cry, I didn't mean to upset you, please don't cry.'

'I'm not upset. It's hormones. I don't care if you shout if it makes you feel better.'

'Oh, dear God, what am I going to do with you? You make me so angry sometimes. Did you see it on the screen again? Is it really OK? Are you really OK?'

'Yes I am, truly OK. It was a bit heartstopping at the time but I'm fine now and so, I hope, is our child.'

Gavin was seething. As soon as he heard the news he was sure it was the shock of the letter from Tony that had caused the threatened miscarriage.

Gavin had had his moments in his younger days and had mixed with more than a few unsavoury characters. He was sure he could call up a name or two if he had to, but would Angie agree? He doubted it, and he weighed up the good with the bad. He didn't want to lose Angie's affection but at the same time he wanted her to be happy in the long run and there was no way that could happen with the lowlife Tony Willmott chasing her tail for the rest of her life.

He decided to broach his solution with Angie first, to see if she would agree to him getting pressure applied on the bastard and if not . . . well, if not he would find a way of doing it anyway.

'Angie baby, I can deal with it if you'll let me. You just have to trust me. I have the contacts to shut him up. I don't mean anything fatal, just a teeny bit life-threatening, enough to frighten him off.'

Gavin had gone to Dave's cottage in Kent where Angie was resting under orders, away from the trappings of a home office.

'No, Gavin. I mean it, it's just too risky for you to be involved. He's a dangerous man – I know that at first-hand – dangerous and ruthless. Perhaps if I negotiate to pay him off with less and a signed agreement . . . He doesn't know where I live . . .'

Gavin laughed. 'Angie darling, you are so naïve sometimes. Whatever you give him he'll want more and more. He'll bleed you dry and then still go to the papers to get some from them. A signed agreement would be as much use as second-hand bog roll. You cannot give in to blackmail.'

'Leave it, Gavin. When I'm back up to scratch we'll think of something, but promise me, no violence. I lived with it, remember, and I hate it in any way, shape or form.'

'OK, we'll talk about it again soon. Meanwhile, look after yourself and baby. That's what's really important. But when you're ready, Angie baby, just say the word. That low-life needs sorting very, very soon.'

Gavin wasn't happy about taking no action but he decided to wait for a while and hope Angie changed her mind.

Two weeks later she got another letter. This time it was hand delivered through her front door while she was upstairs working in her office, completely unaware of who was creeping around out-side her house while she was inside alone.

Well, Gollywog, you're taking your time, aren't you?

£25,000 tomorrow at the latest. If it doesn't arrive then, ready or not I'm coming in to get it, and anything or anyone else that takes my fancy. The tall dark-haired one looks quite interesting, and if you're really lucky I'll let you watch while you wait your turn.

TOMORROW.

Love from TONY.

Angie phoned Gavin.

'I've changed my mind. Something has to be done now. I've had another letter. He knows where I live and I'm absolutely shit scared, not for my career now but for my life . . . and Sue's. Can you get here now?'

Gavin took his life in his hands and broke every speed limit on the drive from Brighton to Fulham.

As soon as he'd read the letter he knew there was no time to waste. Something would have to be done, and fast.

'I'm taking over now, sweetheart. This can't go on. I'm going to make some calls.'

'But, Gavin, what if—'

His face was set. 'No more what ifs. It's too dangerous.' He hugged her, kissed her on the cheek. 'Don't worry, Angie baby, I'll make sure this is the last time Tony Willmott dares to bother you.'

Gavin had worked in some dubious clubs in his time and he knew there were certain bouncers who liked nothing better than a chance to show off their muscle. The favourites were two brothers called Fred and Barney because they looked a mere step away from neanderthal man. Their other nickname, behind their backs, of course, was 'the two missing links'.

They were like peas in a pod – not particularly tall but with shoulders like battering rams and necks that probably measured the same as their thighs. The crew-cut hair and intimidating battered faces always looked incongruous atop beautifully maintained suits, but they could put the fear of God into any drunken troublemaker who overstepped the mark on their territory just by standing close. Gavin knew that they were the answer to Angie's prayers, he just had to convince her.

Chapter Eleven

Even if Angie had seen Tony Willmott shuffling along with his head down on the other side of the street she wouldn't have recognised him. It had been nearly twenty years and the Tony now bore little resemblance to Tony then.

The handsome and arrogant young man was now stooped and skeletal, his once-sleek blond hair a dirty grey, with the hairline receding dramatically, making a caricature of the ponytail that hung matted down his back. He looked like any other of the sad and lonely old tramps that wandered the city streets aimlessly, turning over rubbish bins and searching the kerbs for dog-ends.

However, the one feature Angie would have recognised if she'd got close enough was the eyes. The hatred shone as fierce as ever but now there was a madness in them.

As soon as he had realised the money was missing from the tin under the bed he'd known he was in big trouble. He already owed a substantial sum, and the cash Louise had taken rounded up the debt to nearly five thousand pounds. For once in his life he'd been justifiably petrified.

Fran had come in from work one day shortly after to find him in the trashed flat, his body battered and bruised to a bloody mess and one kneecap shot to pieces. No one in Albemarle Street had heard a sound. Allegedly. The Three Wise Monkeys' sense of self-preservation had kicked in instantly. Hear no evil, see no evil, speak no evil. The neighbours had known nothing.

She didn't want to but Fran knew she had no alternative but to call an ambulance and save his life.

Following a spell in intensive care under police guard he recovered enough to be discharged into the hands of the police, who couldn't believe their luck. Tony Willmott was in actual fact Anthony Bingham, wanted by the police in connection with a hit-and-run in Manchester that had left three young children fighting for their lives.

His sentencing was the day that Fran had breathed a sigh of relief. Once again she could see a future for herself.

Tony's spell in prison had been short-lived, however. The diagnosis 'psychopathic personality disorder' had resulted in him being transferred to finish his sentence in a secure psychiatric unit. Fearing for her life, Fran had left the flat the day before he'd been released and had disappeared off the face of the earth.

Tony blamed everything on Louise and after years of searching for her thought he had finally hit the jackpot the morning she appeared on TV in the guise of Angie Kavanagh. He recognised her, and he wanted to get her – the little black whore who'd wrecked his life.

He watched her walk confidently to the front door of her house, laughing and joking with Dave, who was proudly pushing a huge Silver Cross pram.

He intended to make Louise pay a high price for what she had done to him but he knew he had to be careful this time. He'd been warned off once by the pair of heavies she had sent round.

He'd stayed away for a while – just long enough for them to relax their guard and stop looking over their shoulders. Now he was back, with dark vengeance the only thing on his deranged mind.

Gavin had finally put his foot down. He brooked no more prevaricating from Angie.

'No, this is out of your hands now. I've made some calls and called in a few favours.'

Angie was a nervous wreck. Curled up in the big chair with her dressing gown wrapped tightly around her, she looked again like the vulnerable young girl he had first met.

'Gavin, please, no violence. I hate violence. He is the one that made me hate it.'

'Leave it to me. I will sort it and you can get on with your life. Think about the baby now – that's what you have to concentrate on – but I promise Willmott won't be hurt physically . . . We are just going to scare the shit out of him and make sure he never comes near you or does anything to hurt you.'

Angie was shaking as Gavin went to make the call. She alone knew what Tony Willmott was capable of.

Gavin stayed with her twenty-four hours a day, watching and waiting, ever alert. Dave thought he was just visiting, paying a social call.

Three days after he'd set everything up, the call he'd been waiting for came for Gavin. He smiled as he replaced the receiver.

'Tony Willmott won't be bothering you again, Angie babe. He's seen the error of his ways and doesn't really like the idea of being permanently disabled.'

'Gavin, are you sure? He's a devious bastard . . .'

'I'm sure, Angie. Trust me, you can forget about Tony Willmott.'

Five months later Angie was in labour and on her way to the maternity unit. She prayed for no complications. Twelve hours to recover and then out was what she had requested, and everything going to plan would ensure that. All she wanted was a healthy baby back home with its parents.

It was a bitter-sweet time for her. The joy of giving birth to a beautiful and healthy boy was overshadowed by the memories of the previous child she had borne and the circumstances surrounding that birth. There was no comparison.

Dave had stayed with her throughout, calmly and confidently supporting her and doing all the right things, feeding her ice and rubbing her back, but he looked decidedly shell-shocked sitting by the bed as Angie held the baby to her breast for the first time.

'My son, I can't believe it, my son. Isn't he just the most gorgeous baby you've ever seen?'

Angie smiled sadly as she looked in wonder at the downy head nestling close. She had to close her mind to last time, she knew that.

'Of course he is. We're his parents – he couldn't do much better. Are you sure about the name? You really do like it, don't you?'

'Of course I do.' Dave looked from mother to baby. 'Joshua is just perfect; he even looks like a Joshua.'

'He may be named after my dad but he certainly doesn't look like him. Dad was the tallest, handsomest, blackest man in the world.' She looked thoughtfully into the distance. 'I wonder where he is now.'

'Why don't you try and found out?'

He didn't know that she had thought the same thing many times over the past few months. She had thought a lot about all the people from her past, but mostly Joshua and Fran, her parents. But she wouldn't know where to start to find them after all the time that had passed. Dave didn't know the full story, just the bare bones of her running away from an abusive home and going to Brighton.

It had been a relief to Angie when Gavin's shadowy 'friends' had reported back that Tony was living alone in the flat in Albemarle Street. At least Fran hadn't been party to the blackmail attempt.

'I don't know if I'm strong enough for what I might find. Maybe one day . . .'

Dave suddenly reached across, gently stroking the cheek of the tiny baby. He didn't look at Angie.

'Marry me . . . marry me and save this little man from the name of Joshua Kavanagh-Oliver.'

She looked at Dave lovingly. 'I'll think about it, I promise. Just give me time to get over this.'

He smiled ruefully at her; he had expected nothing more.

Twelve hours later they all went home.

From the minute they arrived back at the house in Fulham there had been a nonstop flurry of activity with visitors coming and going. Gavin and Jemima were staying, and waiting hand, foot and finger on Angie and Joshua, and Sue was nearly as permanent a fixture as when she still lived there. She'd moved in with Giles shortly after his divorce had been settled.

The two friends were on the sun loungers in the garden as Joshua slept in his crib just inside the open French doors.

'I hate you, Angie. You've made me feel so bloody broody. I just love that baby of yours to bits. He's so gorgeous I could eat him.'

'Why don't you then?'

She threw her hands up in horror. 'What? Eat your baby?'

'No, you fool, not eat Joshua,' she laughed, 'have a baby. Both you and Giles are young, free and single – what's stopping you? You need to think about it soon with the old body clock ticking away. Time's getting on for a first baby.'

'You managed all right. Anyway, no offence, sweetie, but I want to be married before I have a baby, married and secure. But more importantly, Joshua can get away with being Kavanagh-Oliver, how could I possibly inflict Portchester-Boughton-Jones on a seven-pound weakling?'

They both laughed so loudly that the baby let out a wail. Angie was up and beside his crib in a flash. She took him out to the garden and lay back down, letting him snuggle into her breast.

Giles and Dave followed swiftly to find out what all the noise was about.

Tony Willmott was in the alleyway that ran along the rear of the gardens. He was peering through a carefully crafted hole in the fence, watching the domestic scene that was unfolding before his eyes. He recognised them all; he'd been watching for weeks now – watching and waiting.

He had stayed away for a while until eventually his urge for revenge had got the better of him, but this time he was more cautious.

Twenty-five grand might just have been enough, enough to move away and forget Louise Jermaine ever existed, but despite waiting excitedly for the money and checking every day nothing had happened. When there'd come a knock on the door it certainly hadn't been the postman making a personal delivery.

Two thugs the size of gorillas had pushed their way in and thrown him into a heap on the chair with the ease of swatting an irritating gnat. He'd frozen, remembering all too well the last visit he'd had from hired muscle.

One of the men had put his face so close to Tony's the man could almost see his tonsils.

'You are a pervert, a fucking pervert, a child rapist, a paedophile.'

Tony had opened his mouth to protest, but before he could get a sound out the second gorilla had wrapped a huge hand round his throat.

'I said, you're a fucking paedophile. Do you know what they do to paedophiles in the nick? They fuck them. They shag the arse off them with anything and everything. Broken snooker cues, table legs, broom handles, over and over again, day in day out, night in, night out. And, just when you think it can't get any worse they strangle your balls with rusty wire until the circulation stops and eventually they drop off.'

Tony had felt the bile rising in his throat and had suffered the indignity of wetting his pants.

The two men had looked at the dark patches that slowly appeared on Tony's trouser legs, and laughed – a frightening growl that had turned his blood to ice.

'One more letter, one phone call or one glimpse of your snivelling little face within ten miles of the lady in question and we'll be back to perform all of that on you personally,' the man still holding Tony's throat had continued. 'But just for fun we'll finish by cutting off your diseased little bollocks and stuffing them down your fucking throat.' He'd let go and Tony had slid to the floor. 'Do you get my drift? Is that clear enough for you?'

'Yes, yes . . .' Tony had been crying. 'I won't go near her . . .'

As they'd left he'd crawled into the corner whimpered like a dog that had been kicked within an inch of its life.

Remembering it all, Tony could feel his head throbbing and his blood boiling. He was close to breaking point. As he watched Angie pull up her tee shirt and help the baby hook up to her breast, the hatred bubbled inside him like a sore that was about to erupt and spew its poison. His instinct was to hurl himself down the garden and kill them all, but even through the fug of his deranged brain he knew that wasn't good enough for him.

No, she had to suffer. She had to suffer the way he had. The way she had made him suffer. She would feel the searing pain as her kneecap was smashed to smithereens and her face was battered to a pulp, and then he would inflict the worst thing of all on her. Just the thought of it gave him an erection and he hadn't had one of those for a long time.

He watched her gazing at the baby in her arms and suddenly a plan began to form.

Angie loved Joshua with a ferocity she had never known before. He was her second chance and she was going to make sure that he received all the love that she had never had a chance to give Skye.

She knew it would soon be time to get back into the mainstream of work but for the time being she was happy just to spend every minute with Joshua, savouring each milestone of his babyhood, no matter how small.

'Wasn't he just perfect? I've never been to a christening before where the baby didn't make a sound. He looked as if he really was interested, taking it all in. He's going to be one bright child, my godson.'

Angie slapped her friend playfully on the arm. 'You are just such a prat sometimes, Sue. He was fed and warm and dry. That's why he didn't cry!'

Dave and Angie had decided to celebrate Joshua's christening with a barbecue in the garden, with just a few close friends and a smattering of Dave's relations.

Gavin had brought Simon, and Jemima had come with her latest boyfriend, a morose young man called Dominic, who was dressed from head to toe in several layers of strange black clothes. He didn't go to the church but turned up at the house for the barbecue.

Dave did a quick double take when Dominic was introduced. He smiled appropriately and then whispered in Angie's ear, 'I wonder if Dracula knows what his son gets up to during the daylight hours.'

She glared at him. 'Stop it, they'll hear. Don't start acting like an old man, it doesn't suit you – and anyway you're one to talk, Denim Man.' She looked up and down in mock horror. 'Jeans to your only son's christening?'

He looked quite indignant. 'You said you didn't mind . . .'

'I don't, but people in glass houses shouldn't throw stones!'

He kissed the top of her head. 'I love you so much . . .'

She smiled up at him. 'I know you do and that feels good. But you can still leave the boy alone.'

The party was in full swing, the sun was shining, the champagne was flowing and everyone was enjoying themselves.

Everyone, that is, apart from Tony Willmott, who was in his usual position, eyes glued to the hole in the fence, the hatred screwing up his face.

He wasn't quite so angry now. He could watch Angie and not boil up to the point of losing control now that he knew in his mind precisely how he was going to exact his revenge. He just had to wait for the right time.

Suddenly, without warning, one of the Siamese cats jumped over the fence and landed full force on Tony's shoulders. He shouted out in pain as the cat proceeded to run down his back, gouging as it went.

'What was that?' shrieked Angie, her face frozen in terror as they all stopped and looked towards the end of the garden.

Before Dave finished saying, 'There's something there . . .' Gavin was off at a run, with Dave then quickly on his heels. They reached the fence in a few long paces and looked over to see a man running down the alley.

Dave smiled and turned to the horrified guests, all watching silently.

'It's OK, it's only that old tramp that's been hanging around. I bet he smelt the barbecue and couldn't resist taking a peek. If he's still there later I'll take him some out.'

Everyone relaxed again, and Gavin and Angie exchanged relieved glances. He went over to her.

'You OK?'

'I am now. For a split second I was worried . . .'

'So was I, but it's only reaction. There's really nothing to be scared of. Tony Willmott is a closed book.'

'Quiet everybody.' Sue clapped her hands like a school teacher. 'I have a couple of things to say. First, I would like to congratulate Angie, my best friend, and Dave, her gorgeous partner, on their beautiful son, and thank them for giving me the honour of being godparent. I hope I do justice to the role as I'm sure will Gavin, Joshua's other godparent. Three cheers for Joshua Kavanagh-Oliver! Hip, hip . . .'

They all joined in gamely. Sue and champagne were always a lively match.

159

'Secondly,' she continued, 'I have an announcement of my own. Giles and I are engaged. We're getting married as soon as possible.'

Angie threw herself across the garden. 'Sue, I'm so pleased for you. Giles, come here and let me kiss you. I'm so happy for both of you!'

They all kissed and hugged and raised their glasses. Suddenly Angie spotted Dave standing apart, looking pensive. She went over to him, putting her arm round his waist affectionately. He pulled away.

'What is it with you, Angie? Why are you looking so happy? I'd have thought it would be sackcloth and ashes at awful news like that. I mean, getting married? Surely that's only one up from going to the gallows.' He looked crossly at her. 'They've both been divorced and are willing to give it a try . . . You've not even been there once!'

She couldn't answer him.

'Are you OK, Angie baby?' Gavin asked. 'You look a bit pissed off . . .'

'Dave's giving me a hard time because I won't get married. Sue put the tin lid on it with her badly timed announcement. I wish she hadn't chosen Joshua's christening as the forum.'

'You know Sue – high on drama, low on tact. She opens her mouth before her brain has even engaged. Don't get me wrong, I adore the woman, darling, but she can be such a fucking airhead sometimes. I can't imagine how she runs a business.'

Angie laughed. She could always rely on Gavin to cheer her up.

He grabbed her hand. 'Come on, let's go and look at my godson-cum-grandson-cum-beautiful boy!'

As they walked into the house Angie knew that Dave was watching them, and could only imagine his bewildered expression. She decided that was just tough. She had always told him how she felt so it was a bit unfair of him to get sniffy over it now.

The decision to get back to work was a hard one for her. She was torn between her total love for Joshua and her urge to get back into the work she loved. Having caught up on her backlog and fitted in a couple of phone interviews she was starting to get restless. She discussed it with Dave one evening when Jemima was there, and she came up with the ideal solution.

'So, you want to go back to work but you don't want a nanny, is that right?'

'Well, yes, I suppose it is. I can't face leaving Joshua with a stranger, even one from a reputable agency . . .'

160

'OK then, what about me? I can look after him during the summer break. I can live in and you can be free to get back into the work mode. How about that?'

'Sounds good to me. What do you think, darling?'

'Dave was hesitant. 'Jemima's very young, you know—'

'Get a life why don't you, Dad? I'm nearly nineteen, for Christ's sake and he is my baby brother.'

Angie felt a warm glow at the way the word just flowed out of the girl's mouth . . . my brother. Not my half-brother, just . . . my baby brother.

It was difficult at first for Angie, trying to combine work and motherhood. It took all her willpower not to rush down the stairs from her office every time she heard Joshua cry, but for Jemima's sake she forced herself to stay put. Even when Dave was there she found it hard to hand over the reins, though he was more than capable and willing to do his share. Angie was so completely besotted with the fair-haired little bundle that gazed up at her with total trust, she found it hard to believe that she could love so much.

'I'm just popping into the kitchen to grab a coffee, Jem,' she shouted up one morning soon after Jemima moved in, trying to sound casual. 'Is everything OK? I thought I heard Joshua cry.'

The girl put her head round the door. 'Of course it's all OK, now stop panicking. Joshua's fast asleep and hasn't so much as murmured. Read my lips: GO AWAY AND WORK.'

'I only wanted a coffee . . .' Angie managed to look hurt.

'No you didn't, you only had one ten minutes ago. Please trust me, Angie. I know what I'm doing. There can't be a single thing that you haven't either told me or written down for me.' Jemima smiled affectionately at Angie as she turned round and slunk back upstairs to her office.

Angie hoped it would get easier when she was out and about more, when the commissions started again in full flow. But at that moment she couldn't imagine staying away from Joshua overnight. He was still only three months old.

Tony shuffled down the street past the house. Two cars were outside again. He had hoped that by waiting and watching a pattern would emerge, a pattern that would help him catch Angie in the house alone with the baby, but just lately the young girl was staying there. He was frustrated; didn't they ever leave the black slut alone? If it wasn't the short fat one it was the boyfriend, or the

161

tall woman, or her boyfriend, or the other man, the one he had heard being called Gavin. He couldn't get his head round it.

He was now a familiar sight in the road and some of the residents even slipped him a pound for a cup of tea. Stupid bastards, he thought, but he still took it.

He had enjoyed the day of the barbecue. Just when he'd thought he'd been sussed and was about to get his feared punishment the boyfriend had found him huddled behind a garden wall and had given him a paper plate of sausages instead. That'd amused him for days.

The time spent aimlessly wandering the streets that ran parallel and adjacent to Lovelace Road gave Tony too much time to think and his fragile grasp on reality was getting weaker by the day. He truly believed Angie to be the prime mover in his downfall, that she had deliberately set him up when she took the money and ran; in his head he blamed Fran for giving birth to her, for allowing a black man to inseminate her. Angie had become the devil incarnate, an evil force to be stopped, to be punished for her wrongdoings. By birth her child was the son of Satan, sent to continue her line; he had to be put down to prevent the further spread of tainted blood. Now Tony saw himself as a man with a mission – one that he was determined to fulfil.

As he walked the streets muttering and swearing to himself he received the sympathetic glances of unsuspecting passers-by. People had become so used to aggressive young beggars on the streets they were tolerant of the shabby, pathetic man who shuffled around and never bothered anyone. He heard them sometimes: 'He's harmless enough . . . at least he doesn't bother anyone . . . such a shame to come to that . . .'

He never made eye contact, he just soaked up all the sympathy and regarded it as justification for dealing with the black whore and her bastard child.

At the right time.

'Angie? Dad?' Jemima called up the stairs. 'Is it OK if I take Joshua to the park with Dominic? He's ever so good with babies; he's from an absolutely huge family – eight kids, in fact, can you imagine it? And he's the eldest.'

Angie and Dave were both in the office planning a joint commission. Dave looked at Angie and opened his mouth wide in mock horror.

'Good with babies? The boy in black? Perish the thought, he probably eats them for supper.'

'Behave yourself,' she laughed before shouting back down to Jemima, 'Yes, of course, but only for an hour or I'll start to panic!'

'Panic?' Dave spluttered, carrying on with his theme. 'I'm panicking at the thought of another seven like him. It must be like the Adams family.'

'Dave Oliver, I'm ashamed of you; he's a really nice boy, he just takes himself a bit too seriously.' Angie looked at him seductively. 'If the house is empty for an hour why don't we play hooky in the bedroom? It's been a long time since we were alone together.'

He feigned innocence. 'Hooky in the bedroom? Never heard of it. What exactly would that entail?'

She sniggered. 'Come with me and I'll show you.'

Tony was peering over the fence, trying to see into the house, when he glanced upwards and saw Angie near the bedroom window. He watched as Dave came over and kissed her gently before unbuttoning her blouse, unhooking her front-fastening bra and releasing her breasts from their restraint.

Just as Tony felt the warmth flowing into his groin they embraced passionately and moved away from the window, out of his line of vision.

He tried standing on tiptoe, then he scrabbled around in the rubbish-strewn alleyway and found several house bricks that he balanced precariously one on top of another to try to gain some height, but it was no good. They were out of sight.

He was enraged. The whore! In full view of everyone. That proved to him that she was truly evil: she was seducing a white man.

The time had to come soon, before she could poison anyone else and ruin their lives. He couldn't leave it much longer.

'Friday night is takeaway night – who wants what?' Dave jumped to his feet. 'Let's have a vote on it. I say Chinese, and I'm buying so that's two votes for me.'

'Pizza,' shouted Jemima. 'Let's call the pizza man.'

'I'm easy,' said Angie, trying not to laugh as Dave winked at her lasciviously. She felt the warm afterglow of comfortable lovemaking, and mentally decided they should take time out more often. 'Dominic? What about you?'

'I don't mind so long as it's vegetarian.'

'Chinese it is then,' Dave decided. 'I win with my two votes and Angie's one!'

'That's not fair . . .'

'Oh yes it is. He who pays the piper chooses the tune. Come on, you two, get your coats and then Dominic can choose his healthy option. Angie, you can warm up the plates.'

They were all laughing as they rushed about getting ready.

Tony watched them leave and saw the chance he had been waiting so long for. Angie wasn't with them and neither was the baby. He knew then they were indoors, alone.

The sound of breaking glass sent a shiver through Angie. It came from the side of the house, the old morning room that was now a day nursery for Joshua. She got to the door just in time to see a shadowy figure climbing through the window right beside the baby's cot where he lay quietly wide awake. Resisting the urge to scream and so frighten Joshua, she ran across and grabbed him, holding him tight to her pounding chest.

'Get out,' she hissed, 'get out now before I scream for my husband. He'll call the police. Get out . . .'

But the intruder continued to climb in as Angie backed towards the door.

'What do you want? Money? I'll get you money, just get out of my house.' She was terrified; she recognised him as the old tramp she had always thought kindly of, and she tried to rationalise to herself that he meant no harm.

Suddenly his feet hit the floor and before Angie could move from the spot he was across the room and behind her, his hand firmly clamped over her mouth.

'Money, Gollywog? You weren't so fucking keen to give me money when I asked before. No, I don't want your fucking money. It's you I want now, you whore from hell – your life and that bastard tainted baby. But first you're going to pay for what you did. You're going to pay a higher price than you could ever imagine in your worst nightmare. Now put the bastard down.'

She was rooted to the spot, literally frozen with fear.

He screamed at her, 'Put the fucking bastard down before I chuck it out the window.'

She moved slowly back towards the crib with his hand still over her mouth. Carefully she laid Joshua down and tried to cover him with a blanket in the vain hope that Tony might forget about him.

He took a bright shiny knife out of one threadbare, filthy pocket and a hammer out of the other.

'One sound from you, whore, and I'll batter the bastard's head to a pulp. Now strip.'

164

Riveted to the spot with terror, she didn't move.

He snarled at her, his face contorted with manic hate. 'I said strip, whore!' He held the hammer over the crib.

Angie quickly removed her clothes and mechanically folded them without realising what she was doing. Her eyes never left Tony's face. She had no fear for herself, only Joshua, who had now closed his eyes and dropped into the world of twitchy half-sleep.

'Tony, please . . .'

'Not a fucking sound. Now get over in the corner away from the bastard, right over there, and don't move an inch.'

He undid his trousers and let them fall to the floor, his eyes never leaving her face.

'Look at this fucking useless leg . . . I said LOOK . . . Can you see that?'

Slowly Angie let her eyes drop to the twisted and scarred malformed limb that he was pointing at. She raised her eyes and nodded silently.

'Now look at the top of my head. See that fucking great scar? See it?' His voice was getting louder, and she prayed the neighbours might hear him and call the police. 'You did that, you WHORE.' He screamed the word. 'You took my money and that's why they did it. It was your fault, and then you have the fucking gall to send a couple of gorillas round to threaten me? To threaten to rape me with a table leg?'

He grabbed the table that housed Joshua's changing mat and upturned it, smashing it to the floor. He continued smashing until he broke one of the legs free.

He had lost it; the tenuous thread that had kept him sane was broken.

Now, Gollywog, guess what I'm going to do to you? I'm going to smash your knees, batter your head, beat you to a pulp and then shove this table leg up your black arse as far as it'll go. But first–' he paused and smiled the vicious smile that she knew so well, a vicious, spiteful smile that made her literally shiver and keep shivering until her teeth chattered – 'first I'm going to do it to the bastard in the cot and you're going to watch . . .'

Angie screamed. She screamed like she never knew she could and threw herself across the room, landing on top of him with a ferocity that took him by surprise, kicking, biting and hitting him over the head with her fists.

All the time she screamed and screamed and screamed . . .

At that moment the front door opened.

Tony stopped in his tracks, then rushed from the nursery and made a dash for the open door, pushing the others out of his way.

Dave and Jemima ran into the room to find a naked Angie shaking from head to toe and clutching Joshua so tightly they had to prise her hands off him.

Dominic gave chase. The agile young man soon caught up with Tony but just as he tried to grab him, Tony lurched away into the road.

The taxi driver had no chance of stopping. The first thing he saw was someone bounce off his bonnet and disappear under the wheels . . .

The general consensus was that it was unfortunate that Angie had just got undressed for a quick shower when the vagrant broke in and found her naked.

It was also unfortunate that she scared him into running out straight under a car. Still, the poor fellow was deranged and it was probably for the best in the long run that he was killed instantly. At least he didn't suffer.

The incident only warranted a couple of column inches on an inside page of the *Evening Standard*.

BOOK THREE

Chapter Twelve

1992

'Mummy, this is Sue Portchester. She is my very favourite person; she looks after my career. And this is Giles Boughton-Jones, her gorgeous partner in both senses of the word. They're engaged, you know. Isn't that just so cool at their age?'

Rebekah Alari smiled charmingly as she made the introductions. Sue wanted to punch her straight between the eyes.

'Sue, Giles, this is my mother, Lauren, and that's Daddy over there. I'll introduce him to you later when he can tear himself away from his friends.'

Sue resisted looking at Giles. It was all a bit too much, super-bitch Alari being cute.

One of the most extravagant parties of the year was in full swing. Rebekah was celebrating her nineteenth birthday and no expense had been spared by her doting parents. It certainly looked to Sue as if it was a success, if the vast number of people there was anything to go by.

It was the first time that Sue had visited the Alari country home, which occupied a large chunk of Surrey countryside, although Rebekah had always made sure everyone knew all about it.

'Sue, did you see my super birthday present outside? I left it there for everyone to see as they came in. I had no idea I was getting it. It was such a surprise when I got up and Mummy and Daddy took me out to see it.' Rebekah was still into little girl mode as she looked expectantly at Sue.

'I certainly did see; would have been hard to miss.' Sue turned to Rebekah's mother. 'That is some birthday surprise for a nineteen-year-old. I do hope Rebekah appreciates it and doesn't come to any harm.'

Lauren Alari was totally oblivious to the undertones of Sue's voice and the veiled hint of criticism. 'Oh, she just loves it to bits already, and she's promised to be careful,' the woman looked adoringly at her daughter, 'haven't you, darling?'

'Oh, I will. I'll be really, really careful – speed limits and all that . . .'

There had been no way of missing seeing the car. As Sue and Giles had driven up the drive that snaked through the grounds of the Alari mansion, there it was, under floodlights, in all its glory.

'For fuck's sake, look at that, why don't you?' Sue had sighed to Giles as it came into view. 'I wonder if they've given the spoilt bitch a loaded gun to make up the pair?'

A brand-spanking-new silver Porsche convertible, decked out in ribbons and balloons, with a professionally printed poster attached to the bonnet had taken pride of place at the bottom of the stone steps that swept up to the front door: 'Nineteen Today. Happy Birthday To Our Darling Rebekah, the best daughter in the world. We love you. Mummy and Daddy.'

'Not jealous, are you, Susie? Don't tell me you wouldn't have given your eyeteeth for one of those at her age.'

'Of course I would, but my parents – and yours, for that matter – were too sensible to hand over a lethal weapon to a kid. Especially one with a psychotic temper like hers.'

Rebekah quickly lost interest in Sue and Giles and disappeared off to hold court in her usual fashion, leaving them standing rather awkwardly with her mother.

Lauren Alari was a twitterer. She went on and on inanely for the next five minutes, extolling the virtues of her daughter. Sue and Giles just stood listening in open-mouthed amazement, unable to get a word in.

They both heaved a sigh of relief as she moved on to welcome more guests. Small and neat, with perfectly coiffured blonde hair and expertly manicured nails, Lauren was hard to age, but Sue guessed she was in her mid-fifties. The wide eyes, full lips and flawless skin hinted at cosmetic surgery rather than youth, but it was the hands that were a positive giveaway to Sue.

'She could do with having the collagen implanted into the backs of hands now her lips are full up,' she whispered sideways to Giles as Lauren Alari tripped away on her impossibly high heels. 'Plastic on legs! I bet she's had everything else lifted and shifted as well – a nip here, a tuck there . . . major construction somewhere else . . .'

'Don't be such a cow, Susie. She looks OK to me. A bit vacuous perhaps, but harmless enough, I suppose. She's laid on a wonderful do for Rebekah. There must be a couple of hundred people here.'

'Giles darling, I'm so glad you're my sleeping partner, in the business sense of the word of course; the company would go down the toilet in five minutes if you had any say in it. You're not just into people, are you? The woman's a pain in the arse and her precious daughter is an ever bigger one. Rebekah's the bitch troll from hell on a good day, and her mother must be barking if she thinks otherwise!'

'You're the one being naïve. She's not trying to convince you and me Rebekah is her adorable and adoring daughter, she's trying to convince herself!' He smiled gently to take the edge off his words. 'Now enough of the bitching, darling. Let's circulate and enjoy this extravaganza instead of ripping the hosts to shreds.' He looked around at the assembled crowd that filled the expansive halls and drawing room. 'There are quite a few familiar faces.'

'Of course there are, sweetie. In this world it's see and be seen that's important. See the photographer over there? This will be splashed all over the papers tomorrow and as they say, one picture is worth a thousand words. Not that I'm complaining. Rebekah is my star, albeit a black-hearted one.'

'LEWIS? Lewis, where are you?' Rebekah's roar was like a klaxon over the party noise. Everyone nearby stopped talking and looked round. She screeched again. 'Where is he? He's supposed to be organising the music, for fuck's sake. It's ten o'clock and not a sound. LEWIS . . .!'

Lauren quickly appeared at her side. 'It's OK, darling, they're setting up now. Some problem with the sound system, Lewis said. It won't be long. Why don't you come out on to the terrace? Daddy's out there with some very important business people who are just dying to meet you. By then the music will be going and all you young ones can decamp to the marquee.'

Sue put her fingers down her throat, making Giles spit his drink down his tie.

'Never mind the "Come out on to the terrace, darling", more like, "Get thee behind me Satan". See what I mean? She needs her face slapped!'

Rebekah was angry. It was supposed to be her day but her parents had hijacked it as usual. Instead of just her family and friends it had turned into a networking opportunity for her father and a social challenge for her mother. There was always a hidden agenda with them. Lewis was the only one who understood, and now Rebekah couldn't find him.

171

She played the game as she had been trained to from as young as she could remember. Brother and sister were both used to being paraded in front of an array of 'useful' people. They were shown off in much the same way as the house in Palm Beach and the apartment in Manhattan. Belongings proved status, advertised success, and Rebekah and Lewis were their parents' belongings, proof of their expansive parenting. Rebekah knew that her success as a model was used by them too: 'My daughter is a supermodel, you know . . . earns an absolute fortune, you know.' It all added to their standing, they thought.

She did the polite rounds of inane formalities on the terrace and then went looking for Lewis. She found him in the marquee, laughing and drinking champagne with the band.

'Hi, Beka, how's it going? The fun will start shortly—'

'I've been looking for you everywhere. How come I get the business bastards and you disappear in here to enjoy yourself? I hate you . . .' She stamped her foot but the effect was lost on canvas.

The young man just laughed; he knew she didn't mean it. 'Because it's not my birthday, fortunately. Cheer up, we can go and round up the interesting people and herd them in here now, and leave the boring old farts outside. If we're selective, Mum and Dad won't venture in so we'll be safe.'

Rebekah was unusually close to her brother. They were chalk and cheese but as close as twins with a mere ten months between them. From as far back as she could remember, Lewis had always been there for her, her security blanket. She knew he loved her unconditionally.

He could easily have resented his younger sister, who had more than her fair share of brains and beauty while he'd been dismissed from an early age as 'a sweet boy but a bit lacking in the brains department', but he didn't. He just adored her, and he was the only one who knew the insecurities of the beautiful young girl that lay behind the façade of poise and confidence.

If Rebekah hadn't quickly acquired the posture of a model she could have been described as gangly. Very tall and thin, at over six foot and under eight stone, there was not an ounce of flesh on her. The minimal skirt of the deep green silky designer dress she wore this evening skimmed the bones of her jutting hips, clinging gently to her slender legs with the halter top that was slashed to the waist displaying a lack of cleavage and an expanse of skinny arms. She wore no jewellery bar a satin choker centred with a white gold and diamond-studded pendant, her birthday gift from her brother.

'Come on, boys. Start up the music as loud and heavy as you can. Beka, you come with me and we'll get this party on the road. You're going to enjoy it whether you like it or not!' Lewis took her by the hand like a child and led her back into the house.

Sue and Giles managed an hour in the marquee but the noise was too much and the company too young, too beautiful and completely up themselves!

The decorations were tastefully co-ordinated, with everything swathed in pink and silver, and the roof filled with shining silver helium balloons that reflected the lights flashing from the stage. Even the barmen and waiters were wearing pink and silver satin bow ties.

'Doesn't it make you feel old, all those supertrendy wealthy young things? We're actually old enough to be parents of nearly all of them. It's just too depressing.'

Giles giggled. He was the one drinking; Sue was driving. 'I would hate to be that age again, all the insecurities and fears for the future. Don't you remember what we were like?' He leant against her gently as he spoke.

'Yes I can. Like we are now without the crevices.'

'Crevices? Where? I can't see a single wrinkle. You look just as beautiful to me now, Susie, as you did at eighteen.'

'Exactly how much have you had to drink, Giles? Come on, I'm taking you home. We'll talk about wrinkles in the morning when you see my naked face on the pillow beside you.'

After they had made their excuses and left and were waiting for the valet to bring their car round, Sue looked again at the bedecked Porsche, still spotlit.

'Isn't Rebekah Alari just the child of your worst nightmares? I'd string her up if she was mine.'

'I feel sorry for the poor kid, I always have done. That is one emotionally deprived girl.'

'Bullshit. You're pissed, sweetie,' was Sue's snorted response.

Rebekah was the centre of attention in the marquee.

As the night went on and the champagne continued to flow, topped up with a selection of dubious substances, the atmosphere was distinctly merry and uninhibited. The exotic buffet remained mostly untouched by the weight-conscious gathering, who danced frantically to the mind-blowing music.

The clue to all the hyperactivity lay in the countless empty water bottles that lay discarded all over the place.

All the Wondermodels, plus a few from other agencies, were out in force, with a plethora of rich young things, male and female, whose parents were busy networking, along with the Alaris.

A hand reached out and grabbed Rebekah's arm. 'Darling, you must come and meet Cormac, the new male model at Essence. He's been dying to get to you but he couldn't break through the crowd. He escorted Zoe but, as you know, she's more into girlies than boys!'

Rebekah crossed her eyes. 'If he wants to meet me he has to come here. Bring him to me, if you like, and I'll cast an eye over him!'

'Promise you won't be dreadful to him. He's a nice guy . . .'

'Moi?' Rebekah pointed at her chest and smiled. 'Moi be dreadful? As if!'

'Yes, you. I know you, you can be just so emasculating, darling. Stay there, I'll go and find him.'

A few minutes later a man appeared beside her.

'I've been told to come and introduce myself. I'm Cormac.'

Rebekah glanced at him, then quickly did a retake.

'Cormac who?'

'Just Cormac.'

She turned towards him and held out her hand, at the same time looking him up and down.

'Well, Cormac no name, care to get me a drink?'

'Of course. I'll be straight back. Don't move from that spot.'

Rebekah was suddenly focused on the young man as he politely made his way to the bar and back. About the same height as she, he was handsome and lean, and moved effortlessly through the throng. He stood out from the crowd – first because he was beautiful and dressed top to toe in black, and secondly because he was black.

Rebekah wondered vaguely how he had managed to get in past her Texan mother, who still had a problem with racial integration. It was OK for the waiters and servers and hired help, but she struggled with total equality.

'Your drink, but before you drink it, can we dance?'

She quickly took the glass and handed it straight to one of the other young men who were all glaring jealously at Cormac, wondering how he had managed so effortlessly to persuade Rebekah to take to the floor.

Moving towards the makeshift dance area, she was very aware of his hand lightly touching the middle of her naked back. Trying to talk over the booming music was impossible, and there seemed

174

little likelihood of a slow number while the floor was full to overflowing.

Very soon Cormac asked, 'Shall I get your drink for you and we can go outside for some air?'

She didn't need asking twice.

'That's better,' he smiled as they walked slowly across the grass in the direction of the summerhouse. 'It's a great party, but not good for conversation. I don't normally get the chance to go to these bashes; I'm not on the A-list, unlike you.'

Taking a readymade joint out of her tiny Gucci shoulder bag Rebekah lit it and breathed deeply.

'You really shouldn't smoke that shit, you know. It dulls the brain.'

'It's better than disintegrating the nasal cavity with snorts of coke. Anyway, it's none of your business. I expect that crap from Mummy but not a total stranger.'

He looked surprised. 'Sorry, you're right.'

'Where are you from?'

He feigned surprise at the question he was always asked.

'London, why?'

'Oh, come on, don't try all that. You know exactly what I mean. In words of one syllable, where did your family come from in the first place?'

He laughed at her candid approach. 'There are three syllables in family. My parents are from Guyana but I was born and bred in London. What about you?'

'Daddy's parents are Italian but he was brought up here, and Mummy's from the Deep South of the good old US of A, but like you I was born and brought up in England.'

'So that's where you get your exotic good looks from – the Italian blood in your veins, and a fiery Mediterranean temperament to match, so I hear.'

She laughed. 'It's hard to keep your cool when you spend all your time surrounded by arseholes, but I'm not that bad, really!'

They chatted comfortably but superficially for a while until they were interrupted.

'Beka, there you are. You'll be in trouble if you don't get back to the party. Dad was looking for you. It's starting to wind down.'

Lewis had quietly appeared in the doorway of the summerhouse and looked quizically at his sister and the guy sitting close beside her.

'Lewis, this is Cormac; Cormac, this is Lewis, my brother.'

Lewis smiled as the young man stood up and held out his hand. 'Pleased to meet you, but I have to drag Beka away or we'll both get it in the neck. We've done the "Welcome to the party", now it's time for "Thank you for coming to the party" – usual nonsense.'

They all laughed.

As they walked quickly back to the marquee Cormac slipped her a card. 'Phone me tomorrow, we'll do dinner.'

'Great, I will.'

They hugged and air-kissed both cheeks as an amused Lewis looked on.

As soon as Cormac was out of earshot Lewis laughed loudly. 'Now that really is guaranteed to send the olds into apoplexy. That's not why you're doing it, is it? Not very fair on the guy . . .'

'No, it isn't why I'm doing it. He's just so cool and gorgeous, and if Mummy and Daddy don't like it – well, that's just an added bonus!'

Sue was jumping up and down shouting, 'Yes, yes, yes,' and punching the air.

'Get me Rebekah on the phone,' she ordered her assistant. 'If we can get her out to Milan by Tuesday she's on the runway. Check out flights and book her in the hotel with the others. Isla's sick or pregnant or coked up, whatever, and Jose wants Rebekah.'

Sue knew this would be good professional kudos for both of them.

The agency was doing well now, well enough for Giles to be considering a move from sleeping partner to wide-awake proactive partner. Now Gabby was paid off and the divorce finalised Sue hoped that they could formalise their personal relationship as quickly as possible. She was constantly thinking marriage, babies and domesticity.

She loved Harry and Emily because they were Giles's children, but they weren't hers and that was what she wanted. Ever since Angie had given birth to Joshua Sue's hormones had been in turmoil, loudly demanding a baby – hers and Giles's.

'I can't get hold of her, Sue. Her mother told me she's in Palm Beach.'

'Palm Beach? Palm fucking Beach? What's she doing there? Oh, never mind. Have you got a number there?'

'Tried that, but the housekeeper said she's out shopping.'

'Keep trying, and check out flights to Milan from there. And if the worst comes to the worst we'll have to charter something but the bitch can pay for it herself. How dare she just take off without a word?'

★ ★ ★

The young couple strolling hand in hand down Worth Avenue were eyecatching even by Palm Beach standards. She was sporting the shortest, tightest white linen dress with shoestring straps, and multicolour-heeled mules that added an extra couple of inches to her six foot. He was casually turned out in beige chinos and a black polo shirt tucked in, his carefully maintained to look casual rasta curls bouncing about at jaw level.

Rebekah kept nipping in and out of the shops, giving her platinum card a pasting courtesy of her father. Cormac was laden with designer carrier bags.

'Go on, Cormac. If you like them, get them. I'll pay.'

He had made the mistake of admiring a ridiculously priced pair of loafers and she was pressuring him to have them.

'No, Beka. I pay my own way and if I can't afford it I don't go there.'

She pulled him round to face her and slowly ran her forefinger down his chest. 'But I can afford it. What's the problem? We're talking a lousy six hundred dollars. You're being so masculine. Would you have a problem with buying something for me that I couldn't afford?'

He stood his ground as she moved even closer to him, looking him straight in the eye. He wasn't going to budge.

'There's nothing that you can't afford, seemingly, so that just wouldn't happen.'

She pulled apart from him and started to walk away sulkily. She wasn't used to being thwarted, and certainly not by a boyfriend. Usually they hung on her every word and looked at her like grateful puppy dogs.

'Look, Beka,' he caught her up, 'if you want to shop for Britain then I don't have a problem with it, really, but I don't need you to buy for me. Come on, let's go and eat.'

'Fuck off, I'm going home. You've spoilt my day now.'

He sighed; she was such hard work sometimes.

They drove back to the Palm Beach mansion in silence. Cormac was getting his first taste of Rebekah's fiery temperament and although he didn't like it he was besotted with her. She had phoned him the day after her party and they had gone for lunch . . . then for dinner, and then they had spent the night at her flat.

She knew he was hooked there and then, and he had jumped at the chance of a few days alone with her. Even if it was at her parents' Palm Beach property.

'Miss Rebekah, Miss Rebekah, there's been one heap of calls for you. You have to phone England right away. Someone's sure getting stressed out trying to get you.'

The housekeeper, Maria, was waiting for them as they drove up. A huge middle-aged black woman, she had been at the house for ten years and knew all the Alari family as well as she knew her own. She took her job seriously and was well paid because the Alaris trusted her to look after the house responsibly all the time, occupied or not.

'Too fucking bad. I'm on holiday.'

Cormac felt very uncomfortable and was about to comment when Maria beat him to it.

She wagged her finger at Rebekah.

'You don't talk bad language like that in front of me, girl. Now you get in that house and make that call. You're one bad-mouthed bad girl. And you be polite, mind.'

It was all Cormac could do to keep a straight face, especially when Rebekah turned on her heel and obediently headed for the phone.

Maria looked at Cormac and raised her eyes to the sky.

'That is one gorgeous child, and I do love her like my own, but she sure as hell needs her hide tanned. Mr and Mrs Alari ain't done that girl no favours by spoiling her so bad. All the money and none of the time, you know?'

Cormac wandered through the house and out to the poolside where Rebekah was stretched out with the phone to her ear.

'I can't go to fucking Milan, I'm on holiday . . .'

He couldn't hear what was being said the other end but it went on for a long time.

'Well, how am I going to get there?' He noticed a slight change in her tone. 'OK, OK, call me back when it's arranged and I'll go, but it's fucking inconvenient.'

She slammed the phone down and looked at Cormac.

'I've got to go to Milan tonight. I'm on the runway for Jose, jet lag and all. I'm getting pissed with this game.'

He wanted to scream and shout. The young man was desperate to succeed, he did everything possible, and if anyone said jump he asked how high, but he was still only on the periphery, still taking anything and everything to make a living. Clients rarely asked for him although they sometimes accepted him if offered. Rebekah, however, was being handed it on a plate and was complaining about it!

'You should be grateful they want you. They certainly don't want me.' He said it lightly but he meant it.

'Well, you go then. They probably wouldn't notice the difference. We're all just mobile dummies to them, anyway.' She looked
at him and relented. 'You're right, darling, I shall go and be
gracious, take the money and run . . . Do you want to stay here
until I come back? I'll only be a few days. Maria will look after
you. She thinks you're wonderful, in fact she fancies you for
herself, she said so!'

He laughed, the tension dissolved as it always did with Rebekah
if you were strong enough to ride out the storm.

'No way! What about your parents? I think your mother would
call the riot police if she found a black man on her property,
unless, of course, he was in chains, picking cotton. Can't I come to
Milan with you? I'd love to get the feel of a big show.'

Without answering she picked up the phone and dialled Sue's
number. 'Rebekah here. Make that two flights to Milan, will you,
sweetie pops? Oh, and could you book a double room somewhere
really super? I'm bringing a gorgeous guy with me, a real hottie.
You'll love him.'

She smiled mischievously at Cormac as she held the phone away
from her ear before Sue predictably kicked off. 'One, two, three,
go,' she whispered. She wasn't disappointed.

Cormac couldn't help but laugh with her.

Rebekah Alari went down a bomb and made it into all the papers.
There were photos of her on the catwalk strutting her stuff in one
of the most outrageous outfits in the collection, along with shots
of her at the party afterwards. The photo of her on the catwalk
with the headline 'The New Pretender to the Catwalk Crown' was
the one Sue gave pride of place to.

Rebekah preferred the front-page tabloid shot of her and
Cormac leaving the end-of-show party, arms wrapped round each
other and heads close together: 'Rebekah and Fellah, It Looks
Like Love'.

She waited eagerly for the call from her mother. She didn't have
to wait long.

'Darling, I saw you in the papers today. Who was that young
man you were with?'

'Which young man, Mummy?'

She had only been back in her London apartment a couple of
hours before the call came. Rebekah was disappointed Cormac
had had to go straight on to a catalogue shoot and wasn't there to
share the fun with her.

'The one on the front page of the newspaper, darling.'

Rebekah could sense the restrained impatience.

'Which one was that?'

'You know which one, darling.'

'No I don't; there's been just so many photos of me I've lost track.' She was smiling to herself now.

'The black man, darling, the black man you were wrapped around.'

One up to me, Rebekah thought. I've made her say it.

'Oh, you mean Cormac, isn't he just divine? He's my new hot date. Would you like to meet him, Mummy . . .?'

Barely an hour after she'd put the phone down on her spluttering mother there was a ring on the apartment intercom.

'Yes?'

'It's me – Lewis. Can I come up?'

'Is this a social visit or a second-hand bollocking from Mummy and Daddy?' Rebekah asked as soon as Lewis appeared at the door.

'You've really done it this time, Beka. Mum was on the phone to me in tears and Dad is furious because he's the one in the firing line. I knew you were doing it on purpose . . .'

Lewis wasn't good-looking but there was a wholesomeness about the gentle blond-haired, blue-eyed young man that made women want to mother and care for him and men be his friend. He was completely open and unthreatening, the opposite of his dark and fiery sister. While she revelled in the limelight he always stood back, watching and admiring her self-confidence. He often wished he had more himself.

He looked at his sister now, waiting for the outburst that always came when she was challenged.

'Bullshit, I admit I did enjoy a bit of a wind-up – she's so easy, isn't she? But I really am going out with Cormac and I really like him. The photos weren't a setup even if they were well-timed.' She looked at her brother, carefully watching his face for signs of the laughter that she could always extract from him whatever the circumstance. 'Was she reaching for the smelling salts and pretending to feel faint? Was she saying, "How could my darlin' daughter do this to her mummy and daddy after all we've done for her? . . . Where did we go wrong? . . . We've given her everything . . . Lewis darlin', this is making me ill . . ."?'

He smiled reluctantly. Rebekah was a natural mimic and could take off their mother's regular hysteria attacks perfectly. He just could not be mad with his sister for long and she knew it.

'Something like that. I've been sent to get all the gen. I'm under orders to report back tonight!'

'How's this for a bit of news for her. How do you fancy telling her that Cormac and I have been shagging at the Palm Beach house? Maria's fallen in love with him, she said she wants him. She told me I shouldn't be screwing around with a black man; that was her prerogative!'

'Shit, Beka, have you got a death wish? Mum has already said they'll suspend the trust fund.'

Rebekah laughed and threw herself full length on to the pristine white leather sofa that nearly stretched the length of the room.

'The same old threats. If it goes the usual route they'll increase it and pray that I'll go away somewhere quiet. Last year we got a month wallowing in Barbados because I was naughty. Where do you fancy this time? It's worth at least three months!'

Lewis looked at her seriously. 'Beka, why can't you just get on with your life and stop wasting energy always trying to put one over on them? I know they're not perfect parents, and they do think money is the answer to everything, but deep down they do love us. They're just no good at showing it other than with money. It could be a lot worse, you know. You should read the papers sometimes and get to grips with the real world.'

'And so endeth the lecture for today. How's the Media Studies course going, by the way? Is that media as in communications, or media as in Mr Mediator for Lauren and Joe Alari?'

'You can be such an ungrateful, selfish bitch. Look around you – who paid for this apartment? Who gave you the money to furnish it? Who paid for you to go to drama school when the convent kicked you out? Who's given you everything you ever wanted in life? Mum and Dad, that's who.' He stood up and walked over to her. 'You've got a fucking good career ahead of you that you wouldn't have had without their money behind you. Just forget the crap from the past and look ahead if you want to be happy.'

She stretched a long leather-clad leg out and, quick as a flash, kicked him hard on the knee. 'Arsehole.' She smiled broadly as her foot connected.

'Vicious bitch,' he retorted, rubbing his knee.

'I know, but you love me really, don't you? It's you and me for ever, isn't that what we always used to say?'

'I suppose so, but what am I going to tell Mum and Dad?'

'Just tell them I wasn't in. Tell them I've gone away. That'll cheer them up no end.'

Rebekah was right.

Her mother phoned the next day. 'Daddy and I have been

181

talking and we know you've been working real hard – how would you like to go down to the South of France for the summer? We'll pay, of course, and Lewis can go with you. You could have such fun, darling. All your friends will be there. The nice friends, I mean, not those awful modelling types. We could rent the villa in St Tropez for you from the Sandersons. What do you say . . .?'

Rebekah picked up the phone.

'Lewis? See I told you. We're off to St Tropez for the summer, how about that? Can't wait. Aren't you glad I'm a nasty piece of work?'

She dialled yet another number.

'Cormac, my man! How does the summer in St Tropez with me and Lewis courtesy of Mummy and Daddy grab you?'

Chapter Thirteen

They arrived at the start of the summer, with Rebekah on a high because she had put one over on her parents again, Lewis on a high because he was with Rebekah and Cormac on a high just because he was there.

Overlooking St Tropez, the villa in the hills was magnificent, all pink and white with huge pillars, several terraces, acres of marble and a vast guitar-shaped swimming pool. Even Rebekah was impressed, but feigned nonchalance in front of the open-mouthed Cormac as the Mercedes glided smoothly up to the high walls and waited for a moment for the intricately designed wrought-iron gates to roll back quietly with a life of their own.

Twisting and turning through a scented grove, the gravel drive led up to the extravagant property that was set into the cliffside overlooking the sparkling blue waters of the Côte d'Azur.

Pristine maids were there to welcome them and whisk their luggage away, with lunch swiftly and silently appearing under the white sunshade on the main terrace. Lewis was first on to the terrace, eager to look out across the sea.

'Beka, come and look at this. This is the most amazing view.'

'Fuck the view, Lewis, look at the size of this room. We can have some top-gun parties here . . . The first thing we need to do is check out who's here already and who's due to come. We can have such a ball!'

Cormac and Lewis exchanged glances and raised eyebrows. The two young men got on well but Lewis was wary of getting too friendly, too close. A wave of sympathy washed over him for the likeable young man who was being sucked in by his sister, but who, he knew, might soon be spat out sharply when the next attractive guy appeared. Rebekah had been doing that from about the age of twelve.

'Who owns this place?' Cormac turned to her, totally overwhelmed.

'Oh, he's a friend of Daddy's. Some big cheese in the music industry who's made a fortune ripping off rock stars. Not bad, is it, for a holiday home?' She laughed at the expression on his face. 'And,' she paused for effect, hands on hips, 'do you know they haven't even been here for three years? They've bought a place in the Caribbean, decided St Trop is no longer exclusive enough. Mummy wants Daddy to buy it, but he says the house in Palm Beach has to go first. He can be such a tight-arse sometimes!'

'Hardly rips them off, Beka. Greg Sanderson is an agent and a good one,' Lewis gently reprimanded his sister.

'Show me an agent who isn't out to rip everyone off. Bloody Wondermodels makes a living off my back . . .' she sneered at him.

Cormac couldn't get his head round the place. He thought he'd had a fairly comfortable upbringing with his father a teacher and his mother a social worker. True poverty was something he saw regularly and his parents were wealthy in comparison. His parents had willingly subsidised their only son during his stint at drama school, and now they were encouraging him in his pursuit of a career in modelling. While not completely approving of his direction they supported him in his choice.

But this was something else, he thought as he looked around. Never in his wildest dreams could he have imagined being in a place so ostentatious.

'Do you think you're going to enjoy yourself?' Rebekah asked him quizzically. 'Let's just hope we don't get too many fucking phone calls. Lewis is all right, though; media students aren't that much in demand, are they, darling brother?'

Lewis took no notice.

Cormac hoped there would be calls, lots of them, otherwise his limited cash would soon run out in this playground of the rich and famous. Rebekah had offered to pay his flights to and fro if need be, and he had reluctantly accepted, but only as a loan and only if he really needed it!

He didn't need it. With only three calls for him during the whole summer he went back to London twice.

Sue called Rebekah nearly every day and the girl became a familiar and dreaded face at Nice airport, stamping about, expecting, and most of the time getting, preferential treatment. But on one occasion Rebekah had refused to co-operate with Sue.

'Sue darling, why do I have to fly all the way to London just to sign some silly old contracts? Can't someone bring them out to me? I'll pay for the ticket, of course . . . In fact, I've just had an idea. Why don't you come? You could chill out for a few days. What do you think?'

Sue couldn't bring herself to say exactly what she thought.

'Rebekah sweetheart,' she forced the words out reluctantly, 'it really isn't very practical, is it? If you want this contract you have to sign. I'm sorry, but that's what you're in this business for, isn't it?'

'And if you want me to sign the contract, and I'm sure you do . . . remind me again of your percentage, darling? No, never mind, I remember it now . . . If you want me to sign it then you'll have to bring it.'

As usual Rebekah won.

Slamming noisily around the flat she and Giles shared, Sue tried packing an overnight bag with three days' clothes plus a few. Giles was getting the brunt of her frustration but this time he wasn't quite the soft sounding board she wanted.

'Susie, it's your own fault. You should have called her bluff in the first place. All the girl needs is someone to say no now and again and actually mean it. No one ever seems to try that. Instead you all pussyfoot about her, terrified she'll leave and go to another agency. She shouldn't have that power.'

'But she's our best earner—'

'So? Find another one, one that gives you and me less grief. The agency is called Wondermodels, not Rebekahmodels; she is not the only fish in the sea. The girl is playing at this, she'll give up soon, anyway, when she gets bored and Daddy will buy her a new toy.'

He watched her throwing her clothes all over the bed.

'I get the feeling that even though you're upset with Rebekah you're secretly looking forward to a few days in the South of France.'

She laughed. 'Maybe!'

Sue looked at the man lolling on the end of the bed, hindering more than helping. He had worn well. As a young man he always bordered on the edge of pretty but he had definitely improved with age.

The floppy mousy hair was now close-cropped, with a few flecks of early grey creeping through, and the skinny boyish face that had once been young and smooth now reflected his years of good nature and was etched with laughter lines around his eyes and mouth. With the few extra pounds that he now carried he looked good.

Sue often wondered why it had taken her so long to realise that she loved him deeply.

'You don't mind if I go, do you?'

Giles roared with laughter. 'Of course not, but rather you than me. Three days with Rebekah and friends will be like six weeks in playschool. You'll have to be Miss!'

She threw a shoe at him.

'I suppose it could have been worse; she could have been digging in her heels in Newcastle. At least St Tropez will be hot. I can top up my tan for the wedding!'

Rebekah had pushed her luck too far and Sue was incensed although she was at pains not to let it show. Arriving at the villa after a three-hour flight delay she found out they were all actually leaving for London the next week anyway.

'Didn't I mention that? God, I'm sorry, Susie, I just never thought. It could have waited until I got back, could it? Sorry, sorry, do you forgive me?'

No I fucking well don't. You've made a fool out of me once again. I want to slap your smug little face and kick your arse all the way back to London!

She thought it but didn't say it. Instead, taking a leaf out of Rebekah's book and smiling her brightest innocent smile: 'Don't give it another thought, Beka sweetie. I'm delighted to be here,' she simpered, confusing the girl. 'This is just the most beautiful house. Aren't you just the lucky one to have been able to spend all summer here? The other girls who have been out told me how absolutely divine it is. I was thrilled to get the chance to savour it for myself.'

Spoilt, ignorant, bad-mannered, devious little bitch, she thought. Boiling in oil would be too good for you . . . Sue carried on smiling as she thought dark thoughts; it made her feel better.

'You've met my brother, Lewis, haven't you? He's my best, best friend, and this is Cormac, my man of the moment. He's a struggling model at Essence. Isn't he the most beautiful thing on two legs?'

While Lewis just nodded and smiled amiably, hands in pockets, Cormac loped gracefully across the terrace, his hair bouncing sexily, and held his hand out to Sue. His black skin, clothed only in a pair of ragged old denim shorts, was shiny with sweat emphasising the six-pack stomach and rippling biceps.

'Pleased to meet you. I hope you had a good flight. The traffic is a nightmare from Nice, isn't it?' He shook her hand firmly and smiled. 'Can I get you a cold drink?'

A light bulb went on in Sue's brain as she subtly looked Cormac up and down. This delectable young man has got it, she thought. With a little training, who knows? He could replace Rebekah in the earning stakes . . . He's got manners as well and, fingers crossed, not a multimillionaire overindulgent father!

'I'd love an ice-cold anything, and then we must talk. You may be just the person I'm looking for.'

'Mac, I am getting totally pissed off with you. You're spending more time with that old woman than you are with me and we've only got a few days left.'

Cormac turned round to see Rebekah in the doorway, wearing her sulky face again. She could be so unbearable sometimes but he was besotted, and when she walked towards him wearing nothing but a shiny silver thong, and trailing a matching sarong in one hand, he just couldn't keep his hands off her . . . and she knew it!

Deliberately putting on her model walk she swayed over to him, her hair casually piled high on her head, caught up with a clip and kept in place with sunglasses pushed back. She moved close enough for her naked breasts lightly to touch his arm.

One glimpse of her glistening sun-oiled body and he was reduced to a gibbering idiot. He reached out to touch her but she nimbly moved out of reach, her catlike smile spiteful.

'Go and screw the old woman instead,' she whispered as she swept out of the room.

Sue couldn't hear what was being said but she could see it all through the tinted glass of the expansive wall-to-wall terrace windows: Cormac's devoted gaze and Rebekah's tormenting of the guy. Sue wanted to shake the silly boy.

In the two days she was there Rebekah had been on top form: Susie darling, let me show you where to have fun. You do remember fun, don't you? . . . Susie darling, let's charter a cruiser for the day. We can watch the plebs with no money down in the harbour gawping at us in envy . . . Susie darling, shall we do Cannes? . . .

Susie darling, this . . . Susie darling, that . . . It took all of Sue's willpower to keep her hands off the girl's throat and shout: Don't fucking call me Susie darling . . . But she kept her cool with effort; no way was the girl going to know how much she was getting up her nose!

Looking around the villa when she'd first arrived she'd been horrified that three youngsters had been given the run of a multimillion-pound house with no supervision.

187

'This is a beautiful house, how come you three are here on your own?'

Rebekah laughed. 'Mummy rented it for us to get me out of town and away from Cormac. She is just so racist, she went absolutely apeshit when she found out he's here with us. It was just such a hoot!'

'I'm sure it was, Rebekah; I'm sure it was a hoot. Golly gosh, I wish I could have pulled a stunt like that when I was nineteen. Imagine being able to get a good . . .' she paused and looked all around her, 'I don't know, probably fifty grand out of the jolly old parents without lifting a finger, and then putting one over on them to boot. What a jape!'

Rebekah laughed long and loud.

Such was the girl's arrogance she didn't even pick up on the sarcasm but Lewis and Cormac did. Both had the good grace to look uncomfortable.

Sue had decided there and then that she would try to sign Cormac. It wasn't good to have all your eggs in one basket. After spending time talking to him she knew the boy had potential and was hungry to succeed. Rebekah Alari had taught her that one without the other was a waste of time.

Now, ready to climb in the Mercedes waiting to take her back to the airport, Sue smiled at Cormac, who was holding the door open for her.

'Don't forget, come and see me as soon as you get back and bring your book with you. I'm sure we can sort out something beneficial for both of us.' She kissed him on both cheeks and held both his hands in hers a fraction longer than was necessary, just to irritate the sullen Rebekah.

Having shaken hands with Lewis, Sue then turned her attention to the girl.

'I want you in my office at ten o'clock on the dot next Monday. We have to talk. Giles will be there as well. I've phoned and arranged it already.'

Rebekah smiled. 'Sorry, darling, no can do. I'll be too knackered. I'll try and pop in later in the week when I've got a free moment—'

She was sharply interrupted. 'Oh yes you can do, darling, and you will do, because if you're not there ready and waiting on the dot of ten you're out of my agency for good, off the books, and there isn't another decent one that will touch you with a bargepole with your track record. BE THERE!'

Quickly getting into the car, she slammed the door and, as the car purred off down the drive, she glanced back to see Rebekah's expression.

Laughing so much as she related it to Giles, Sue could hardly get the words out.

'Sweetie, she was totally gobsmacked. That's the only word for it, gobsmacked. Mind you, I felt sorry for the lads. Their lives wouldn't have been worth living!'

Much to everyone's surprise Rebekah turned up, suitably apologetic and promising to behave herself from then on.

'See, Susie? Just be firm with the girl. She'll come out OK. After all, she's still only a kid really. Now give me all the gen on this Cormac before he comes in,' Giles said afterwards.

Unfortunately they weren't privy to the conversation Rebekah had with her parents.

'Daddy, it was just so unfair, you should have heard her.' She turned to her brother. 'Tell him, Lewis, tell him – wasn't she really rude to me in front of everyone? She is just so jealous of me.' She glanced slyly in her father's direction. 'And, of course, she's jealous of you, you're a rich and important businessman.'

'I wouldn't say she was exactly rude, Beka.' Lewis was trying to tread the fine line as always. 'Severe is more like it, but, be fair, you had upset her.'

Glaring at him for not fully supporting her Rebekah turned back to her parents. 'She was rude, fucking rude.'

Lauren Alari paled. 'Darlin', you mustn't speak like that in front of Mummy and Daddy. It's not polite.'

Rebekah looked down at her feet to hide the smile playing on her lips. 'I'm sorry, Mummy, but it was just so humiliating, you can't imagine. I want Daddy to do something about it.'

Sue had nearly been right. Rebekah *had* been gobsmacked, but only for a moment. Then she decided to pay Sue back, and started plotting and planning. She also decided that surprise was the best form of attack so for the moment she would play the game, be co-operative and compliant, wait until Sue thought it was all OK and then . . . WHAM . . . she'd hit her right where it hurt.

'Exactly what do you want me to do, precious?' Joe Alari asked.

'I want to use my trust fund to set up my own agency, the biggest and best. I want Wondermodels out of business. Why should that ignorant bitch make a penny out of me?'

Joe Alari was impressed with his daughter: that was the language he understood, the sort of initiative he admired. He hadn't got where he was without being ruthless. The high hopes he'd had for his son had quickly dissolved when he discovered the boy had the impetus of a snail. No way could he ever follow in his father's footsteps, he just didn't have the killer instinct.

But Rebekah? Suddenly he saw a potential heir to his business throne. The girl could be the epitome of charm or vicious and vindictive. She also worshipped on the altar of the god of big money: she had all the qualities he admired.

'But, honey,' her mother interjected, 'you can't have that until you're twenty-one.'

'I can if Daddy agrees, and you will, won't you?' She gazed at her father, the loving gaze she had perfected that always without fail got her what she wanted.

At five years old she would sit on his lap and gaze at him, her big brown eyes looking unwaveringly straight into his. At ten she would snuggle up close and gaze at him. Now she only had to gaze across the room in total adoration to get anything she wanted.

Joe Alari looked from one to the other.

'Mummy is right, sweetheart, but I'll do a deal with you. We'll be partners. I won't interfere, I'll get you a business consultant and I'll fund you until you're twenty-one. Then I'll hand over to you hook, line and sinker and it will be all yours, my darling. How does that sound?'

Rebekah had won. She didn't really want her trust fund anyway; she much preferred spending her father's money.

'That's wonderful, Daddy. I love you so much.' She scooted over dramatically and gave him a hug and an exaggerated kiss on the cheek.

'Come on, Lewis, we've got a lot to do.'

'Count me out. I have to get back to college, sorry.'

'Fuck college, Lewis, you're coming in with me. I need you.'

Joe Alari suddenly saw a flaw in the plan.

'Darling, Lewis is right, he has to get back to college. This is his career you're talking about. We'll do this between us, don't worry. When Lewis finishes college we'll see.'

Lewis wanted to laugh. More perceptive than Rebekah, he knew his father didn't want him, didn't want him to be part of it, which he didn't want himself anyway. As far as he was concerned the whole thing stank, but he wouldn't say anything. He never did.

'You go to Wondermodels and we're finished. You can just fuck off for good. I don't want you there. Read my lips; I don't want you at Wondermodels.'

Cormac didn't understand. He thought she would have been pleased – assignments together, more time together. He had yet truly to understand Rebekah.

190

Lewis did and thought he could read the signs. Cormac had been used, the summer fun was over, there wasn't a lot of mileage left now the parents had been suitably shocked, so it was on to the next one.

'Why not? Just give me a straight answer. Tell me why not. You have to tell me—'

'I don't have to tell you anything, arsehole.'

Cormac suddenly reached his point of no return. One insult too many had been hurled his way.

'Let me tell you something instead then, Lady Rebekah. You can fuck off, not me. YOU. I've had it with you, you obnoxious cow. I'm going to Wondermodels and I'm going to make it on my own, not courtesy of Daddy's bankroll—'

Lewis interrupted him. 'That's not fair—'

Cormac turned to him, his face showing the pain behind the anger.

'Shut up, you wimp. You're nothing more than a devoted pet poodle. I've seen more backbone in a bar of soap. You two are the perfect match, do you know that? She shouts, you jump. Jesus, it's almost incestuous. The only thing you don't do together is shag – or not that I know of, anyway. I'm out of here. I'm not into threesomes!'

Jumping up out of the chair, he kicked the coffee table out of the way and was across the room in a few long paces. The slam of the sitting-room door was followed shortly by the crash of the front door.

Cormac had gone and he had no intention of going back.

They looked at each other in amazement, then Rebekah started to laugh long and loud, completely unaware that Lewis wasn't joining in.

He suddenly wondered if everyone saw them like that.

'Giles, I'm really worried. That new agency, The Two As, is poaching a lot of our models. Suddenly they're all finding legitimate ways out of their contracts, or at least the cash to buy their way out. Are you sure you don't know who's behind it? The fellow fronting it has as much knowledge of the modelling business as the newsagent on the corner, but the money must be coming from somewhere. They're spending a fortune pulling everyone away. We're in trouble.'

'I really can't find out. I've tried but I always pull a blank. I think it's a big business trying to get in on the act undercover.'

Sue was frowning, her attractive and open face for once wearing a very worried expression. She didn't understand it.

Now she and Giles were full working partners all their livelihood was tied up in the business. She knew they were hardly on
the breadline but their house in Docklands was nearly completed
and there was no way back out of the purchase now, and to cap it
their wedding was imminent.

But just as their outgoings were increasing their income was
decreasing slowly and surely. The steady drip, drip, drip of models
and bookers leaving for The Two As was draining their finances
and, more importantly, their reputation.

Giles was more optimistic than Sue.

'At least we've still got Rebekah and Cormac, although they're
the only two "names" left. They earn more than all the others
between them. That guy was a find, you know. I can't understand
why Essence didn't do more with him, he's a dream. Mind you,
even Rebekah is behaving well now.'

'Yeah, right! So long as she and Cormac are kept apart. Why does
the bitch have to fight with everyone?' Sue laughed humourlessly.

Giles pecked her on the cheek affectionately. 'Perhaps this is all
just a hiccup. We've had a good run, we'll just have to ride out the
storm. Meanwhile, the wedding – is it all going to plan?'

Sue and Giles were getting married in a little over two weeks
and everything was set. They were flying out with a small group of
family and friends to Florida for the wedding on the West Coast
and then staying on for a brief honeymoon. There was going to be
a huge celebration bash for all-comers when they returned.

'Yes, I think so. Flights are booked. Angie and co are flying with
us and the children into Miami and a limo will meet us at the
airport and drive us to Captiva Island. The rest are following the
next day into Fort Myers and they're picking up hire cars.'

'Did the resort confirm? Any hiccup there and we're in bother.
It'll be too late when we get there.'

'God, you are such a panic artist! All OK. A luxury apartment
for us, accommodation for fourteen adults and three children and
the wedding package. I've left the lot to them, now all we need are
our clothes and ourselves.'

'Sounds good to me. Let's just enjoy our wedding and worry
about The Two As when we get back. The girls are going to hold
the fort, we'll sort it out after the honeymoon!' He smiled at her.
'Don't worry, be happy!' He put on a silly voice. 'That's my motto!
We've waited too long for this to let it get spoilt.'

They stood up and fell into each other's arms, oblivious to the
audience of staff looking through the clear glass door.

★ ★ ★

'I now pronounce you man and wife.' The officiator smiled at them both and then looked at Giles. 'You may kiss the bride.' They stood under the raised flower-covered arbour in the middle of the pristine lawns as the sun set over the Gulf of Mexico and kissed slowly. The timing was perfect. Several dolphins even chose that moment to leap out of the water as if on cue.

It had all gone according to plan. The romantic hotel resort that nestled at the top end of Captiva Island did the wedding party proud with their attention to detail so all everyone had to do was be there dressed and ready. And ready they were.

Sue and Giles had both chosen white: Sue a floaty romantic strapless creation that fluttered around her ankles in the gentle sea breezes that wafted the scent of the real flowers in her highlighted hair. Giles was very naval in his white suit and shirt, contrasting with a loud flowery tie bought in the island boutique that morning. They both looked deliriously happy.

Following the family kisses and hugs they walked over to where Angie and Dave were sitting, with Joshua wriggling furiously on his mother's lap. Angie smiled up at them.

'Congratulations. This was a wonderful idea, it is just so romantic . . . how did you find it?'

'We like this coast, and last time we were here we rented a house on the island and decided this would be it when we did get married and here we are!'

Sue leaned forward and lifted Joshua up. 'Hello, little man.' She looked at Angie. 'With luck he'll have a companion soon. We're going to start trying right away . . .'

Dave feigned shock. 'What here? Now? Not in front of my Joshua, surely.' He looked at his son. 'Joshua, avert your eyes, young man. You're not old enough for all of this.'

They all laughed; even Joshua joined in, giggling happily without knowing why.

'Do you know,' Sue was close to tears, 'this is the happiest day of my life and I'm just so pleased you're here with me, Angie. You've always been a special friend, truly special. We'll always be friends, won't we?'

'Of course we will, and you've done far more for me than I can ever repay you for – more than you'll ever know.'

'No tears now, girls,' Giles interrupted, 'today is a happy day.'

'But we are happy,' they chorused in sync. 'That's why we're crying!'

Dave had learnt by now that it was a waste of time mentioning marriage to Angie. They were happy, they had Joshua, he was grateful for that. He hoped one day she would relent. He would just have to bide his time.

They celebrated till dawn in the restaurant overlooking the sea that twinkled with the lights of the passing fishing boats and superyachts. Everyone agreed the wedding was a great success. The guests stayed for a few days before heading back home, leaving the happy couple to enjoy some time on their own for their honeymoon.

'I love you, Mrs Boughton-Jones, I really love you. We're going to have a wonderful life together . . .'

'I know! We're going to have lots of babies and live happily ever after.'

They looked into each other's eyes and wondered again why it had taken them so long to find each other.

They were walking along the beach, holding hands and watching the sun rise as the pelicans swooped down into the clear motionless sea for their breakfast.

'It's so perfect, I've never been so happy.' Sue looked out across the white sands towards the sea. 'It's so peaceful here – no phone calls, no models, no make-up and no clothes . . . well, nearly no clothes!'

Giles bent down and picked up a small, perfectly formed shiny shell. He handed it to her. 'A present for you.'

She laughed as she took it. 'I shall treasure it always, a reminder of the last day of a perfect honeymoon!'

The newlyweds arrived back in England to the cold and damp, traffic jams on the M25 and jetlag.

Giles ceremoniously carried Sue over the threshold of the flat, although she insisted he would have to do it again when they moved into their new house. There was a mound of post that the cleaner had piled neatly on the table, awaiting their return, and the answerphone was flashing furiously.

Giles went to press the button but Sue stopped him.

'Not a chance, sweetie. We don't start work again until tomorrow. Today is still honeymoon.'

They walked arm in arm into the bedroom, smiling at each other, but were both fast asleep as soon as their heads hit the pillow.

'Come on, Sue, we really must get up now, first day back. There'll be all manner of problems waiting for us. I'll put the kettle on, you can cook the toast! God, Captiva seems a lifetime away already. No more pancakes and bagels, cookies and ice cream, no key lime pie . . . just toast and marmalade!'

Giles kissed her lightly and went into the kitchen.

Opening the post with one hand, he pressed the answering machine with the other, listening at the same time as opening envelopes and drinking tea and trying to sort the relevant from the purely social. The messages ran through but the last one got his full attention.

He stopped what he was doing and rewound to make sure he had heard right. He had.

'Sue,' he called urgently, 'I think you'd better come and listen to this.'

She came through and he turned it on again.

'Hello, Susie sweetie, Giles darling, it's Rebekah here. Hope you had a lovely, lovely wedding and that you have a lovely, lovely marriage. NOT. Shame you won't have a business now, though. The Two As, The Two Alaris, father and daughter – between us we've fucked you, cleaned you out. We have left you all your has-beens – oh, and you've still got Cormac. I wouldn't touch that dickhead with a barge pole. Bye, sweeties, enjoy the rest of your honeymoon. Good luck with finding gainful employment. Kissey, kissey, kissey.'

Sue was incensed. Her beloved business that she had started from scratch ruined by an overindulged child and her rich father. She shouted, she swore and then she sobbed until she was cried out, her face bloated and her eyes mere slits in her face.

'She doesn't really mean it, does she? Tell me she doesn't mean it . . . the bitch . . .'

A few phone calls confirmed that she did mean it. The Two As had bought, bribed and blackmailed everyone worth having with offers they couldn't resist.

Giles was at a loss. He'd never seen Sue like that ever – sunny Sue, who rose above everything and smiled, never vindictive and always happy.

He phoned Angie for help and for once Angie assumed the driving seat. Sue had pulled her through everything that had happened to her. Now it was her turn to be strong for her friend.

'Right, let's be rational. We'll sort out a game plan to get the business back. Don't worry, we'll thing of something. First things first, is it all true?'

'YES,' Sue and Giles answered in unison.

'Can you afford to bribe them all back?'

195

'NO.'

This time it was Angie with her fingers crossed behind her back. This was going to be one losing battle, she could sense it.

'Would you like me to take out a contract on Rebekah Alari? Pay someone to shave her head and force-feed her until she's fat?'

Sue managed her first watery smile since the message.

'Angie, can't you write a really poisonous feature on her and spread it all over the Sunday supplements? That might make her think again . . .'

Angie looked apologetic. 'I'm flattered but I think you overestimate my power. No one would touch anything dubious about Rebekah at the moment. She's the golden girl and her father is too powerful. But give it time . . . a little bit further up the tree and they'll all be fighting to push her off. I know that's not a lot of help at the moment, though . . .'

'Too right it's not, but thanks for coming to our support. We do appreciate it!'

Angie felt completely helpless. Just as her star was shining bright, Sue was in the depths of despair and there was nothing anyone could do except be supportive.

Chapter Fourteen

1995

Rebekah was bored and that meant she was hanging around
Lewis. He adored his sister – always had and always would – but
now she irritated him a lot of the time.

'Lewis darling, leave all that and let's do lunch.' The little girl
voice that all her life had got her what she wanted was in full
swing. 'Those out there' – she waved a hand dismissively towards
the door – 'they're paid for that . . . please?'

'Beka, I'm sorry but no. There must be friends you can ask,
people like yourself with fuck all to do all day. I'm working and I
still want to prove myself to Dad. He's sure I'll screw up.'

Petulantly beautiful she moved to perch carefully on the corner
of his desk, the skin-tight jeans tucked neatly down her cowboy
boots allowing little room for movement.

'And prove yourself to me, honeybun. This is my business, in
case you've forgotten.'

His eyes narrowed as he looked up for the first time since she'd
come into the office.

'Then you come and sit in this desk and work eighteen hours a
day, seven days a week, and I can do lunch . . . do dinner . . . piss
around all night with airheads and cokeheads, and fuck off to
New York in some silly bastard's Lear jet at the drop of a hat . . .
how about that?'

'God, you are just so not funny and so very boring now . . . OK
then, I'll find someone else who's up for it. There's plenty who
would drop everything for me, the lovely Cormac included. Yes,
that's who I'll phone, your precious superboy model.'

'Jesus, Beka, why can't you leave the poor guy alone? You don't
really want him, you're just proving that you can whistle him up
any time you fancy.'

She smiled and blew him a kiss. 'I know, and he comes every time, in more ways than one! Bye, little brother, don't work too hard!'

Despite everything he smiled affectionately as she wafted out of the door and theatrically waved to him with her mobile phone already clamped to her head.

The Two As was now the most successful agency in town but no thanks to Rebekah.

After about a year of struggling and losing money hand over fist, Sue and Giles had admitted defeat; they knew they didn't stand much chance against the Alari millions. But as soon as Rebekah heard that she lost interest in the business. Aim achieved, vengeance wrought, satisfaction gained, suddenly it was no fun playing any more.

Lewis had helped Rebekah behind the scenes in the beginning and when she copped out he carried on and was now running The Two As by default. Joe had no input. He had bought his darling daughter a new toy and it was up to her what she did with it.

Rebekah also didn't give a damn about her own modelling any more. She was a full-time It girl and discovered that was loads more fun than actually working. Better still, she had brought Cormac back to heel when Wondermodels hit the wall.

Meanwhile Sue and Giles were in the middle of another crisis.

'Giles, what are we going to do? I can't believe this has happened to us. It's not bloody fair, nothing has worked out since we got married. Maybe that bastard ex-wife of yours has put a hex on us, or even that Daughter of Satan Rebekah Alari.'

There were no tears, Sue was too distraught even for that. Giles was at a loss. He was upset but his pain wasn't as great; he had two children.

The loss of the agency had been almost forgotten, so completely overshadowed had it been by three miscarriages, followed by a barrage of tests the results of which Sue and Giles had just received, three years after their wedding.

The news wasn't good although not completely hopeless, but Sue couldn't be convinced.

'Susie sweetheart, I just don't know what to say. We can keep trying. Maybe next time?'

'Don't be so fucking thick, Giles. I'm thirty-seven with fibroids the size of fucking grapefruits and they're talking hysterectomy. What next time are you talking about exactly?'

'It wasn't definite – the hysterectomy, I mean. Just agree to go into hospital and let them have a look. There may be a way round it – they said that, didn't they? That's their job, let them do it.'

'It's just so stupid. Angie didn't want to get pregnant and did it without even trying, but me? Oh, I know I can get pregnant easily enough but can I stay pregnant? Not a chance. Just take a good look at me, Giles. No job, no baby, I don't know why you stay with me. I'm a failure.'

'You're not a failure, and I stay with you because I love you. Babies aren't what they're cracked up to be anyway . . .' As soon as the words were out he knew he had said the wrong thing, he hadn't meant it to sound that way. He then proceeded to carry on putting his foot in, compounding his unintentional tactlessness. 'If we'd known this was going to happen it would have been worth putting up more of a fight for the agency, but with you wanting to get pregnant and get out anyway . . .' He was floundering and he knew it the moment her hand contacted with his face.

'Insensitive arsehole. I'm going to bed but don't think you're following me. You're in the spare room!'

Giles had found no problem getting a good job in a city bank again after Wondermodels, and had quickly settled back into the old routine, but Sue had gone to pieces. Angry and bitter she had thrown all her energies into the new house and trying to get pregnant. She discovered it wasn't as simple as she thought.

Wondermodels was quickly sidelined in the obsession that took over her life. She wanted a baby then and she continued to want a baby. Now more than ever. Each miscarriage pushed her nearer and nearer to the edge.

Lewis had felt a distinct twinge of guilt when he heard that Wondermodels had shut up shop. He hadn't approved of what Rebekah was doing but as always she had worn him down and he had been sucked into it. But now that she had dropped out he found he was enjoying the challenge, the chance to prove himself to the great Joe Alari, the business superhero of the Western World . . . and completely useless father figure.

Although pleased that he had been given the chance he was paranoid that his father would find out about his secret life, the life that no one, not even his sister, knew about.

After Cormac had shouted at him and virtually accused him of sleeping with his own sister, Lewis had wanted to rush out after him. He wanted to stop him in his tracks and say, 'You've got it all wrong, Rebekah is my sister, the only woman I've ever been interested in, but only as my sister. I am gay!'

But he couldn't. He couldn't admit it to anyone because he knew that would be the end of his chance at The Two As if Joe had anything to do with it, and probably the end of his trust fund too. He couldn't even confide in Rebekah. One good row with one or other of the parents and she wouldn't be able to resist throwing it at them.

Joe Alari was as homophobic as his wife was racist and Lewis's secret was a black barman called David. A triple win, David was gay, he was black and he had no money, all the things that Joe and Lauren Alari despised, but Lewis thought he was in love with him.

'Cormac, my man,' Rebekah twittered down the phone, 'how do you fancy lunch? To see and be seen at The Vienna?'

He wanted to say no, he wanted to say, not a chance you're a user, but the words didn't come out. He heard himself say happily, 'Yeah, sure, shall I pick you up en route?' As soon as the words were out he smiled wryly to himself.

'She who must not be thwarted', as he and Lewis called her affectionately behind her back, had hated it when he finished with her and had quickly made sure he was reeled back in. Now she picked him up and dropped him as the mood suited her but he was hooked; he was addicted to her as much as the young dropout who slept near his flat was addicted to heroin. When the chance of a fix came along he took it although he knew it was dangerous.

The Vienna was packed but Rebekah had prebooked so they were whisked straight to a table near the centre of the restaurant. The 'see and be seen' table.

She marched to the table with Cormac following meekly behind as she looked from side to side, flamboyantly waving and blowing kisses as she passed by the other tables. Everything Rebekah had learnt at drama school and on the catwalk held her in good stead for her performances. She was her own best PR and would probably have made a wonderful actress if she had been motivated.

Cormac was used to it now, but when he'd first started mixing in those circles it amazed him that so many of the 'in' restaurants and nightclubs in London were actually quite dowdy and ordinary. The Vienna was no exception apart from there being a 'face' at every other table.

Rebekah put her elbows on the table and leant forward.

'Cormac darling, you're not cross with me, are you? You've been an eensy bit quiet.'

He smiled. Experience had taught him not to show too much to her.

'Of course I'm not. Why should I be?'

'I just wondered if you were miffed that I went off to New York and then, silly me, forgot to tell you.'

He knew she was lying, that she was jerking him around, but he didn't respond.

She carried on, 'I really did forget, you know. Justin sprung it on me out of the blue so I couldn't say no now, could I?' She was still waiting for a reaction.

'Justin time, so to speak? No, of course you couldn't, I understand that. Did you have a good time?'

'It was absolutely fucking marvellous. His Lear is just the greatest – designer interior, all beige leather and mahogany, and a huge circular bed, no less, black satin and silk, a real love plane.' She looked sideways, slyly watching his face for changes. 'We actually went to do Christmas shopping but I didn't get many presents – well, not for anyone else. I got heaps for me, though, and the scent launch party was just out of this world. EVERY-ONE was there . . . you should have seen it! Top gun!'

He tried to sound casual. 'Are you seeing him again?'

'Christ, no! Well, not for a while, anyway. His wife went ape when she saw the pics in the papers. He's been grounded!' She giggled hysterically. 'Imagine, a forty-year-old superstar being grounded. Mummy and Daddy couldn't even ground me when I was ten!' She ran her manicured fingers up his bare arm and looked him in the eye seductively. 'Do you want to know what else we got up to?'

'Not really, that's your business. We're both single, no commitment, we can both do exactly as we like.'

She glared at him petulantly; he felt pleased with himself. Once upon a time he would have been nigh on hysterical and unable to hide it but now he was learning. He was successful in his own right, he could be cool, calm and collected. It was hard but he could get her at her own game occasionally.

Until, of course, she beckoned seductively. Then all his principles tumbled about him like a house of cards.

Now she looked at him seductively . . . he melted!

'I think it's time we took another holiday, together, just the two of us. No one's at Palm Beach at the moment—'

He banged his hand on the table. 'Not Palm Beach, not St Tropez, not New York, not anywhere courtesy of your parents. If we go anywhere then I pay. I can afford it now and I don't want freebies from anyone, certainly not your parents.'

'Ooooh,' she grinned sarcastically, 'you are just so assertive sometimes, Mr Do It All By Myself! Well, I can afford to go anywhere I like but I can't see the problem with taking what's on offer. Still, if it makes you happy . . . How about that adorable little resort in Barbados? Where we did those mag shots? I know the manager there, he's always good for a discount . . .'

Cormac laughed; he really didn't want to but he couldn't help it and that was the reason he kept going back for more. However much of a bitch Rebekah was to him sometimes, she could always make him laugh in the end.

'Not a chance, I'm not going anywhere where you know "someone" either. How about Mexico? That's hot right now in more ways than one.'

'Done. When are we going?' She pushed her salad around her plate a little more before moving it to one side and lighting a cigarette. 'Come on, when are we going? Tomorrow?' she continued.

'You jest! I've got two shoots before I can get away.'

'Aren't you pissed off yet with all that modelling lark? Being at every bastard's beck and call? I've got my life back now, darling man, and it's just great. I can do whatever I want and wherever I want, even a mile high up in the sky!'

'So could I if I had access to unlimited funds like you, hon, but I have to work. Anyway, I actually enjoy it.' He paused for a second for effect; she had taught him well. 'I know what I forget to tell you. I've got two TV auditions, one for a commercial and another for *The Bill*. How does that grab you? Top gun, eh?'

When she shrugged and stubbed her cigarette out with a flourish he knew she was seething. Mentally he clocked up one to him for a change.

'*The Bill?*' she sneered after a lengthy pause. 'Who wants anything to do with loads of crap? I'd sooner take to the streets and sell my body!'

He smiled. 'You don't have to do that. I can afford it. How much for the afternoon, madame?'

They hurried back to Rebekah's apartment, nearly getting down to it in the back of the black cab. As Cormac kicked the front door closed with the back of his heel she was already ripping his shirt open and fumbling with the buttons on the 501s.

They didn't even make it into the sitting room, let alone the bedroom.

★ ★ ★

Rebekah was still angry. Even an afternoon of frantic sex hadn't cooled her down so she went back to the office, after Cormac had finally left, to vent her anger on her brother.

'How the fuck have you got him television auditions? What about me? I want to be on television. Why can't you get me any auditions?'

'Do you really want me to spell it out for you?' He counted down slowly on his fingers for effect. 'First, you're not on the books any more, you've retired ... so you said. Secondly, I couldn't trust you to turn up or behave, and thirdly, sweetie, your temperamental reputation precedes you so no one would want you anyway. Sorry, but that's the bottom line. You did ask!'

She said nothing, she just sniffed, picked up the water jug from his desk, tipped it clean over his head and walked out.

She wasn't so keen on the new truthful Lewis; she much preferred the old doormat.

Sue had changed completely. As she rattled about in the Docklands house all day with all the time in the world to think, she became introverted and unsociable unless the subject was miscarriages or infertility.

She wouldn't see Angie because Angie had Joshua, and she wouldn't have Emily and Harry there any more than was absolutely essential because they reminded her of what Giles already had and she didn't.

One of the reasons for buying a big house had been for Giles's children to be able to come and stay more often, but it hadn't worked out. They were sidelined by the preparing of a fully decorated and expensively furnished nursery that had become a shrine with a wardrobe full of baby clothes, a cot full of cuddly toys and every possible baby accessory off the shelves of Mothercare.

The glossy fashion magazines were replaced by baby books, pregnancy was Sue's only topic of conversation and the kitchen became a macrobiotic haven, with vitamins and supplements on the dining table where the condiments used to be. Nuts and pulses became the staple diet, along with anything that had the word 'organic' on the label, and Giles was convinced that one more mouthful of sugar-free, salt-free, vitamin-fortified muesli would make him throw up then and there. Nothing passed their lips indoors that wasn't from the health food shop in Kensington which had its own shiny catalogue and delivered to the door.

Giles was convinced Sue was turning into a crank, but she still had the ability to surprise even him, he discovered.

'Susie, this really is going a little bit over the top, don't you think?' he challenged her one evening over dinner.

He had tolerated the majority of her quirky ideas but the thought of a joint visit to an astrologer was too much.

'Darling, Christiana is wonderful. Everyone goes to her, apparently. Just by talking to us she can predict the optimum time for conception to ensure a healthy pregnancy. Miscarriage is all to do with phases of the moon. Christiana says we just timed it wrong, that was why we lost the babies. You just have to come with me, you have to!'

'When are you going back to the hospital?'

She ignored him and continued flicking through the latest book that had arrived by post.

'Susie, you have to go back. This is your health we're talking about. Try the treatment they've suggested. They said they might be able to shrink the fibroids, please give it a try. It might just work and then there's no reason for a pregnancy not to continue—'

'I'm not going back. I'm not going to have them cutting me open and mutilating me. Now are you coming to the astrologer or not?'

'Not unless you agree to go back to the hospital.'

'Forget it . . . Oooh, I know what I did forget to tell you. I was reading an article today about overseas adoption, you know Eastern Europe, China, all those sort of countries. I've asked them to send me the information, what do you think . . .?'

Giles was at a loss to know how to deal with this person he no longer knew. He tried to think of a solution.

Often he stayed out later than he knew he should; it was just too difficult to face going home.

It was on one of these occasions, when he was having a drink with a co-worker in a Soho pub that he saw, across the other side of the room, tucked in an alcove and deep in conversation with a man, Lewis Alari.

Giles found his eyes being drawn to them and after a few drinks he became angry. It was common knowledge that Lewis was now running The Two As, the agency set up by Rebekah to ruin Sue, the agency Rebekah didn't even want now it had served its purpose.

Fired up and ready to go over and have words, he suddenly stopped in his tracks, unable to believe his eyes. Lewis hadn't seen him, but from his vantage point at the bar, and with the help of the mirrors on the wall, Giles could see clear as a bell what was going on.

He watched fascinated as Lewis gently trailed his hand up his companion's leg and slowly touched the bulge in his tight white jeans. His hand rested there for a few seconds before making its way back down to the knee where it stayed until the other man took hold of it. Both men were by then head to head, nearly mouth to mouth, and clasping hands under the table.

Giles moved round to get a closer look at the young black man Lewis was with. He didn't recognise him although for one awful moment he had thought it was Cormac. He smiled to himself. So the great white macho Joe Alari not only had a spiteful little bitch as a daughter he also had a gay son, who was now almost making love to a black man in public.

'Excuse me,' Giles said to his colleague, 'there's someone over there I have to speak to. I shan't be a minute . . .' He made his way across the bar as inconspicuously as possible until he was just a few steps away from the alcove. The two men were deep in their own world, hands entwined and knees touching. Another couple of paces and Giles was beside the table.

'Well, well, well, if it isn't Lewis Alari, the third A who doesn't even warrant a mention. Aren't you going to introduce me to your friend?'

The two men moved apart like scalded cats, but it was too late, Lewis knew he'd been caught out.

Giles laughed. 'On second thoughts, don't bother. I know the score but does the bankrolling Daddy Alari, I wonder.' He turned and walked back across the bar, smiling to himself.

David Orince looked at the man sitting opposite him, the man whose bed he frequently shared.

'Who was that, Jono? Why did he call you Lewis something or other?'

'I don't know.' Lewis shrugged his shoulders and feigned surprise. 'I've never seen him before. He must have mistaken me for someone else.'

'Lewis? Lewis? Wakey, wakey. The lights are on but no one's in . . .' Her singsong voice brought him back.

'Sorry, Beka, it's been a long day. What were you saying?'

She was in his apartment again and he was getting fed up with it. Feeding the cat and watering the plants when he was working away was one thing, letting herself in at any time of the day or night was taking the piss. He had got in from the pub in a state of panic after seeing Giles to find her having a bath!

He had no life of his own; his was inextricably tied with

205

Rebekah's but, again, it was one-way traffic. He didn't have access to her apartment. He was expected to call first, 'just in case I'm *in flagrante*, darling!'

It never occurred to her that he might want a bit of *in flagrante* himself.

'I was just saying again that I fancy doing something on TV. Can you sort me out something? Puleeeese, darling?'

'Oh, grow up, Beka. The little-girl act is getting a bit wearing now. You're twenty fucking two, for Christ's sake.'

'Who rattled your cage tonight then? It's my business, don't forget, and if you can do it for Cormac you can bloody well do it for me. Take note, I can sack you any time I want.'

'Well, sack me then. I really don't give a shit.'

He was worried. Worried because Giles had seen him and worried that word would get back. Then Beka wouldn't need to fire him, Joe would ensure it happened without a doubt – and disown him, and shut down the trust fund . . . It all flashed before him.

'What's Mr Grumpy doing tonight then?'

'Not a lot with you hanging around. Haven't you got another poor sucker to harass?'

She smiled sweetly. 'I thought I'd keep my brother company, unless you'd sooner I left? I will if you want . . .'

Guilt swept over him. Rebekah was good at creating that.

'No, it's OK. I'm sorry, just a bit stressed out, you know. I'll see what I can do about TV, maybe a commercial or something, but I can't promise.'

'Oh, brother dearest, I love you so much.' She flung her arms around his neck and kissed him. She'd won again!

'Did I tell you Cormac and I are off to Mexico for a week all on our own? I'd invite you if I could but he'd just kill me.'

'That's OK, Beka. I've got too much on anyway.'

Lewis wasn't really concentrating. He knew he had to speak to Giles before he went ahead and bought the new studio flat, the secret hideaway where David would live and to which he himself could go backwards and forwards without a soul knowing.

Providing Giles didn't blow the whistle first.

Giles was in a quandary. He wasn't usually malicious but he was feeling quite vindictive. The Alaris had caused him a lot of grief and now he had the weapon to get back at them but couldn't quite bring himself to use it. He would be taking himself down to their level, he thought, fighting with his principles . . . and yet . . .

'Giles, are you listening to me? I went to the homeopath today and you'll never guess what. I explained to him about our problem and he's given me these drops. We both have to take them in herbal tea three times a day. They strengthen the sperm and thicken the womb lining. He sounded really optimistic . . .'

The more Giles listened to Sue the more he wanted to get a sawn-off shotgun and blast the Alari clan into oblivion. At least if Sue still had the agency it would be a distraction from this baby obsession that was getting worse by the minute.

A plan formed in his mind. Blackmail and violence weren't in his nature, but perhaps a little leverage wouldn't go amiss.

'Lewis Alari, please. Tell him it's Giles Boughton-Jones.'

The pause was quite long before he was put through.

'Lewis here. What can I do for you? As if I didn't already know.'

'I think you and I should have a talk. Shall I come to your office or would you prefer somewhere anonymous? Somewhere out of the way where we won't be seen?' The sarcasm was heavy.

'I haven't got anything to say to you—'

'Oh, I think you have, I really do think you have. So now where's it to be, Lewis, office or out?'

Lewis and Giles had met up in a motorway service station, both anonymous businessmen stopping en route for a bite to eat.

They exchanged casual pleasantries, each trying to assess the other like two rival stags about to lock horns.

'OK, I'll go first,' Lewis suddenly said. 'Tell me what you want and let's get it over with. I'm sure you're not here to congratulate me on my choice of partner. So I'm gay, so what?'

'Lewis, I don't care who you're screwing, be it man, beast or the Queen of Sheba, what I do care about, passionately care about, is my wife. The Alaris en masse nailed her to the wall. Rebekah had a stupid little squabble with Sue and you all closed ranks to help the silly girl become even more of a spoilt brat than she already was.'

'You didn't put up much of a fight as I remember rightly—'

'Maybe because I knew the Alari millions were strong competition and it was better to go gracefully than via the bankruptcy courts.'

'It wouldn't have come to that—'

Giles banged his fist on the table making Lewis physically jump.

'Get yourself into the real world, Lewis, the world of mortgages, bills, ex-wives and school fees. Sue and I may be comfortable, but filthy rich? Endless funds? No way.' He leant forward, his face ruddy with controlled anger. 'We were newly married and about to start a family – or so we thought anyway – we had to have security

207

and the Alaris took that away from us. How old are you? Early twenties? And you've never gone without anything in your life.'

Lewis made eye contact for the first time. 'Never gone without financially, I agree, but in other ways? You are far, far better off than me or Beka. I bet you'd never swap your childhood for ours, no matter how many millions went with it. I know she is a high-maintenance drama queen but that's how she was brought up. Tantrums and fighting dirty get you what you want – the Alari code of conduct.'

Giles was intrigued.

'What about you then? Did you stamp your feet and get what you wanted too?'

Sadness passed over the gentle face of the intense young man sitting opposite him.

'No I didn't. I was frightened of my own shadow and quivered and quaked behind Beka whilst she fought for both of us. Emotionally we only had each other. It's still the same now and I love her more than anything else in the world, spoilt brat or not!'

Giles briefly smiled. 'Does she know you're gay?'

'No, she doesn't, not because she would mind but because she wouldn't mind and wouldn't sweep it under the carpet. She would laugh and then she may just announce it.'

'So what's wrong with that? We've close friends with a gay couple who don't hide it, don't announce it, don't do anything, they just are, and they're happy!'

Lewis sneered. 'How the fuck do you know how they just are? What about their parents? Were they happy too? My father, the great Joe Alari, would beat me to a pulp and then he would probably castrate both me and David with his bare hands. My mother would be behind clapping him on. That's how happy they'd be about it.' He paused. 'This is getting a bit like *Little House on the Prairie*. Tell me what you want and get it over with.'

Giles leant back and folded his arms.

'I've done my homework in the last few days and the feedback is that you are The Two As and you're good, despite being young enough to be my son . . . almost. Rebekah has long lost interest. I want you and me to buy her out and then for you and Sue to be joint partners.'

'Or what?'

Giles sighed. 'Or nothing, probably. I'm not sure. I want to back you into a corner and threaten to blow the whistle to Daddy but I don't think I've got it in me to be a low-down, dirty-dealing, muck-raking blackmailer. My name isn't Joe Alari.'

The two men parted back at the door. As they shook hands Lewis smiled.

'I'll give it some thought. It actually sounds like a good idea to me . . . Now Beka . . . that's a whole different ball game.'

Rebekah went berserk, as he had guessed she would.

'What do you mean, you want to buy me out? You've lost the plot, Lewis. I own The Two As and you work for me, period. No question. Go and start your own fucking business.'

'Beka, I might just do that. I do all the work, I run it hook, line and sinker. You don't even want The Two As, you never really did. You couldn't get anyone else to do what I do without being in on it. All I'm asking is that you think about it. You and I both know Dad doesn't give a shit whether you sell or not. It's no different to him buying you that car that sits doing nothing while you swan about in cabs.' He watched her, studying her body language for hints. He knew her so well. 'Just think about it.'

'Not a chance, brother, not a chance.'

'Beka, listen to me and think about it logically. I'm not going to carry on building the agency up without something more than a weekly wage and no name on the headed paper. You don't really want it any more. Be honest, you put one over on Sue and that was it. Sue was good and she and I together could be a good team. Please, Beka, think about it for me – just for me. I can do it if I'm given the chance, I know it!'

Over the next few days they batted back and forth for so long Lewis couldn't remember how many times he'd pleaded with her, but he knew she was weakening.

Finally, at the end of a half-hour argument, Rebekah waved her hands in the air with a dramatic flourish.

'Tell the old woman to apologise to me first . . . and I want TV, preferably *The Bill*!'

Lewis knew he was nearly home and dry. He phoned Giles.

'Are you some sort of lunatic? Are you teetering on the brink of insanity?'

Giles had expected a better reaction from his wife. He was bewildered by her torrent of abuse.

'I don't want The Two As, I don't want Wondermodels, I don't want any fucking agency, all I want is a baby . . . Fucking men, you have no idea, do you?'

She packed her bags and left that night. She turned up on Angie's doorstep. 'I've left Giles. Can I come and stay with you? Please?'

Chapter Fifteen

The change from model to TV actor was easy for Cormac with his dark good looks and drama school training. It was this that had led to the first couple of bit parts but now he was becoming popular with casters and viewers alike, and set to be a hit.

Rebekah didn't like it one little bit. She felt sidelined by both Cormac and Lewis. She wasn't happy, she wasn't the centre of attention.

'I don't understand how you keep getting parts and I don't. I've had drama training, I've been a top model and I'm beautiful, why won't they use me?' Crossing her legs and folding her arms she was back in sulky mode.

Cormac and Lewis looked at each other. Neither wanted to answer her.

'Why not do some more modelling? You've still got a good few years ahead of you if you want to do it. They still want you . . .'

'What and kowtow to you and the old woman? No way. If you really want to work with her that's up to you, but I'm not. I told you that.'

'Well, you can cut off your nose to spite your face if you want but we've got work to do so hop it. The quicker you go and let us sort this contract out, the quicker Cormac will be free to hang on your every word,' Lewis smiled.

'I'm bored. I still want to go to Mexico but your little pet Chihuahua is still too busy.'

'Why don't you go to Palm Beach? Take a couple of girl friends and enjoy one last fling there before it's sold.'

Rebekah's eyes lit up. 'Good idea, brother dear. I might just do that. The olds aren't there, are they?'

'Christ no, I wouldn't wish that on you, would I?'

'Cormac, my man, how about Palm Beach?'

He threw a cushion at her.

The deal over The Two As had gone through far more easily

than either Lewis or Giles could have imagined. Rebekah had backed down on the apology from Sue and signed off without a second thought. Ever the butterfly flitting from flower to flower, to her the agency was history. Palm Beach was on the agenda.

Sue was a completely different matter. She went to Angie's and stayed there, refusing to have anything to do with Giles, and driving Angie and Dave to distraction by lying about the house all day and treating Joshua as if he was her own.

Eventually, in desperation, Angie told Giles to get over there and sort it out or else; the nanny was threatening to leave and the daily was threatening grievous bodily harm with a vacuum cleaner. They had tried tender loving care, they'd tried persuading her to go to the doctor, all to no avail. Now they decided drastic action was called for.

Giles came round and they pointed him in the direction of the sofa and left him to it.

'I'm sorry, Sue, but I told you I was going to buy into the Two As and I have. We've renamed it ABJ models and Lewis is still managing mostly on his own. He could use your help and experience, there's nothing you don't know, and I'm struggling right now . . .'

'Why are you telling me? I don't even want to see you, let alone hear about anything to do with the bastard Alaris. I like it here. Dave and Angie understand me.'

'I'm sure they do, and I know you think I don't, but you're in danger of outstaying your welcome, sweetheart. Please come home – come home and we can try and get through this.'

'I want a baby, I want to get pregnant . . . that's all I want.'

'Well, it's not going to happen while we're on opposite sides of London. I'm not that well-endowed.'

For the first time in months Sue laughed at something he'd said.

Angie heard the laughter from the other side of the door and hoped for the best. Much as she loved Sue dearly and would do anything for her, just now she was only one step away from throttling her.

'I'll think about it, Giles, but I'm not going within a mile of that bloody agency, OK?'

'Whatever you want . . . Just come home. I love you!'

She went home to Giles the next day, adamant that she didn't want to know anything about ABJ, but her curiosity soon got the better of her.

212

Giles had invited Lewis round to supper to try to break the stalemate. He knew Sue would get on with the young man if she really got to know him as a person, not an Alari.

Lewis brought her flowers, kissed her hand and listened sympathetically while she went on about her medical problems. Giles had said a silent prayer of thanks when he realised Angie had persuaded Sue back to a normal diet, and the meal was delicious although she did insist on regaling Lewis with all the details of her gynaecological problems over the salmon.

Inevitably the subject turned to ABJ and although Sue pretended total disinterest, Giles could tell she was taking it all in.

She came to life when Rebekah's name came up.

'How can you even mention that name to me? The grief she's caused—'

'I know.' Lewis took the bull by the horns. 'I know what she did and I know it wasn't a very moral thing to do but Beka is a very complex person. She's been made that way. My father is, as I'm sure you know, a very ruthless businessman and she's been trained to think the way he does. Win at all costs is how we were brought up.'

'You don't seem like that and you were brought up together. Why's she like it and not you?'

'I had the advantage of not being beautiful and clever!'

Sue's questioning was aggressive but Lewis took it seriously and tried to explain about their relationship and their upbringing. She wasn't convinced but she did agree to go into the agency one day and have a look around . . . providing, of course, Rebekah wasn't going to be there.

'You're OK, she's off to the house in Palm Beach for one last fling before my father sells it and decamps to the other coast. They've bought a place in Naples on the Gulf of Mexico, with a boat dock. He now wants a cruiser to go in it.' Lewis laughed good-naturedly. 'See what I mean? Rebekah doesn't stand a chance really!'

Rebekah was in Palm Beach with three other girls from the original Wondermodels. Not close friends – she'd never had a close female friend – but girls she knew well enough to holiday with. Not friends at all in fact, just girls who were more than happy to freeload off Rebekah, whom they didn't even like!

'Beka darling, couldn't we head for Miami for a few days? That's where it's at now. Don't get me wrong, Palm Beach is a dream and we love the house, but it's just so sort of sedate. Come

213

on, we can check out South Beach and the guys, really party . . . What do you say?'

Sasha simpered at Rebekah while Marina and Cathy looked on innocently. Sasha was the one they had voted most likely to talk Rebekah round and they couldn't go without her; she was the one with the platinum card and the limo!

'Is it going to be Miami?'

Rebekah was torn. She didn't like being used but at the same time she enjoyed being magnanimous. She also wasn't totally convinced they wouldn't go without her.

'You're on. Look out, South Beach – and I've got an even better idea. Let's hire a convertible, a real cool tanning machine, and do it in style.'

They booked into a suite in the trendiest hotel in the art deco district of Miami and within five minutes were out cruising. Four beautiful young women in a bright white convertible with the hood down attracted a lot of attention and before the end of the day there were a selection of offers to choose from.

They argued among themselves and wrote them all down; then, giggling hysterically, picked straws. They had all agreed the format for the night: dinner at the trendy Tuxedos on Ocean Drive, followed by a night on the tiles at Shadows, the exclusive night-club. The one thing they couldn't agree on was who with, hence the straws.

Marina won.

'Christ, Marina, those guys were such dorks and so old! I mean, what kind of guy poses in a thong when he's got a paunch like a six-months-pregnant woman?'

'Seriously rich guys, darling, seriously rich.'

Everyone laughed again and even Rebekah joined in.

'I'll suffer it tonight for you, sweetie, but tomorrow I get to choose.'

Marina shook her head gently to settle the dead-straight, platinum hair that may just have had a single hair out of place, and crossed her long pale slender legs.

'Rebekah darling, they may be dorks and they may be old, but they are rich old dorks and up for spending. What more do you really want?'

'A lot, Marina. But for tonight we'll settle on them. Just don't expect me to shag any single one of them; it would be like having sex with your own father, totally gross!'

'It's OK for you, Beka, you can afford to shag the poor, we can't. We have to make choices and if it's a straight choice between a darkly tanned, well-oiled washboard belly with no money and a flabby millionaire then the well-oiled belly can slide away back to where it came from.'

Their laughter echoed out over the balcony.

All beautiful, classy and designer-clad, the four girls looked stunning together and that was all that was needed in Miami to gain entry to the clubs and eateries of the moment. This was the city of beautiful people, and the competition was great, but all four knew the password and intended to use it.

They had arranged to meet the men safely and neutrally in the restaurant.

The Philadelphia four, half of a party of eight, were on a boys golfing holiday, allegedly! They certainly hadn't been on the golf course that day. They'd been posing in their pouches on the beach and pulling Rebekah and her three companions!

The girls were late and the men had just about decided they weren't going to turn up. Heaving a combined sigh of relief, they watched appreciatively the four beautiful and desirable young women climbing out of the car outside. Little did they know it was only by the grace of the straws that they were the chosen few!

Handing the car over to the valet, Rebekah confidently took the lead. As far as she was concerned these men were arseholes and she was along only for the ride.

Rebekah looked at the four men grouped around the large table with the girls. They were all still on small talk, the pros and con of Miami Beach.

Ritchie, Lou, and Ralph, she guessed, were all businessmen – she recognised the manner, the attitude, from her father and his friends – but the fourth man, Dan, seated beside her, was harder to evaluate. He was with them but apart, not as raucous, not as gawping.

'You weren't at the beach today.' Rebekah's tone was accusatory as she looked him up and down.

'That's correct. I was playing golf all day. Something else came up for Charlie, so here I am.'

'Yep, something sure did come up for Charlie,' laughed one of the others, 'his wife! She'd hopped a flight and come to surprise him.'

They all roared but Rebekah could see Dan's laughter didn't quite reach his eyes.

'Are all you bastards married?' A stunned silence fell over the group as Rebekah asked the question in the sweet, smiley way that the other girls knew pre-empted the turning of the knife. They had hoped she might behave for a change.

A solitary voice eventually broke the uncomfortable silence.

'I'm sure as hell not,' Dan spoke softly with a smile.

Three pairs of female eyes were on him instantly but he was looking at Rebekah. Leaning back in her chair and rocking it on two legs, she glanced around the whole restaurant before letting her eyes wander back and rest on him.

'Why not? Do you have a problem we should all know about?' she laughed, and the tension was broken, the conversation restarted.

Intrigued but clever enough to look disinterested and let everyone else do the questioning, she eventually found out that he was Dan Silverman, a plastic surgeon in private practice in Philadelphia, aged forty-two, divorced, three children, addicted to golf.

Sasha, Marina and Cathy each hoped they'd hit the jackpot. Suave and sophisticated, single and a plastic surgeon to boot – what more could a girl want? They were all getting ready to slug it out but sadly Dan only had eyes for Rebekah, and towards the end of the evening she felt herself being drawn irresistibly.

His wavy black hair was cut short and tight against his head, emphasising the lean tanned face, but the decider came when he stood up to his full height and was taller than Rebekah in her heels!

The deep green eyes rarely left her face, and when they danced at the nightclub and he held her lightly but firmly, she could feel the muscular body moving with her and was instantly turned on.

Aware of three pairs of envious eyes boring into her back Rebekah moved closer and Dan's hold tightened slightly. She knew the other girls were furious. They had the rich but lecherous, married merchants; she had the most eligible man in Miami that night.

Old habits die hard and Rebekah left Dan wanting more that night and went back to the hotel with the girls, but the next day she took him back to Palm Beach.

Running up the winding marble stairs past a disapproving Maria, they went to bed and stayed there for two days, fuelled up by alcohol and cocaine.

Dan was a seduction expert and knew exactly what to do. He flattered and fussed her but at the same time took charge. For the first time Rebekah was not in control of the lovemaking.

She was used to men who adored her totally and were so

216

pleased to be with her they let her do whatever she wanted. Dan was different, he was assertive and demanding. When he reached over and poured a glass of chilled champagne she held her hand out for the glass but instead, he gently dribbled it over her naked body, his eyes never moving away from hers for a second.

She shivered ecstatically and decided at that moment that she was in love.

The girls weren't happy when they got back to the house in Palm Beach.

'You're one selfish bitch, Rebekah Alari, just pissing off and leaving us. We had to get a cab back.' Cathy had been voted spokeswoman to tell Rebekah her fortune but she had bitten off more than she could chew. Rebekah just laughed at them!

'Pissing off and leaving you? *You* wanted to go to Miami, *you* wanted a good time and you had it, courtesy of me. Who paid your fucking hotel bill? I did. Who paid for the fucking convertible? I did. Mind you, a pickup truck might have been more appropriate, that's all you wanted to do. Who's fed and watered you for a week? I have. Now piss off back to London and leave me alone . . . freeloaders, the lot of you.'

'It looks to me like you're the one who picked up, not us,' Sasha smiled sweetly, 'and don't forget, you invited us, no doubt because no one else could bring themselves to go on holiday with Lady Alari!'

Rebekah picked up a cut-glass ashtray and threw it in the direction of the girls.

'Arseholes, all of you,' she screamed.

Laughing hysterically they went off to pack.

Dan hadn't uttered a sound during the outburst. He stayed silent until they had left the room.

'Wow, that was some mean attack. I'd best stay on the right side of you, you're one wildcat.'

She laughed. 'You'd better. That was nothing. You should see me when I'm angry!'

Three days later, on the spur of the moment, and high on champagne and cocaine, Rebekah and Dan chartered an executive jet and flew to Las Vegas.

The next day they were married in the Chapel of Love and the ceremony was witnessed by Elvis Presley and Marilyn Monroe lookalikes.

The first thing Rebekah did when she and Dan got back to Palm Beach was to phone Lewis.

'Hi there, brother dear, guess what. I just got married!'

Lewis was stunned. He decided Beka had really gone over the top this time and told her so. She listened for a while, then put the phone down.

She phoned her mother whose questions came in the order she thought of them.

'Is he rich? . . . Is he white?'

She never asked his name and it never occurred to her to ask her daughter if she was in love. A white, wealthy plastic surgeon from Philadelphia was good enough for her to be able to boast to all her friends and hold her head up high.

Rebekah laughed humourlessly as she imagined the Alari phone lines hot with the news.

'Cormac? Lewis here. Look, I'm sorry but I've got some bad news for you. Rebekah got married in Las Vegas yesterday . . . No, I don't really know any details . . . Yes, I know you're upset, so am I. I'll ring you again if I hear any more . . .'

The jungle drums rolled and within hours everyone knew.

Sue phoned Angie at 7 a.m. Angie answered the phone with a voice that was thick with sleep, cursing herself for not putting the answering machine on.

'Angie, you'll never guess what the Daughter of Satan has done now. She's married some American plastic surgeon in Vegas. She's known him less than a week, Lewis told Giles . . .'

'That's nice,' Angie struggled to reply. She was having a lie-in.

'You're not listening to me, are you? He's American, she'll be upping sticks and going to live there, won't she? It's an omen. As soon as she's out of my life things will get better, I just know it. I bet Mummy Alari is over the moon. Her very own plastic surgeon son-in-law. She should be a challenge for him – cut and shut, lift and shift, inflate and deflate – his options are endless, a full-time job in fact . . .'

Angie was making faces at the young child sharing her bed. Dave was away and she had three days off to spend with her beloved Joshua. He had clambered in with her at the crack of dawn and snuggled down beside her in the warm.

Rebekah Alari and her escapades were of no interest to her at that moment but she faked enthusiasm because Sue sounded the closest she had been to her old self in a long time, and nearly back to her witty bitchy best.

'I wonder what possessed her? She normally uses and abuses

218

them and leaves them in her wake . . . I wonder what he's got?' Angie asked the question half-heartedly. She was wide awake now and so was Joshua.

'Obviously soul mates. She would have related to him instantly. He's good with a scalpel, she's good with a knife in the back . . . simply made for each other, a match made in hell!'

Angie was really laughing by now and Joshua joined in.

Sue was in full flow now: 'I've got it. He sees her as a challenge. He's going to open her up and look for a heart.'

'Sue, shut up, that's enough. Listen, do you want to come over this morning? Joshua goes to nursery at ten. We can go shopping for three whole hours. It's been a long time since we did that.'

'Sounds good. We can even fit in a coffee and raise our mugs to the emigration of the black-hearted beast. See you in an hour.'

Thank God for that, Angie thought as she wrestled with her beloved son, who didn't want to get dressed. Sue was stepping back from the abyss, thanks to that silly, silly girl. Now all she had to do was persuade her to go back to the hospital. Angie felt optimistic. Her own life was going so well she really wanted the same for Sue.

Looking at Joshua, with his thick fair hair and innocent wide eyes, she couldn't imagine what it must be like desperately to want a baby and not have one. Neither of hers had been by design, and she wondered again at the irony of life.

Rebekah was in shock. It had seemed such a fun thing to do at the time and so romantic. Dan was gorgeous, they'd had great sex and it had seemed such a good jape, another opportunity to shock the olds, but the drug-free realisation that she was married and expected to go and live in Philadelphia was something else.

She knew that wasn't what she wanted. She wanted to keep her life in London, her easy, flirty lifestyle, partying at night, shopping by day, and jetting off all around the world on a whim. She wanted him with her, not her with him.

'Dan darling, I really can't pack up and move just like that, any more than you can. It's going to take time . . .'

They were back in Palm Beach but were due to fly out the next day and both were still booked on separate flights, she to London, he to Philadelphia, and still arguing about it.

'We're married now, honey. You're my wife and belong with me. I want you with me, not in London. I want to introduce you to my kids. You're their stepmother now . . .'

The statement made her blood run cold. Stepmother? She hadn't even thought of that.

'But they don't live with you, do they?' She couldn't believe she hadn't thought to ask that question earlier on.

'Fifty-fifty. They come over Friday after school and leave Monday morning; weekends are dedicated to my kids, so are the school vacations. You'll just love them, honey, they're great kids.'

Rebekah's mood was sinking by the second.

'How old are they?'

'Here, look, I've got a photo of them in my wallet.' He dug down into his pocket. 'That's Carrie, she's thirteen, Dan junior next to her is ten and the cutie at the front is Abby, she's just six.'

Rebekah looked at the photo in front of her in horror. She hated children!

What had she done? Why hadn't she thought about it? Trying to work her way back through the fug of drink and drugs she vaguely remembered that it had been his idea that they hotfoot it to Vegas and he was the one who had produced the cocaine. Had he used as much as her? She couldn't remember. How much had she told him about herself? She guessed she may well have shouted her mouth off about Mummy and Daddy's millions, the houses, the trust fund . . .

In a single moment of clarity she suddenly made sense of the situation. He was after her money . . .

Cursing her stupidity and realising she had really dug herself into a deep hole this time, she tried to think on her feet. If she could get home then her father would sort it out for her; he always did.

'They are beautiful, Dan darling, and I can't wait to meet them but I have to go to London first. Couldn't you grab a few extra days and come with me?'

'No way. I have appointments booked. I have to get back to my patients. I hate to disagree with you so soon, honey, but I'm sorry, you're coming to Philly with me tomorrow. No argument.'

He smiled at her and, taking both her hands in his, pulled her down towards him. For the first time she saw an edge, a slight veiling of the eyes, and a hint of cruelty in the handsome face. No argument? Who did he think he was?

She smiled sweetly. 'Sorry, Dan, but that's not an option, I'm afraid. I'll go to London and then when you have a window in your busy schedule you can fly over and meet everyone – my parents, my brother, Lewis . . . Then we can arrange a more permanent—'

Mid-sentence she felt a punch in her stomach. The fist had appeared so fast she hadn't seen it coming. Reeling back, she registered his expressionless face.

'Now, my gorgeous bride, I'll just change your flight while you pack. You'll love Philadelphia, I just know it!'

Catching her breath, Rebekah tried not to cry. No man had ever made her cry, apart from her father, and there was no way this one was going to.

'I'll get Maria to help me.'

'I've given her today and tomorrow off. I said goodbye to her for you, though. She told me you needed taking in hand,' he smiled his most charming smile, 'and that's what I'm doing. Now, no more nonsense.'

At that moment Rebekah hated herself for being so stupid.

Trying still to look casual, she turned and went up to her bedroom. She tried the phone but it was dead. Panicking now, she ran in and out of all the rooms trying all the phones but there was nothing: all the receivers were silent.

Mobile, she thought, but then remembering it was downstairs in her handbag she decided the safest thing to do was carry on playing the game. She could raise hell at the airport.

She heard Dan coming up to the bedroom so she started packing.

Lewis had called Cormac into the office to hear the tale from Sasha.

The young woman had the face of an angel and the body of a goddess but when she was excited her accent was pure East End, loud and raucous, and her laugh had everyone putting their hands over their ears and cringing. Right now Sasha was excited.

'I don't think the poor bastard knew what had hit him. She was all over him like a rash from the minute she set eyes on him. He didn't have a chance. But then neither did the rest of us.' She cackled like a manic cockerel. 'Mind you, I never for one second imagined this. I thought he was from the company of Shaggum and Leggit, like the others . . .' She stopped as they looked puzzled. 'Shaggum and Leggit?' she repeated it slowly. 'Oh, for fuck's sake, bonk' em and run – you must have heard of that one?' Looking from one to the other she raised her eyes and her hands in sync and spoke to the wall. 'Men? Who needs 'em?'

'OK, Sasha, cut the gags and get on with it.'

She told them all she knew.

'Oh well,' Cormac sighed, 'that's that. She must have known what she was doing, I suppose. I hope she'll be happy. I just wish it had been me.'

'They'll be back tomorrow, then we'll know more. I would imagine Mum and Dad are killing the fatted calf as we speak. It's

221

quite a coup for them after all her other antics.'

Cormac's expression rapidly changed from hurt to angry.

'Are you saying I was just one of her antics?'

'No, of course not, but you know what the parents are like . . . appearances are all. I'm sorry, I'm as bewildered by all this as you.'

After Cormac had left, Lewis wanted to cry. How could she have done that after everything they'd been through? He couldn't believe it hadn't occurred to her to tell him beforehand, give him the chance to be there with her.

Rebekah didn't have her handbag within reach. It was down by Dan's feet in the footwell. It contained everything she needed – phone, passport, credit cards – it was just a matter of getting it.

'Rebekah, I've phoned my ex-wife and told her to make sure the kids are going to be at the airport to meet us. The nanny will bring them over to pick us up.' He looked at her out of the corner of his eye. 'What's the matter, honey? You're not mad at me, are you, for a little tiny push?'

Rebekah Alari had been to drama school, she had acted up for years, now she decided she would really perform. The bastard would regret that punch. She had decided she wasn't just going to make a scene and get away, she was going to nail him.

'Shit no, honey, I never even felt it, and when I thought about it I knew you were right. A wife's place is with her husband and I really want to meet your kids. If they're anything like their daddy – wow. No, it's just that . . .' she paused, 'I could really use a fix right now. Have you got anything on you?'

'Hell no, we're going through the airport. You dumped yours, didn't you?'

'Of course I did, that's why I was asking you. Never mind, I'll cold turkey. I don't suppose you do anything at home? You know with the kids around?'

He laughed. 'Honey, I do anything I want, just not at the airport!'

They checked the hire car in and then walked on to the concourse. All the cases and her bag were on the porter's trolley that Dan was keeping a close eye on. She guessed he thought that once he got her safely to Philadelphia he would be home and dry.

'I need to use the ladies' room, can I have my bag?'

'No, honey, there's nothing you need—'

'I need my make-up purse. Just look at my face. Suppose someone recognises me? I'd just die! Can you get it for me?'

She held her breath as he fumbled in her bag and handed her the small innocuous black velvet purse.

Kissing him gently on the cheek, she whispered happily, 'Back in a sec, darling.' Then she paused and looked him straight in the eye. 'Whatever did I do to deserve a man like you?'

Make-up my arse, she thought grimly as she locked herself in the cubicle and opened the purse that contained enough cocaine for several parties and a clutch of pre-rolled joints. Taking a cigarette packet out of her pocket, she emptied it into the bin and carefully compacted the coke and joints into the packet before putting it back in her jacket pocket.

Dan was pacing nervously outside, his face grim, as she came out.

'Didn't you say you were going to do your face?'

'You should see the queues in there . . . I couldn't even get near the mirror. I'll have to keep my head down and touch up on the plane!' She hooked her arm through his affectionately and he smiled at her.

'Look after my ciggies, will you? They ruin the line of my jacket.' She smiled widely and kissed him as she slid the pack into his pocket.

As soon as the police officer drew level with them she started screaming, 'Help! Someone help me! I've been kidnapped, help . . .' The screams echoed around the building and as Dan reached out to put his hand across her mouth he was wrestled to the floor.

She looked down at him on the floor and then knelt beside him. 'Right, Dan the Man, no one fucks around with Rebekah Alari and gets away with it,' she whispered.

She thought she could dine out on the story for months. In the end she dropped the kidnap charges – they would have been hard to prove as she and Dan were married – and Daddy would, no doubt, sort the divorce out.

She was happy, though. As she explained to her brother, it was enough for Dan to be charged with possession and struck off. Who wanted a plastic surgeon who was a cokehead?

'Lewis darling, it was just such a hoot. He really thought he could drag me off to Philadelphia, spend all my money on his debts and habits, and get an unpaid babysitter into the bargain. The man was totally barking! The best part is that Mummy really thinks I should have gone with him and become a little wife, crazy old hag!'

Lewis looked at his sister sadly as she made light of the situation.

'You really have to take some responsibility in your life, you know, Beka. You did take a total stranger home with you and you quite happily trotted off to Vegas with him and then married him, for Christ's sake. Now that was barking if anything was.'

'Sweetie, you're so hard on me . . . I got myself out of it, didn't I?'

'Maybe, but with a bit of straight-thinking instead of your usual high drama there could have been a simpler solution. You're lucky you weren't raped or even murdered for your money. He was obviously desperate . . .'

'Oh, do shut up, Lewis. You're like the prophet of doom. I take after Daddy, I'm invincible!'

For all her bravado her brother could see that Rebekah was actually quite shaken up but like a true Alari she couldn't bring herself to admit to weakness, to admit that her error of judgement could have had dire consequences.

Chapter Sixteen

1999

'Cormac darling, come back to bed. I want you NOW.'

The white silk nightdress was short and low cut, and as she stretched herself catlike towards him across the huge wobbly water bed he was sorely tempted.

'I can't, I really can't, I'm late already. I can't disrupt shooting again, I'll get fired.'

Fighting his urge to get back on the bed he continued throwing his clothes on.

Rebekah's voice changed from persuasive to demanding. 'Let them fire you, then. I can keep the both of us. You don't need the goddamned money, fucking male ego . . .'

'It's not male ego, hon, it's personal pride.'

'Personal pride?' she laughed humourlessly. 'It's the same thing, dickhead. I hate you . . .' Jumping back up on the bed, she pulled the sheet over her face.

'And I love you too. I'll see you tonight.'

Cormac pulled the sheet down from her face and kissed her on the mouth quickly before she had a chance to bite his lip, and then covered her up again.

'Bastard,' she shouted at his departing figure. 'I'll find someone else to shag . . .'

Rebekah had taken longer than she cared to admit to get over the incident with Dan. It wasn't what had happened that worried her, it was the fact that she had made a mistake and everyone knew about it, Rebekah Alari had never been wrong, up until then.

Cormac had been very hurt and it had taken a while for her to get round him, and that was really annoying. Good old Cormac usually responded to the whistle immediately.

Eventually he caved in, as he had always known he would, but the relationship was subtly different.

Cormac was more assertive, Rebekah more needy and just a touch insecure.

'Daddy? It's Beka, are you and Mummy at home? I thought I'd come and see you, stop overnight maybe?'

That would teach Cormac, she thought happily; she would be out, make him wonder where she was, reel him in again.

Without leaving a message for him she quickly dressed and left in her new sporty BMW. She had given Cormac the Porsche, threatening to dump it in the Thames if he got on his high horse and refused. He had known that she would without a second thought; sentimentality over belongings was not one of her strong points.

Driving down to Surrey she thought back over the past few years. She would be twenty-six soon; maybe Lewis was right, maybe it was time to pull back and reassess her life. Just lately she was bored. Her life was a nonstop round of lunches, launches, events and shopping. It was getting repetitive. Even half a dozen holidays a year were no longer exciting. There was no doubt that she had enjoyed herself, and Cormac and Lewis were always there to bail her out when she enjoyed herself too much, but there was no substance any more.

She wanted something else and as she gunned the car up to over a hundred, hood down, hair flying, she decided what it was.

Joe and Lauren Alari were at home. Since having a heart attack the previous year, Joe had slowed down and was now making his wife's life a misery by being around her more.

Screaming up the gravel Rebekah swung the car round to a halt outside with a handbrake turn that brought her father out to see what was happening. She ran to the steps and threw herself into his arms.

'Daddy, it's so good to see you, I've missed you . . .'

'And I've missed you too, my precious.' He looked over her shoulder. 'I'm pleased to see you've come on your own. Mummy was worried you might bring that man friend of yours.'

'His name is Cormac and the only reason I haven't brought him is because he's working . . . working hard, I'll have you know, and making pots of money being famous on television. I thought you approved of work?'

Joe Alari was short and chubby, cuddly even at first glance, but could also present himself as quite menacing, his bald shiny pate totally at odds with his black bushy moustache.

He looked at his daughter and raised his eyebrows but made no comment as they walked arm in arm up to the entrance.

'Where's Mummy?' Rebekah wasn't really surprised her mother wasn't there to greet her.

'She's in the pool, doing her laps. You know Mummy – fifty laps a day to keep her figure in shape . . . Doctors said that's what I should do, exercise.' He laughed loud and sarcastically, 'Huh! What do they know! I get all the exercise I need raising a brandy glass to my lips and a phone to my ear! Come on, let's get Gladys to rustle up something to eat while we go and find your mother, then you can tell us why you're here. There always has to be a reason, sweetpea, doesn't there?'

She knew her mother didn't want to see her – ever since the fiasco with Dan she had been cold towards her daughter. Rebekah knew it was because Lauren Alari had been ecstatically happy one minute: 'My daughter's married a rich American plastic surgeon', then mortified a few days later: 'He was a conman'. It was all too much for the woman to whom appearances were everything.

Joe and Rebekah walked together into the poolhouse and sank down on loungers by the edge of the water.

'Is she ever going to come out of that pool?' Rebekah asked her father as they watched the woman furiously swimming back and forth in front of them. 'If she's not out soon I'm going, ignorant old hagbag!'

'Don't you talk about your mother like that.' He spoke the right words but smiled as he said them.

Rebekah pointed to the pool. 'Look, she's surfacing. Call the Norwegians and their harpoons!'

They both laughed, making Lauren feel even more hostile as she saw them together. She stepped out and put on a towelling wrap before taking a seat beside them.

'Well, hello there, honey. I thought you'd forgotten all about your Mummy and Daddy. We have to read about you in the papers nowadays to know what's going on.' She didn't so much smile as bare her beautifully capped teeth.

Rebekah smiled back, equally falsely. 'I wanted to talk to you and Daddy about something . . . Cormac and I are going to get married. We love each other and want to do it properly. You're always telling me to find a nice man and settle down – well, I have found him.'

She waited expectantly for the explosion but none came. Lauren just looked at her in disgust.

'Darlin', if you're expecting to upset us then you'll be disappointed. There's nothing else you can do to trash the name Alari any more than you have done already. Marry the man and take his name then we don't have to go through any more shame, you won't be an Alari.'

Rebekah looked insolently at her father. 'Daddy? What have you got to say? Do you agree with that?'

'I do agree with your mother. Nothing much surprises me any more with you or your no-good fairy brother—'

Rebekah was on her feet in a flash, stamping her designer boot on the mosaic-tiled floor.

'He's not "no good" as you put it. He's a fucking sight better than all three of us put together. He's not been tainted like the rest of us by the bloody Alari money.'

'No? Well he's still quite happy to support himself and his boyfriends with Alari money. I haven't noticed his trust fund winging its way back to me.'

'And why should it? It wasn't set up with the proviso he could only have it if he was straight . . .'

Her father was quietly angry, which Rebekah found harder to deal with than all-out warfare.

'Maybe it should have been . . .' He sighed as he said the words.

Lauren was sitting on the edge of her chair, picking delicately at her nails. She spoke without looking up.

'Bad blood will out, Joe darlin'. I told you, it always does!'

'What the fuck does that mean?' Rebekah looked from one to the other.

Joe spoke quickly. 'Stop swearing, Rebekah. You know what she means. Your mother never really thought I was good enough for her pure American bloodline. Mind you, the money helped ease her into thinking I might just be acceptable.' He spoke to his daughter but his eyes bored into the top of his wife's head, and still she didn't look up. 'You want to marry Cormac, you go ahead. We'll give the biggest and the best, just like we always have, but after that you're on your own. I'm not saving your neck this time when it all goes pear-shaped, which it will.'

'What about Lewis? I want him there.'

Still glaring at his wife Joe answered quietly, 'Of course he'll be there . . . but no boyfriend. That just turns my stomach.'

Rebekah didn't stay the night. There was a tension between her parents that she couldn't quite fathom and, anyway, she wanted to get back to Cormac, to work on him.

When she went to the bathroom she stopped outside the door

and listened, the same way she always had; it was hard to break old habits. Her father's voice was quiet and menacing.

'Don't ever do that to me again or I'll break every bone in your man-made body . . . It's too late now, we agreed.'

Rebekah fleetingly wondered what he was so upset about but she soon forgot it. Now all she had to do was convince Cormac he wanted the full Alari wedding bit.

ABJ agencies were on the up. Sue had never really got back her enthusiasm so Giles returned to it himself, and he and Lewis had revamped, reorganised and dramatically expanded the business. Now they covered everything from modelling to TV and films to showbusiness in their three offices. Business was booming.

As soon as he was a full partner in the agency and he had nothing to lose, Lewis had gone to see his parents and explained that he was gay. Their reaction was predictably explosive but he felt better with it out in the open, even though David had gone off with someone shortly afterwards and screwed him out of the studio flat!

Lewis and Giles were deep in discussions when Rebekah flung the door open and marched in; the secretary knew better than to try to stop her.

'I've been to see Mummy and Daddy to tell them Cormac and I are getting married . . .'

Lewis looked shocked. 'Cormac never told me, I only spoke to him today.'

'Cormac doesn't know yet,' she smiled at him, 'but he'll agree, he always does. Anyway, they're going to give me the biggest and best – even you are invited – and then I'm never to darken their door again. Sounds fair enough to me!'

'You are such a hypocrite!'

'That's right, brother dearest, Joe and Lauren Alari have taught me well!'

Giles was listening with interest. He had become quite close to both of them in an almost paternal way. Rebekah looked at him.

'What about you and the old woman? Are you going to come?'

Giles was the only man who never ever took the bait, much to Rebekah's disappointment. He just smiled. Sue could never understand why he was so fond of Rebekah, and Giles could never really explain it himself other than to say that he could see the lost and lonely child behind the façade.

'It'll depend when it is. Don't forget Sue's expecting a baby soon.'

'Oh shit, yes, now that's a good one. Fancy still shagging at her age . . . How old is she, did you say?' Rebekah continued to try to rile him.

'Not for you to know, darling, not for you to know!' He laughed and tugged her hair affectionately.

Sue was on bed rest. After several minor operations and much disappointment she had conceived, and they were cautiously optimistic, having passed the danger period for the first time.

Lewis interrupted. 'You're way ahead of yourself, Beka. Cormac isn't the walkover he used to be. I can't see him agreeing to an Alari wedding. He knows they don't like him.'

'He'll agree when he knows it's that or nothing, but I'll skin you if you breathe a word to him. I know how to handle him, you'll see!'

She was off again, waving and smiling regally as she went.

'She's something else, your sister.' Giles laughed as Lewis looked bemused.

Rebekah had called up one of her hangers-on, as she called them, and gone out to dinner. She wanted to make Cormac stew a little and keep him on his toes so she turned off her mobile and stayed out until 3 a.m.

She expected him to be in bed pretending to be asleep when she got in but as she crashed into the apartment he threw the sitting-room door open before she even got to it.

'Where have you been? I've been trying to call you all night . . .'

'Oooooh, is the super-cool Cormac jealous?' she giggled.

'You've been drinking, how pissed are you?'

'Don't worry, darling boy, I got a cab. I've left the car . . . somewhere . . . I can't quite remember where, though . . .'

'Listen to me, Beka. I've been trying to get you and so has Lewis. Your mother and father have been in an accident. Your father had another heart attack at the wheel of his car and ran into the brick wall at the house. They were just on their way out . . . Rebekah, it's serious. I'll take you to the hospital, Lewis is there already.'

They got straight in the Porsche and he gunned it round the motorway.

She was stunned. It was only that morning that she'd been there with them, winding them up and enjoying it.

'Tell me what happened again. Fuck, I can't believe it.' She put the window down and stuck her head out, trying to sober up and get her brain back into gear before they got to the hospital.

'As far as the doctors know – and it's sketchy because neither of them is conscious – your parents were on their way out but they never even reached the main road. The hospital think your father had another heart attack and his foot jammed on the accelerator. They hit the property wall full force. They've both got multiple injuries, according to Lewis, both on the critical list. I'm sorry, Beka, I really am . . .'

'I was horrid to them today . . .'

He smiled sympathetically. 'They're used to that, that wouldn't have made any difference. Your father had a dodgy heart and wouldn't do as he was told. Another attack was inevitable.'

'They asked for it, though . . .' Rebekah still had to have the last word.

An eerie silence hung over the long corridors and their footsteps echoed as Rebekah and Cormac made their way to the Intensive Care Unit at the Surrey hospital. Once they were let in the security doors the signposting was clear and they quickly found the ward that housed the desperately ill.

The nurse directed them to a door beside the nurses' station and then went off to get them a drink while they waited.

Lewis was in a small lounge alone with his head in his hands, a cold cup of coffee beside him. He looked up as the door opened and almost jumped into Rebekah's arms. Cormac watched help-lessly as they hugged and cried together.

Joe and Lauren Alari were both still down in the operating theatres and Lewis had no more information on their condition. All they could do was sit and wait.

By the time morning dawned the couple were both back from post-op but still unconscious, still critical. Joe's condition was worse because of the heart attack, but Lauren had suffered facial injuries as well as internal damage.

It was going to be a long wait.

'Do you think we ought to go to the house and get them a few things? I don't know what they'll need . . .'

'Leave it a while, Beka. They don't need anything at the moment and it might be tempting fate, they're both so ill.'

The three of them were sitting on the small wall outside the building, drinking murky coffee out of polystyrene cups while Rebekah chain-smoked.

She was aware that she looked ridiculous in her body-skimming silver Lycra dress and high strappy shoes but she hadn't stopped to change. She looked down at herself.

'I can't spend all day in these clothes, they just look so dumb in

231

here. I'm going back to the house in a while to change. I've got clothes there. Are you coming?'

Lewis shook his head. 'We can't go together, just in case. You go and I'll phone you if anything changes.'

Cormac drove Rebekah to the family home. It was only the second time he had been there and the first time in daylight. He was overawed at the extravagance of it all.

As they drove up, the first thing they saw was the demolished wall and the remains of the Daimler that was still in the grounds but unrecognisable where the emergency services had cut Joe and Lauren out.

Rebekah shivered as Cormac drove slowly past.

The housekeeper quickly opened the door as she saw them drive up. She was desperate for information but concerned for Rebekah at the same time. The woman had worked with the family for over twenty years and there wasn't a lot that got past her but she was also the soul of discretion and fiercely loyal to them all.

'Now you come with me, young lady, and I'll run you a hot bath. Then I'll cook you both some breakfast before you go back to the hospital. Now no arguing, come along.'

Cormac went into the kitchen while Gladys hustled Rebekah up to her old room.

She settled for a quick shower and hairwash to get rid of the smell of the hospital that lingered on her like a spray of scent, all the while picturing her parents inside the mangled wreckage outside. She felt sick.

Without even bothering to wrap a towel around her dripping hair she went out on to the galleried landing and shouted down.

'Cormac, come up here a minute.'

He rushed up the stairs two at a time to find her naked and damp, a wildness in her eyes. She started madly tearing at his trousers as she pulled him into her bedroom, her room since she was two years old. Cormac responded instantly as he always did when he was near her.

Afterwards, as they were getting dressed, he looked around him for the first time at the sheer opulence of the room that was almost the size of his parents' house. It was more like a showroom than a place for a young girl to sleep in.

'Let's get married.'

Cormac wasn't sure he had heard right. 'Pardon me?'

Rebekah carried on getting ready to go back to the hospital.

'I said let's get married. What do you say?'

'I say that I don't feel right discussing this in your parents' house while they're desperately ill in the hospital.'

'You're such a pompous shit sometimes, you know. Why can't you just say yes and be done with it? You know you want to.'

'This doesn't feel—'

She interrupted him sharply. 'Do or die time, Cormac my man. Yes or no. You won't get another chance.'

He watched her sit down in front of the ornate mirror and start putting on her lipstick, before carefully smudging her kohl and reaching for the hotbrush for her hair. Anyone else would have been horrified but he understood her now, her insecurities and the love-hate relationship she had with her parents. Deep down she was still a little girl seeking attention in any way she could get it.

'All right then, yes. Now let's get back to the hospital. Lewis is on his own.'

She kissed him lightly on the lips.

'I knew you'd say yes.'

No you didn't, he thought, you were petrified I'd say no!

Lewis stood up as they walked back into the waiting room. Rebekah didn't say anything. She just looked at her brother, asking the question with her eyes.

'They're hanging in there. Mum will probably be OK but Dad is still critical. It's going to be a while before they can say any more but both of them have come through the surgery.'

Rebekah, Lewis and Cormac spent most of their time at the hospital over the next few days until the news was better.

Joe had two broken legs and several broken ribs and would have heart surgery as soon as he was well enough. The paramedics had just got to him in time. Lauren was a different matter. The internal damage had been repaired but her face and neck had taken the full force and she was going to need extensive plastic surgery.

It seemed that Joe had been in a filthy temper and had roared down the drive before she'd had a chance to put her seat belt on.

Rebekah had laughed grimly at that. 'I know a good plastic surgeon!' Lewis silenced her with one threatening look but Cormac understood. The débâcle with Dan the surgeon had hurt Rebekah – not so much what had happened but her mother's reaction to it: 'Darlin', you're being very silly. He is a plastic surgeon!' Her daughter's wellbeing, as always, was secondary.

Joe Alari was transferred to a hospital in London and his wife to a specialist unit in Essex. Lewis and Rebekah took it in turns to visit

233

each of them but now they were on the mend she was getting impatient.

'Mac darling, we have to start arranging the wedding—'

Lewis interrupted her sharply. 'I can't believe you just said that, Beka. At least wait until Mum and Dad are out of hospital. I presume you're still expecting them to foot the bill?'

Lewis was angry; he had taken it all far worse than his sister.

'I thought I was doing them a favour, saving them the worry . . .' The little girl voice was really irritating him lately.

'Don't give me crap. You just want to do it your way and present them with a *fait accompli* – well it's just not on.' He looked at Cormac. 'Tell her, she'll listen to you.'

Cormac knew she wouldn't so he stayed silent.

'I'll compromise with you, Lewis sweetie. I'll just start making enquiries and get going on the guest list. Don't worry, I'll include all the arseholes and hangers-on that Mummy would want. Daddy won't give a stuff, he never does, and Mummy can get her teeth into it when she's up and about.'

'Bitch, you know that won't be for months and months. Her face is still a mess.'

Rebekah roared with laughter, hard humourless laughter.

'That face of hers has been under the knife so many times, why should once more make any difference? She'll be ordering what she wants in no time, a little bit off here, a little bit transferred to there . . .'

'Shut up!' Cormac and Lewis retorted in unison.

Rebekah was at the house collecting all the things that her parents had asked for. She decided to get the address books and start the list, regardless of Lewis and Cormac. The dress was already being designed and the venue chosen – it was just a matter of waiting for her parents to get better.

It gave her a feeling of satisfaction to be inside her mother's rooms, the study that had always been a no-go area for the children when they were growing up. 'This is Mummy's private room,' Lauren would say before locking the door.

Well, today I've got the keys, Rebekah thought happily, and today I'm going to have a really good nose about.

Rebekah Alari loved prying, and her imagination went into overdrive. Maybe she would find love letters from secret admirers or proof that her mother indulged in strange rituals at midsummer; maybe she was a witch after all. She was quite excited at what goodies might be hidden behind the locked door.

Nothing it turned out, so she had to content herself with flicking through the huge leather-bound address book that lay on the locked bureau and looking for secret codes. Still nothing. She decided her mother really did lead a boring life after all.

She picked up the book and an envelope fell out from the back. Bingo, thought Rebekah gleefully, the key to the bureau, but she still found nothing apart from proof of how much her mother spent, but that was no secret anyway.

Lauren was short, Rebekah tall so she had trouble getting her long legs out from under the custom-made bureau. Her knees brushed the underneath as she manoeuvred them out and she felt something sticking out. Reaching under, she found a small lever, and as she pulled at it a small compartment hidden in the intricate marquetry popped open . . .

Lewis picked up the phone. Rebekah was incoherent at the other end and his first reaction was that something had happened to one of the parents.

'Get to the house now, Lewis, get to the fucking house . . .' She was sobbing so loudly she couldn't get her breath.

'What's happened?'

'Just get here, Lewis, just get here . . .' That was all he could make sense of, and there was no calming her down. The more he tried the more hysterical she became. 'Just fucking get here . . .'

By the time he arrived Rebekah was in her mother's bedroom, carving knife in hand, attacking the clothes in her wardrobe. The rest of the room was already trashed. She was screaming like a banshee while Gladys watched helplessly from the doorway.

Lewis grabbed her from behind with a bearhug and held her in an iron grip until he felt her relax a little. Letting go, he took the knife from her hand and led her to the bed.

'What's all this about, Beka? Tell me . . .'

Silently she walked back into her mother's study, over to the bureau, and handed Lewis a wad of papers. The large envelope she had found them in lay on the floor.

He flicked through them once, then the second time he scrutinised them more carefully before looking at his sister, his face ashen.

Amid the legal documents and newspaper cuttings were the adoption papers for Rebekah and Lewis.

Neither of them were Alaris but, worst of all, the brother and sister weren't even siblings. Their whole lives had been a lie.

BOOK FOUR

Chapter Seventeen

Rebekah looked at the cutting again. She knew the words off by heart but still she had to keep reading it.

She wanted to tear it into shreds, to put all the papers back in the desk where she had found them and pretend nothing had changed, pretend that she was still Rebekah Skye Alari, daughter of Joe and Lauren Alari, sister of Lewis Alari, but she knew that couldn't happen. That was just a fantasy.

BABY ABANDONED IN TOILET
(Pictured on right with Mrs Smith who found her.)

Only a few hours old, this baby girl was found in a toilet cubicle yesterday at Brighton Hospital by Jeanette Smith, a nurse at the hospital. She is being cared for on the maternity unit and police have appealed for the mother, who may be in need of urgent medical attention, to come forward.

The baby was discovered in a carrier bag wrapped in a shawl. The mother left a note giving details of the date and time of birth and naming the baby, who doctors say is of mixed race, Skye.

The cutting was from the front page of a newspaper and dated 21 November 1973. The day before that was Rebekah's birthday.

The knocking on the door and the shouting continued, but she didn't, couldn't respond.

'Beka ... Beka ... open the door, please open the door. PLEASE, we need each other, please open the bloody door ...'

She could hear that Lewis was crying, hear that he was as distraught as she, but she couldn't get up off the bed, which was now covered with the letters and papers she had found in the bureau.

By the time Lewis had got to the house the impact of what Rebekah found had hit her fully in the stomach, making her

239

physically sick. She had retched and retched until there was nothing left, until a red haze had descended on her. She'd gone down to the kitchen, come back up with the carving knife, and attacked anything and everything, cutting and slashing with the strength of ten men.

By the time Lewis had got there she didn't even remember doing it but she did remember the contents of the hidden drawer. She had snatched them back from him, run into her old bedroom with them and locked the door.

'Last chance, Beka, before I get someone to break it down . . . I mean it, NOW OPEN IT.'

This time she heard his voice in the distance and something clicked in her brain. This involved him as well as her.

She unlocked the door and turned straight back to the bed.

Literally running across the room, Lewis threw himself down beside her, clutching her close to him.

To him she looked ten years old again. Whenever Rebekah was truly distressed she would curl up defensively in the foetal position, facing the wall and wrapping her long arms tightly around her legs. He had a sudden flashback to the day that Lauren had picked them both up from school and told them, 'Mummy and Daddy have got a surprise for you both, my little darlin's. Daddy is in the stables.'

Excitedly they had bounded out of the car and hared round to the stables to find Joe Alari with two ponies, a rein in each hand, looking as pleased as punch and eagerly waiting for their reaction. It had taken a few minutes for them to register the empty stables behind him.

'Where are Puffin and Champagne?' Rebekah had asked.

'I sold them, sweetheart. You don't need two ponies each and they were too small . . .'

Rebekah had been inconsolable. Joe Alari just hadn't understood that Rebekah loved her pony to bits, that he was her confidant, her best friend, not just a belonging. She went into the foetal position then and stayed like it until she was threatened with the doctor. She never rode again from that day.

They cried together now as they had then, both betrayed, but Lewis feeling his sister's grief as much as his own.

'How the fuck could they do that, Lewis? How could they do that to us? All these years and never so much as a hint—' She stopped mid-sentence and looked at her brother. 'Now I know what the cow meant the other week. She was on top form, you know, the usual – me a slut, you a fairy – and she said something

240

strange. She said, "Bad blood will out." Daddy waffled round it but I bet that's what she meant and that's why they had a row. He thought she was going to say something . . . Bastards, bastards, I hate them . . .'

Her face contorted with rage, she picked up the limited edition porcelain birthday dolls that were set out in a neat row on the shelf above her bed and systematically, one by one, smashed their faces against the wall. Lewis didn't try to stop her. He knew she had to vent her fury, the fury that was always greater than his.

As always the affable, easy-going young man's pain was more for his sister than himself. He waited until she had finished.

'Beka, we have to decide what we're going to do. We can't tell them we know; they're both too ill, the shock might kill them.'

'Good. That's just what they deserve after what they've done to us.'

Lewis looked at her but didn't say anything. At that moment he could very nearly have agreed with her.

Gathering up the papers that were all over the bed and taking her by the hand like a child, he led her through to the bathroom and gently wiped her face with a cold flannel. Pulling her hair back, he took her face in both hands and looked at her.

'Beka, we'll get through this together. Maybe they had a good reason for keeping this from us—'

'Bullshit. There's no reason they can come up with for this.'

Lewis splashed water on his own face and walked her back to the bedroom.

'Come on, we're going downstairs and we're going to read all this properly. Poor Gladys is nearly hysterical. We have to let her see that we're OK.'

There was no doubt about it. Rebekah and Lewis were both adopted in 1974 by the Alaris from Dr Barnardo's in London. The letters were all the proof they needed: 'Dear Mr and Mrs Alari, Re: the adoption of Skye and Lewis . . .'

There were letters, copies of formal documents and the full birth certificates that removed any shadow of doubt that may have been remaining. And, of course, the yellowing newspaper cutting, carefully clipped and dated.

'I'm Skye, aren't I? I'm the baby found in a fucking toilet, abandoned . . . I'm not Rebekah Alari, the daughter of Mr and Mrs Fucking Alari, I'm Skye, dumped in a toilet, mixed race, Skye . . . look at the date of birth.'

'Beka, I don't know what to say except that it affects me too . . .

241

I don't know who I am. Neither of us is who we thought we were.'

She looked at him, her face frozen in horror as the implication of what he had said hit her.

'You're not my brother . . . Lewis, you're not even my brother!' The words came out in a howl. She started shaking from head to foot as the shock of it all took effect. Over and over again she said it, getting more hysterical by the second. 'You're not my brother, you're not my brother, Lewis, you're not my brother . . .'

For the first time in his life he hit Rebekah, short and sharp around the face. She stopped and stared at him.

'You hit me, you bastard.'

'That's right, I hit you. Now look at me properly, look into my eyes . . .'

Holding her hand to her face she did as she was told. There was something in his voice that she'd never heard before – an assertiveness that told her for the first time their roles were reversed. Lewis was now the leader; he was telling her what to do.

'You are Rebekah and you are my sister. Blood tie or no blood tie, you are my sister. I love you, nothing can change that. Do you understand me? Nothing can ever change that.'

Lauren Alari continued to improve and Lewis continued to visit her but Rebekah wouldn't, couldn't.

She visited her father once but the strain of not being able to confront him was too much. She desperately wanted answers but his heart surgery was looming and Lewis had made her promise to keep quiet.

Looking at him lying in the hospital bed, covered in wire and tubes, both legs in plaster she felt detached from the man she had always known as her father. He looked so small and weak she almost felt sorry for him, but at the same time she wanted to rip the tubes out and shriek, 'Die, you bastard!'

When she was awake she fantasised about doing just that, but when she was asleep she had nightmares about being trapped in the lavatory bowl, and as the water came flushing down it was Joe Alari, her father, who pulled her out.

Rebekah had moved in with Lewis after the discovery, telling Cormac they wanted to be close in case of any emergencies. Cormac had been so understanding she felt guilty at not confiding in him but she and Lewis had agreed. Nobody was to know until they had the opportunity to confront their parents together. All four of them together. They knew it could take a while.

'Lewis, what are you going to do?' Rebekah asked him one

morning. 'Are you going to look for your real parents? You stand more chance of finding them than I do. Nobody knows anything about me but you could be different, you could find out.'

Lewis had thought about it. He had thought of nothing else – his birth parents, Rebekah's birth parents, why? How? What did they look like? Were there any other children? Brothers or sisters neither of them knew they had? The questions went round and round in his head, but he knew what he was going to do. He had decided.

'I'm not going looking, Beka. Mum and Dad are the only parents I have and they have always been there. I don't want to know anything else. They are it, for better or worse!'

She swung round, her eyes dark and spiteful. He knew that look only too well.

'Why do you always have to be such a wimp? They've crapped on us from a great height and still you stick up for them . . . arsehole!'

Glaring at him, she opened her mouth but before the words came out he continued, 'Look at it this way, Beka. You and I were both, for whatever reason, not wanted, lost property as it were. Where would we be now without them? Probably have spent our lives in children's homes and be out on the streets now with all the other kids who spent their lives in care . . . They didn't kidnap us and drag us off into the night, they adopted us and brought us up. Is that really such a sin?'

'You've changed your tune, brother dearest . . . Oops, I forget, you're not my brother, sorry!'

Without responding, Lewis turned and walked out of the room but not before she had seen the hurt on his face. Mortified she ran after him.

'Lewis, I'm sorry, I didn't mean it.'

He turned and looked back at her.

'That was a step too far, Rebekah, even for you.'

At that moment she hated herself even more than she hated her parents, but she knew Lewis didn't really understand how it was for her. He had always been easy-going and good-natured, but she knew she was a selfish temperamental bitch – she knew it, she just couldn't help it.

It had always been said that she took after her father, but who did she really take after? 'She's an Alari' had been the excuse for so long but now she knew she wasn't an Alari; she wasn't anybody. If they weren't Alari genes that made her the way she was, then whose were they?

The ring on the intercom made her jump.

'Lewis,' she shouted, 'can you get it? Someone's outside.'

She heard him go into the hallway and press the buzzer. 'Hi, come on up.'

'You're not letting anyone in, are you? Look at the state of me.'

'You're OK, it's only Giles.' He looked round the door at her, the coldness still in his eyes.

'I'm sorry, Lewis, I really am. You know I didn't mean it . . .'

He didn't answer her.

Giles was holding a bottle of champagne.

'Hi, guys, how are you both? How are your mum and dad? Any more news?'

Lewis answered quickly, pre-empting any smart response Rebekah might come up with.

'Nothing new, it's slow but sure.'

'Do you want to hear my news? I've just come from the hospital. Sue had the baby today, a little girl!'

Lewis walked over and shook his hand.

'That is really good news. We could do with some of that, couldn't we, Beka?' He shot her a warning look that told her to at least pretend.

'Yeah, great, congratulations. I'm pleased for you both.'

Giles looked surprised. He was used to her sarcastic and sometimes vicious tongue but the monotone she used now was different.

'We're pleased – well, actually we're over the moon. She had a Caesarean but we were expecting that, just not so soon. We've named her Elizabeth, she weighs six pounds and she's a little doll! Harry and Emily can't wait to see their new sister. I'm picking them up in the morning. I did try phoning . . .'

Rebekah was aware that his eyes kept flicking back to her while he was talking, the concern in them apparent. She wanted to shout at him, tell him she didn't give a toss about his baby, his wife, his cute little family.

She wondered if he would be talking to her, sitting in the same room as her, offering champagne to her, if he knew she wasn't Rebekah Alari, daughter of Joe, of Italian descent, but Skye, an unwanted mixed race baby dumped in a public toilet? She realised he was bemused by her appearance – the pyjamas, the lack of make-up, the dishevelled hair – but she didn't care. She really didn't care what anyone thought.

'How are the wedding arrangements going, Beka, now we've beaten you to it and we can both be there?'

244

'I'm cancelling it. I'm not getting married to Cormac, or to anyone. It's all off!'

'You two had a tiff? Sue and I rowed constantly before our wedding, everyone does.'

'No, we haven't had a tiff, as you call it, it's just off, that's all. No wedding, so you can put your top hat away again.'

She saw him look questioningly at Lewis, who merely shrugged his shoulders as if to indicate he knew nothing.

Reaching down the side of the sofa, she pulled out a silver tin and slowly and carefully went through the motions of rolling a joint, concentrating completely on the job in hand, or so Giles and Lewis thought.

'God, that takes me back,' Giles sighed reminiscently. 'I remember when Sue lived in her first flat, in the same building as her friend Angie. We used to be out on the tiles and then go back to one or other of the flats and smoke dope until the air was blue. Those were the days. Now we're all parents and sane and sensible.'

He looked at Rebekah. 'Sad really when you have to grow up and face reality.'

Her head shot up, her eyes wild and alert.

'What do you mean by that? Tell me what you mean. What do you know?'

Lewis was beside her like a shot. 'Hey, it's all right. Giles was generalising.'

He put his arms around her, hugging her close. He looked at Giles, who was totally bewildered by the outburst.

'Take no notice, Giles. She's a bit stressed out. You know, the business with Mum and Dad and now the wedding's off – it's all a bit much.'

Giles, like Lewis, had a kind, gentle streak running through him that sometimes made him a bit slow on the uptake, but even he knew there was something desperately wrong with the girl. He recognised the scared eyes, the body hugging, and the shaky hand clasping a joint with the desperation of a drowning man clinging to the last piece of wood in the sea. The girl was on the brink of a breakdown. He had seen it with Angie all those years ago.

'Right, well, I'd better be going. I just wanted to tell you both myself. I'll see myself out. I'll speak to you at the office tomorrow, Lewis. I'll be backwards and forwards for a few days, like yourself. We can sort it all out then. Bye, Rebekah.'

She half-smiled at him and went back to concentrating on her

245

carefully constructed joint. Although he wondered briefly again what could be up with her his mind quickly went back to Sue, in hospital with baby Lizzie.

When Sue had grudgingly agreed to hospital investigations and treatment it was a double-edged sword for Giles. He'd prayed for it to be successful but at the same time he'd been all too aware that if it failed Sue would be back where she'd started.

He smiled to himself as he remembered her throwing open the door to his office and flying in at full speed.

As soon as the pregnancy had been confirmed Sue had been advised to rest, and the next seven months passed painfully slowly. Sue had anticipated miscarriage every single day. She'd been in and out of the loo, checking constantly for the dreaded bleeding, completely distraught at the mildest stomach pain and completely neurotic right up to the day of admission for her prearranged Caesarean delivery.

Giles had stayed with her throughout, at the top end, as he cheerily described it, and he knew he would never forget the expression on her face as their tiny daughter was handed to her for the very first time.

'We've done it, we've really done it. Look, isn't she just beautiful?'

They had both cried as they looked at the perfect little person in her arms.

Giles had sighed. 'Yep, my darling, we've done it at last!'

As time went on and Lewis was rushed off his feet, alternating between the two hospitals where his parents were, the office and Rebekah, he could feel his compassion for his sister wearing a little thin. He gently tried to tell her so after coming home and finding her once again curled up in a ball on a beanbag staring into space with a joint in her hand.

'I know it was a shock – it was for me too – but there is absolutely nothing we can do to change things.'

He was aware that as usual he was the giver and she the taker. Some things never change, he thought wryly, as he cajoled and soothed her. There was no one to offer sympathy and a listening ear to him.

'Life goes on. Mum and Dad are on the mend and when they're both out of hospital we can talk to them, but in the meantime I have to go to work and you have to try and get yourself back together. Nothing has changed has it? Not really!'

'Fuck off. How come you're suddenly a fully paid-up member of agony aunts anonymous? You just don't understand how I feel.'

'Yes I do, Beka, I really do. You're feeling sorry for yourself.' He stood his ground despite the ferocity of her glare. 'Well, that never did anyone any good.' He paused before continuing, 'They were asking after you again, you know. They think you're too busy enjoying yourself to visit. They think you don't care, especially Dad. They haven't even got each other at the moment.'

She glared at him. 'Sweetie, I think you've mistaken me for someone who gives a shit!'

He picked an imaginary piece of fluff from his sleeve and then looked away from her into the large mirror over the fireplace. He ran his finger through his still blond hair.

'No, Rebekah, I think I mistook you for someone who was grown-up.'

As the weeks went by, Rebekah felt increasingly isolated.

She had told Cormac not to visit and to her annoyance he didn't; Lewis was always out rushing around – suddenly she realised she had no one. No close girlfriend to confide in, no other family, it was just her and Lewis and she had alienated him.

Thinking back over her childhood she wondered if her parents had ever really loved her. Had they gone to the adoption society the same way they went to the car showroom? The estate agents? The supermarket? Had they suddenly thought, I know, let's go and get a baby. We've got everything else, now let's get a baby. That one there, he'll do, he's blond like me . . . Oh, darlin', while we're here we might as well get two, save making another journey. Look at that one, she's dark like you, honey . . . we'll take the pair. Is there a discount for two?

Her mind was racing.

Why a toilet? Why abandon a baby in a toilet? Because her mother thought of her as waste matter? Something to be discarded into the sewerage system?

Why? Why? Why? Lewis really didn't understand how she felt. His papers showed he was put up for adoption; he had a chance to find his mother and ask her if he wanted to. She had nothing, just a yellowed newspaper cutting. Suddenly Rebekah knew she had to go to Brighton, visit the hospital, the scene of the crime.

The speed cameras flashed behind her as she put her foot down and roared down to Brighton. Oblivious to everything except the hospital, she left several near misses and a lot of angry motorists in her wake.

For the first time in weeks she had dressed with care and applied a touch of make-up to disguise the gaunt face that stared back at her. Since the accident she'd shed half a stone that she could ill afford to lose. Her slender arms and legs were now stick thin, her hip- and cheekbones protruding like dangerous weapons; she looked ill, she knew it and she didn't really care.

The hospital was easy to find but Rebekah hadn't given any thought to the time lapse. The new extensions and layout had included the building of several new toilets. She was confused, and angry with herself for not planning it better.

Finding the cafeteria, she got herself a coffee and thought up a plan.

'I wonder if you can help me. My name is Annie Jones and I'm writing a book about abandoned babies. I understand there was one abandoned here in the toilets over twenty years ago, about 1973 I think. Where can I find some information?'

Standing at the information desk Rebekah felt her heart thumping so fiercely she was convinced the young woman in front of her could hear it.

'I'm sorry, I don't know anything about it. I've only been here for six months. Why don't you try Maternity? They might know something. Go up in the lift to the third floor and ask the security guard. He can point you in the right direction.'

By the time she had spoken to four people who knew nothing she was starting to get frustrated and thinking about giving up, but she struck gold with the fifth she was directed to.

Mary O'Hara was a career midwife, never married and totally dedicated to her work. Her retirement was looming and she made no bones about the fact that she was dreading it. After thirty-five years at the same hospital, she had delivered more babies than she could ever begin to count.

She took Rebekah into a tiny office no bigger than a broom cupboard, and settled her well-padded hips on a stool. She looked about sixty and her uniform was starched and pressed, the silver buckle on her belt glistening. Mary was a nurse from the old school who despaired of the lowering of uniform standards.

The long iron-grey hair was pulled back into a severe bun that did little to enhance the face that was actually quite kindly, motherly even. She smiled widely as she talked.

'I remember the baby – ooh, it must have been over twenty-five years ago. She was brought into the unit. I wasn't on duty at the time but I came in the next day and met the poor little mite. Pretty

248

little thing, she was, masses of dark hair, looked like a wig.'

The woman laughed and then paused. 'You say you're a writer, why do you want to write about this?'

Rebekah knew she had to keep a sharp hold on her tongue. She didn't want to exchange pleasantries but she did want information. She smiled nicely, trying to sound professionally distant. No emotions, she told herself, just be interested.

'I was asked to do it. It's not something I've ever thought about really, but now I'm getting into it, it's a fascinating subject, don't you think? How did you feel about a mother abandoning her baby in a public toilet?'

'Oh dear Lord, I was so upset, just so sad for the poor mother. She must have given birth on her own, alone and scared, and then brought the baby to the safest place. She did make a phone call, you know, she didn't just leave her and run.' She stopped for a moment, trying to remember, her face screwed up in concentration. 'She left a note as well, and gave the wee mite a name. They never traced her, though, and she never came forward. It was so sad. I never knew what happened to the baby. She was taken to the children's home and then I heard she had been fostered and that was it.'

The elderly nurse brought herself back to the present. 'Now tell me, what's your book to be called? I'd love to read it.'

'It hasn't got a title yet but I'll send you one.'

'Oh, that would be so kind. But don't be too hard on the poor young mothers, will you? Who knows what goes through their minds at a time like that, and then probably for the rest of their lives – never forgive themselves, no doubt. Don't forget, there but for the grace of God . . .' Again she paused. 'Oh, and all that rubbish in the papers about dumped in a carrier bag – stuff and nonsense, that was. The little thing was in a strong sturdy canvas bag, like those that were all the rage at the time, and wrapped up warm in a brand-new shawl. Made me think the mother was only a young wee thing herself.'

As Rebekah forced herself to smile and shake the woman's hand she remembered the key question.

'Can you just tell me which toilets? Are they still there?'

'Yes, of course they are, down the end of the corridor in the old building just before the exit.'

'Thank you again for all your help.'

As she turned to head in the direction of the old part of the hospital the nurse called her back.

'I know what I didn't tell you. We never found out if it was a coincidence, but every November on the baby's birthday, I heard that someone places a pink rosebud in the cubicle.'

Rebekah could feel the rising excitement that threatened to turn into panic.

'Did you ever try and find out who she is?'

'No, by the time we realised the roses may be connected with the baby too much time had passed. The baby was gone – why try and cause more pain? No, let the mother have her private moment, it's all she has. So sad, so very sad . . .' The woman's voice faded as she spoke; even Rebekah felt moved by her concern for the mother. HER mother.

Standing in the small cubicle that the nurse had indicated, she knew she was one breath away from breaking down. She had to get out. She vowed to herself she would come back on her birthday and keep watch, and then she'd knife the fucking bitch right between the shoulder blades.

Collecting her car from the car park, she raced back to London.

When she got home she checked through two weeks of mail that lay unopened on the dresser, looking for invitations. She knew there would be several from all over the world, there always were. Private parties, launch parties, charity functions – Rebekah Alari, It girl 1999 was high on every invitation list. Her photographs always got into the papers and so did the party hosts by default. That was how it worked.

A couple of invites were out of date but there were two for that night: a jewellery launch and a fund raiser. She hesitated and then decided on both.

She was dressed, made up, hair blowdried and out just before Lewis got in, her taxi passing him on the corner. She kept her head down as they crossed but, deep in thought, he never even looked in her direction.

Tonight she was going to party and party, and enjoy her secret, the secret she was convinced would mean her exclusion from the A-list. After all, she thought, what publicity was there to be gained from inviting a mixed-race bastard with no background to a launch of the latest exclusive diamond jewellery? What interest would she be at a fundraiser if she wasn't an Alari with access to Joe Alari's millions?

She partied and drank champagne like it was going out of fashion, she snorted cocaine until her nose burnt and the room spun, and topped it all up with tequila slammers and the best skunk on the market.

Rebekah was flying.

She had no recollection of stripping off in the street outside the top London hotel and physically assaulting the two policemen sent to deal with her. The arrest and night in the cells was all a blur although she did remember Lewis bailing her out the next day and pulling a few Alari strings to get the charges dropped and keep the publicity to the minimum.

What they didn't see, until it was too late, was the paparazzo photographer who was waiting outside the hotel snapping away, who followed them to the flat, snapping away, and who then followed them to the hospital. When he was eventually spotted, Lewis threatened to kill him but he just laughed.

Rebekah also remembered Lewis taking her home and being very, very angry.

Then it all came back to her, the events of the day before – Brighton, the kindly nurse, the toilet, the pink rosebud.

Her alcohol and drug levels were still so high that it didn't take many painkillers and sleeping pills to push her over the top into unconsciousness. Lewis took her to hospital himself and stayed with her while her stomach was pumped.

It was 11 a.m.

The grandfather clock in the hall loudly chimed eleven times. Joshua still enjoyed counting the chimes if he was nearby.

Angie was working in her office and Kate, the nanny, was in charge for the school holidays, but even upstairs Angie could hear him shouting the numbers in time to the rhythm.

'Nine . . . ten . . . eleven . . .'

She felt a chill in the warm room, like a blast of cold air, and suddenly she felt an incredible urge to throw up, a pain in her throat that made her want to retch. She controlled it and it was gone as suddenly as it had come.

Odd . . . She didn't think she'd eaten anything dodgy.

Chapter Eighteen

Oh, how the press loved it, with most of the tabloids carrying photos either of Rebekah in her silk G-string and Wonderbra dancing in the middle of the street, fighting with a red-faced young policeman, or leaving the police station with her coat over her head, accompanied by Lewis.

The gleeful headlines made unhappy reading for Lewis and Cormac but were entertaining to everyone else – except, of course, Joe and Lauren Alari, still in hospital but more than capable of reading the papers with steam coming out of their ears.

The Fall of the It girl . . . Rebekah Alari, daughter of multi-millionaire businessman Joe Alari and his wife, Lauren, was arrested last night for disturbing the peace outside an exclusive London hotel. It is alleged that she was under the influence of drugs and alcohol. Her brother, Lewis, Managing Director of the ABJ modelling agency, was on hand to bail her out after a night cooling her heels in a police cell . . . She was later taken to hospital after a suspected overdose.

All the newspaper stories were in a similar vein.

Lewis left the hospital and gave waiting reporters a few quotes that sent them away happy for the time being. 'Rebekah is well but staying put for a few days' rest, following her accidental mixing of alcohol and prescription medication that caused an allergic reaction.' No problems; no big story. The problem was that no one believed it.

Under cover of darkness that same night a nondescript small, dark saloon slipped quietly to the back entrance of the hospital where Rebekah was waiting silently with a nurse. Wearing a tracksuit and enveloped in a huge shawl, her gaunt face free of any make-up, Rebekah was nearly as nondescript as the car.

After checking that there were no lone paparazzi hiding in the shadows, cameras at the ready, she slid quickly into the passenger seat and Lewis drove her straight to an exclusive private clinic in London to be treated for nervous exhaustion.

Everyone had agreed she would be safer there, away from the public eye.

'Look, Dave, that Rebekah Alari has been up to nonsense again.'

Angie passed the paper to him across the breakfast table but Joshua snatched it first.

'Who's Rebekah Alari?'

'Just someone that Auntie Sue and Uncle Giles know. Now give the paper to Dad.'

The boy carried on reading, pretending he was interested. Seven years old, with light brown curly hair and sparkling eyes, he was like his mother in looks but his temperament was more Dave's, gentle and kind but with a strong mischievous streak.

'I'm reading it . . .'

Angie and Dave exchanged smiles over the boy's head.

'No you're not, now pass it over, buster, before I take you outside and string you up by your ankles.'

Joshua passed the paper to his father with a big sigh. Dave skimmed it briefly.

'She doesn't know when to stop, that girl. She'll be dead by the time she's thirty.'

'I can't understand it. She's had everything handed to her on a plate. Never mind silver spoon, more like eighteen-carat pure gold. I feel sorry for her parents. How much would you like to bet that Sue will be on the phone before the day's out?'

Dave smiled wryly. 'I wouldn't waste my money.' He turned his attention to his son. 'Come on you, time for school. Don't forget Jem is picking you up. You've got the whole weekend with her.'

'I know that. We're going to have pizza and chips and chocolate-chip ice cream,' he looked from one to the other, 'AND we're going to have popcorn at the pictures . . .'

'Well,' laughed Angie, 'so long as she clears up when you chuck up then that's OK, isn't it?' She cuddled her son close and kissed his forehead. She loved him so much it frightened her sometimes.

Kissing Angie on the cheek, Dave shepherded Joshua out to the car.

'See you tonight,' he shouted as he got in the car. 'Back about seven probably!'

She waved until the car was out of sight and then settled down for a peaceful half-hour with the papers before getting down to work.

Skimming again the lurid details of Rebekah's latest escapade she sighed to herself. What a waste. She had been born with looks, talent and unlimited money, the best of everything, but for some reason it wasn't enough.

The phone rang and Angie smiled to herself; she knew without doubt who it was.

'Angie, have you seen the papers? I nearly scalped Giles. He knew about it and hadn't told me! He actually said I was a gossip!'

'Well, he's right, you are. What else did he say?'

Sue tutted in exasperation. 'Reckons he only knows as much as was in the papers. He had the nerve to say it's none of our business. I said, "But you work with Lewis, it is our business." Do you know what he said then?'

'I can't imagine, go on.'

'He said he didn't discuss all our personal problems with Lewis at the time so why should Lewis discuss Rebekah with him? Daft bastard!'

Angie laughed. They may all be a lot older and a bit wiser, but the easy-going relationship between the friends hadn't changed at all.

'How are her parents? Are they still in hospital, did he say?'

'Heaps better, apparently. Well, until they saw the papers, that is. Guaranteed for a setback now, I'd have thought. They're both due to head back to the Alari mansion shortly with a team of nurses. They don't do anything by halves, that family. Lewis is the only normal one. Apparently even he is exasperated by it all . . .'

Angie felt her interest waning.

'How's Lizzie doing?' Angie knew that was a good way to change the subject. Sue was completely besotted by her baby daughter and loving every second of being a mum.

'Angie, she is just so adorable, worth every single stitch and some more. When are you coming over? She's changing every day, you won't recognise her soon . . .'

Sensing a hint of reprimand Angie felt a twinge of guilt. She was working so hard lately there wasn't even enough time for Joshua.

'Soon, Sue, I promise, after we get back from Scotland.' Suddenly her guilt got the better of her. 'Unless you want to come over for an hour this morning? Get Giles to drop you off – it's not too far off his route – and I'll run you back. I'd love to see Lizzie again.'

Now she would have to work into the night to catch up and it was supposed to have been a free evening for her and Dave.

Angie opened the door to find Sue holding the baby and Giles laden like a packhorse with what looked like every baby item Lizzie would need for six months.

'Quick coffee before you go, Giles?'

'Only if you're not going to grill me about Rebekah . . . I've told all I know, honestly!'

Angie laughed as they staggered through to the new conservatory on the back of the house.

'Come on, Giles, now we've got you captive, tell all. You're not going until we have every single gory detail!'

'I've already told Sue everything. Rebekah went out on the town, drank too much, no doubt coked too much and was off her face. Come on, you guys, we've all done it ourselves, just that no one was interested in us. Who would have bothered to take any photos if it hadn't been Rebekah? The press are hyping it up. She'll be out of hospital tomorrow and back to normal. Trust me, a nine-day wonder!'

'I can't believe she was out whooping it up when her parents were still in hospital. Christ, it's only been a few weeks since they were at death's door. Self-centred bitchtroll!'

Angie could see Giles was getting a bit heated.

He snapped at Sue, 'Leave the girl alone. It's none of our business. It's Lewis I really feel for. He doesn't know if he's on his head or his heels.' He clapped his hands together in the same way he did to mark the end of a business meeting. 'Anyway, enough now, I'm going to work. There's no end of crises to resolve as you, my dear wife, should understand only too well. I've even recruited Cormac to help out. He's the only person I can trust and he's not working on anything at the moment. I really need you back in harness, Susie. You can bring Lizzie with you.'

Sue ignored him and smiled at Angie. 'I hear the wedding's off as well – before it was hardly on, even. I wonder if Giles has any info on that?'

They all laughed and Giles got up quickly.

'No comment. Goodbye!' Giles kissed Sue and Lizzie and was still laughing as he closed the front door.

'There's far more to this than meets the eye, sweetie, I just know it. I've heard it before: ooops, I accidentally took too many prescription drugs, emphasis on *prescription*, on top of a teeny little drink . . . I didn't mean to do it. Bullshit, that self-absorbed mare never did anything by accident.'

Silently Angie agreed, Rebekah Alari appeared to be a total control freak and now she was out of control. But why?

Summoned in true Alari fashion, Rebekah and Lewis were on their way to see Joe and Lauren. Although still a patient at the clinic, Rebekah was free to come and go as she pleased, but this was her first outing.

Despite fighting against it in the beginning she was actually settling in to the clinic, the routines, the sessions and the company.

'Wait till I get my hands on them, bastards, and they've got the fucking sauce to expect us to want to see them?'

'Sorry, Beka, but it has to be done. They've both been home a fortnight now and you've not been near. It looks as if you just can't be bothered. We have to get this out in the open, but *please* remember Dad's heart . . .'

'What heart? Did they give him one? He didn't have one before the accident, did he?'

Lewis looked at his sister out of the corner of his eye and his lips tightened as she started again. She didn't realise how much he was hurting, how close he was to breaking under the strain.

'Just shut it, Beka, shut it. You're like a bloody parrot, same thing over and over again. It's just getting too fucking boring for words.'

'Stop the car . . . I said stop the bloody car, I'm getting out,' she screamed at him, pummelling his shoulder with her fists.

To her surprise he pulled straight over on to the hard shoulder.

'Go on then, get out.' Looking straight ahead with both hands firmly on the wheel, he revved the engine in neutral.

She didn't move.

'Well, go on then. I'm not sitting here all day while you make up your mind. Get out and walk but mind the cars, won't you?'

Silently she stayed where she was and eventually he pulled away again.

'Lewis, why are you being so horrible to me? You're all I've got now. Even Cormac hasn't been to visit me.'

He sighed in exasperation. 'You said you didn't want him to. You told him to fuck off and never come near you again.'

'I know but I didn't mean it. He should know that.'

He very nearly laughed.

Rebekah felt sick as they pulled into the drive, she hadn't been near the property since the day she found the papers and she could feel a panic attack coming on just at the sight of the building.

'I can't go in there, I can't face them . . . You go in, I'll wait in the car.'

Lewis was gentle but firm. 'You can. We'll both go in together but please let me do the talking. It's no good you going into one of your tantrums, that won't do any of us any good. Now deep breath, we're going . . .'

Joe Alari was in his wheelchair on the terrace in the sun while Lauren was in the drawing room with the doors open, sitting in the shade. When Rebekah and Lewis went through Joe turned his chair around and held his arms out to his daughter.

'Sweetpea! I thought you'd forgotten about us. Come and give your daddy a big hug . . .'

Rebekah held back, rooted to the spot in panic for a few seconds before Lewis gave her a subtle push. The embrace was fleeting but Lewis detracted from it by going over to his mother and making a fuss of her.

Rebekah looked at both her parents. Lauren was still in light bandages on her face and wore very dark glasses, the only indications of the accident. Other than that she was meticulously groomed as always. Not a hair out of place, not a crease in the lounger suit, but Rebekah was shocked at Joe; he looked so old and shrivelled.

'How are you feeling now, Mum?' Lewis clasped Lauren's hand as he spoke but his eyes stayed on Rebekah, silent and frozen, unpredictable.

'We're doing OK, darlin', but your sister has given us both a setback with her behaviour and not a word of apology . . . not a visit in weeks, even . . . and now all this – the shame of seeing you in the newspapers like a common call girl. I just don't understand you . . .'

Lewis took his sister's hand and held it tightly, encouraging silence for the moment.

'Mum, Dad, before we get into all that we need to talk to you. Can we go inside and shut the doors? It's private.'

Joe Alari looked at his wife and raised his eyebrows.

'My, this looks expensive, both of you being so serious!' He laughed as he said it.

Rebekah pushed her father's chair through into the drawing room and shut the long French windows firmly, resisting the urge to slam them. She watched as they all took up their places. It reminded her of a murder mystery whodunit party, nobody sure what was coming next.

Joe took the lead as always. 'Well, come on then, out with it. What do you want . . .?'

Rebekah spoke for the first time. She didn't look at anyone, she didn't raise her voice, she didn't move a muscle but she could feel her blood pressure rising slowly but surely.

'We know.'

Lauren asked, 'What do you know, darlin'?'

'You tell us, Mummy dearest, what it is that we should know but we didn't and now we do.' Her voice was low and sarcastic.

Joe and Lauren looked at each other.

'You'll have to tell us, sweetpea,' Joe said. 'We don't have a clue what you're talking about.'

He smiled at them, and Rebekah guessed that neither of them really did know what she was talking about.

'Lewis and I are adopted and you never told us.'

It was impossible to judge Lauren's face behind the bandages and glasses but her voice was confident.

'Whoever told you that nonsense? Dear Lord, I've never heard anything like it. Where did that come from?'

That was it, Rebekah could hold on no longer, the rage erupted.

'From the fucking drawer in your fucking bureau that's where. We know everything, you lying bastards, you lying, lying bastards . . .'

Lewis held her back, he alone could see the pain in his father's face as he visibly shrunk further in his chair.

'Are you tellin' me you've been in my study? Going through my things? How dare you?' Lauren's self-righteous indignation made Rebekah laugh.

'Oh, I dare and I did, and I cut up half your clothes and trashed your room but good old Lewis here helped Gladys clear it up. Didn't you even notice you'd hardly got any clothes?'

'Gladys said they were at the cleaners, a water leak or something. And how did you find that drawer? I've not opened that in over twenty years—'

'SHUT UP, ALL OF YOU.' Joe Alari's voice boomed through the room and the stunned silence was instant.

'I really don't give a toss about clothes and bureaus and the whys and wheres. I care that you know, that you found out this way . . . Now let's all talk about this sensibly and like adults, which we all are.' He waited for a second. 'Rebekah, is this what all that nonsense in the papers was about? Is it?'

She nodded.

'Right then, that's that out of the way. Now, are we adults or are we not?' He looked at the three faces. 'OK, let's talk.'

What Joe really meant was that he would talk and they would listen, and they did. Everyone always listened to him. Joe took on the role of storyteller as his wife sat silently at his side.

'When your mother and I first got married there was never any doubt that we both wanted a big family. We were comfortable, even then, and we wanted children, lots of them, but it wasn't to be. We saw all the top doctors but no one could find anything wrong.

'We decided that we would adopt. Now that's a long story but, anyway, we were approved and told about a baby boy who had been given up for adoption but, for various reasons, was still in a foster home at sixteen months old.

'Now we'd always imagined adopting a tiny baby, but when we saw you, Lewis, there was nothing we could do. We fell in love with you instantly. You toddled over to us and tried to climb up our legs, you came to us, you chose us, we loved you instantly.'

Joe smiled at Lewis but he was busy watching Rebekah; she just carried on looking at her feet.

Joe continued, 'However, for nearly six months of your short life you had been sharing foster parents, bedroom, toys, everything with another baby – you, Rebekah, but you were still called Skye then. As dark as Lewis was blond and as truculent as he was passive, both so different but you were like brother and sister even then, as if it was meant to be. From the minute we saw you, you were our little girl and Lewis was besotted with you even then. We had to fight, boy, did we have to fight, because you were the most wanted baby in England after all the press coverage, but we got there in the end and we adopted both of you. It all seems so long ago, as if it happened to someone else. You *are* our children—'

Rebekah interrupted: 'Why didn't you tell us? Why did you let us live a lie?'

'We intended to tell you, in the beginning, but we wanted you to be our own children so much I suppose I wished it on ourselves. We moved soon after and no one knew except my parents and that was that. You forget so quickly and then when you do remember it's too late.'

'Why did Mummy say, "Bad blood will out?" That was a dig, is that what you think? Bad blood?'

Lauren said nothing so Joe answered for her.

'Hand on heart, sweetpea, how often have you said something you don't mean? When you're shrieking "I hate you, I hate you", as you often do, do you really mean it?' He looked at his daughter but she was silent. 'Well? Do you?'

As Rebekah continued to stare at her father, Lauren spoke.

'Darlin', I'm sorry. You just pushed and pushed and I could have cut my tongue clean out my mouth as soon as the words were out. I love both my babies.' She paused. 'Now look, you've made me cry. I'm not allowed to cry . . . my scars . . .'

Joe turned to Lewis. 'You're quiet, son. Haven't you got anything to say?'

'Not really. I don't mind as much as Beka does.'

'Perhaps we weren't good parents but we—'

'Too right you weren't,' Rebekah snapped. 'We came in somewhere below the houses and above the horses, about level with the cars by my reckoning . . .'

Joe ignored her outburst.

'We may not have got it right but it had nothing to do with your being adopted. We just made a few mistakes along the way, as any parents do. None of us is perfect and if we had our time again, who knows?'

On the drive back to the clinic Rebekah was on top form.

'Lying bastards, they still can't admit they were fucking useless parents. "Mummy loves both her babies" – what a load of total crap. They don't realise what they've done to me . . .'

Lewis let her carry on. He couldn't be bothered to argue. Rebekah had never been reasonable in her life and he knew that, ironically, that was because she was Joe Alari's daughter.

She was surprised to see Cormac waiting in the lounge of the clinic when she got back.

'What are you doing here? I told you I didn't want to see you . . .'

Lewis sighed as Cormac got up and walked straight out. Lewis followed him out, muttering as he went, 'Give it a rest, Beka. You're in danger of becoming a first-rate, top-of-the-tree, top-gun bore!'

When they were in the corridor, Lewis said, 'Please go back in, Mac. You know she's not well, give her a chance.'

'I'll give her a chance when she's honest with me, honest about what all this is about—'

Lewis interrupted, 'Ask her. I'm sure she'll tell you in her own time but this is big, really big, and she's still out the window with it all . . .'

Rebekah was looking for Peter, the really nice man with the gambling addiction who was in the clinic courtesy of his probation order, but he had left just before she'd got back from her parents'. Had enough, walked out, gone.

She would miss him. Sharing her spiteful sense of humour, he made her laugh with tales of his embezzling habits that got him into court in the first place.

He was great fun, and she enjoyed making him laugh with outrageous tales of her antics with drugs and sex, her overdose and her night in the cells. She even told him about the débâcle with Dan the Man. Exaggerating as she always did when telling a good story to a good listener, she really made him laugh out loud at the tales of all the celebrities she socialised with.

He had even sneaked in some dope, and they had puffed away sneakily under a huge tree in the grounds, whispering and sniggering together, like two naughty school children behind the bike sheds for an illicit cigarette.

He was such good company and now he was gone and she was depressed. He had understood her. He had always wanted to listen to her.

The headlines that weekend wreaked havoc. 'DRUG ADDICT IT GIRL REBEKAH IN CLINIC FOLLOWING SUICIDE ATTEMPT' – the whole story, the life and times of Rebekah Alari, plus a lot more, spread across three pages of a tabloid Sunday newspaper.

Rebekah had unwittingly provided the gambler with his funds to hotfoot it back to the casino. He'd sold her out.

Angie was checking her answerphone messages.

'Hello, this is Lewis Alari. Giles Boughton-Jones suggested I contact you. Please can you phone me as soon as possible? I'm in New York with my sister.'

Giles had phoned Angie soon after the story had appeared.

'I want to ask you a favour. I take it you've read all the stuff about Rebekah Alari? Is there any chance you could do a sympathetic interview with her? Let her put her side of the story?'

Angie had been surprised. She'd been wondering how to get an interview with Rebekah and now it was being handed to her on a plate.

'I'd love to get the chance to interview her but I can't guarantee it would be sympathetic. Everyone's trying to get her side of the story – why me?'

'Lewis said she's in a bad way – so is he for that matter – and my advice, for what it's worth, was to speak out instead of hiding away, set the record straight. Most of it wasn't true, you know . . . Oh, she was in the clinic all right, but not for the reasons they said. She's not a junkie, just mixed up.'

262

Angie had smiled affectionately; Giles would find some redeeming features in the devil himself.

'Come on, Giles, he was wired up. The whole thing is on tape, it was almost verbatim. She blew the whistle on everyone, even you!'

'It was a setup, you know how it works. He didn't wire himself up.'

'I'll do it if it's an exclusive. She's not to talk to anyone else and I want Dave with me for photographs. I also want a free hand and I want a watertight agreement. I can do without having Joe Alari on my tail forever afterwards . . .'

'I'll get back to you and I'll get Lewis to contact you.' He'd paused. 'She's not a bad kid, really, not once you know her. No one really understands her, apart from Lewis, of course.'

Angie had laughed.

'You're the only person who could say that, Giles. You're such a nice man, do you know that?'

Lewis had collected Rebekah from the clinic and they'd headed straight to Heathrow for a flight to New York and the Alari apartment on Park Avenue.

Rebekah didn't want to talk to anyone, she just wanted to crawl away. It was the worst time of her life. She could see her lifestyle slipping away – who wants to invite someone to a party who's going to kiss and tell at the first chance?

'I'm not a drug addict, I don't shag everyone I meet, and I didn't OD – well, I did, but that's not the point. Why did they write that shit?'

'Because that's what you told the arsehole and he taped it, and it's a great story. It's just a bloody miracle you didn't launch into chapter and verse on the baby in the toilet business.' Lewis stopped and looked at her. 'You didn't, did you?'

'Of course I didn't. I don't think I did, anyway.'

Lewis could see she was thinking about it. 'You can't have,' he reassured her. 'They would have used it by now . . . No, damage limitation is what we need now. Giles suggested an exclusive with Angie Kavanagh, she's fair.'

'Fair? She's a friend of the old woman, Sue bloody Portchester, bloody Boughton-Jones – how can she be fair? Sue hates me, everyone hates me now . . . not even Cormac will talk to me. He thinks I'm a cokehead who's shagged every rock star in the history of the world behind his back.'

Rebekah was pacing the floor, up and down, round and round, just like the big cats in the zoo, ready to lunge at the first movement.

263

Lewis wondered if she could hold out much longer without medical help. Maybe he should call Cormac and try to persuade him to come over. He was one of the few people they could trust.

'Well then, take the opportunity to set the record straight. Go formal, give them just enough and then they won't dig any further. They're all after you, Beka, to find out the gory details. It's not fair on Mum and Dad for the rest of it to come out. Go for the sympathy vote: you were upset over the accident and went over the top. Angie is your best chance if you don't want it all laid bare across the tabloids.'

'Fucking ring her then, and see what she's got to say, but I don't promise.'

'Dave darling, how do you fancy a trip to New York?'

He looked at Angie suspiciously. 'Work or play?'

'Both, if we play our cards right. An exclusive with Rebekah Alari for both of us. Providing it comes off I've sold it already. Big bucks, honey, big bucks for both of us. After the interview we can stay on for a week, have a romantic holiday all to ourselves. Joshua can either stay with the nanny or go to Jemima's.'

'Aren't you worried Rebekah's using you? Setting you up as her mouthpiece?'

'I'm not in the least worried. I know she's going to try to use me but that's always half the fun of celebrity interviews, the hidden agenda. There always is one if they want to speak to a journalist!'

'Sounds good then, when are we off?'

Dave hadn't changed at all over the years – still denim man with a ponytail and not a hint of a receding hairline although the blond was now grey and the waistline was slightly thicker. Angie still loved him dearly but she often wondered at how lucky she was to be with someone she liked and someone whose company she enjoyed. He rarely mentioned marriage now and she knew that with time she was weakening. She wanted to be married to him but the thought of the relationship changing was just too unbearable to consider.

Rebekah was the talk of the town. Every newspaper had picked up on the story to some extent. It even warranted serious editorials on the pros and cons of a socialite, spoilt little rich girl. There were quotes from everyone she had ever upset who had thrilled to the chance of turning the knife, plus unlimited, unsolicited advice from doctors and psychologists on TV. The whole episode had turned into a three-ring circus. It was a nightmare.

Rebekah's life was laid bare and this impacted on everyone close to her.

Joe and Lauren Alari had taken off to Florida with their nurses to the new house in Naples, where armed guards dissuaded anyone from getting too near. The Alari parents weren't even talking to Lewis, let alone Rebekah, who'd described them as the parents from hell!

Lewis had phoned Giles, who in turn phoned Cormac, who phoned Lewis. His immediate response was, 'No way, man, no way.' Then he booked a flight.

He had known all along he would go but just for once he wanted to be in control if only for a little while. He wanted her to need him, to love him the way he loved her, not just jerk him around for fun.

'I hope Josh is OK. It's a long time for both of us to be away together . . .'

Dave and Angie were flying high over the Atlantic en route for New York.

Dave patted her hand on the armrest and smiled reassuringly.

'He's going to be fine. He's got two of them at his beck and call, he won't even miss us. Now, how are the notes going? Do you know where you're at with it yet? It would be nice to get it over with double quick and then enjoy ourselves. It's been ages since we escaped to the jolly old big apple for a dirty weekend.'

He put his arm round her and pulled her close. 'I love you, Miss Kavanagh.'

'And I love you, Mister Oliver.'

'Let's hold hands and watch the movie, pretend we're in the back seat of the Odeon. We could even snog a little?'

'No way, José, I've got my reputation to think of. Just look at the bother our little Miss Alari has got herself into by not being discreet.'

Lewis Alari rang Angie at her hotel.

'Does one p.m. tomorrow suit you? . . . I'll meet you in the lobby.'

He put the phone down and turned to Rebekah.

'It's all set now, there's no going back. Let's get it over and done with and get on with our lives, all of us. You're the only one who can dig yourself back out now.'

Cormac arrived in New York that evening and went straight to the apartment. Rebekah looked at him and welcomed him in her own inimitable way.

'You took your fucking time. Where have you been?'

The words from her mouth didn't match the look in her eyes. He knew she was pleased to see him and he was pleased to see her, she just hadn't got a clue how to show it.

They were all awake all night and for the first time Cormac was party to the whole sorry story. The two men tried to persuade Rebekah to sleep but she was hyper and chain-smoking, her nervous energy keeping her persistently on her feet. They did hold their ground on one thing: despite her constant demands they refused to let her have alcohol for fear of a hangover. Everyone knew that as much depended on the photographs as the actual words.

If Rebekah Alari didn't want all her secrets laid out then they knew she had to gain Angie Kavanagh's sympathy and put her own side of the story across.

Chapter Nineteen

Angie Kavanagh still got a buzz from an exclusive, still enjoyed putting one over on the opposition by getting in there first. The media circus were in New York staking out the Alari apartment and trying to get quotes from anyone who would give them. That was what kept a good story running.

As she was getting dressed she pictured their faces as she upstaged them once again. One of the secrets of Angie's success was the attention she paid to detail; she had learnt over the years that it was the little things that put people at ease when she was interviewing them and clothes were important. Expensive but understated, and never overshadow or overpower your interviewee. That was her motto and she stuck to it.

'How do I look, darling? Suitably fashionable, but not mutton, et cetera, et cetera?'

Dave cast a fleeting glance in her direction. 'Great, you look great. Cab's due in five minutes, let's get all this stuff down to the lobby.'

Angie smiled. 'Your enthusiasm underwhelms me.'

She didn't really need his opinion, she knew she had chosen well. The dark green designer suit and white collarless blouse combined with black tights and kitten-heel pumps were stylish and businesslike at the same time.

Denim man was in jeans as usual and a matching shirt. His only concession to the New York autumn was a battered beige body warmer with more pockets than he could ever use, and an old pair of thermal gloves he had bought in Russia years before.

They went downstairs together, an unlikely combination of workmates both laden with all the equipment needed for one interview and one set of photographs.

Lewis was waiting in the marble-floored lobby of the Park Avenue apartment building when they pulled up. He waited until they were through the doors before greeting them.

267

'Hi, pleased to meet you again. Can we go straight up? I am just so pissed off with having my photo taken by every passing camera . . .'

No one spoke as a mirrored elevator the size of a small room whisked them silently and swiftly up to the penthouse. Angie had never formally met Lewis or Rebekah, although they had often passed each other by at social dos in the past; she may not have noticed Lewis but everyone noticed Rebekah. She stood out like a shining beacon and eclipsed everyone around her. This time was no different.

Introductions and small talk over, Angie settled down into an easy chair, almost, but not quite, opposite Rebekah; she wanted to keep Lewis in her line of vision as well. Whatever was going on he knew about it as well.

Dave pottered about in the background, setting up his equipment, seemingly oblivious to the conversations, but Angie knew he would be listening.

Rebekah was ready and waiting to launch on to the current crisis. She had a prepared speech ready almost, but Angie wanted background first from the key person, not from cutting and clipping. With double indemnity of pencils, pads and cassette recorder, as well as copious notes and questions, she started dipping and delving, prompting when she needed to but otherwise just listening.

As the session wore on Angie found herself warming to the girl. Her caustic wit was very observational, if occasionally spiteful, and at one point the older woman felt obliged to interrupt.

'Rebekah, please remember I'm a journalist. Don't say anything you don't want me to repeat; off the record comments I find hard to deal with!' She laughed as she said it but the warning was there; if you don't want it printed, don't say it!

'OK then, I'll try and be good!' She reached over the antique occasional table the size of a single bed and took a hairband from the fruitbowl. Twisting the long shiny hair up on to the top of her head she fastened it tightly into a ponytail.

'Don't worry, Dave darling, I shall adjourn to adjust myself before you get to shoot me . . .'

The flirty, girly smile didn't go unnoticed by Angie. It was second nature to Rebekah, and despite the circumstance she still couldn't resist doing it. Angie could see why the girl was so very unpopular with women and adored by men!

The interview flew by and Angie was still in the dark.

She believed Rebekah when she said that a lot of what she told

Peter the gambler was bravado, related to impress him and make him laugh, but the rest of it didn't make a lot of sense: the timing wasn't right. The incident outside the hotel and the overdose were too long after the Alari accident. It had to be something much bigger that made her kick off. Angie was still thinking about it when Rebekah went to get ready for the photos.

'Look, Lewis,' Angie said, 'you're not going to make me look a fool over this, the pair of you, are you? I've been doing this for too long. I know when there's a hidden agenda . . . I remember a certain royal interview when the Duchess stated categorically that she was not pregnant and then announced it formally a few days later. The interviewer took a lot of flack for that.'

'Honestly, Angie, Rebekah just wants to put her side of the story and then let it die down. It's all a lot of nothing, really. She's been stupid but she's paying a high price for it: exclusion from the A-list she loves and total disappointment from the parents. I think she's learnt her lesson about adverse publicity.' He found it hard to look Angie Kavanagh in the eye as he continued, 'She told you she's going for therapy, didn't she?'

'She did,' Angie smiled wryly, 'for drug abuse, for alcohol abuse, for stress, for smoking, for allergy tests, to find her true self . . . shall I go on?'

'OK, OK, Rebekah isn't known for doing things by halves . . .' He raised his eyes to the ceiling before bursting into crazy laughter. 'She's mad, totally off the wall, but I love her!'

Rebekah came back into the room and Angie watched the inveterate model in action. She was impressed. Not a movement nor an expression betrayed anything other than what she wanted to portray. The girl was one hundred per cent professional.

Angie always used a check list to make sure she got all the facts right. While Lewis made the coffee she went through it with Rebekah.

'Can you spell Rebekah and Alari for me. I hate to get spellings wrong . . . Your home address? Just so that I can send you a copy prepublication to check for discrepancies . . . Date of birth? No hiding the true age, thank you!'

'November 20th 1973.'

Angie's pencil stopped on the page.

'Sorry?'

Rebekah repeated it. By now she was bored and it showed in her voice.

'November 20th 1973, twenty-six next birthday. I'm too young to start lying about my age, but if you ever ask my mother add on ten. She likes to pretend she was a child bride!'

Angie carried on down the list. The date had fazed her but she soon got back on to an even keel even though it had reminded her of the past.

But soon it got the better of her. She had to ask, had to put her mind at rest.

'Is Rebekah your real name?'

'Of course it is, Rebekah Alari . . .'

Go for broke, Angie thought, go for broke. That's what journalists do . . . 'Are Joe and Lauren Alari your birth parents? You're not adopted or anything?'

Rebekah sat frozen in time and Lewis nearly dropped his cup. The colour drained from their faces.

'What sort of dumb fucking question is that? Are you saying I'm not who I am? I am Rebekah Alari . . . daughter of Joe and Lauren Alari. How dare you insinuate otherwise?'

Angie didn't look up. 'Sorry, just another routine bit of nonsense.'

She stood up and collected all her belongings that were spread over the table.

'Right, Dave, have you done? Let's go and leave Rebekah and Lewis alone. They've probably had enough for today!'

She looked at them: they were both almost in shock.

'Thank you for your time. Are you staying here long? Where shall I send the copy?'

Lewis saw them out and when he got back to the apartment Rebekah was going crazy.

'You said something, you fucking idiot, you told Giles and he told the old woman, Angie Kavanagh's best friend . . . Now it'll be all over the paper: Rebekah Alari, the baby nobody wanted, the baby dumped in a fucking toilet. Everyone will feel sorry for me but no one will want to know me.'

'I swear to you, Beka, I haven't told a soul. She can't possibly know anything or she would have asked about it. Now forget it, you're being paranoid. Cormac will be back shortly. I'm going to call in the caterers. Let's really push the boat out and celebrate the start of the end of all this. I have to get back to London tomorrow, it's not fair on Giles.'

'Ring for Cormac now. If he's speaking out I'll crucify him myself.'

'You know he wouldn't say anything. Anyway, he only knew last night. Now forget it, it'll soon be over.'

★ ★ ★

270

Angie had sent Dave out to the deli for a takeaway; as soon as he was gone she picked up the phone.

'Gavin? It's Angie, I'm phoning from New York. I need a favour . . . Can you get yourself up to the public records office in London tomorrow and check out Rebekah Alari? I need to know if she's adopted or not and anything else you might find. You know Dave and his fate and karma and meant to be crap? Well, I'm beginning to believe in it. When you call back don't give any info to Dave, just pretend it's a social call.'

The call came the next day and Angie could feel the big black cloud that had been absent since Tony Willmott's death threatening to engulf her.

'Rebekah Skye Alari, dob 20 November 1973. Adopted May 1974. Surely this doesn't mean what I think it means, does it?'

'I think it does, Gavin. I think Rebekah Alari is my daughter. How's that for a particularly evil twist of fate? The odds on winning the lottery jackpot three weeks running are better than that. What am I going to do?'

'Nothing Angie baby, absolutely nothing. You may be wrong. We'll talk when you get back. Another few days is neither here nor there in the scale of things.'

Dave misread the signs. He thought Angie's withdrawal and preoccupation was because of being away from Joshua.

'There's no need to feel guilty, you know.' He turned towards her in the four-poster bed.

'Guilty? What should I feel guilty about?' Suddenly she was alert, aware of his presence beside her, she had been so lost in thought she had almost forgotten he was there.

'I thought you were feeling guilty at leaving Joshua for so long, for having a holiday without him. He's having his own holiday you know.'

'Sorry, darling, I was miles away. It's not Josh, I was just thinking about Rebekah Alari and how sad it all is. She shouldn't have to justify her behaviour to the world. She's just young and silly and been spoilt rotten. I would hate to have my life dissected over Sunday breakfast in every household, have total strangers passing judgement on me as if they knew me.'

Dave pulled himself up on to one elbow and looked down at her, his eyes twinkling.

'Excuse me? What did I say this morning? And what did you say? Can you remember?'

'So you were right, as always. But I was right as well, you know.

271

If it wasn't me it would be someone else. I didn't get her into this situation. If it's anyone's fault it is her parents'.'

'Not necessarily. Look at Lewis, he's quite well-adjusted considering.'

'Mmm, I suppose so.' She paused and looked up at him. 'How would you feel if my life was suddenly up for public analysis? There are things that wouldn't stand too much scrutiny.'

Dave was distracted now, his mind on better things than Rebekah Alari. He leant forward and kissed her hard and long.

'I'd manage! Now let's get down to some really interesting business . . .'

Angie pretended to respond. She tried really hard but her mind was elsewhere. The time had come to tell Dave everything, she knew that. The problem was, how?

Just that morning all had been right with her world – Dave, Joshua, Jemima, her career . . . this could rip it all apart. And what about Rebekah?

She tried to imagine how the tall beautiful girl who had postured and pouted in front of Dave's camera could possibly be her daughter, Tony Willmott's daughter, a child of rape, a baby abandoned at birth.

Angie prayed she was wrong. After all the years of trying to picture Skye and wondering where she was and what she was doing, and hoping one day she would find her, the reality was too frightening to contemplate.

Right now she needed Gavin, good sensible Gavin. He would know what to do.

They were expecting Jemima to meet them at Heathrow but instead Gavin was there. Angie spotted him as they came out of the customs hall and threw herself at him, leaving a bewildered Dave with all the luggage.

'Hiya, you two. I'm in London for a few days so thought I'd save Jemima the journey. How was New York, my most favourite city in the whole wide world? I'm in the wrong job, you know . . . Next you'll be trying to convince me it was all work and no play!'

Angie was so pleased to see him she wanted to cry but there was nothing she could do, nothing she could ask him until they were alone.

Her chance came when Dave offered to drive his daughter back to Kent and Joshua jumped up and down, pleading to go as well.

Dave tried to dissuade him.

'Don't you want to spend the evening with Mummy? She'll want to hear all about your holiday and she can tell you all about ours. We went right to the top of the Empire State Building.'

'I want to come with you and Jem, please . . .'

Any other time Angie would have felt hurt but she desperately needed to speak to Gavin.

'You go, sweetheart. We'll talk about it all when you get in.'

As soon as they'd gone, Angie and Gavin made themselves comfortable on the sofa.

'Now, Angie baby, I can see you're stressed out. Tell me why you think Rebekah Alari could be Skye. It all sounds a bit far-fetched to me, a teeny bit overimaginative . . .'

'I hope I am wrong, Gavin, I really do, but what if I'm not?'

He pulled her close as he always had done in times of crisis.

'If you're right or wrong we'll deal with it, but either way you must tell Dave. Then at least he's prepared. You don't have to tell him about Rebekah, that's speculation, but tell him about Skye.'

Angie fidgeted with her clothes, straightening her jumper, pulling up her socks, the way she did when she was fifteen and Gavin first met her. She still looked the same to him, vulnerable and childlike; he wanted to hug her and make it better but he knew he couldn't.

'Come on then, Angie baby, let's have a brainstorming session and see what we come up with. Now, Rebekah Alari was adopted, her date of birth is the same as Skye's, and her middle name is Skye . . . is that enough?'

'How much more do you want? That's more than coincidence, surely? Gavin, I'm so confused. I often think about her and imagine meeting her but this . . . And if it is her, well, can you just imagine if that got out?'

Gavin smiled. 'Everyone would feel sorry for you – the daughter from hell.' They both laughed but Angie had more than that on her mind.

'Just supposing it is her, and I tell her, she's going to want to know about her father. What do I say? He was a drug-dealing psychopath who married my mother and beat the crap out of her, raped me and then tried to murder me and Joshua. But it's OK because now he's dead, run over outside my house. How can you wrap that up?'

'Somehow you can, but you're still jumping the gun. It's all hypothetical; there are no concrete facts. Do you think she knows she's adopted?'

Angie laughed. 'I'm bloody sure she does, but I don't know if she knows the background – if it is her, of course!'

'Well, Angie baby, my advice to you, for what it's worth, is to tell Dave the facts, only the facts, and then you're over the first hurdle. Tell him tonight. I'll stay if you think it will help . . .'

'No, that might make it worse. He'll think we're ganging up on him. I'll tell him tomorrow. Now give me your news. I know you've got some.'

Gavin was surprised. 'How do you know that?'

She planted a gentle kiss on his head. Gavin was looking older now. He was grey and quite chubby compared to the lean young man she'd first known, but she loved him dearly, her nearly father.

'Because I know you, silly. You've got excitement written all over your face!'

'All right then, you win. I'm selling the café and moving to London to live with Simon. He's younger than me so he can work and keep me in my old age. I'm going to retire, I think!'

'But that's brilliant! Oh, I'm so glad. We'll be able to see each other all the time too!'

When Gavin finally left, Angie ran herself a hot bath, and as she lay back trying to soak the stress away, her mind wandered back over the first fifteen years of her life. BA, she thought to herself, 'Before Angie', the life of Louise Jermaine.

There was Fran, her mother, who put herself before everyone else, Joshua who left her and never came back, Daniel the baby brother she adored, Sharon her best friend, and Nancy, more of a mother to her in a short space of time than Fran ever was.

She realised it was an impossible dream to think she could erase the past, pretend it had never existed.

Old Mrs Anderson suddenly appeared in front of her: 'Be sure your sins will find you out.'

Angie knew there were two options open to her. The first was to ignore it all. Skye would never be able to trace her birth mother. There was no information at all for her to go on, nothing that could lead her to Angie. The second was to tell Dave and risk her relationship, and tell Rebekah and ruin her life maybe.

How do you tell someone that she was born from rape? Especially someone who had lived the life that Rebekah had lived, wanting for nothing?

Eventually she decided on a course of action and opted for a bit of both: tell Dave and then try to find out if Rebekah was looking for her mother. If she wasn't looking then it was best to let it lie. But how could she find out?

It was only as the knocking got louder that she realised Joshua was outside the door.

'Mummy, I've got to go to bed in a minute. Come and talk to me . . .'

'Be out in a minute, darling. Sorry, I didn't hear you come in.'

Wrapping a bathrobe tightly around her, she went through to tell Joshua all about New York. She carried on talking even after the dark eyes had fluttered shut. She watched him cuddling his comfort blanket with one hand while the other was instinctively making its way to his mouth. He hated sucking his thumb but during the night he always did.

Angie thought about Rebekah Alari and wondered again if it was remotely possible.

'Dave, there's something I have to talk to you about, something awful, so awful you'll probably hate me; something I should have told you a long, long time ago.'

Standing in front of him almost to attention she took a deep breath. She had delayed the evil moment as long as she could. It was now or never. She knew she might never get up the courage again. Before telling him she had crept up into the attic and retrieved the tote bag that held all her secrets and taken it downstairs.

'This sounds serious. Don't tell me you're married?' His joke fell flat and his expression changed the moment he looked at her face.

'Sorry, that was a bad joke. Go on then, tell me what's wrong.'

She opened her mouth and the words tumbled out. She was desperate to tell the story before she lost her courage.

'My name isn't Angie Kavanagh. I was born Louise Jermaine. When I was nearly fifteen my stepfather raped me and made me pregnant. I ran away to Brighton, had the baby and abandoned her in the toilet at a hospital. I stole my stepfather's drug-dealing money and he came after me and blackmailed me. He was going to go to the papers. He was the so-called tramp who broke into the house. He was going to murder me and Joshua.'

She didn't even pause for a breath. There she thought, it's done, out in the open at last.

Dave didn't say a word for a moment. She could see he was trying to absorb what she had said.

'Let me get this straight: you had a secret that you kept from me, then you put all the family at risk to keep that secret? Joshua and Jemima? You were prepared to sacrifice them for your career?'

Once the tears started she couldn't stop them. The gasping sobs made it hard for her to speak coherently.

'It wasn't like that. Gavin said—'

His face was red with rage. 'I might have known bloody Gavin was in on it.'

'That's not fair . . .' She tried to keep her voice down, aware of Joshua upstairs sleeping peacefully.

'It's not bloody fair that you couldn't trust me, or did you think I'd go to the papers as well and endanger your precious career?'

'I hoped you'd understand. I know I should have told you but it got harder and harder. I'm sorry I didn't tell you but I'm not going to apologise for what happened. That wasn't my fault, you bastard, it wasn't my fault, it wasn't my fault . . .' She knew she was at the point of hysteria, about to lose control, but she couldn't stop. Hurling herself at him she battered his chest. 'It wasn't my fault . . . I didn't ask to be raped . . .'

It was almost as if Dave suddenly came to his senses and realised what he was doing. He grabbed her and held her so tightly she couldn't move.

'Calm down, calm down, I'm sorry, calm down and we'll talk, I love you, I'm so sorry . . . ssshh, it's OK.'

They talked into the night, jet lag forgotten, and she showed him the old newspaper cuttings that she had kept – every cutting from every paper that had reported the abandoned baby.

'No one knew, not a soul. I had never told anyone but when I got the first letter from Tony I panicked. That's when I told Gavin. I had never said one word to anyone until then. Perhaps I thought if I didn't speak about it, it hadn't happened. In hospital I never even told the psychiatrist.'

'You should have told me, Angie. You really should have trusted me. I'm sorry I was angry but I still feel so hurt. Don't you know me better than that?'

She didn't answer.

'Why are you telling me now? Why tonight? Has something happened?'

Suddenly he was alert. She could see his brain was trying to make sense of the timing, and she could tell he was suspicious.

'I just thought it was time . . .' Even as she said it she knew it was inadequate.

'Don't lie to me, Angie, tell me. Is she looking for you? Are you looking for her?'

'Neither Dave, truly, but . . .' She hesitated and looked at him, trying to think on her feet, to decide the best thing to do for everyone.

'But what?'

'I think I've found her by accident.' She took a deep breath. 'I think she's Rebekah Alari!'

Dave spluttered his coffee down his shirt. In any other circumstances his face would have been laughable, he was so stereotypically stunned.

'You are joking? Tell me you're joking . . . Oh shit, now I understand the question, that stupid question you've never asked anyone before that I know of . . . are you adopted or anything? Cool and calm as you like. What the fuck made you think of that?'

'Her middle name is Skye, the birthdates are the same, and then I checked: she was adopted. It all fits, Dave. What am I going to do?'

'Fuck knows.'

Angie smiled for the first time. 'That's twice you've used the F word; and you keep telling me not to swear! You tell me that swearing is a sign of an inadequate grasp of the English language, no one needs to swear ever according to the gospel of St David!'

'You always did bring out the worst in me.' He looked at her and laughed. 'Rebekah Alari, the bad-mouthing, tantrum-throwing, foot-stamping Rebekah Alari – the most spoilt brat in the history of the world, according to the gospel of St Angie and she could be all yours!'

'That's not even remotely funny.'

'No, I know it's not, but sometimes you just have to laugh.'

That night Angie dreamt vividly, strange and disjointed dreams of Fran and Joshua, of Daniel when he was a baby. None of it made any sense but when she woke up the first thing she did was elbow Dave in the back.

'I've made up my mind, I'm going to go back. I'm going to find my parents and brother and I'm going to shoot those demons down once and for all.'

Taking his face in her hands she shook him gently.

'Wake up, Dave? Are you listening? Do you still want to marry me?'

Angie Kavanagh's exclusive interview with Rebekah Alari was being published that weekend. Rebekah and Lewis were back in London and the family, friends and colleagues all had their fingers crossed that there was an end in sight to the tabloid tittle tattle.

'It'll be OK, Beka. A nine-day wonder and then it's over. Everyone will forgive you because you were set up. Done and finished and back to normal, praise the Lord and bang the tambourine.'

'Lewis, shut up, you're getting on my nerves.'

'Thanks a lot. My life had been totally disrupted because of you. Giles is fed up, Mum and Dad are really pissed off and instead of "Thank you, Lewis, for digging me out of the mire yet again" I get, "Shut up, you're getting on my nerves." Selfish bitch.'

She looked at him in surprise. 'Who's pushed your buttons, brother dearest?'

'You, Rebekah, you. Now go away and grow up. I've had enough.'

Putting his head down and making a play of getting on with his work he was aware of her heading out the door and slamming it hard behind her.

Rebekah had wanted to talk to Lewis but her pride as usual had got the better of her and she just had to storm out.

She wanted to talk to her parents but again her pride got in the way. She wondered if she could bring herself to fly to Naples and crawl over broken glass in sackcloth and ashes. She was confused. Her prime concern had been her reputation, her loss of status and the desire for no one to find out about her, find out who she really was, but now she found the emphasis shifting.

Over and over again she found herself thinking about her mother, who she was, why she had abandoned her baby, and she also thought about her father. What part did he play in it? Did he know? The anger had been replaced with a burning desire to find out about herself. What did 'mixed race' mean? Was her mother Black or Asian? Where was she from? What about her father? What was the combination that had left her with an olive complexion and thick, deep chocolate-brown hair?

She couldn't understand why Lewis had no urge to find out about himself, why he was content to be an Alari; she wondered if it was easier for men than women.

The problem was she didn't have anything to go on to start searching. She already knew everything there was to know and it wasn't much. Her only hope was the hospital on her birthday next month.

The woman with the rosebud – she was her only connection to her birthright.

'Did you say what I think you said this morning? Did you really ask me if I still wanted to marry you?'

'I did. Do you?'

'You know I do.'

'Then the answer's yes. Now there's no secrets and lies, the answer is yes!'

'When?'

'Whenever you want.'

'Where?'

'Wherever you want.'

'Are you sure about this?'

'I've never been more sure of anything.'

'What about the demons?'

'I'm going to deal with them this week. I know, how about Edinburgh at Christmas?'

'You're on!'

Angie made a list.

1. Go back to Albemarle Street to try to find Fran and Daniel. Someone must know.
2. Find Nancy Aberlone – maybe she hasn't moved.
3. Contact Sharon. Nancy will know.
4. Go to Barbados and find Joshua. His family will know.

Chapter Twenty

It was teatime when Angie parked her car at the end of the street of her old nightmares. She had remembered it as a scruffy but neighbourly street but now there was something intimidating about it as well. Trying to look confident, she set the car alarm and started walking down towards the flats.

The groups of baggy-clothed youths hanging around watched her defiantly as she walked away from her Mercedes. The same youths who would have balked at the idea of a school uniform were dressed identically, all their faces sinisterly shielded by base-ball caps. Angie knew instinctively that if she was too long at least part of her car would be missing by the time she got back, if not the whole thing. She couldn't help thinking that if he was still alive Tony Willmott would be dealing drugs with these youngsters. She wondered fleetingly just how many lives he had ruined indirectly.

The first flat she went to was number 3, her home for the first fourteen years of her life. The block had obviously been redecorated recently and all the front doors were bright canary yellow. Some of them had hanging baskets and big terracotta pots outside their doors, and there was now a security door at the entrance. It all looked a lot nicer than she had expected when she walked down the road – almost an oasis in the semiderelict street. She could feel herself shaking as she rang the bell and waited.

A young girl with a baby in her arms and another, not much older, clinging to her legs opened the door.

Angie smiled politely. 'Hello, I wonder if you can help me. I'm looking for Fran Jermaine or Willmott who used to live here. Have you any idea where I might find her?'

'Not a clue. Who wants to know?' The girl looked her up and down suspiciously. Angie was pleased she had dressed down in jeans and a sweatshirt.

'I'm her daughter and I'm trying to find her ... We lost touch ...'

281

'Dunno, I've only been here a year and before that it was boarded up for ages, waiting doing up.'

'Is Mrs Anderson still upstairs?' Angie knew she was clutching at straws; Mrs Anderson would be ninety-odd if she was still alive.

'Never heard of her. Sorry, but I've got to go, dinner's cooking. Try number forty-four. They've been here about twenty years.'

The couple at number forty-four just about remembered Fran but hadn't a clue where she might have gone.

'Sorry, love, try the pub on the corner. They might know something.'

By the time Angie had tried the pub and nearly every house and flat in the street she was feeling deflated and annoyed with herself for being so optimistic. Although she had felt apprehensive about facing Fran in one way, it hadn't occurred to her that no one would know where she was.

'Barry!' She said the name out loud. Of course Barry would know; he was Daniel's dad.

Angry at herself for not thinking of that first she rushed back to her car. Heaving a sigh of relief that it was still in one piece, she drove the short journey to Barry's house, hoping against hope that he still lived there.

'Hello, I'm looking for Barry Wright who used to live here. Does he still?'

'No, sorry.' The man looked her up and down appreciatively. 'He's moved away, gone to Suffolk.'

'You don't know his address, do you? I really need to find him.'

'Why? Why would you need to find Barry? He left a long time ago. Good riddance is what I say.'

'Please, if you do know, please tell me. It's important.'

She looked at the young man properly for the first time. Tall and lanky, he was not good-looking but had a certain charm. He moved from the shadow of the dingy hallway on to the step and for the first time Angie saw the bright red hair.

He leered at her and leant on the porch doorframe, his arms crossed in front of him.

'Tell me why it's important? Tell me who you are and I'll think about it.'

'Is your name Daniel? Are you Barry's son?'

'Tell me who you are and why you want Barry.' She could hear the impatience in his voice.

'If you're Daniel, I'm Louise, your sister.'

The man wasn't the least bit fazed by the announcement. He just looked at her.

'Why do you want Barry, then? He's not your father.'

So he did know what she was talking about. Angie started to feel irritated with the arrogant young man who was smirking at her now.

'Look, do you mind if I come in? I don't like talking about this on the doorstep.'

'Sorry, no way. Mother wouldn't like it.'

Her heart pounded. 'Do you mean Fran? Is Fran there with you?'

He laughed, an unpleasant rasping laugh that almost frightened her.

'Don't be bloody stupid. Fran was never my mother. Sally brought me up and as far as I'm concerned she is my mother.'

'Fair enough, but why can't I come in? She was always nice to me when I visited you . . .'

All Angie's quickly raised hopes of a tearful and happy reunion with her brother were evaporating. She couldn't figure it out.

'That was probably before my father left her for the second time and took off with Fran the slapper again.'

Angie could feel the tears filling her eyes.

'What about you then? I'm your sister.'

'No you're not. After all these years you're just a stranger. I don't have a sister, I'm an only child.'

He walked inside and carefully shut the door in her face.

This time she hammered on the door, banging and banging until he came back.

'Please tell me where they are. I need to know. I want to talk to you, explain what happened . . .'

He opened the door a fraction.

'Forget it. Now piss off before I call the police.'

'Daniel, please, I know that what I did may seem wrong to you, but at least give me the chance to explain, then you can tell me to piss off . . . please?'

'I'll meet you in McDonald's in the High Street at seven o'clock.'

Again he shut the door abruptly. She could only hope that he turned up.

Walking the two familiar streets to the High Street, the same route that she'd taken when Daniel was a baby in his pram, Angie could feel her mood swinging from despair to elation and back.

She had found Daniel, her baby brother, who was now a grown man she didn't even faintly recognise. An unlikeable young man such as she would never have expected him to become in a million years. However, she was certain he knew where Barry was, though

283

surely he wasn't with Fran again. Not after everything that had happened.

It sounded incredible, but then again if they were together, and Daniel told her where, then she had at least found two of them. That left only Joshua, Nancy and Sharon.

Carefully choosing the window seat she waited impatiently for Daniel, not completely convinced that he would show.

He appeared round the corner at twenty past seven.

'I thought you weren't going to come . . .'

She looked at him closely but the only identifying feature she could see was the red hair. Other than that she thought he was right – they were strangers.

'I said I would. Now tell me what you have to and then I must get home. My mother isn't well.'

'Can I ask what's wrong?' Angie tried to make eye contact but he was having none of it.

'Nothing for you to worry about. I look after her.'

Angie told him briefly the reasons for her leaving, although she didn't tell him about Skye.

'I know Tony Willmott by reputation. He was a nasty bastard if ever there was one. Dad wouldn't let me go round there, but then Fran moved away and not long after Dad followed, stupid bastard that he is. Mum was devastated. She's still not got over it.'

'Do you keep in touch with them? Please tell me . . .'

He sighed. 'I don't keep in touch but I know the address. They're in Lowestoft.' He passed her a piece of paper with the address and phone number on. 'Now, if that's all . . .?'

'No it's not, Daniel. I really would like to get to know you. Can we at least try and mend some bridges? Here's my address and phone number . . . at least give it some thought.'

'I'll give it some thought but I'm not promising anything.'

They walked back to the car together and she kept looking at him, trying to feel something, but all she was really aware of was a deep sadness. She knew she had left it too late. They would never be able to have a true brother-and-sister relationship.

She wasn't sure whether to kiss and hug him or what, so she settled for offering her hand.

'Please keep in touch!'

'We'll see. I have to consider Mum first and foremost.'

The house was silent as she let herself in. Joshua was in bed and Dave was working in his office, magnifying glass to his eye as he studied a sheet of photos.

'I've found Daniel and I know where my mother is. She's in Lowestoft with Barry Wright, Daniel's dad. I'm going up there tomorrow.'

'Do you want me to come with you?' He still didn't look up but paused in what he was doing.

'Oh, yes please. Today was shit and I think tomorrow is going to be worse.'

The rain beat down on the windscreen, nearly bringing the wipers to a halt but Angie and Dave carried on until they reached their destination, a tiny bungalow in a quiet cul-de-sac just outside town.

'This doesn't look like the right place for Fran,' Angie said. 'She'd die stuck away somewhere like this. It must be wrong, Daniel must have sent us on a wild goose chase. Come on, let's go home.'

'Uh uh, you don't know that. Now are you going to knock or shall I?'

Her fear was so intense Dave could feel it in the car.

'I don't think I can. I want to go home. Take me home. I'm going to let it go, this is all too much for me, Dave. I'm frightened I'm going to crack up again!'

'If that's what you really want . . .'

'It is. Come on, let's go. I can always come back another time. Maybe I ought to phone first next time.'

He put the car in reverse and was just about to back up when the front door opened.

'Fuck, I think that's Barry . . . yes it is. What shall I do?'

'Just get out of the car and go and see him. It's easier than knocking on the door.'

Opening the door, she swung her legs round, climbed out as if on autopilot and walked over to him just as he got to the gate.

'Hello, Barry.'

He looked at her, slightly puzzled.

'Barry? It's Louise, remember me? Fran's daughter.'

His face broke into a huge smile. 'Of course, little Louise. I knew you'd turn up one day. I told Fran, one day she'll just come walking back in. Come in. Your mum's inside. How did you find us?'

'Daniel told me.'

'Ah, the dreaded Daniel. I'm surprised you got anywhere with that little sod. He won't have anything to do with me or your mum. He's a real mummy's boy. Sally's ruined him. He might be my son but he's not a very nice person.'

Angie thought that was probably because of his background but didn't say anything. She turned to the car.

'Dave, come and meet Barry, Daniel's dad. Barry was good to me.'

Dave got out of the car and shook hands with the man. Angie was surprised at how old he looked, she had to keep reminding herself that it was twenty-six years since she'd run away.

They walked inside the bungalow and the first thing Angie noticed was how clean and tidy it was, nothing like the hovel in Albemarle Street.

'Fran? Put the kettle on, we've got visitors.'

Angie went into the lounge just as Fran was carefully getting up from the chair. She was shocked as she saw the woman stumble and nearly fall over when she looked at her.

'Louise?' Fran looked at her in amazement. 'It is. Barry, it's Louise. Where the fuck have you been all these years? I've been worried sick about you!'

Louise knew Fran was pleased to see her when she sat down quickly, folded her arms under her huge breasts and glared at her.

'You've got a lot of explaining to do, young lady. You've caused me no end of aggro and worry. Then you swan up here, cool as a bloody cucumber—'

Barry intervened. 'OK, Fran, that's enough. You know you're pleased as punch to see her – we both are, Louise – we're both just happy to see you're all right.' He turned to Dave. 'Come on, we'll go and make the tea, let those two sort themselves out.'

Fran looked older, there was no getting away from it, but she was still done up to the nines in a skin-tight sweater and a short black skirt, with her red hair piled up on top of her head. Angie guessed it was dyed now but still it was Fran; she would have known her anywhere.

The one noticeable addition was the two sticks propped up on the chair. Fran's right leg was stiff and straight in front of her.

'Well, come on then, girl, tell me what happened, why you did a runner, although with hindsight I think I can guess. Did Tony beat you up? He went ape when he found out you'd had his money. Why'd you do it, babe? Caused no end of problems, that did.'

Louise looked at Fran, her mother, and wondered how much she should tell her. The years had mellowed Angie's feeling of pure hatred for the woman who should have protected her, and now she wondered if she could really lay that amount of guilt on her.

'I'll tell you about it later. You tell me about you and Barry. How did that happen? I saw Daniel and he is really anti, and how come you ended up here, away from the bright lights?'

As they were talking Angie realised that she and her mother were having a conversation for the first time ever. Angie told her about her life now, and about Joshua.

'So you've done all right for yourself then. Joshua, your father, always said you would and you're telling me I'm a grandma? That's a turn-up. I thought Danny would have done something by now but that bloody old hypochondriac Sally never lets him out of her sight long enough for him to meet anyone. I've not seen hide nor hair of him since we moved here.'

Still puzzled, Angie asked her about the move.

'Well, babe, after Tony did this to my leg, among other things – he beat the shit out of me with a baseball bat – I knew I had to get away before he got out. Your old mate Nancy came up trumps for me. She gave me the money to get away and then Barry followed—'

'Nancy?' Angie interrupted sharply. 'Do you mean Nancy Aberlone, Sharon's mum?'

'Yeah, of course. Good friend she's been to me. She'll be over the moon when I tell her you've surfaced at last. After all that with Sharon we got quite close, both losing our daughters an' all.'

'What do you mean? Where's Sharon then?'

Fran looked at her and smiled sadly. 'Of course, you wouldn't know. Sharon died. She had leukaemia, died when she was only eighteen.'

Overwhelmed with guilt, Angie was speechless. Lively, happy Sharon, who wanted to be an air hostess and find a nice boyfriend; big Sharon, who had bounced into her life and made her laugh during the bad times. She just looked at Fran open-mouthed as she carried on.

'Anyway, Nancy and I got quite close. She wasn't so bad after all, you know, and she missed you. Always asks if I've heard from you!'

The afternoon passed in a flash and the parting was on quite good terms, considering. Everyone promised to keep in touch.

'I quite liked your mum. She's not bad really, is she? Certainly a character. She made me laugh. It did seem odd, though, hearing them call you Louise, you don't look like a Louise, you look like an Angie. What made you choose that name?'

Dave was trying hard to jolly her out of her moroseness. They were on their way home to London and Angie was silent. She hadn't spoken a word since they'd left.

'Why didn't I tell her?' Angie asked suddenly. 'After everything I went through I still spared her feelings. It was always like that, it was always as if I was the mother and she was the daughter. Why couldn't I throw it all at her?'

'Because, Angie Kavanagh, you're a genuinely nice person, that's why, and anyway, she suffered enough herself because of that psychopath. Sometimes the past is best left at what it is, the past. If you can't change it there's no point in raking it over.'

She was quiet again for a moment, deep in thought.

'I have to ring Nancy. I can't believe Sharon is dead. She was my best friend, more like a sister, and I wasn't there for her . . . that bastard Tony Willmott, he ruined so much for me.'

Dave didn't answer. He knew she had to work through it herself. After a few minutes she spoke again.

'What am I going to do about Rebekah?'

'Is that a rhetorical question or do you want an answer?'

'I probably don't want one but I need one.'

'Talk to a professional about it, someone who understands adoption. Get some proper advice from people who know and understand these things.'

She murmured a sort of response. She had suddenly decided what she was going to do.

She dialled the number three times before she finally let it ring.

'Hello, Lewis, this is Angie Kavanagh. I want to talk to you about something in strictest confidence.'

Lewis Alari was curious as to what Angie Kavanagh could possibly want with him and not with Rebekah. He assumed it was to do with the interview but he didn't know what. He was intrigued.

She met him at his new office, and when she was shown in, carefully shut the door behind her.

'Is everything confidential in here? No bugs or anything?' She smiled as she said it but she was aware of agents and their recording habits. They were always paranoid about being misquoted.

'Of course not, but is this business or personal? If it's personal, would you sooner go somewhere else?'

'No, I'm fine here, thanks, so long as we won't be disturbed.'

Angie was impressed by the young man opposite her. No one ever had a bad word to say about him. Popular and successful, he won a certain sympathy from everyone with Rebekah Alari as a possessive sister.

Rumour had it that he never had a social life because he was always on call for when Rebekah snapped her fingers. It was common knowledge that he was gay but he was rarely seen with anyone and he certainly wasn't out and about on the gay scene.

'I'll be honest with you. I want to talk to you about Rebekah but I don't want her to know; if that compromises you then I'm sorry but I need your word that nothing I say will go any further.'

'I don't think I can commit to that. If it concerns Rebekah then I really think she has a right to know.'

Angie could see that she had his interest. She hated what she was about to do, putting her personal life first, but she had to know and she was prepared to lie.

'OK, well, I'll leave it to you to decide. You know I queried whether Rebekah was adopted? Well, I've heard on the grapevine that someone has got wind of that, someone who has been around for a long time, who has tied up dates, been gathering information on her.'

Watching his face she saw his guard go up. She was right: he knew something. Now she had to get it out of him. She needed to know and there was no other way to find out.

'They have this idea that Rebekah may be the baby who was abandoned in 1973, in Brighton. It could be a big story. Rebekah has always made such a fuss about being an Alari; she's also made herself very unpopular with a lot of people—'

Lewis interrupted angrily, 'Why are you talking to me about this? It's all total crap, complete bullshit. Rebekah is who she says she is and that's that.'

'Lewis, listen to me. It's easy enough to find out these things. So you and Rebekah are both adopted – what's the big deal? Why the secrecy?'

'The secrecy is because we have only just found out, by accident, and all this shit is going to push her right over the edge. She's close enough as it is.'

Stopping suddenly as he realised just what he'd said, he tried to regain his composure by going on the attack.

'What's in this for you, Miss Angie Kavanagh? A big follow-up? Are you miffed because we didn't lay our lives bare to the great interviewer? Why should we?'

'Oddly enough, I agree with you, but Rebekah has always played with the press, made a good living out of the press and, when it suited her, been perfectly obnoxious to anyone and everyone. Now she's seen as fair game – she's done it to herself unfortunately – there are a lot of people who would love to knock her off her self-made pedestal.'

He was baffled. He couldn't figure out exactly what she was after.

'And you're not one of them? You still haven't answered me, what's in it for you?'

'Nothing.' She looked down as she lied again. 'There's nothing in it for me. I just wanted you to know, then you can decide what you want to do.' She paused and looked up again. 'Now she knows, is she going to try to find her birth mother? Is she looking? Is she the Brighton baby?'

'Now I'm not going to answer that. It's not my information to divulge and I don't know if she's looking, but if she is, and if she finds her, then the woman had better beware: Rebekah may well stick a knife between her shoulder blades.'

Angie felt a shiver of apprehension. She remembered what had happened to Sue and Giles when they'd upset Rebekah.

But she was convinced she was right and that Rebekah and Lewis both knew.

'Can I ask you one more question? Has Rebekah either got, or seen, the note that the mother wrote and left with the baby?'

'No she hasn't. There was just—'

He looked horror-stricken as he realised he had walked straight into a trap. He stood up sharply and kicked his chair back.

'You bitch. That was below the belt. Now get out. I really thought you were an OK person but you're the same as the rest.'

'No I'm not, Lewis, and I promise you nothing will go beyond these four walls. Please trust me. I know it's a lot to ask but please trust me, I'm on Rebekah's side.'

The wedding was back on, and on the surface Rebekah was putting her all into it. The church was booked for the weekend before Christmas, the formal reception and the big evening party were arranged and the invitations prepared from the guest lists that topped three hundred altogether. The Alari machine was in motion and there was no stopping it. The marriage itself was secondary to the wedding day, an Alari spectacular.

Rebekah viewed it differently. While she was talking to caterers and florists the one thing in the forefront of her mind was: will my real mother turn up? Even she knew it was an irrational thought. She had no idea what she looked like, and the woman probably didn't know who she was, but time and again it flashed through her mind, a romantic image of a woman huddled at the back of the church, her collar turned up. She imagined walking up the aisle on Cormac's arm and spotting her, a little mousy woman in a raincoat. What would she do? Hit her? Spit at her? Or sweep graciously past, carefully ignoring her? Would they fall into each other's arms? She wasn't sure. It changed from day to day, her fantasy, her obsession with the woman who had abandoned her.

No one was aware of it. Rebekah never spoke about her mother to anyone. She knew they wouldn't understand. Not even Lewis knew what was going on in her head.

Cormac had told her to forget the past, Lewis thought she had overreacted, and Joe and Lauren were pretending none of it had ever happened. On the surface she did the same and they all thought she was being her usual butterfly self, that now the furore had died down, thanks to Angie's feature, Rebekah was on to the next thing, her wedding, planned to be the biggest and best of the year.

For the first time in her life Rebekah was hiding her feelings. She wanted this all to herself. In fact she was quite pleased with how she was dealing with it.

No one knew she had been in contact with Barnardo's, with the adoption agency. It was a dead end really because they held so little information – no more really than she had gleaned from the newspaper cutting – but she had got a copy of the note that had been left with her, the note written by her mother. All it revealed was that she was probably young and probably cared.

Rebekah had shared this with no one. She was waiting for her birthday.

The day was planned with military precision. There was no way anyone was going to find out she was going to Brighton to stake out the toilets. That made her laugh, the one and only Rebekah Alari, loitering around public toilets. The press would love that!

It was difficult because it was her birthday and birthdays were holy days to the Alaris. Down to the mansion for a late breakfast, open the presents, then a family lunch that lasted all afternoon – four times a year the ritual was carried out and it was always the same and no excuses were allowed. Even Cormac was summoned this year, despite Joe and Lauren's disapproval of him!

Rebekah knew she wasn't going to the birthday spectacular but was saving her cop-out until the day before.

There was no way she wasn't going to Brighton that day. It was the only positive thing she had connecting her to the woman who had given birth to her and then dumped her, the woman she knew she had to meet face to face and ask, WHY?

Angie hadn't told Dave about her annual pilgrimage to Brighton. She thought it was something that, when spoken out loud, would sound silly, but she didn't want to lie to him any more. She had promised him.

'Dave, if I tell you something do you promise not to laugh?'

They were sitting side by side in companionable silence after Joshua had gone to bed.

'Oh dear, I hate it when you say that.' He laughed nervously and put his arm around her. 'OK, I promise, out with it . . .'

'Every year, on Skye's birthday, I go to Brighton, to the hospital, with a pink rosebud. I know it's silly, and even more silly now I know who the baby is, but I can't bring myself not to go. I've been doing it for so long . . .'

'You really are a great big sentimentalist, do you know that?'

'I do, but I'm also superstitious. It's crazy, especially now, but you know how hard it is to break away from rituals, don't you?'

Pulling her close, he took her hand. 'In that case go, but why don't we make a day out of it? I'll drop you off and go into town, then we'll meet up afterwards for lunch. How about that? A romantic day by the sea in November!'

She smiled and leant over to kiss him. 'I love you so much, Dave, do you know that?'

'I hope you do. We're getting married at Christmas.'

'I know, and guess who else is getting married at Christmas? Sue told me today, Rebekah and Cormac, but that's going to be the wedding of the year, unlike our quiet little gathering . . .'

'Do you want the wedding of the year? If you want it you can have it.'

'Fool! I suppose I would like to take a peek at Rebekah's, though. Do you think I could get away with it?'

Dave shook his head. 'No, no, no. Not a good idea. Let Sue tell you all about it afterwards.'

Angie had booked it all up: they were going to Barbados at the beginning of December for a week. She wanted to try to find her father before the wedding on 22 December, four days after Rebekah's. The letter she had sent to Joshua remained unanswered, and she had no idea what she would find. She just prayed fiercely that nothing had happened to him as well.

She had carefully avoided mentioning Joshua in front of Fran and Barry. She knew there was a lot of time to make up and a lot of wounds to heal. Twenty-six years was too much emotion to cover in one afternoon.

The next meeting with Fran and Barry was arranged to take place at the house in Fulham, to introduce them to young Joshua, and also Jemima, whom Angie always considered as her daughter.

It had been hard enough explaining to them that suddenly a

grandmother was going to appear but she knew she also had to talk about Barry and Daniel.

Easy-going Jemima was no problem. She and Dominic, the boy in black, who was now her husband, both thought it was terribly romantic, but Joshua was different. He wanted answers and Angie knew he would be mercilessly firing questions at Fran, who hardly qualified as tactful or maternal! The thought of the visit made Angie palpitate.

But first she had to get the visit to Brighton out of the way. She tried to persuade herself not to go and she had almost convinced herself that it was a nonsense after all the years that had passed, but there was just something inside her that made her want to remember the day.

She wanted to relive the day she had given birth and then given her baby away, almost punish herself for it, and the only way she could do that was actually to be there. Other mothers celebrated birthdays with their children and she knew that couldn't happen so Brighton was the next best thing – the only thing she had in common with Skye, her daughter by birth, whom she still couldn't equate with Rebekah Alari, model, It girl and trust fund queen!

Chapter Twenty-One

November 20 1999

Angie and Dave dropped Joshua off at school and then headed off to Brighton. Instead of the motorway, they went the pretty way, stopping for coffee and cream cakes in one of the little villages. They found a flower shop and giggled like schoolkids at the woman's reaction to Angie's request for a single pink rosebud. In the end they bought a bunch and she spent the rest of the journey picking through them, trying to choose the best one.

'I know it will get trodden on, picked up and taken or swept up at the end of the day but this is a sop to my guilt. Do you think I'm mad?'

'Of course not, just a wee bit deranged, that's all.'

'Thanks a lot.'

They were both laughing and Angie suddenly thought how nice it was after all the years to share the day with someone.

'Does Gavin know you do this?'

'Shit, Dave, I'd forgotten about Gavin. I wonder how Fran will react to him? She'll have a fit when she realises he's gay. Oh God, she's bound to say something awful . . .'

'I'm sure Gavin can rise above all that although I think he's bound to feel jealous of her. You're going to have to tread carefully so he's not made to feel excluded . . . surplus to requirements.'

She carried on picking at the flowers. 'Gavin doesn't know I do this. I always said I was going into town for a look round . . . Don't tell me you're jealous? Feeling excluded? Surplus to requirements?'

He smiled as he concentrated on the lane ahead of him.

'Touché! Sorry! Now shall we have lunch before or after?'

'After, then I'll be able to relax.'

★ ★ ★

Once again Rebekah had to fall back on her excellent drama training. Luckily she had tossed and turned all night and then at 4 a.m. given in and headed for the coffee machine and a pack of cigarettes.

Cormac stirred briefly as she got out of bed.

'Where are you going?' he mumbled as she crept out with her dressing gown over her arm.

'I don't feel too well, I'm going to get a drink. You go back to sleep.' She could have saved her breath. He was asleep again before she answered.

By the time six o'clock came she was hyped out on caffeine and coughing like a bronchial old man as she lay on the sofa with a bucket beside her. She heard Cormac moving about and suddenly he appeared beside her with an elaborately wrapped present and a card the size of a billboard. He kissed her gently.

'Happy birthday, Beka darling. What got you up during the night? Birthday excitement?'

Deliberately not smiling back she groaned. 'No, I really don't feel well. I've been sick more times than I can count and my stomach really hurts. I must have a bug . . .' Rebekah pulled her legs up tight to her body and lay there in agony, clutching her stomach and moaning. 'Can you just open it for me.' She gave him a watery smile but as he came over to sit near her she cried out dramatically and pushed him away. 'Don't get too close in case you catch it, whatever it is I've got . . .'

Even Rebekah Alari felt mean as she saw the concern written all over Cormac's face but she had to do it. He stood up.

'We'll have to cancel going to your parents today, darling. You're just not up to it . . .'

'No, don't do that. I'll probably be all right later. Just pass me my present. I've been looking forward to this.'

The elaborately wrapped flat packet contained two Concorde tickets to New York for the next weekend and a piece of paper that read: 'I Cormac, owe you, Rebekah, dinner at the Windows On The World on Saturday night.'

'Oh, thank you, darling, that's wonderful . . . Oooooohhhh, my stomach. I have to go to the bathroom . . . Oh Christ, I really have to get over this quickly if we're off to New York.'

She did herself proud. She packed Cormac off with Lewis, pleading to be left to sleep it off and promising to follow down later. They weren't happy to leave her but she insisted it wouldn't be fair on Mummy and Daddy for none of them to go.

'Don't phone me. I'm going back to bed now but I'll phone you later and let you know how I am and when I'm on my way.'

Dressing quickly and inconspicuously in black jeans tucked in her boots and a big, baggy jumper with her hair tucked inside, she rushed down to her car and roared off, aiming to get to the hospital by ten. She hoped that wasn't too late.

She made it in record time and rushed straight in to the cubicle: nothing was there. She suddenly realised that she couldn't stay inside for the whole time, someone was bound to notice the permanently locked door.

There was a small cafeteria nearby and she found that by sitting on the very end chair and turning it round slightly she could see down the corridor and across to the door. The best she could was alternate between the two and hope she didn't miss the woman.

She knew she could dismiss anyone noticeably under forty and that it was unlikely to be someone over sixty.

Taking out the book she had brought with her, she pretended to read it.

Dave dropped Angie at the hospital entrance.

'I'll meet you back here in an hour, is that long enough?'

She leant through the open window and kissed him.

'God, yes, bags of time. See you then.'

She watched the car pull away and slowly made her way through the grounds to the old building. Stopping at the entrance she sat on the wall as she had done so many times in the past and lit a cigarette, just watching the cross section of people who walked up and down the well-trodden stone steps.

She told herself this would be the last time; in a few weeks she would be married to Dave. Fran and Barry would be there, so would Nancy, and if her search was successful maybe even Joshua. She had sent an invitation to Daniel but had not had a reply. All the loose ends were slowly being pulled together and it was time to move on.

Skye a.k.a. Rebekah was getting married as well to that nice, handsome Cormac. It was ironic that he was black, that made her smile wryly. She knew that Rebekah and Cormac would never face the hostility that Fran and Joshua had, and that their children wouldn't have to suffer the torrents of abuse that had rained down on the young Louise.

Rebekah had led a fairly charmed if spoilt life: she was rich and beautiful, she'd travelled the world, been doted on by her adoptive parents and, most of all, she had the faithful Lewis as a brother. Not bad for the daughter of poor little Louise Jermaine.

Angie lit another cigarette and smiled conspiratorially at the other people on the wall, all doing the same thing – a quick puff to pluck up the courage to go in for whatever reason.

Rebekah had been there for just over two hours and had jumped up and down more times than a jumping bean.

'Are you OK, dear?' The WRVS lady, who served the teas, had been watching her doing a regular trot back and forth to the ladies. Rebekah had been aware of her eyes following her.

'Fine, thank you. I'm just waiting for someone. I was early and now they're late.' She leant forward to the woman and whispered, 'I've got a bit of a bladder problem, you know. I'm seeing the doctor this afternoon . . .'

The woman smiled sympathetically and bustled away. Rebekah wondered how long it would be before that little snippet was passed on to the other elderly lady behind the counter.

She tried again to imagine just what she would do if she did see the woman, if she did catch her with her bloody pink rosebud, an annual peace offering to compensate for what she'd done. She hated sitting there in public, watching and waiting for this person who was her mother, someone she didn't know from Adam.

How can anyone not recognise their own mother? Supposing she didn't come? Supposing she had died in the last year? She would never, ever know anything about herself. That thought frightened her more than anything. She crossed her fingers, screwed up her eyes and wished as she used to wish as a little girl.

'Please let me find her today. I promise I will be good for evermore if you let me find her today.'

Angie knew there was always a lull at lunchtime between out-patients clinics. All she wanted was just a few minutes without someone banging on the door shouting, 'Are you OK in there?' Just because it was a hospital it didn't mean that everyone in the lavatory was about to pass out!

She decided she would go in at one fifteen precisely. One more cigarette first.

She thought back to how she had felt that day twenty-six years ago. It had seemed like the end of the world for her. She had felt so alone and rejected she had just wanted to die, literally, and then along had come Paolo and Gavin, followed a few years later by Sue and Giles, and then of course Dave and little Joshua, truly the light of her life.

There was only one way of looking at it: she wouldn't wish her childhood on anyone, but without it she wouldn't have everything she had now.

Looking at her watch she stood up and walked up the steps into the building, turned left and made her way down the corridor that still smelt exactly the same year after year. Or was it her imagination?

Rebekah bought a can of cola at the shop.

'I hope you don't mind me saying, dear, but if you have problems with your . . . you know what, then cola isn't a good idea. It's a diuretic; it'll make you go more than ever!'

Resisting the urge to punch the woman straight between the eyes Rebekah just smiled.

'I know, that's what I need before my appointment!'

Just as she was about to sit down again she saw her – Angie Kavanagh walking straight towards her. Sitting down quickly, she held her book up in front of her face but the journalist wasn't looking her way. Turning just before she reached the cafeteria Angie went into the toilets. Rebekah wanted to scream and shout and smash the place up, followed quickly by Angie Kavanagh's face. The fucking bitch had followed her. She knew, and she had followed her, fucking journalists. Now she wouldn't be able to confront the woman, not with the press hot on her trail.

She kept her face down and waited for Angie to reappear, but after a few minutes she had to go and look.

There was no one in the washroom so Angie had to be in a cubicle, her cubicle. What the fuck was she waiting in there for? Then again, maybe it was just a coincidence, maybe Angie was visiting a sick relative . . . She heard the flush and hotfooted it back to her vantage point.

Angie walked out back down the corridor and Rebekah saw her turn towards the exit. She was torn between chasing after her and ripping her throat out, and staying where she was for fear of missing the woman with the rosebud.

She hesitated for a second but the rage bubbling away inside her erupted and she hurled herself out of the chair. Kicking it away fiercely she grabbed her handbag before running full speed down the corridor, pushing her way through the incoming visitors.

Shouldering open the heavy, old-fashioned door, she saw Angie Kavanagh getting into a car and smiling. She leaned over and kissed the man in the car. Dave, the photographer.

Suddenly it was too much for Rebekah. Taking the steps three at a time she threw herself in front of the car.

'You fucking bastard two-faced bitch of a woman, how could you do that?' Screaming and crying she beat her fists on the bonnet and aimed kicks at the car body with her boots.

Angie was frozen to her seat, unable to believe what was unfolding in front of her. She couldn't have moved even if she wanted to but Dave jumped out and pulled Rebekah off the car.

A crowd was gathering to watch the fun, and faces were appearing at the windows. Dave realised it was only a matter of time before someone called the police so he grabbed hold of the still screaming Rebekah, putting both arms around her and pinning her arms to her side, trying to avoid the kicking boots that were lashing out at the car.

'Calm down, Rebekah, just calm down. The last thing anyone needs is the police, and even more publicity . . . Calm down and get in the car.'

'What? With her? You're fucking joking. I'd rather be dragged off in a police car—'

'No you wouldn't, now GET IN THE CAR.' Dave was in control and suddenly Rebekah sagged against him.

'I have to go back inside, I have to. I can't leave now, it's my only chance . . .'

His voice softened. 'Get in the car. Everything will be OK, I promise.'

Angie watched the drama with detachment. It was a bit like being in the cinema with everything happening in front of you but not being part of it.

Rebekah had been waiting for her. She had found out somehow and she was waiting, waiting for her to show up. Rebekah knew!

Dave got into the back with Rebekah and cuddled her tight.

'Angie, move over and drive. Let's get out of here.'

'My car's here . . . I can't leave my car . . . I have to see her . . . please help me.' Rebekah could hardly get the words out.

'Don't worry, we'll come back. Let's just get away from the crowds before security show up.'

Angie still didn't move.

'ANGIE, drive the fucking car, will you?' Dave bellowed at the top of his voice.

Angie suddenly came to life. She clambered across to the driver's side and they roared out of the gates. She headed by instinct to Paolo's, the only place she could think of. Parking up outside she turned around for the first time and saw Dave still holding a sobbing Rebekah tightly.

'I'm sorry,' Angie said. 'I am just so sorry, I never meant for any of this, I didn't want it to be like this, I just—'

'Fuck off. You've ruined everything, you interfering bitch. This was my only chance and you've fucked it up.'

Shaking her head, Angie tried to make some sense of what Rebekah was saying.

'Please, Rebekah, let me explain. I'm so sorry, I didn't want this to happen . . . I wasn't going to tell you—'

'Then you shouldn't have followed me!' She spat the words out.

It didn't make sense, why did Rebekah think she had followed her?

'But I didn't follow you. I thought you were waiting for me. Why would I follow you?' Angie couldn't get her head round any of it.

'For another fucking story, of course. I'm just surprised this bastard wasn't sitting on the cistern with his camera at the ready.'

It was Dave who suddenly realised what was going on.

'Stop it, the pair of you. Rebekah, tell us what you were doing there. This is nothing to do with work, this is personal and totally secret. Why were you there?'

Rebekah's distressed cries reminded Angie of herself the day that Tony had raped her. The girl was in pain, real acute pain.

'Rebekah, did Lewis tell you I went to see him? Did he say anything to you? Please, I need to know.'

'Lewis? What's he got to do with this? No, I didn't know you went to see him. What did he tell you?'

'Nothing at all. Lewis is loyal to you. Please tell us why you were there at the hospital.'

Rebekah wailed, 'I wanted to find my real mother. I wanted to see her, to see what she was like and now you've screwed it for me, I may never get another chance.'

Angie and Dave looked at each other. Rebekah didn't know who Angie was.

'Right, I can't leave you two alone,' Dave decided. 'Angie go inside and get three coffees, go on. I'll stay here with Rebekah. Strong and black . . . go on, it's OK.'

Dave smiled encouragingly at her. He was still holding Rebekah, his arms around her, enveloping her like he would a child.

'Can you let go long enough for me to get a cigarette out of my bag? I won't kill her . . . yet!'

Dave thought that sounded encouraging. The touch of sarcasm meant that Rebekah was starting to think straight again. He let go of her.

'So, are you going to use the story? Earn yourself another few grand off my back?'

He ignored the barbed remarks. 'I'm just going to help Angie with the coffees, or do you feel up to going inside? It's warmer in there.'

'Whatever, so long as I can smoke.'

'Come on then. I'm sure we can find a nice quiet table where we can talk.'

'Why the fuck would I want to talk to either of you?'

'I think you do, Rebekah, I really think you do! Come on, before Angie brings them out.'

They got to the door just as she was coming out.

'It's too cold in the car. We've come in to find you. Rebekah wants to go and repair her face first, can you point her in the right direction?'

Silently Angie pointed to the door in the corner and then quickly sat down.

'What am I going to do? She doesn't know, she hasn't pieced it together. Shall I tell her? Quick, help me.'

'It's up to you but not in haste and not in temper. You both need to calm down first.'

They drank their drinks in silence. Angie felt strange being in the café as a customer, not knowing anyone. It wasn't even called Paolo's any more; it was The Nosherie, which she thought was really naff.

In the lavatory, Rebekah was trying to make sense of what was going on. It was almost surreal. If Angie Kavanagh hadn't followed her then why was she here and why did she keep apologising? Why wasn't Dave taking photographs? Something was wrong. There was a piece of the jigsaw in her mind missing and she knew she had to find it.

She wondered if it was too late to go back to the hospital. Maybe her mother wasn't going there, after all. Maybe the nurse had got it wrong and it was all a wild-goose chase . . .

'Rebekah, I swear to you, I did not follow you down here. I had no idea you were going to be at the hospital, and I certainly wouldn't use something like that anyway, I swear I wouldn't.'

Angie could tell Rebekah didn't believe her. She looked around the café and it was empty bar a bedraggled little old man in the corner, with a mug of tea, and a glazed expression on his face.

'Then tell me what you were doing there. I don't believe it was a fucking coincidence. Tell me everything – I do have a right to know.'

'OK, I'll tell you. I know that you and Lewis were both adopted and I know that you were the baby abandoned at the hospital today twenty-six years ago. Now tell me what you know.'

Rebekah hesitated. She didn't want to give any more information than she had to.

'That's right, and I came down to the hospital a couple of months ago and found a nurse who was there at the time. She told me that every year a woman visits and leaves a pink rosebud. That's what I was waiting for. I wanted to see her, find out who she was, but you ruined it . . . You shouldn't have been there. Why were you there?'

Angie looked at Dave, waiting for either a nod or a shake of his head, but he just shrugged his shoulders. She knew it was her decision. She took a deep breath.

'I was there because it was Skye's birthday. I was taking the pink rosebud, Rebekah. It was me you were looking for. It was me who left you at the hospital. I am your mother, Rebekah, but I swear to you I didn't know until the day I interviewed you in New York. No one knew that I had a daughter up till then, not even Dave, I . . .'

Her voice tailed off as she realised Rebekah was about to faint. Dave was on his feet and round the table in a flash, pushing her head down between her knees but he was too late. She slumped to the floor in a heap.

Rebekah felt the room swimming around her. She was floating. What was it that Angie Kavanagh had said? Did she really say that she was her mother? She thought that she might wake up in a minute and find it was another dream, another fantasy like all the others she had woven over the past weeks.

The voices started to get clearer.

'Come on, Rebekah, wake up. Come on or we'll have to call an ambulance. Wake up, will you?'

She could see Angie's face coming into focus and slowly the room stopped moving. They helped her up and got her back on the chair, one of them sitting either side of her to prop her up while the man behind the counter looked on.

'Is she pregnant?'

'Something like that,' Dave replied without looking at him. 'Can we have a glass of water over here, please?'

Dave dipped his handkerchief into the glass and dabbed her lips and forehead. Rebekah smiled weakly.

'I hope that's clean.'

Angie heaved a sigh of relief and immediately burst into tears,

303

making Dave throw his hands up in despair.

'I really can't take a lot more of this, you know. Can we sort it out, do you think?'

Rebekah looked from one to the other of them. She was still in shock and wondering what was happening. How could Angie Kavanagh possibly be her birth mother? How could she have met the woman, spoken with her and been in the same room as her for hours without knowing? Rebekah's fantasies never included one where there wasn't an instant bond that they both recognised. How could a mother and daughter not know each other by instinct?

Silently she looked at Angie. For once Rebekah was lost for words.

Rebekah was angry and Angie was upset so they all agreed that the best thing to do was for them all to get back to London as quickly as possible and sort it out then. The drive back to the hospital was fraught with high tension and neither Angie nor Rebekah said a word.

'Now, Rebekah, no arguing. You've had a shock so I'm going to drive you back in your car and Angie can follow in ours,' Dave suggested. 'We'll all talk when we get back to London.'

'I want to talk to Angie on my own. I'll go with her. Don't worry, I won't force her off the road or anything.'

He had reservations but Angie agreed with Rebekah so he had to concede and hope for the best.

'Tell me again what you said in the café and then explain to me how this fucking awful mess has happened. This is like some godawful nightmare that I can't wake up from . . .'

'Trust me, Rebekah, I feel exactly the same. This isn't how I planned it to be – not that I had planned anything. All I had decided was that if you didn't want to know about me then I was going to leave well alone. But you were looking, weren't you? Otherwise you wouldn't have been at the hospital. I had no idea you knew about my visits. If I had then I probably wouldn't have come.'

She glanced over at the girl beside her, scrunched up in the seat looking nothing like the Rebekah Alari that everyone loved to hate. This was Skye, her daughter, her own flesh and blood, and she didn't know her.

The girl turned to her. 'How could anyone abandon their baby? Tell me, how could you bring yourself to do it?'

'Now isn't the time for all the details, but I had a good reason. I was only fifteen and it was the only thing I could think of at the time. What were you doing at fifteen?'

'Believe it or not, I certainly wasn't out shagging and getting pregnant.'

'That's not how it was. When we get home we can go through all the nitty-gritty of it all, but not here, not on the motorway . . . it doesn't seem right somehow.'

Rebekah laughed, a dry humourless laugh that echoed in the car.

'And what you did to me was right? Tell me, Miss Self-righteous Kavanagh, how many other bastards did you dump en route to your super career?'

Angie kept her voice even. She knew the girl was hurting and wanted to lash out at her, make her pay for the hurt.

'I only had one other child, Joshua. He is seven. Dave is his father.'

'Is Dave my father?'

Angie smiled at her sadly. 'I wish! I'd give anything for him to have been the father of my first baby.'

They drove on in silence. Angie was aware of Dave in the car behind them and she could see his worried expression in the rear-view mirror. She waved to him reassuringly.

'Oh fuck, I forgot the birthday ritual. Everyone's there except me. Mummy and Daddy will be going ape by now.'

Rebekah dug into her handbag and got out her mobile phone, quickly pressing the keys.

'Hello, Mummy? It's Rebekah . . . I know . . . I know . . . I'm sorry . . . Yes, I feel a lot better now but I don't think I ought to drive. I've only just woken up . . . I know . . . I know . . . Listen I'll be down first thing in the morning . . . Tell Cormac I'll see him later. Love to Daddy and Lewis.'

She turned to Angie. 'I told them all I had a tummy bug and had to stay in bed and sleep it off. Poor old Cormac has probably had the full force of the Alari clan with no backup, apart from Lewis. Do you know Lewis isn't even interested in finding his birth parents? I can't understand it. How can anyone not want to know?'

Looking out of the car window she watched the countryside flashing by, watched the other cars transporting their occupants to wherever they were going that day.

'It doesn't really change a lot does it? Mummy and Daddy are still Mummy and Daddy and I'm still Rebekah Alari, spoilt little rich girl. You're still Angie Kavanagh, writer extraordinaire . . . I thought I'd feel different somehow. There is one other thing, though. What about my father?'

'I knew you would ask that. I'm sorry but he was just a boy I met at a party. It all went too far, too much alcohol too young, you know the scenario . . . I don't even know his surname.' Angie smiled sadly at her. 'One day I'll tell you all about the rest of my family but not now. It's too soon, too much to take in.'

The girl beside her, her daughter, looked silently out of the window.

Angie just hoped everything would be all right in time. It had to be. They could never be mother and daughter – it would always have to be just a shared blood bond – but at least they could get to know each other and be on the periphery of each other's lives.

Dave was right. Some things are meant to be, and fate gives them a helping hand.

Epilogue

There was barely a dry eye in the church as Rebekah walked down the aisle on Joe Alari's arm. The cream velvet cape with its wide fur-trimmed hood swished gently behind her as they slowly made their way down to the altar with four little bridesmaids and two pageboys walking studiously behind.

As she reached Cormac, looking very aristocratic in full morning dress, she dramatically removed the cape and handed it to her mother, who was wearing the biggest hat imaginable.

Rebekah's dress underneath was simple: a plain cream ankle-length tight sheath with elbow-length sleeves but cut very low at the front and slashed to the waist at the back, allowing her waist-length hair to hang perfectly in the V. The slit up the back just about allowed her to walk in the white strappy sandals with tiny diamanté stones on the toe strap that matched the diamonds twinkling in the tiara holding her hair back from her face.

Rebekah looked stunning, the catwalk queen at her very best.

Sue leant slightly towards Angie standing next to her.

'Only Rebekah Alari could get away with a stunt like that at her wedding . . . the wicked queen shedding her cloak!'

Angie smiled and whispered, 'Isn't she absolutely beautiful?'

'No need to go over the top, darling. This is the bitchtroll from hell we're talking about.'

Angie carried on smiling, trying hard not to grin like the Cheshire cat.

The invitation had been a shock to her, a total bolt out of the blue. Sue was surprised as well, maybe even a bit miffed; she had been looking forward to relating it all to Angie afterwards.

'Why would she ask you?'

'Probably because I did that interview that got her off the hook.'

Angie and Rebekah had talked and eventually agreed an uneasy truce. No one was to know about their relationship apart from

307

Lewis and Cormac, whom Rebekah told, and Dave and Gavin. There was still a lot of explaining to do but Angie was determined it would be done properly and Rebekah had actually agreed to some joint counselling.

There was a long road ahead for both of them.

When Angie received the invitation to the wedding for her and Dave she couldn't have been more excited if there had been a million-pound cheque inside the envelope. It was another small step on the long and bumpy road.

The ceremony was over, and Rebekah and Cormac were slowly walking back up, smiling and nodding at everyone on the way.

When they were parallel to the pew Rebekah made eye contact with Angie and smiled, a secret little smile that made Angie's heart pound in her chest as she smiled back and winked at her daughter.

Sue looked at Angie sharply, and muttered out of the corner of her mouth, 'What was that look for? . . . Oh, for God's sake, Ange, just look at your face, mascara everywhere. How can you possibly shed a single tear? I know, it's tears of sadness for poor old Cormac. He doesn't know what he's letting himself in for!'

They weren't invited to the family reception so Angie, Dave, Sue and Giles went off for a pub lunch and a rest at their hotel before heading for the Alari mansion for the evening party.

Rebekah and Cormac greeted them at the entrance hall.

'Mummy, Daddy, this is Angie Kavanagh, the writer, and her partner, Dave. They're getting married next week, as well you know.' She didn't make eye contact this time. 'Angie, Dave, these are my parents, Joe and Lauren Alari.'

Angie couldn't speak so Dave jumped in to fill the silence.

'You've got a beautiful daughter there, Mr and Mrs Alari. You must be proud of her.'

Lauren Alari twittered, 'Oh we are! We've had our moments with her – oh Lord, have we had some moments – but we love her, don't we, darling? Mummy and Daddy both love you.'

Angie could only imagine Sue's expression behind her so she didn't turn round, she just reached forward and gently squeezed Rebekah's arm and then took Cormac's hand.

'You two have a happy life, won't you?'

Angie couldn't believe how fruitless their trip to Barbados had been. Jermaine was a popular name and the district he had written about in his letters was long gone, a sprawling resort hotel in its place.

They reached dead end after dead end and Angie was depressed.

'What are we going to do? Everything else has worked out but I need my dad, I want him at my wedding. I can't believe I was so naïve. I'm a writer for God's sake . . .'

'Sweetheart, there's not a lot you can do. How about an ad in the local paper? Someone must know him.'

They contacted the local weekly paper and placed an ad but it was due out the day they were returning home. They gave all their details and hoped for the best.

Angie was convinced Joshua would hurl himself into the airport lounge at the last minute but he didn't appear, and the atmosphere on the flight home was morose as she accepted that her father had gone for good. She had left it too late.

Angie and Dave's wedding day arrived. Because there were more guests than they had originally planned they decided on a cere-mony at the local registry office followed by a small reception at home and a belated Scottish honeymoon in the new millennium. Even so, the guest list was short and sweet: Jemima and Joshua junior, Sue, Giles and Lizzie, Fran and Barry, Nancy and her husband, Gavin and Simon, and Lewis.

There was still no contact from Joshua senior and Daniel hadn't even responded to his invitation.

Rebekah was on her honeymoon in Hawaii but Angie knew she wouldn't have come anyway. The emotions were still too raw.

Dave had been persuaded into slacks and a jacket, Angie was in a white and black designer suit that cost far more than she'd wanted to spend but Sue could be very persuasive. No jeans, she said, and absolutely no little black utility dress!

They were all gathered at the main entrance to the registry office at five to eleven waiting for their names to be called for eleven o'clock.

Angie reached her hand out to Nancy.

'I wish Sharon could have been here.'

'Oh, I'm sure she is, Louise. I'm sure she's up there watching, trying to figure out why you're still so slim!'

Angie went over to Gavin.

'Gavin, I wouldn't have any of this without you and Paolo. You're so special to me . . .'

'Angie baby, you're something really special yourself and I love you!'

'Angie, have you got a second . . .?' Lewis pulled her to one side. 'Rebekah asked me to give you this, but please don't cry. Sue will kill me!'

She opened the envelope and pulled out a wedding card: 'To Angie and Dave. You have a happy life as well. Rebekah Skye.'

There was a small package inside the card; Angie opened the tissue paper carefully to find a heart-shaped brooch set with diamonds.

She blinked back the tears and put the card into her handbag and the brooch on her jacket, the first gift ever from her daughter. She touched the silver cross around her neck and the gold charm bracelet on her wrist gently, hoping Sharon and Paolo were both watching as little Louise came full circle.

'KAVANAGH AND OLIVER?'

As they all turned to walk in to the small office a huge familiar shadow appeared in the doorway.

'DAD! What are you doing here?' Angie screamed and threw herself at him, the make-up completely forgotten as she burst into tears. 'How did you know?'

Fran appeared at her side as father and daughter looked at each other, trying to take in the changes the years had brought.

'If you'd asked me instead of just pissing off to the other side of the world without so much as a word I could have told you the old bugger was only in London. Silly cow, never did think first, did you?'

Everyone laughed as father and daughter hugged for the first time in thirty years.

'KAVANAGH AND OLIVER!' The voice was louder now, and they all trooped in and took up their places.

'Did you know about this, Dave? Why didn't anyone tell me?'

'I did know. I thought it would be a nice surprise, icing on the wedding cake so to speak. Are you happy?'

'It's a lovely surprise and I am very happy. I love you Mr Oliver. Now, let's go and get married.'